Snowed in for Christmas

Claire Sandy

PAN BOOKS

First published 2015 by Pan Books
an imprint of Pan Macmillan
20 New Wharf Road, London N1 9RR
Associated companies throughout the world
www.panmacmillan.com

ISBN 978-1-4472-9929-5

3 5 7 9 8 6 4 2

A CIP catalogue record for this book is available from the British Library.

Typeset in Sabon LT Std by Palimpsest Book Production Ltd, Falkirk, Stirlingshire
Printed and bound by CPI Group (UK) Ltd, Croydon, CR0 4YY

Snowed in for Christmas

Claire Sandy lives in Surrey with her husband, her daughter and their dogs. Before she wrote books, she made radio jingles and sold wool (not at the same time). Now she has her dream job as a novelist, having already written *What Would Mary Berry Do?* and *A Very Big House in the Country*.

This book is for Elinor Lawless,
one of my favourite colleens

*A snowflake begins life as a tiny droplet
of super-cooled water which freezes in the sky
to create an ice crystal.*

*If you're not careful, something similar
can happen to your heart.*

LONDON

December 13th

Only twelve days to go.

How, thought Asta, *does Christmas creep up on me every time, even though I spend most of the year looking forward to it?*

Each and every December, it was as if Christmas jumped out of a cupboard shouting *Surprise!* Asta was thinking so hard about wrapping paper, and batteries, and whether or not the gravy stains in her red tablecloth would come out, that at first she didn't hear the supermarket cashier's joke.

With her surname, you became immune; Asta had heard them all before.

'And are you?' the woman giggled as she looked at Asta's debit card. 'A looney, I mean?'

'Sometimes,' Asta replied, distracted, struggling to pack the toilet rolls, soup cartons and Christmas crackers hurtling towards her on the till's conveyor belt. A London Looney, transplanted from her native soil, she itched to blurt out, 'Actually, where I come from there are *loads* of Looneys,' but that would only make matters worse. It didn't help that she'd strung scarlet baubles through her earrings.

Trudging home with Kitty beside her, Asta was replaying

the conversation in her head, editing the dialogue so that her hilarious repartee left the cashier dumbfounded, when something stopped her in her tracks.

To the naked eye, they were simply sheds. A conga line of wonky DIY huts, shivering in the drizzle outside the garden centre. But these sheds possessed magical powers: they sent Asta time-travelling, whizzing her back two decades to touch down in the middle of a far-off summer afternoon.

❄

Asta feels the dry warmth of Etienne's palm in her own. She hears the drone of bees in the waist-high grass. She watches Etienne's face smudge out of focus as he leans down to whisper, 'Tu es sure?'

'Oui, I'm sure,' Asta answers in that summer's mongrel dialect.

The rope ladder dips and spins, then holds as she clambers upwards.

Panting, Etienne is close behind. His excitement is contagious, his expectations terrifying. Asta's bare foot slaps on the rough wood of the treehouse floor.

'So.' Etienne has to stoop in the jerry-built cube. He blocks the light from the square unglazed window.

'So,' repeats Asta. Her nose is full of the juicy smell of untreated wood; her mind is full of Etienne. His beauty, the feeling he ignites in her: the step she's about to take. Asta is eager, impatient. It's a moment she's fantasized about, probably imagined all wrong . . . she reassures herself that it's probably like riding a bike.

Oh, hell, she remembers. I can't ride a bike.

'Mu-um! We can cross!'

The hum of London traffic reasserted itself. 'Sorry, darling.' Asta picked up the plastic bags lolling like drunks at her feet.

Kitty sprinted over the crossing, the rolled cuffs of her Topshop jeans precisely calibrated to satisfy the teen fashion tyrants of Chelsea. Asta marvelled, as she had countless times over the years, at just how she'd managed to conjure up such a gorgeous creature from her own shabby genetic bits and pieces. Although she had, of course, had help on this front.

'What,' asked Kitty as Asta caught up with her at the entrance to their block, 'was so fascinating about those sheds? You were in a trance.'

'Thinking of getting one.' Asta stabbed the security code into the keypad with her nose (don't try this at home) and they shouldered a door each.

'Eh? For our tiny balcony?' Kitty's voice echoed in the concrete stairwell, as 'Mistletoe and Wine' floated through a closed front door.

'They reminded me of something.' *Someone.* Asta wrestled with the contrary lock of their third-floor flat. 'It's not important,' she fibbed.

'Anyway, Mum, can I?' Kitty returned to the debate that was dominating the run-up to Christmas.

'It's *may I*,' said Asta, as haughtily as she could manage while falling through the suddenly co-operative door.

'*May I*, pretty please, share a flat with Maisie?'

'No.' The carrier bags were unfeasibly heavy.

Gibbon-armed, Asta struggled to the tiny kitchen and swung them up onto the worktop. '*Nein. Non.* And, er . . .' Asta had exhausted her knowledge of foreign languages. 'Ninchen,' she improvised.

'Ninchen?' Kitty looked doubtful.

'Why don't you unpack the decorations?'

The tactic worked. Raised by her mother to be bonkers about Christmas, at sixteen Kitty was still young enough to be distracted by tinsel.

'I *love* this year's theme.' Kitty danced away with two of the bags.

'Modern brights,' said Asta pompously. Last year had been Victoriana, the year before Cupcakes. Very little about their life would impress *Elle Decoration*, but whatever their financial situation (over the years, it had swung from so-so to *yikes* and back again), the Looney ladies had a fresh theme for each Christmas.

Goose fat, thought Asta. Then, wildly, *ham?* Her mind would lurch like this until the Big Day, all the things she hadn't done ganging up on her.

Mistletoe, she thought as Kitty spilt the bags onto the low white coffee table. *Stuffing.* Colour exploded in the small white room. Decorating such a confined space, Asta had kept the palette neutral. She loved their orderly, comfortable flat, but she also loved the way Christmas forced its tacky way in every year.

'I wish it would snow,' sighed Kitty, jiggling a set of bright orange sleigh bells. 'Snow makes everything magical.'

'And disrupts public transport. And makes the pavements treacherous.'

Tearing the netting off the diminutive tree – real, it *had* to be real – Kitty attacked her favourite topic from another direction.

'If Maisie and I shared a flat, you could bring boyfriends home, Mum.'

'Boyfriends?' Asta let out a snort that reminded her, disconcertingly, of her Aunty Peg. No woman in her right mind would aspire to be like Peg, so she converted the snort into a girlish *ha ha.*

'I know you go on dates, Mother dearest.'

'I don't. Well, I do, but . . . shut up.' The parenting manuals on Asta's shelves sighed to themselves as she blushed. 'You're too young to live on your own, Kitty.'

'Am I, begorrah, to be sure?'

'Oi! Less of that!' laughed Asta as she pulled out the foldaway dining table. Her accent was still indisputably Irish after nearly two decades as a born-again Londoner, but she'd never uttered a 'begorrah' in her life. Asta wanted to fit in. She'd come a long way: her Irishness was consigned to the past. Along with the treehouse.

A stickler for accuracy, Kitty pointed out, 'I wouldn't be living on my own, I'd be with Maisie.'

'Hmm.' Asta, like her own mother, had perfected the art of painting a lurid picture with a well-timed *hmm.*

'What's wrong with Maisie?' Kitty was high-pitched, affronted. 'She's my best friend.'

'And her mum's *my* best friend. Maisie's like a daughter to me. But she's more streetwise than you.'

'Maybe if I hadn't gone to Lady Toffington's school for Toffee-Nosed Toffs I'd be streetwise too.'

This was an old argument. 'It wasn't easy finding the fees, you know.' This was quite an understatement.

'I loved school, really; you know I did. But it's time for me to get a taste of real life.'

Don't mention the F words. Further education was an even bigger bone of contention than this mythical flat. It was absurd, in Asta's view, to squander the chance of qualifications for the sake of a 'real life' which wouldn't be half the fun Kitty anticipated. 'Real life,' she said carefully, 'is overrated.'

Kitty rolled her tigerish brown eyes as she laid cutlery and glasses on the tiny tabletop. 'I'll never find out, if you never let me experience it.'

'Darling, I'm really, really proud of—'

Kitty cut her off, her hands flying to her ears, the nails bitten and pink like tiny shells. 'Don't do the *really, really proud of me* thing. I know you are, Mum, and that's great, but . . .' The look of distress was almost comical on Kitty's young, crease-free face. 'I want to be messy, make some mistakes, find out who I am.'

'I know exactly who you are. You're my favourite girl in the whole world, the one who's getting a French Fancy for afters.'

'It'd better be a pink one.' However bloody the mother–daughter skirmish, a truce could always be brokered by Mr Kipling.

After a balanced, nutritious and rather dull dinner, Asta shooed Kitty away to her bedroom with an 'I'll clear up.' She folded the dining table, then the chairs: every inch mattered in their bijou flat. Sometimes Asta wished she could fold herself up, too. Square and bright, the flat was rescued from blandness by the home-made cushions on the threadbare sofa, the photo-montages that hid the damp patches on the walls and the well-thumbed books in flat-pack bookcases that seemed permanently on the verge of collapse.

With just the small sitting room, two boxy bedrooms leading off it, a galley kitchen and a minuscule bathroom that was funny if you were in the mood (Asta was rarely in the mood first thing in the morning), the two women lived in an ordered, almost Japanese way. The tidiness of their little empire made Asta feel safe; Kitty sometimes muttered that she felt hemmed in.

The block had improved since Asta had first viewed it in 2000, with Kitty on her hip and her heart sinking. They'd rented throughout the estate's slow gentrification, and nowadays there was no graffiti helpfully reporting that 'Debs is a slag', no more *eau de wee-wee* wafting up the stairs. Asta was glad, even if the flat's rehabilitation meant that she had *absolutely* no chance of buying it (whereas previously she'd simply had no chance).

'Mu-um!' The familiar two-note siren summoned Asta to her daughter's door.

'What, O noble product of my loins?'

'I've got nothing – no, listen, seriously, don't laugh – I've got nothing to wear.'

'Apart from the clothes on your bed, the floor, the chair, every surface in this room?'

'God, Mum, they're the *rejects*. Nothing goes with anything else. Everything makes me look fat.'

'As if!' hooted Asta, sucking in her tummy.

Kitty held a gingham top between finger and thumb as if it was rotting. 'This gives me pig arms.'

Your arms, thought Asta, *could have been sculpted from Carrara marble by Michelangelo.* Reassurances were no use here. Mothers (according to Kitty and Maisie) were so

9

biased that their compliments were rendered null and void. There was no point eulogizing the gently rounded hips, or the skin that glowed like a (very pretty) atomic reaction. Kitty wouldn't want to hear that the spot where her neck met her back looked so vulnerable it made Asta want to weep. Asta risked, instead, 'Your jeans look great with that grey top, you know, the strappy thing with the bow bit.'

This was, heaven be praised, the elusive right thing to say.

'Mum, you're a genius!' Kitty rummaged through the debris and slipped the garment over her head, turning this way and that in front of the mirror. 'Hmm.' She concentrated on the strappy-thing-with-the-bow-bit with the ferocious intensity of a bomb-disposal expert. 'It'll do.' Fussy, but not vain, Kitty took her wobble-free thighs for granted. She hadn't read the small print about such attributes only being on loan from Old Father Time. Asta knew, though – her bottom *really* knew – and the knowledge added poignancy to the sight of her apple-fresh daughter dragging a brush through her dark, waving hair.

'French hair!' beamed Kitty, meeting Asta's gaze in the mirror. 'Proper French hair, isn't it?'

Asta's indulgent smile became forced; this was a tightrope moment. All she could do was balance, wobbling, on the rope until it passed. Sometimes the moment came and went in an instant.

This time, it didn't. Kitty stepped nearer to the mirror to peer at her own face. 'Am I like my dad?'

'A little.' Asta felt the pause stretch. In the mirror, her own pale face over her daughter's shoulder had the look of somebody passing through airport security with a bumbag full of heroin.

'Which bits?' Kitty regarded herself sideways. 'My nose is like yours, isn't it?'

'Just like mine.' Asta began to tidy the chic jumble sale on the floor.

'My mouth . . . is my mouth like my dad's?' Kitty pouted at her reflection.

'Erm, actually, I think you've got my da's mouth. As it were.' This was so painful: Asta could barely remember Etienne's features. The one snap she had – much pored over by Kitty – was a full-length shot of a lean, golden-skinned boy with a riot of dark hair around an indistinct face. He'd laughed just as she'd clicked the shutter. One of his loud barks, like an otter. An otter having a really good time. 'You're more like my side of the family.'

'I've definitely got his teeth, though.' Kitty gnashed her large, white teeth happily. 'Haven't I?'

'Maisie'll be here any minute, and this room's a tip.'

'Maybe he's where I get my running from.' Kitty had effortlessly out-galloped her classmates every sports day, leading to a half-serious belief in the Looney household that she was an Olympian. 'Was he fast?'

'Very. It's nearly seven, sweetie.' Asta attempted to be honest when Kitty asked these questions, lapsing into make-believe where necessary. She hoped that by satisfying the small requests, she could plug the dam of Kitty's curiosity. For now, 'my dad' was safely in the past tense: one day he'd burst into the present, and Kitty would hear the details Asta held back. Details no girl would want to hear about her father.

'I Googled Etienne de Croix.' Kitty said it boldly, with a silent *so there*. 'There's hundreds.' She faced her mother, biting her lip. 'How can we narrow it down? One of them must be him.'

'Yes, I guess so.' Asta's heart trembled, as if she had a hamster in her bra. The doorbell rang and she whipped out of the room, grateful to the bell for saving her. For now.

Angie barged in ahead of Maisie, pressing a bottle of wine at her hostess, making for the sitting room at speed and carrying on that evening's quarrel. At a lower volume her voice could be liquid and calming, but in full cry it was a screech: '. . . walking around, looking like a prostitute, tummy out, wiggling your bony ass, no way madam, who am I? *Who am I?*' She turned, bellowing at Asta, who took a step back before Angie answered her own question.

'I am Maisie's *mother*.' Angie stressed the word. 'And no mother lets her daughter walk the streets like a hooker on heat!' Angie looked around her, adding in a casual way, 'Got any nibbles?'

A bowl of olives on the coffee table was swiftly handed to her: Asta knew better than to deprive her friend of calories. Hugging Maisie, a skinny Venus in denim whose body language screamed *whatever*, Asta dared to referee. 'What's the row about this time?'

As Maisie opened her mouth, Angie shrieked, 'My girl child wants to pierce her belly button!' Angie snorted, as if Maisie had expressed a desire to go a-mass-murdering. 'Over my dead, cold, lifeless body!'

'Is Kitty ready to go?' Maisie, accustomed to her mother's teacup-based storms, loped out of the room. Soon there were loud whoops and hellos and kisses from Kitty's room; the teenagers saw each other most days, yet always greeted one another as if returned safe from a war.

Fetching a corkscrew, Asta said, 'We haven't had the

body-piercing stand-off yet. I'm still recovering from the tattoo wars.' Kitty had wanted a cherub on her ankle; Maisie had hankered after a heart. Asta had said, 'It might be better to wait until you're older'; Angie had thrown a vase and declared she would kill Maisie, then Kitty, then herself.

'My house, my rules.' Angie shook her head, the dozens of tiny plaits in her hair waggling like a modern-day Medusa.

'You can take the girl out of the Caribbean . . .' smiled Asta, pouring a healthy glass of supermarket plonk for her guest.

'It's our way. I ain't changing. I ain't becoming no mealy-mouthed little *yes miss, no miss* mother.' Angie nodded, talked and drank all at the same time, all movement from her dancing hair to her massive bosom to her eloquent eyebrows. 'My girl's growing up straight and true. I don't need no parenting manual, I lay down the law. I'm not *modern.*'

Sometimes Asta just liked to bask in the glow that came off Angie's fire. On paper, the ebullient, opinionated, chatterbox woman was a nightmare. In the flesh, she was the staunchest friend and ally Asta could wish for. It was all about love, as Asta had discovered early on, when a small ad offering a room for rent had brought her to Angie's door.

A newcomer to London, Asta had thought, 'Ealing! Like the comedies,' but there'd been nothing funny about the tall, neglected house on the end of a sooty terrace. Down in the basement she had found Angie and Maisie, defeating the damp and the mice with roaring fires and the smell of pot roast.

That night, Asta had collected her belongings from the home of her second cousins twice removed in East Molesey. She'd worn out her welcome: Celts are contractually obliged to take in relatives, but a teen on the run who'd given birth in their loft had stretched their generosity to breaking point.

Angie referred to these events as 'when I took you in'. Asta was apt to remind her, 'I did pay rent! I wasn't a stray cat!' even though they both knew that Angie had taken one look at the mother and child on her doorstep and reduced the rent, despite the fact she was only letting the room in a bid to make ends meet.

That, thought Asta, *is stuff that binds people for life, even more than blood or genes.*

Angie lacked malice, a deficit she made up for with fire-power. Once you were in her sights, once she'd decided that you were 'hers', then your every move was scrutinized, judged, commented on. But – and it was a big but, as Asta had discovered – you were also protected, worried about, defended and surrounded by love.

And noise. Angie could do nothing quietly. She crashed and banged and shouted and sang. Having been brought up in Ireland, Asta was accustomed to background noise, to an endless loop of comment and criticism. *The accent's different*, thought Asta, *but the sentiment's the same.*

The girls had left, unflatteringly keen to be gone. On one side of the small sitting room Tom Hanks was making Meg Ryan cry with joy: on the other side, two women were ignoring him as they opened a second bottle of wine and upended a family bag of ready-salted crisps into a bowl. Tinsel was Sellotaped around the edge of the coffee table; the transformation of the flat had begun. A crêpe-paper

Father Christmas dangled from the light fitting, a little wonky, like the women in the room.

'So. Your date.' Angie waved a crisp the size of a satellite dish. 'Are we talking same-old-same-old, or did you manage to behave like a normal person this time?'

'Don't know what you mean.' Asta, ignoring the expostulation and the meteor storm of potato shards, knew exactly what Angie meant. 'The date was . . . fine.'

'Are you seeing him again?'

'Well, no.'

'You did it again!' Angie slapped her thigh. It was a large thigh, and it made quite a noise. 'This is becoming a pattern.'

'Nooo.' Asta laughed that off, knowing she sounded unconvincing.

Angie hoiked her magisterial breasts and ticked off a list on her fingers. 'The bloke from the wine tasting: one date, hot sex, no replay. The guy who drove over your bike: one date, hot sex, no replay. The man we met at the lost property office: one date, hot—'

'OK, it's a pattern,' Asta capitulated. 'Except you're wrong about the hot sex.'

Stopping mid-tick, Angie said, 'You didn't ravish him? Really?'

Sinking lower into the cushions, Asta took a consolatory sip of vile wine. 'I can't really remember,' she whispered. 'I was very, very drunk.'

'Then it's unlikely you played Cluedo.' Angie shook her head, more sympathetic than disapproving, which made it worse somehow. 'Hon, you've gotta straighten this out. You need a man.'

'What you've never had, you don't miss.' Asta played with the baubles at her ears and wished somebody could explain how her life had panned out this way, how she'd reached the grand old age of thirty-three, acquired a flat, career, daughter and debilitating Haribo habit without acquiring a significant other. Other people managed it; it couldn't be that hard. *Stupid* people did it: even that girl from her hairdresser's who thought feng shui was one of Victoria Beckham's children had a partner.

'I'm going to unravel you.' Angie put down her wine glass and looked stern.

'Will it hurt?'

'Why do you drink on dates?' Angie folded her arms, scrutinizing Asta. 'You don't drink much at other times but you get hammered on dates.'

'I was beyond hammered this time.' Asta remembered everything perfectly right up until the fourth tequila shot. Then it went out of focus, but she did recall the fear on her date's even features as the sedate Asta morphed into a wildcat and tugged him onto the dance floor to showcase her funkiest moves. Asta had to face the fact that there hadn't been a dance floor in the crowded bar; she'd been twerking between the tables. 'When we got back to his place I bullied him out of his underpants.' Asta went hot, then cold as she forced herself to be frank. 'I think we broke a coffee table.' She peered out from under her fringe. 'I get the fear, Ange. And I knock back the drinks to fend it off.'

'Fear of what?'

The window of frankness banged shut, leaving the one dark corner that Angie's searchlight never reached in shadow. 'I'm just a tart, aren't I?' said Asta, miserable suddenly.

'Sweetheart,' said Angie, taking one of Asta's hands in her own. Her dark skin was dry, cool. 'You're no tart. You're pure of soul. You are good and true. Don't pull that face, you *are*!' Angie could 'do' emotional scenes such as these without flinching. 'Give yourself a break. Relax, and allow some man to get to know you.' She dropped Asta's hand and it lay on the cushions, a five-fingered fish out of water.

'Never mind me,' said Asta, keen to deflect the spotlight her friend always shone on her love life. So far, Angie had swallowed the red herrings Asta had strewn in her path, but that state of affairs couldn't last forever. Sooner or later, Angie would guess who Asta pined for. 'What about you? You're not exactly drowning in suitors!'

Beaming, Angie toasted Asta with the murky wine. 'I wouldn't have a man in my life if he came with a free gift attached.'

Asta savoured her friend's familiar double standard. 'Not even a teeny weeny little man, just for weekends?'

'Don't need one. Don't want one. Don't like the way they smell. They can't stack dishwashers. Each and every one of them would dump me for a snog with somebody off *Hollyoaks*.' Angie's imperious disdain was something to see. 'Nope, I don't need no man.'

'But I do?' queried Asta. 'Just so I know.'

'You definitely do. You're romantic.'

'I am not!' Asta defended herself without being quite sure why. It seemed wrong, somehow, to be defined as romantic when you had rent to pay, a daughter to rear and a future to plan. 'I'm sensible, logical, hard-headed.'

'You're Irish. Romance comes as standard.' Angie seemed certain of her facts. But then, she always did. 'You need a man to sweep you up in a bear hug, kiss the end of your nose, make you feel special.' Angie sniffed. 'All that shit.'

Asta sighed. 'Hmm,' she agreed dreamily, 'all that shit.'

She shook herself. *I have no time for goo.* When she imagined long walks in the countryside, roaring log fires, Sunday lunch *à deux*, it was like hearing of life on a distant planet. Quite a dull distant planet. She sat up, changing the subject. 'This time next week, Oona will have arrived. We must keep her out of trouble this time. She has a boyfriend now.'

'Poor fool, whoever he is.' Angie and Asta's cousin Oona had a love–hate relationship. They'd negotiated a peace of sorts, but without Asta to bring them together they'd have sprung apart like magnets. Oona, as family, boasted a prior claim, but Angie could point to fifteen years' worth of daily contact. 'I'll do some callaloo.' Angie nodded, smug. 'Oona loves my callaloo.'

'Yes, she raves about it in her emails,' said Asta, keen to encourage the *entente cordiale*. Oona's messages were too infrequent for Asta's liking. The two women had grown up next door to each other back in Ireland, inseparable until Asta had 'left' (as she liked to put it) or 'run away in the night like a big hairy eejit' (Oona's description).

'When are you going back, babes?' Angie turned the sound down on the credits of the neglected film.

'To Tobercree? I'm not,' laughed Asta. 'As in never.'

'Seventeen years is a long time to stay away from home.'

'I'm home now,' said Asta mulishly. 'Right here, on this sofa.' She smiled. 'With you.'

'Kitty deserves to meet her family.'

'I'm her family. And so are you, come to that. She sees Oona once a year.'

'Oh, always an answer.' Angie picked up the bottle and scowled at it for being empty. 'There's me, scrimping and saving to send my child halfway across the world to Trinidad every two years, and you could jump on a plane to see your mother and your sister for four pounds ninety-nine. Are you too mean to spend four pounds ninety-nine on your own daughter?'

'Yes,' said Asta, unapologetic. 'As you well know, Kitty's the reason I left. My shameful teen pregnancy, shock horror, et cetera. I swore I'd never expose her to all that petty moralizing. Besides –' Asta hesitated, not proud of this train of thought – 'if we went to Ireland, it'd spark questions about her father. If Kitty tried to find him . . . I couldn't bear it, Ange.'

'It has to happen!' Angie was a realist: her vision was HD, not rose-tinted. 'Why don't you trust that girl?' Angie had been on Kitty's side ever since she'd first held her as a tiny baby. 'She's sensible.'

The weight of what Asta had left unsaid about Etienne bore down on her. 'Nag me again in a few days' time, Ange. I'll remind you.'

'Oh, you won't have to remind me,' said Angie. 'Got any Twiglets?'

Sitting in bed, propped up on pillows, Asta massaged costly gunge into her cheeks with grim determination. The face cream promised results. *I should think so too, at that price.* Either she woke up looking sixteen, or she'd demand a refund.

Sixteen. Her daughter's age. Asta lay back on her pillows and let out a long, slow breath. The age she'd been when her daughter was conceived. Asta had been too young to appreciate her youth, a dimly remembered Nirvana of touching her toes effortlessly, when 'responsibilities' meant remembering to feed her stick insect. (She hadn't: Mr Twiggs had suffered his own personal Irish Famine under Asta's bed.)

A stereotypical colleen, Asta had pale, freckled skin, eyes of a dainty china blue and a small tilted nose that belied its ladylike design by honking when she laughed. It was a tidy face, with a self-contained look, as if its owner had just heard a joke she wasn't quite ready to share. Both she and her daughter had dark hair, a shade beneath black, but Kitty's rioted while Asta's hung sleek and straight.

Aiming the remote at the portable TV balanced on the chest of drawers, Asta silenced the babble of late-night current affairs. Sometimes she fell asleep to its comforting drone, but it left her feeling vaguely pitiful, as if the newsreader was her pretend boyfriend.

It was awfully quiet, though, without her lovely newsreader boyf.

Under the covers, Asta's mobile squawked. She jumped, anticipating, as would any Irishwoman worth her salt, that a phone call late at night means bad news.

'Hello? Yes?'

'Hiya.'

'Oh, Oona. I thought it was the police.'

'Or the hospital,' laughed Oona, who was *not* worth her salt. 'Or maybe feckin' Interpol. Howaya?'

'Grand.' How easily the Irishisms slipped out. Asta would never have said 'grand' around Angie. 'Have you booked your flight? I bought new pillows for the sofa bed. Last time you were here, you said you'd slept in better gutters. And Angie's asked us round for dinner. I know you hate her callaloo, but just—'

'Ah. Now.' Oona sighed. 'You see . . .'

'I don't like that tone.'

'I can't come,' said Oona all in one breath.

'No-oo!' Asta felt as deflated as a six-year-old denied that last, delicious-looking cupcake. 'But you always come over for three nights before Christmas.'

'Pressures of work prevent me.'

Asta shook the phone. 'Work? As in . . .' She frowned, puzzled. '*Work?*'

'I've got a new job. Very lucrative. And Christmas is my busy period.'

'So did they give you the push from the chemist's?' Asta knew that Oona paid more attention to slipping lip-gloss testers into her handbag than to her customers' skincare needs.

'How very dare you?' laughed Oona, who was uninsultable. 'I've branched out. I'm making a fortune.'

'Doing what?'

'If you come over, you'll find out.'

This was familiar territory; Asta ignored the bait. 'Can you visit in the new year instead?' Oona's annual appearances marked Asta's regression to teenagerdom. They would both talk and gossip and sit up all night laughing. Londoners don't laugh as much as the Irish. 'Late January's good. I could take a week off.'

'You can take *any* week off. That boss of yours lets you do what you like.' This, too, was familiar territory. 'He's mad in love with you, you know.'

'That's about as likely as . . .' Asta was too tired to conjure up a sparkling simile. 'As something extremely unlikely.'

'Don't cancel your time off. Use it to come over here.' Oona's voice had subtly altered, as if the phone was tapped and she was speaking in code. 'Your family needs you.'

'Eh?' As far as Asta knew, her mother and sister had simply healed over the spot where she used to be. *I didn't even leave a dent.*

'Things were rough for them after you scarpered.' Oona called a spade a spade: if necessary, she called it a shovel and hit you with it. 'Well, now they need you. They need somebody to sort things out. I'm sworn to secrecy, so don't ask me to tell you more.'

Asta didn't want to play. *Londoners might laugh less, but at least they don't play manipulative mind games.* 'Oona, please tell me if there's anything seriously wrong.' Asta tried to remember the last time she and her mother had spoken. With a stab of something shaped like shame, she realized it was many weeks.

'Sworn to secrecy,' repeated Oona. 'Your ma would kill me.'

'Is anybody ill?' Asta's grip tightened on the phone.

'Sworn to secrecy.' Oona hesitated. 'But no, nobody's ill.' Both women laughed, the bubble of tension dissolved. 'I'd make a grand spy, wouldn't I?'

'Gossip, woman, give me gossip, not family turmoil. Did your Declan tell his mammy about you yet?'

'Yeah! She's taken to her bed and is refusing all nourishment except a small boiled egg morning and night. Apparently she's writing to the pope.'

'Poor Declan.' Asta remembered him from school, a blocky, uninteresting boy with glasses and the choppy haircut popularized by Victorian lepers. He'd grown into a nerdy teen, a mummy's boy who tailed his dragon of a parent to mass and wore her hand-knits to parties.

'Declan is many things, but he is not poor. He has the love of a good woman, and yes, that would be me,' said Oona in answer to Asta's snigger. 'There's many men who would kill for unfettered access to my erogenous zones 24/7. Did I tell you he's a demon in the sack?'

'My ears! My ears!' Asta wished it could be unheard. The thought of Declan getting jiggy with it was problematical. 'Does his mammy knit his Y-fronts?'

'Scoff all you like.' Not only uninsultable, Oona was unembarrassable. 'What that man doesn't know about my clitoris isn't worth knowing.' She ignored Asta's groans. 'Oh! Listen! There's an Englishman in the Big House again. And he has an arse you could write poems about.'

'High praise indeed.' Asta frowned. 'Has he modernized the house?' A vision of Tobercree's Big House came to her, its elegant Georgian lines blurred by ivy, its broad front door peeling. 'It's such a beautiful building.' Effortlessly superior, the Big House (always respectfully capitalized) had stared down from the hill throughout Asta's childhood. A relic of a patrician past, when English landowners called the shots and built themselves grand homes to live in, it had been decaying genteelly for decades. 'Is that Declan I can hear in the background?'

'Yeah. I'd better service him once more before I send him home to boil an egg for the mammy. Ta-ra!'

Alone again without the busy bleat of Oona's voice, Asta leaned over to peer at the alarm clock. 11.29. Her stomach tightened. 11.30, Kitty had said. 'At the latest, Mum.' Asta plumped up her pillows, straightened the duvet, closed her eyes.

It was years since Asta had had the dream. Tonight, after seeing those sheds, that distant summer had crept a little nearer. Perhaps, she thought, opening her eyes again with a feeling of dread, the dream would return. She hoped not,

23

and picked up a tattered paperback, an Edna O'Brien she'd read already.

Beyond the linen blind, Chelsea was getting its second wind. Pubs were closing, club queues were forming and minicabs driven by men who came from no known country were touting for business. *Teenagers are out there*, thought Asta, *vomiting down their far-too-short skirts, half mad on alcopops, passing their STDs around like crisps.*

The jangle of a key in the front door, just as the digital figures on the clock clicked to 11.30, did more for Asta's features than a cream ever could.

It's a dream and she knows it. But she doesn't quite know it; the knowledge is elusive, like the figure she's chasing through the long grass. Shimmering like smoke, he – and it is a he, the dream-Asta knows this – is always just ahead, never close enough to grab.

They're plunging deeper into the woods. They're drawing close to something which isn't in front of them, but above them. It glowers over them, waiting.

Asta fears it, but she desires it too.

December 14th

'No,' repeated Asta for clarity. 'There's no Asta here.' She waited for the baffled response on the other end of the line to run its course. 'Well, you must have misheard her. Like I said, there's no Asta here. Bye.' She put the phone down on the man she'd ravished just two nights before and jumped at the sound of a male voice behind her.

'Another suitor getting the Looney cold shoulder?'

'Conan!' Asta put a hand to her heart. 'When did you get up? You frightened the life out of me.'

The morning sunlight flooding through the floor-to-ceiling windows gave Conan the silhouette of a sleepy grizzly as he bumbled across the coveted panorama of the Thames in his dressing gown. His apartment, which doubled as Asta's workplace, was a discreetly swanky affair in a high-rise, monied Chelsea ghetto.

A painfully chic Christmas tree, black with white balls hanging from it, stood in a corner, the flat's only concession to the season. Unless you counted the wind-up Santa by Asta's computer.

'Coffee.' His New York twang lengthened the vowels. 'I need coffee.'

'Hung over?' Asta was wry as she joined him at the sleek stainless-steel stretch of the kitchen area. 'You don't have time to be ill. You're expected at the magazine in two hours. I laid out your blue suit and I emailed your column and put a copy in your man-bag.'

Over the snotty gurgles of the espresso machine, Conan said loftily, 'It's not a man-bag, it's a document case.' He gave her a hard look as he realized something; he hadn't finished his column, which meant that, once again, Asta had written it for him. 'Thank you,' he said. 'And FYI, I'm *not* hung over, Mother Superior.' He closed his eyes and rubbed his receding but still exuberant black curls. 'To be precise, I'm still drunk.'

'Did you get what you wanted at the French Embassy party?' Asta leaned against the massive fridge that only ever held her lunch box and a magnum of champagne.

'Don't I always?' yawned Conan. 'Lots of naughty people, doing naughty things to or with other naughty people.' Gossip formed the backbone of Conan's journalism. 'Answer the question, Asta dear. Who was that on the phone?'

'Nobody.'

'A nobody who liked you enough to track down your boss's number. Because –' he leaned forward to poke her on her shoulder – 'you won't answer the nobody's calls on your own phone.'

'Some people can't take a hint,' mumbled Asta, pulling a lever and pressing a button on the coffee machine, which seemed to be having some sort of fit.

'Give the poor sap a whirl.' Conan accepted the coffee and downed it in one, holding out the cup to be refilled. 'Mother Superior's just a nickname, you know. You're not obliged to live up to it.'

'He's not right for me,' sounded better than the more

truthful *I'm too shamefaced to see him again*. There was no escaping Conan: when Asta returned to her desk he padded right along behind her, perched on a corner and disturbed a pile of documents. 'Careful!'

'Sorry.' Conan shifted, and knocked her sharpener to the floor. 'I guess you had sex with him and that's that, just like the other *blokes*.' He savoured the British word.

'How do you know that?' Asta stared pointedly at the screen of her Mac, tapping a key here and there to little effect. 'And, um, it's not true,' she added, hastily.

'I have ears. I hear what you tell that Angie character.'

'Twenty-first-century women have sex, Conan: hold the front page!'

'I'm aware of, and grateful for, the modern woman's take on sex.' Luckily Conan's smugness was tempered by his charm, or Asta would have brained him with a stapler long ago. 'But most women don't have sex once with each partner.' He leaned towards her to say, *faux*-shocked, '*On the first date*.' Enjoying her discomfort, he added, 'You sure like bucking stereotypes.' Conan moseyed towards the master suite. 'I thought all good Catholic girls kept themselves pure as the driven whatever until they bagged a husband.'

'I'm not,' said Asta, 'a good Catholic girl.'

'I'm gonna shower,' said Conan.

'May I expect a running commentary on your every move all day?' Asta knew he liked her to be waspish: Conan nurtured a fantasy that his position as London correspondent of *Boulevard*, a prestigious New-York-based monthly that peddled a sophisticated mix of current affairs and social flim-flam, was actually an old-school journalistic career. To this end, he cast Asta as his indispensable, wisecracking dame of an assistant. Asta liked this casting and played up to it, delighted when he called her 'Kid'.

They disagreed about Conan's career. Asta considered his gossipy column a waste of his talents; she loathed the airbrushed byline photo which shaved years (and all intelligence) from his handsome face. His occasional insightful pieces on modern culture were more to her taste, but Conan was too busy attending society parties – and recovering from them – to buckle down.

Conan was satisfied with his lot, however: he had champagne on tap and a trusty Girl Friday to tidy his hung-over prose.

'Oh, before I forget.' Conan ducked back out of his darkened lair of a bedroom, the shower hissing in the background. 'You know how you're always, and I do mean *always*, nagging me to give you an assignment all of your very own-io?'

'Ye-es.' Asta paused, head down, stooping to pick up the expense forms Conan had spilt. She waited for the sting in the tail: much as she loved Conan, he'd installed a shatter-proof glass ceiling above her head.

'I might just have an article for you to write. Ah, thought that'd make you look up, Mother Superior. Book us a table for two at Bob Bob Ricard and I'll reveal all over lunch.' Taking in her expression, he jutted out his lower lip, disappointed. 'Why aren't you jumping up and down with foolish joy? Why are you looking at me like that?'

'Because,' said Asta slowly, 'you're naked, Conan.'

'Ah.' He glanced down at himself, and grinned at her. 'At least now you know what all the fuss is about.'

'You didn't have to phone me, Mum. I was up. I've been up for hours. *Days*.'

Yeah. Right. Asta could hear the effort her daughter was making to sound like somebody who hadn't just crawled out from under her duvet. 'Please, sweetie, take a look at the sixth-form prospectus I left by your bed.' Asta did her utmost not to sound like a nagging mother, but somebody had to motivate Kitty; despite her excellent brain she'd failed her GCSEs first time around, and had just re-sat them all.

'I might drop by this afternoon,' said Kitty.

And badger me some more about this mythical flatshare. 'Lovely.'

'If Conan doesn't mind.'

'Does Conan ever mind?'

'Nah,' laughed Kitty.

Kitty was always welcome at Conan's. He'd known she and Asta came as a pair when he'd offered Asta the job thirteen years ago

The interview had been brief. Asta had sat, taken aback at the opulence of her surroundings. 'You look a bit young,' Conan had said, pulling down his dark glasses to take her in. 'I need somebody reliable and mature and organized. Because,' he'd sighed, 'I'm none of those things.'

'I'm older than I look,' Asta had claimed, damning her freckles. 'I've done this sort of work before.' No thunderbolt had struck her down for this deliberate lie; perhaps the Ten Commandments hadn't reached Chelsea. 'I'll organize you to within an inch of your life.'

That had made him chuckle, and that was that. Conan had offered the wary young Irish girl a job as his Girl Friday there and then, with no mention of references.

'What's a Girl Friday?' Asta had asked.

'Somebody to look after me. Sort me out.' Conan had pulled a look Asta would come to recognize over the years: it worked on the bright young gels he hung out with, but the head down, eyebrows raised, little-boy-lost expression did nothing for her. 'I need help, but I can't bear the idea of having somebody in my apartment. I'm not easy to live with.'

'Hmm.' Asta had been confused. Conan was holding out a trinket, but she was scared to reach out for it. 'Girl Friday isn't a proper job description.'

'OK, OK. *Jesus*.' Conan had shrugged. 'Call yourself a PA, then. I don't care, so long as you come in every day and do your organize-y thing. Now. Money. Let's see, I'll pay you . . .' Conan thought for a moment and then suggested a figure which, although modest, had been beyond Asta's greediest dreams.

'And Kitty comes too?' Asta had been defiant, fearful that this was the deal-breaker.

'Well, she'd better.' They'd both looked down at Kitty, contentedly picking her nose. 'She's obviously the brains of the operation.'

'A commission?' Angie was using her work phone voice. It was lower, more constrained, as befitted a senior social worker. 'Why go to a fancy restaurant to discuss a job?' She gasped, an extravagant noise that sounded like a hot-air balloon taking off. 'Maybe he fancies you!'

'That's a hell of a leap. Conan eats in fancy restaurants twice a day.'

'Not with *you*. Wouldn't that be funny? If Conan suddenly

declared himself over the starter?' Angie hooted, then coughed self-consciously and returned to her work voice. 'It's about time *somebody* got through to you. I'm a single mum to the ends of my fingertips, but you, Asta . . . there's a whole chapter of you waiting to be read.'

'I'm not doing so badly as a single mother,' said Asta quietly. It was her one real achievement, steering Kitty through the labyrinth of childhood.

'You're doing brilliantly!' Angie was horrified at being misunderstood. 'Kitty's a credit to us.' Angie often slipped in an *us* when praising Asta's daughter. 'But it's time for Mummy to get some action. To pick up where she left off. Find some lurve.'

'I've got Kitty and Maisie and you, so I'm well off for love, thanks.' Oona's cryptic comments about the Looneys 'needing' her popped into Asta's head, and she felt herself wobble, as if her shoes were too high.

'This is fancy,' said Asta.

'Is it?' Conan looked around him at the Art Deco restaurant interior. He took in the mirrored alcoves, the ankle-deep emerald-green carpet, the glittering tableware. 'I suppose it is,' he said, and flicked open the heavy menu.

Even without the twinkling lights snaking around the room and the lush, bedecked tree in the corner, Bob Bob Ricard was a festive place. 'I love a booth.' Asta bounced on the green velvet banquette in their deluxe cubbyhole. 'Love it, love it, love it.'

The waiter, in pink blazer and soft grey trousers, was

too well trained to raise an eyebrow at her bouncing. Instead he placed a champagne cocktail in front of her.

'I didn't ask for—'

'I did,' said Conan. 'Drink up, Mother Superior. And shut up. I'll do the talking today.'

'Lunch. Champagne.' Asta looked dubious. 'Are you about to sack me? Kill me? Ask me to marry you?'

'None of the above.' Conan sipped his whisky sour. 'What do you want to eat? The eggs Benedict is very good.'

As she debated lobster vs oyster (and longed for a Cornish pasty), Asta peeped at the other lunch guests, taking in the businessmen wearing pastel ties that clashed with their florid jowls, size-zero women with brittle laughs, a couple so demonstrably in love that they looked like an advert for a dating website. She watched Conan study the menu, great head down, a look of concentration on his broad face that he could never summon up for his work. He had the bulky build of his Irish forebears, shoehorned into bespoke tailoring and garnished with discreet signifiers of status: a serious watch, gold cufflinks, a diamond on his pinkie. His whole bearing sang of wealth, health, entitlement, as if his sense of self was dry-cleaned every night while he slept.

In the intersection between two speckled mirrors, Asta saw a jigsaw of her own reflection. They made an odd couple. She sported an almost terminal case of bed hair, and her cashmere-mix cardi (it boasted a whole eight per cent of the precious stuff) was showing its age.

Presently, after prawn cocktail and pie, Asta said, 'So. What about this article, then?'

'You're the only person I'd trust with this assignment.'

That last word set Asta a-wriggling. She was glad she'd

worn her black trousers: they were far more assignment-y than her customary jeans.

'It will involve travel. And exploiting your contacts.'

Wondering who these contacts might be, Asta nodded. Her pen was poised above a new notebook she'd ceremoniously unwrapped that morning. 'Is it a filler?' she asked, and then, more hopefully, 'Or a one-page piece?'

'Neither. It's for the Europe in Focus section. At least three pages. With photos.'

Putting down the pen, Asta frowned. 'Are you codding me, Conan?' Her accent and jargon veered towards Ireland whenever she was discombobulated.

'No, I'm not *codding* you.'

'That's the first section of *Boulevard* I turn to.' Full of flavour and colour, Europe in Focus was sometimes searing reportage on conflict, at other times a lighter piece, like the one Conan had recently turned in on Morris Dancing. Asta took a slug of her cold white wine. It tasted like angel cake might if it came in a glass. 'I'm too green for this gig.'

'I know. My bosses agree, believe me. But this is tailor-made for you, Asta. I've stuck my neck out and convinced them to commission you.'

'Why?' Asta was suspicious. Conan, for all his brotherly interest in her well-being, had always been loath to further her career. 'You don't really want me to be a writer. You want me tending to your needs, night and day, like a Geisha. Explain, O'Rourke.'

'With pleasure, Looney.' Conan sat back, chest out, arms laid along the back of the banquette. 'It's about Ireland.'

'Right.' Asta chewed her lip. She could do Ireland. She was perfect for Ireland. As long as it wasn't Tobercree.

'Tobercree, to be exact.' Conan beamed. 'See? Perfect! Am I good to you or am I good to you?'

A bitter taste flooded Asta's mouth. So this commission was nothing to do with the thousands of words she'd written for Conan, nothing to do with her creativity, her energy, her ideas. It was a simple case of her place of birth. 'Why,' she asked slowly, 'would *Boulevard* be interested in Tobercree?'

'It's a one-horse village, I'm guessing?'

'It couldn't muster up a whole horse.'

Conan laughed. He didn't seem to notice how low Asta had sunk on her banquette. 'You really don't know about the phenomenon?'

'Eh?' said Asta, stupidly. Tobercree had no phenomena; it didn't even have a hairdresser's.

'They have a statue there, of some saint, in the church. Catherine, is it?'

'Yes. I know St Catherine.' Asta pulled a face. 'Well, I don't *know* her. We don't go clubbing together. What about her?'

'Your little saint's been crying. It's all over the media.' Conan frowned. 'Hey, don't I pay you to keep up with the zeitgeist so I don't have to?'

'Yeah. Sorry. Must have missed it.' The truth was that Asta mentally pixellated any Irish news story. She was an exile, and any mention of her homeland made her itch. 'I've heard of crying statues. There was one in Wicklow my mum used to visit with her friends, in a minibus, as if they were off to a rock concert.'

'Crowds are flocking to your no-horse village. The statue cured a deaf girl. Just like that. TV news teams from all over the world have covered the story. A little fly speck on the map of the back of beyond is suddenly famous. Sorry, kid, no offence. I know it's your home.'

'This is my home,' said Asta quietly.

'At the eye of the storm is the parish priest. My instincts tell me he's the man with the plan. He's pulling this scam. 'Cos it has to be a scam, right?' laughed Conan, rhetorically. 'Statues don't cry. Every adult knows that.'

'Not the adults in my family.' Asta could imagine her mother and sister's excitement at having a real live boo-hooing statue in the local church: they'd be like heroin addicts, strung out and wild-eyed, up all night.

'Trouble is, the priest won't talk. Doesn't give interviews. Says the saint can talk for herself. An expert in Irish blarney.'

'Yeah, that sounds like Father Dominic.'

'You know him!' Conan looked ecstatic.

'Wish I didn't.' Asta had evicted Father Dominic from her thoughts long ago.

'I think this guy's lining his own pockets.'

'Wouldn't surprise me.'

'Take Kitty with you. We want a nice in-depth portrait of the village. An investigation into how educated men and women can believe in such Dark Ages superstition. But you have to nail it, Asta. You have to find out *how* the priest makes the statue cry.' He gestured at her with his empty glass. 'You're the ace up my sleeve. A bona fide Catholic miss who grew up just down the road. You go in under cover, find an "in" to the shonky priest's house, steal the story and fly home to your very own byline.'

'I already have a ready-made "in" to the priest's house.' The flat delivery belied Asta's words.

'You do?' Conan looked delighted, the way he'd looked

when Asta had told him his third fiancée had sent the ring back.

'My Aunty Peg is the priest's housekeeper.'

'Hallelujah! So she'll help?'

'You've obviously never met my Aunty Peg.' Asta conjured up her relative, head to toe in black with a scowl to curdle milk. 'She's not the most helpful woman in the world.'

'But it's a fantastic start. You can exploit her.'

'Again, you've obviously never, et cetera.'

'There are strings attached.' Conan attempted sternness. 'You report to me. I help shape the piece. That's the deal, that's the way I sold your involvement to the high-ups.'

Asta cleared her throat. 'Conan . . .'

'Why do I get the feeling I'm not going to like your next sentence?' Conan frowned, a proper frown that transformed his blithe face.

'Sorry, but I can't do this.'

There was a long silence. Asta could practically hear Conan's cogs whirring; he knew her too well to try and dissuade her. 'Do I get to find out why?'

'Not really. It's a long story. It wouldn't make sense.' Asta was wittering: she put the brakes on. 'Bottom line . . . I can't do this.'

In Conan's disappointed face, Asta read all the favours he'd done her over the years, all the perks, all the under-standing about shooting off early because Kitty was ill, or third shepherd in the school nativity. Conan had upped her salary when Asta had fretted about affording private educa-tion ('Might as well get Kitty beaten up by a better class of bully,' he'd said), he'd tolerated Kitty trundling around his apartment during the school holidays, he'd thrown Asta a lifeline when she was about to drop from the fatigue of cleaning strangers' houses all day, every day.

'Is that all I get?' Conan leaned in. 'Asta, this is an amazing opportunity. I deserve an explanation. No, goddammit.' He slapped his open palm on the table, the uncouth noise drawing looks from every direction. 'I deserve a *thank you, Conan* and a *I can't wait to get started*.'

Asta couldn't bring herself to supply the explanation Conan needed, so it was best to say nothing.

'Hey! Cheque, please.' Conan motioned to the waiter and threw a wad of notes onto the table. 'I'm out for the afternoon, Asta.' He was out of his seat, avoiding her eye. 'When you get back, book me a first-class ticket to the nearest airport to Tober-whatsit for the sixteenth, and sort me out the best hotel in the area for seven nights.'

The lunch meeting, and Asta's brief black-trousered moment as a woman with an assignment, was over.

Snatching a moment between meetings to call, Angie was direct. 'You've blown it.'

'I haven't!' Asta defended herself, knowing that Angie was right. By refusing to explain, she'd managed to both hurt and annoy a man who was an important strut in the fragile framework of her independence. Conan would never offer her another assignment. 'Well, I have. But let's draw a line under it, eh?'

Drawing lines under things was not Angie's style. 'We don't have knights on white steeds, you and me. If there are going to be roses around the door in our old age, then we have to buy them. And plant them. You're a role model for your daughter, Asta. How will she feel when she realizes her mum is a coward?'

'I'd rather be a coward than a corpse,' muttered Asta, resurrecting a phrase from her childhood.

'Plus, it's great timing. Didn't Oona say something about your family needing you? What manner of person ignores that?'

'A person who knows all about emotional blackmail. The Looneys have PhDs in the subject.' Asta was uneasy, despite her flippant answer. *Nobody's ill*, she reminded herself. They'd got along fine without her all these years; a few more wouldn't make any difference.

'You must grab this opportunity with both hands!' Angie was evangelical, zealous, bloody frightening. 'Show Kitty her homeland. Well, one of them.'

'Don't you remember what Father Dominic called her? My family didn't defend her. Or me. They were ashamed. Of Kitty. Of my beautiful girl.' Asta pursed her lips, stemming the flow. This was old dirty laundry she'd sworn never to air again.

'People change,' said Angie.

'Not my family.'

'Look, you're being a fool, and I don't hang around with fools. Sort it out.'

Angie's tough love is particularly tough, thought Asta as she put the phone down and dialled the travel agent to book Conan's first-class flight to Ireland.

'Look at the way it catches the light!' Kitty was a small child again as she twirled the fuchsia bauble. She placed it on the tree, reconsidered, moved it, stood back, moved it again.

Looney Sr and Jr took dressing the tree very seriously.

'Do they have Christmas trees in France?' asked Kitty, unwrapping the angel from layers of tissue paper. Whatever the theme, the angel she'd made in primary school was a constant. Tattered now, she bore the marks of her years with grace. 'Do you think one year I'll spend Christmas there? With my dad?'

Asta was stuck for an answer. An honest *Of course not!* was too frank, but she was weary of half-truths. Kitty was showing initiative now; she could imagine her daughter booking an EasyJet flight and doorstepping a random French man with a *Bonjour, Papa!*

'Turn off the lights!' Kitty fizzed with excitement. This was their ritual; the room must be made dark before the tree lights were switched on, and then – *ta-daa!*

'It's the best one ever!' Kitty said this every year. And she was always right.

Christmas had officially broken out in the tiny flat.

Unable to settle, Asta tried to outrun her misgivings with a bath and an episode of *30 Rock*. Nothing worked. She felt guilty about Conan. She felt guilty about Kitty. She felt guilty about feeling guilty.

Picking up a copy of *Boulevard* at random from the tottering pile by her bed, Asta flicked through it, stopping at a piece she hadn't read before.

'Face Your Demons!' said the headline, beside the byline photograph of a psychologist who turned in a few thousand words for every issue. She was a highly strung woman who Conan had bedded once and then forgotten, and a high proportion of her articles seemed to be about toxic men and how to avoid them; but this particular essay spoke directly to Asta. The psychologist – who was much older than her byline photo suggested – argued that carrying bad feeling about past events could cripple people emotionally.

Amen to that. Asta visualized her heart bandaged up and leaning on a crutch.

One way to deal with them, according to the essay, was to put them in writing, as if composing a memoir. In that way, you could confront them safely, then close the book and put them away. The past would no longer have any power over you.

Asta wondered if the psychologist – or 'that psycho', as Conan had referred to her after she bombarded him with emails – might have a point.

Dragging out a writing pad, she settled herself on her bed, lit a scented candle for no good reason other than *why not?*, and began.

When I heard his name, my heart swelled. Etienne de Croix. *I liked him so much that I avoided him like the plague.*

Invaded by twenty French exchange students, Tobercree's pheromone levels threatened to blow it into the sea.

The incomers weren't like the natives. I'd kissed some of the local boys and they'd left me neither shaken nor stirred. The French boys murmured to each other in a low, smoky rumble when we girls walked past. They didn't shout Hey, me mate fancies ya!, *they didn't vomit over their own feet at the church disco, they didn't go puce if somebody said 'breast'.*

The French boys smoked. And they laughed with a throaty hurr-hurr-hurr. *They were impossibly glamorous, and they scared me.*

Oona nabbed Jean-Paul before the other girls were out of the starting blocks. He had kinky, greasy black hair, a leather coat and his own personal Gauloise fog. While they smouldered at each other, I was busy ignoring his friend Etienne.

Etienne loped behind Jean-Paul, not in a subordinate way, but amused, watchful. I was mad about his hair. It was longish, curling, dark, and it fell across brown eyes that were always on the ground. Was he shy? Or just rude? The boy sparked questions in me and I found myself watching out for him.

Like the chat who got the crème, Oona paraded Jean-Paul like a new handbag. I grew accustomed to his limited conversation ('Do you like ze Cure? I like ze Cure. 'Ow big are your boobs?') and I looked the other way when he and Oona snogged as if they had ten minutes to live.

All the while, I resolutely cold-shouldered his best mate, and practised writing Asta de Croix in curly hand-writing.

Nobody at home noticed my new obsession. Gerry, my big sister, was getting married in a couple of months, and everyday life had been sucked into a vortex of marquee prices, cake tasting and bridesmaid bullying.

Ma was nuts about her prospective son-in-law, absorbing any amount of his sycophantic compliments. I was neutral about Martin, finding him too vanilla to hold my interest when there was so much else to think about.

The day of a planned boat trip, eleven mixed Frogs and Paddies, was moodily grey, but we went ahead anyway. The Irish learn young not to let the weather spoil their fun. After a hissed conference between Oona and Jean-Paul, I *realized my cousin had taken matters into her own hands. I found myself alone in a creaky rowing boat with Etienne.*

Red-faced, I pushed away from the shore, avoiding the eyes I wrote poems about. I let Etienne take the oars; display was important to these French boys.

The little flotilla headed out from the cove, bobbing and wheeling. Laughter floated over the water. Our boat was silent.

Perhaps, I thought, those moody foreign films are true-to-life and French people really do communicate mutely, with loaded looks and breathy grunts. We were on the sea for forty minutes and our script went like this:

Etienne: So . . .

Asta: Yeah . . .

Etienne: I like . . . boat.

Asta: Me too.

[Thirty-nine minutes' silence]

Etienne: I want to kiss you.

Asta: OK.

After Etienne kissed me, he held me really hard. As if he meant it. Over his shoulder I could see the glorious scoop of the cove floodlit by the setting sun.

I could also hear Oona whooping, but I blocked that out.

Over the next few days, Oona would warn me not to fall for him, because 'they're fecking off home in a few weeks'.

'I'm not falling for anyone,' I'd say. And it was true. I didn't love Etienne. I adored him and enjoyed him, but above all I lusted after him.

It was quite something, lust. In the clumsy arms of my yokel boyfriends I'd never understood what all the fuss was about. Now, I got it. It was like sitting on a rocket, like your insides going through a spin cycle, like being possessed. It was pure, clean, as cool as snow and as dangerous as fire.

Half a lifetime later, I can still smell him.

Gauloises plus rumpled cotton, warm from his body. Around the edges a slightly ripe, musky smell, like a peach left out in the sun.

Etienne's feelings for me matched my feelings. We were un-lovers. He would bury his face in my skin, greedily breathing me in. He traced the line of my lips with a gently calloused finger and stood up in excited expectation when I turned the corner . . . but I knew he didn't love me.

It was what it was. And what it was was lovely.

One evening on the bridge, Etienne and I were accosted by Father Dominic, his blood-shot eyes on our clasped hands.

'I hope you two aren't up to any monkey business,' he thundered.

Funny he should say that . . .

I decided to have sex with Etienne precisely because I didn't love him. Etienne was sensitive, perceptive. I trusted him. Sex with Etienne would be funny and romantic. And just a touch soppy. My first time should be all those things, but I didn't want it capitalized: if we'd been in love it would be my First Time, and the pressure would be too great.

Huddled against him, a driftwood fire crackling at our feet and Oona shouting at Jean-Paul behind us, I broached the subject.

Etienne's surprised smile cut a white slash through the dark. He kissed me. It felt like drowning. He said, 'We don't have to, you know.'

And I did love him, a little, for saying that.

My place was out of the question. Ma would feel it in

her bones if the deed was done between sheets she'd laundered.

Etienne's lodgings with a family of thirteen were a no-no. I didn't want our momentous tryst to take place in the top bunk above red-haired triplets.

Then I thought of somewhere so perfect that I squealed. When I told Etienne about the abandoned treehouse, deep in the woods, he squealed too, but in French, so it was more elegant than the noise I made.

It felt wrong not to tell Oona. She knew everything about me, and I knew all about Oona, from her favourite TV programme to the fact that she slept with her long-gone mum's nightie under her pillow. It was disloyal not to tell her; but I knew Oona's heavy-handed commentary on something so special would dent the magic.

The big day arrived. I barely registered Gerry's breakfast-table tantrum about a great-aunt who hadn't RSVP-ed. Coming over all symbolic, I put on a silky white T-shirt to meet Etienne at the dark brow of the woods. Through the long grass, into the clearing I remembered from childhood games . . . and there it was. The rickety treehouse Da made for me and Gerry. We didn't have Da for long. Sometimes I wonder if things might have been different if he'd been around when my troubles began. He was a good man, my da, and he loved me.

He wasn't much good at building treehouses, though.

'It's falling apart,' laughed Etienne.

'It's pretty, though, isn't it?' I needed him to see its beauty.

'Oui, vair pretty.' Etienne chucked me under the chin: no Irish boy had ever done anything so sentimental. 'Comme toi.'

I felt a rush, as if all the feelings I'd ever felt were ganging up in my head.

'Tu es sure?'

'Oui, *I'm sure.*'

Not just sure; I was impatient.

Asta laid down the writing pad. She could give up now, leave out the rest, nobody would know.

I'd know. Asta began to write. She would finish the job.

Shy about undressing, we hid against each other. Tussling with the condom broke the mood: Etienne giggled so hard tears came out of his narrowed eyes. The laughter soon gave way to breathless words with no real form or language.

Nature took over. We were two creatures, weightless and innocent, discovering a new way of communicating.

Etienne said my name. I whispered his.

The next day, he went home.

Facing demons took stamina, but it was worth it for a dream-free night. Asta crept between clean sheets, leaving the fairy lights around her mirror switched on. Their cheerful, celebratory twinkle was the last thing she saw before she fell asleep.

Asta embraced Etienne in the long grass. They looked up and the rickety treehouse loomed over them, casting a rat-coloured shadow in the summer afternoon.

When Etienne placed his foot on the rope ladder, the structure above them tilted.

Asta shrieked, but Etienne held out his hand. He was fearless.

'Come,' he said, and in his face Asta read a dare.

December 15th

'I mean it, KitKat, if you don't get out of bed I'm opening today's little door on your advent calendar and stealing the chocolate.' Before she had time to make good her threat, Asta's phone cheeped.

Why aren't you at work yet? (Or is that also too complicated to explain?)

Ignoring the sarcasm, Asta politely informed Conan that she never started until midday on Tuesdays. She refrained from adding *as you'd know if you ever got up before noon*, because she didn't want to stoop to his level. Conan was accustomed to having her there, a constant figure in his landscape, sitting erect at her desk, putting right the never-ending messes he made.

'Kitty!' she bellowed. 'A tiny chocolate shepherd! Yum!'

Asta wanted to text Conan again, beg him to extinguish his bad mood. He was a constant in *her* landscape too; a burly, good-tempered giant she relied on to always be the same. Running late. Smoking too much. Slightly hung over. This chilly Conan who stabbed out sarky messages wasn't to her taste.

'I'm unwrapping him! The foil's coming off!'

Despite the starlet girlfriends, the engagements, the leg-overs in the lifts of five-star hotels, Asta thought of Conan as *hers*. She gave him something the long-legged pedigree lovelies couldn't: she challenged him.

Or at least, that's how Asta had always seen their relationship. This change in the weather made her reappraise matters. *Maybe*, she thought, *he'll sack me and replace me*.

Asta didn't hear Kitty clomp into the kitchen and snatch her shepherd. She'd been whisked to a tundra, a Conan-free place where she had an ordinary job and an ordinary boss.

Her stomach plummeted to the flat below. Her plan would never pan out if Conan let her go. Asta needed him to wake up one day and realize that he loved her the way she loved him.

Moving about the cramped kitchen, boiling an egg, toasting multigrain bread, stepping around the teabag Kitty sent plunging to its death on the lino, Asta allowed herself the rare luxury of pondering Conan the man as opposed to Conan the boss.

The former was every bit as maddening as the latter, but Conan the man had lit a fire in Asta's loins the moment they'd met, and it had never quite gone out. Thirteen years of practice had enabled her to box up her attraction to him and stow it somewhere in the loft of her brain. She had neatly packed away her appreciation of his dashing looks, and how his bungling touched her heart, and her silly need to make him laugh. All these things were of no use to her. Not until he woke up, like a big, hairy sleeping beauty, and smelt the coffee.

'Door,' she said at the sound of the bell.

'God-duh,' said Kitty. 'I do *everything* in this house.'

A moment later, Conan and his enormous overcoat seemed to fill the kitchen.

'How do you live in such a tiny flat?' He leaned against the fridge, disarranging the Christmas fridge magnets. 'Guinea pigs have bigger hutches.' He swiped up the toast soldiers bound for Kitty's boiled egg and popped them into his mouth, chewing and talking at the same time. 'Nice dressing gown,' he said to Kitty. 'DKNY?'

'Primark,' said Kitty, twirling.

'On you it looks designer.'

'Conan,' said Asta, breathless at this ambush, 'what the hell are you doing here?'

'A simple *hello* would suffice.' Her boss folded his arms and enjoyed her discomfort. 'So, Kitty, you on drugs yet?'

'You're so evil,' hooted Kitty, swatting at Conan. He was probably, thought her mother, the nearest thing she had to a father figure, God help her.

'Christ, is that your tree?' Conan peered into the sitting room. 'Or is it from a dollhouse?'

'We can't all order our trees ready-trimmed with sterling silver balls,' said Asta, a touch more waspishly than an employee on the naughty step should. Trying to conceal her joy at having Conan's tousled glamour in her home, she came over all school-marm. *He's forgiven me*, she thought.

'Have you bought Kitty anything from me for Christmas?' asked Conan.

'Not yet.'

'Here, KitKat.' Conan pulled out his wallet and flicked through tenners like a racecourse bookie. 'Buy yourself something unsuitable.'

Asta's knee-jerk reaction was, 'Conan, that's too much.' The wealth that dripped like molasses from Conan's fingertips had never been part of the attraction. In fact, a little financial hardship might have helped Conan develop some practical skills. *But then*, she realized, *he wouldn't need me so much*.

Kitty didn't share her mother's attitude to money. 'Fifty pounds!' Her face lit up with the wholesome, hideous greed of the average teenager. 'Thank you!' She threw her arms around Conan, and his face lit up too.

'Guess where I'm going tomorrow?' he asked as Kitty tucked the money into her dressing-gown pocket.

'Timbuctoo?' said Kitty. 'Brighton?'

'Tobercree.'

Kitty stopped tucking, her eyes wide. 'Get off,' she barked. 'That's where Mum's from.'

'Don't I know it.' Conan wandered out to the sitting room, dwarfing the fixtures and fittings. 'Do you think you'll ever go there?'

'Erm . . .' Kitty looked at Asta.

The expression in Kitty's eyes was a slap in the chops to Asta. She knew that foxy little face better than she knew her own, and she read fear there.

That clinched it.

'Conan,' said Asta. 'You're not going anywhere.'

Asta had passed down to the next generation, along with her nicely shaped nose and her weirdly shaped knees, a fear of going back. She refused to subject Kitty to a life sentence of pointless angst.

The fear had to be faced. And whupped.

'Pack a bag, KitKat. We're off to Ireland.'

Over endless mugs of coffee, plans were laid.

'Will it snow?' asked Kitty. 'It'll snow!' She answered her own question, drumming her heels with joy. 'It always snows in Ireland at Christmas.'

'Ireland's a real place, you know. It's not a snow globe.' Kitty's enthusiasm alarmed Asta. The fly-blown village could only disappoint after such a build-up. 'It usually rains at Christmas.'

'So,' said Conan, who had taken his coat off to reveal trousers twice as expensive as the sofa he sat on. 'The plan is?'

Referring to her clipboard, Asta read out the agenda they'd cooked up. 'One: infiltrate Father Dominic's house via Aunty Peg. Two: examine statue close up, and discover how he makes her cry. Three: investigate money trail.'

Conan interrupted to say emphatically, 'It's all about money. See where it's being spent.' He waved his hand, grandly, as if Asta was a courtier. 'Carry on.'

'Four: interview the believers and the healed. Five: confront Father Dominic with the truth about the statue.' Asta ended with an audible gulp. She'd left Father Dominic behind aeons ago, and the thought of seeing him, let alone confronting him, filled her with soup-like dread.

'Pepper the article with quotes from ordinary people.' Conan drew air quotation marks, as if he didn't quite believe in these fabled creatures. 'You've booked the flights, yeah? Going out on the sixteenth and coming back on the twenty-third?'

'You heard me do it,' said Asta. 'Can't it wait until after Christmas?' Christmas had always been a golden full stop to each year for Asta and Kitty, no matter how hard the previous twelve months might have been.

'Deadlines, doll,' said Conan apologetically.

'But I won't be able to do all the little last-minute things.' Asta felt cheated, as if Christmas would happen behind her back. 'When will I wrap? And I haven't bought the pudding yet. And—'

'And shut up,' said Conan.

Packing done; arguments about packing done; items Kitty had smuggled into her case extracted; time for bed. Asta kissed Kitty on her cheek, a cheek which smelt of Body Shop cleanser and youth, and whipped out her laptop.

A search for *Tobercree crying statue* unleashed pages of results. Hopping from one to another and skim-reading, Asta learned a lot. The sheer number of weeping statues worldwide amazed her – apparently they were a 'thing'. Some were merely splashed surreptitiously with a combination of oil and salt, but others were ingeniously fitted with tubes leading to a small reservoir of water which could be pumped through to the eyes at the appropriate moment.

The local paper proclaimed: 'IT'S ST CATHERINE GIVEAWAY WEEK IN THE TOBERCREE CHRONICLE!' A respected national broadsheet linked the miracles to the recession.

Some more hopping from link to link, and Asta found a nun's blog: 'Tobercree is lucky to have such a marvellous parish priest, who works day and night to put them on the map.' She closed the page. *Try being an unmarried mother in Father Dominic's parish, and then see how* marvellous *he is.*

'Mu-um!' called Kitty from her bed. 'I'm too excited to sleep! It's like Christmas has come early!'

Asta put aside the laptop. She wouldn't sleep either. Dread of the dream was only part of it. Tomorrow she'd confront faces she hadn't seen for seventeen years. Would she be welcome?

And the questions that Tobercree would spark in Kitty would have to be answered. Asta punched her pillow as if it was to blame and then settled down, determined to keep the dream at bay by sheer force of will.

The treehouse floorboards are rough beneath her bare feet. Beyond the uneven square of the window, the woods have grown dark. Kissing Etienne, Asta can't see his features; they slide away from her.

The feeling of foreboding, of something coming through the woods, is lessened slightly by the movement of his lips on hers, so Asta kisses him harder.

They both freeze as her name is called from the forest floor.

TOBERCREE

December 16th

From seat 17a, thirty thousand feet in the air, Ireland didn't look as if it had changed at all.

'It really is green,' grinned Kitty, leaning over her mother's lap to squint out of the absurdly small plane window. 'The Emerald Isle isn't just a cliché.'

'Nope.' Asta peered through the clouds. The rain wasn't a cliché, either. The land below looked abundant and pleasant, a reliable lowerer of blood pressure for weary travellers.

Apart from the one in seat 17a.

'Wait 'till I tell Maisie we went to the airport in a *limo*. Conan's brilliant, isn't he?'

'Brilliant,' agreed Asta, her sarcasm skating over Kitty's head. Conan had promised to be *in* the limo to see them off, but once again, his hangover had won.

A hug – however brotherly – from him would have set her up for this adventure. The next few days would demand a lot of Asta; already she missed the reassuring timetable of her London life, her daily interaction with Conan. *Will he miss me?*

The answer was an emphatic 'not on your nelly'. Tonight would be business as usual; he'd be out partying, chatting up blue-blooded models and passing out in the taxi home.

'Mum, I can't believe I'm going to meet Grandma.'

'She came over when you were born.' Asta remembered that tense fortnight well.

'On the phone she always asks me the same things. How am I? How's school?'

'She's not good on the phone,' conceded Asta. 'You'll meet your Aunty Gerry as well.'

'What's Gerry short for?'

Jesus, thought Asta, *my own daughter doesn't know the basics about her closest relatives.* 'Geraldine.'

'Is she nice?'

'She's lovely,' said Asta. Gerry wasn't all that lovely, but Kitty could make up her own mind about that. 'And there's Oona, of course. She's dying to catch up with you.'

'I'm a bit nervous, actually,' admitted Kitty, rolling up her copy of *Heat* and tapping the tiny fold-down table with it. 'What will they make of me?'

'They'll love you, darling. Like I do.' Asta hoped that was true: when Kitty had been a mere bundle of cells, there'd been precious little love on offer. Cautiously, she added, 'They're a funny bunch,' hoping to provide some armour against the mixed reception they were bound to receive. 'But we can escape them at the hotel. In seven days we'll be home and in the new year I'll treat us to a proper holiday.' *Boulevard* was generous: the fee would send them somewhere hot and un-Irish.

'Mum,' said Kitty, uncertainly.

'Yes, love?'

'Tell me something *nice* about Tobercree.'

'I've told you hundreds of nice things about Tobercree!' Asta was shocked.

Kitty shook her head, her eyes big.

'Let's see.' Asta was dismayed by her own parenting skills. 'There's the cove. A sweep of fine sand, with dunes. I love dunes. And the woods. They're dark and deep and wild. The hills are gentle, covered in gorse. And, ooh, the castle! It's a ruin, spooky in the moonlight. And the village is really cute.' This felt like too little, too late. 'It's a typical Irish village.'

'OK.' Kitty had the Looney skill of investing humdrum words with layers of meaning. She listened as the crackly tannoy instructed them to buckle up. 'Mum,' she said with a gulp. 'We're there!'

And I, thought Asta, *am right back where I started.*

'There they are!' A cry went up as Asta and Kitty exited the customs section of the tiny airport, trailing their wheeled suitcases like curmudgeonly pets.

'Mum?' Kitty quailed as a mob surged towards them.

'It's OK, it's just . . . Looneys.' Asta braced herself as the tidal wave of relatives hit. Suitcases were whisked away, faces thrust into their own, small babies jiggled for their approval.

'Ah, look, Asta's the image of her grandmother, God rest her soul!'

'And is that little Kitty! All grown up!'

'Did youse eat on the plane?'

'Have you no fellas with you?'

'Did you buy them shoes in London?'

'Do you remember me?'

Asta struggled to stay upright as Kitty was jostled from her side to have her hair strenuously admired by a troupe of old ladies. 'Hello, hi there, hello,' she smiled, knowing how Paul McCartney must have felt during Beatlemania.

'Asta!' A small, bird-faced woman with ferociously bright eyes, like her mother but much older, broke through. 'Come on, love, we've a minibus waiting.'

'Mum?' Asta stared rudely. Where had all the lines on Ma's face come from? Why was she portly? And why was her fabulous flaming red hair completely white?

Ma stopped short, one arm through her daughter's. She gestured at Kitty. 'So that's . . . herself?'

'Yes, Mum.' Asta swallowed. 'Kitty! Come and meet your grandmother.'

A deafening 'Aww!' went up as Kitty escaped the old ladies and approached Ma, her feet slow. Ma's arms shot out, and Kitty was squeezed until she gasped.

'Aunty Peg!' Asta's greeting teetered between delight and horror. 'You don't look a day older!'

'Hmm.' Peg Looney had looked one hundred and four since childhood, with her unforgiving bun of jet-black hair. 'You're back to re-break your poor mother's heart, I suppose?'

A thousand retorts died on Asta's tongue: nobody cheeked Peg. 'I've come to see the family,' she fibbed. 'Hopefully no organs will be broken in the process.'

'Come on, youse lot.' Ma turned decisively for the exit, her arm around Kitty. 'Quickly, Assumpta!' she chided Asta.

Kitty's sneakers halted, almost tripping her grandmother and their hysterical disciples. 'Assumpta?' she repeated, staring at her mother.

'Yes. Get over it.' Asta sped towards the sliding doors, glad that what lay on the other side would distract her daughter.

'Snow!' yelped Kitty.

'Yes,' said Ma proudly, as if she'd personally arranged the weather. 'It's been snowing all morning.'

'Isn't it lovely, Mum?'

'It's an airport car park,' muttered Asta. The sketchy flakes fluttering to the ground alarmed her, even though they disappeared like a magic trick as soon as they landed.

Oona leaned against the bonnet of a minibus, a chauffeur's cap jauntily balanced on a nest of titian curls and ringlets augmented by the worst hair extensions Asta had ever seen. They hung like road-kill from her cousin's head.

'Yay!' Oona bounced gleefully on the spot, and her 40DD bosom bounced with her. Soon Asta was clasped to that bosom and was being jiggled and tickled and generally manhandled as the Looney entourage bundled into the back seats. 'You came! You came! You came!'

Respect for personal boundaries is not something the Irish are famed for. Asta was black and blue from being poked and jabbed by the time the minibus coughed them all out onto Tobercree's main street. She was, apparently, fatter, thinner, taller and smaller than the mob remembered. The lack of a man was *tsk*-ed over, the beauty of Kitty agreed upon, and the breaking of Ma's heart re-confirmed.

'Where's Gerry?' Even with the changes that seventeen years can wreak, none of the squawking women resembled Asta's sister.

'Couldn't make it, love.' Ma marshalled the men of the party to carry the luggage. 'Pressure of work.'

Hmm. Gerry worked four days a week in Tobercree post office.

'Did you really grow up in a pub?' Kitty gazed up at the sign: *Looney's Saloon Bar and Lounge.* 'Cool,' she decided, surprising Asta.

Anything but cool to Asta's eyes, the pub was a facsimile of countless others, with its solid brick frontage and traditional etched-glass sign in flowing Victorian script. But it was clean, well-kept and prosperous-looking – the prettiest and best-run pub for miles. As if set in nostalgic aspic, it sported overflowing geraniums in its window boxes, Guinness adverts in its windows and gleaming brass fittings on the door that Asta had dashed through a million times. She paused a moment, quiet amidst the whirlwind. The pub was at once so familiar and so alien that she was overwhelmed. It was unexpected, this poignancy, and as salty as it was sweet.

'Mum,' she said, 'perhaps Kitty and I should freshen up at the hotel first.'

'Sure, I cancelled the hotel,' said Ma blithely, throwing open the doors. 'What would you be staying at a hotel for when you have your old room here?'

'But . . .' Asta was so busy staring, transfixed, at the saloon bar that she couldn't argue.

So vivid in all her childhood memories, it had sneakily reinvented itself behind her back. No longer a smoky cavern of dark wood and prehistoric carpet, it was decorated in a pleasing palette of Farrow and Ball greys. The walls were – Asta gulped – *greige.* The *Irish Times* dangled from brass rods and a shabby-chic blackboard promised 'gastropub bites'. A minuscule man in a flat cap, a throwback to the bar's origins, took his seat on a distressed stool and regarded the cappuccino maker with hatred.

'Honestly, Ma, I don't want to put you to any trouble . . .' It was a token effort; Ma had outflanked Asta.

Behind the bar, Ma administered beer and crisps to the multitude. Above her head hung swags of paper chains, and tinsel wound like a boa constrictor around every light fitting and chair-back. There was no restraint; forests of poinsettias bloomed under a sun of massed fairy lights. Ma's only theme was 'overkill'. Artificial snow on the windows framed the real stuff falling outside. It could be noon or midnight beyond the doors, but in here the ambience would be the same until the new year. Looney's Bar was Christmas Central.

'Kitty,' hissed Asta, retrieving her daughter from a huddle of young people, some of whom she recognized as bewilderingly large versions of toddlers she'd babysat. 'Are you, you know, OK, sweetheart?' She examined her daughter's face with its two bright spots of feverish pink on the cheeks. 'It's all a bit much, isn't it?'

'I've got cousins!' Kitty squealed. 'There's Liam and Theresa and Joanna and . . . It's mad!'

It was good-mad, apparently, rather than the very-bad-mad Asta had feared. 'They're not your cousins, strictly speaking . . .' Asta gave up with a smile: they were all tenuously related, and in Ireland that made them cousins. 'It'll calm down later,' she promised, not sure that it would.

'God, hope not!' Kitty stretched out an arm to take the Guinness offered to her by Liam, or it could have been Pat. Or maybe Jim. 'I have to taste it, Mum,' she said, pre-empting any maternal comment. 'I'm discovering my Irish roots!'

Two brimming bowls of Irish stew were put down on a pine table. 'Eat,' said Ma.

Asta gulped. That was a lot of stew for a teenager raised on udon noodles and grilled chicken.

'Made that meself this morning.' Ma watched them as they took up their spoons.

Watching Kitty push the stew around her plate, an old lady muttered, 'I hope the poor child isn't one of them vegetations.'

Taking a bite, Kitty announced, 'It's fab.'

'*Fab!*' echoed the audience.

'Sis!' screamed a figure in the doorway, her arms thrown up in the air. 'Would you look at you! I thought you'd be skinny,' beamed Gerry, 'but, God love you, you're not!' She turned to Kitty. 'And this beauty,' she said, her head on one side, 'must be Frenchy.' The air chilled in the bar. 'I mean, Kitty. *Céad míle fáilte*, love, or are you sick of hearing that already?'

'What does it mean?' Kitty stood up to accept her aunt's embrace: it looked as if a heron was making off with its dinner. Gerry was tall, long-limbed and spare, with a bouncing ponytail of dyed yellow hair.

'It means a hundred thousand welcomes.' Gerry turned to Asta. 'Does she not study Irish?'

'It's not madly useful in London,' said Asta. 'And hello, Gerry,' she added pointedly, holding out her arms.

'It's good to see you,' said Gerry, to nobody in particular as she ignored Asta's arms and cast about for a chair. 'And about feckin' time.'

Standing up, Oona said, 'Come on, Asta.' She winked as she saved her from Gerry. 'Walk me to work.'

'Be back at one sharp, madam.' Ma spoke to Asta as if

the last seventeen years hadn't happened and Asta was still a biddable teenager. 'I'm doing a roast.'

Out on the pavement, Oona tucked a proprietary arm into Asta's.

'It's colder here than Chelsea.' Asta whipped out a scarf to wrap about her neck. *But it's warmer too*, she thought as a passing woman, head down against the sleet, winked at her and said, 'I see you've brought the snow with you, Asta!'

Smiling politely, Asta whispered, 'Who was that?'

'Neil's granny, you know, Dymphna's aunt, the one who had the cat with the gammy eye, her son married a woman who owned a goat, she used to—'

'OK, OK, thanks.' Asta had forgotten how intricately people were knotted into Tobercree's landscape. She looked around her almost fearfully as they promenaded up the slushy slope of the main street: Asta was time-travelling again.

Tobercree had an untidy outline on the map, unfurling eccentrically up the benign slopes of its valley. The main thoroughfare wandered parallel to the river: water and street met at the southern end by way of the ancient stone bridge. From there the village petered out into meadows and dunes and then, finally, the homely curve of the cove.

In the other direction, the edge of the village was defined by the church, a large twentieth-century structure of ribs and spines, filled in with modern stained glass glowing like Quality Street wrappers. Its spindly finger of a spire beckoned.

Or, if you were Asta, it *accused*.

'The street's busy for a Wednesday afternoon,' commented Asta.

'Nah, this is nothing. Some days we have coaches backed up to the bridge. Hiya!' sang Oona to a man on a bike, his face muffled against the weather. The people they passed, on the whole, smiled at them. Soon Asta relinquished the eyes-down expression she habitually used on Chelsea's pavements.

Above their heads, swags of green and red lights hung across the road. The Tobercree Christmas lights had been a highlight of her year when she was a child. To an adult, they looked endearingly amateur.

'Monaghan's the butcher,' murmured Asta, counting off the familiar shopfronts, all strung with multicoloured bulbs and garnished with blow-up Santas. Tobercree took Christmas seriously. 'Gaughan Toys and Fancy Goods.' There was no Next, no River Island, no Monsoon: this was no identikit high street. 'O'Toole's hardware. Ceslowski fruit and veg?' She looked to Oona, puzzled.

'A Polish couple took it over when old Billy Hartigan died beneath the hooves of a crazed bull.' Oona didn't break step, as if such a death was commonplace. 'They're lovely.'

'Murphy's Bar.' Asta still felt a residue of the sneer Ma had insisted they wear while passing their competitors. 'The Pop-In Minimart.'

'Your ma protested about the Pop-In selling porn mags.' Oona laughed at the memory. 'Her placard said, "*Do we really need to see bottoms et cetera whilst buying our milk?*"'

'Good for her.' Asta stopped, pointed. 'A beauty salon! In Tobercree!'

'So?' Oona bridled on her village's behalf. 'It's not just Londoners who deserve fake tan. They do half-price Botox every second Friday.'

Botox and Tobercree: this did not compute. Asta shook her head, then let out a sentimental mew at the poster advertising ice creams in the newsagent window (a window strangely unchanged: Asta could swear the handwritten card offering a 'nearly new hampster cage, best offer excepted' had been there the day she scarpered). Names of long-forgotten ice pops and ice creams thrilled her. 'HB Icebergers!'

'Stop pointing at everything!' admonished Oona. 'You're like a tourist.'

'That's exactly what I am.' Asta looked up, beyond the low-rise roofs, and located a shimmering white square in the distance. 'I liked the Big House ramshackle,' she said. Even at this distance it looked sharper, newer than she remembered. 'I hope this English bloke with the four-star bum hasn't ruined it.'

'No, it's gorge. No expense spared,' said Oona, as cocky as if she'd personally overseen the project. 'And the bum is *five*-star. Even you'll fancy this bloke.'

'What do you mean, even . . .' Asta decided against picking that apart. 'What passes for shagadelic these days?'

'Tall. A looker.' Oona paused and looked Asta up and down, as if she found her wanting in some way. 'Actually, nah, you wouldn't go for him. He's not a wuss.'

'I don't go for wusses.' Asta defended herself indignantly. Conan wasn't a wuss. *If only*; she might have made more progress if he had been.

'Of course you do,' said Oona, as if it was common knowledge, all over Wikipedia, that Asta Looney went for wusses. 'You like them all wispy and poetic. Bed-wetters. Like Coldplay.'

'And you're basing this on what?'

'Etienne.' Oona faltered halfway through his name, aware

she'd strayed into dangerous territory. 'He had hair like a girl.'

'That was a long time ago. Perhaps my taste has changed.'

'It won't have changed that much. This English fella's a bit of a mystery. Very . . .' Oona groped for an adjective. 'Very *male*,' she said eventually. And approvingly. 'Yup. Too strong a brew for you.'

Asta halted, puzzled. 'What happened to the mill?'

'Jaysus, you know nothing about this place, do you?' Oona pulled up the hood of her quilted jacket. The snow was redoubling its efforts. 'The mill closed down ages ago.'

Like a missing tooth in the mouth of the bright high street, the big utilitarian building was dark. There were no carnival lights strung in its empty rooms, no Christmas tree flickering in its depths.

'I loved the mill,' said Asta, as sad as if somebody had died. 'I had my first Saturday job there.'

When the girls were teenagers, the old mill had been a multi-storey outlet for Tobercree Woollens. Riding the economic boom known as the Celtic Tiger, the small knit-wear company had expanded and found itself in demand all over the world. The mill complex was a draw, bringing tourist money to the village and supplying jobs for locals.

'It had a lovely cafe,' said Asta wonderingly, looking at the deserted facade as if gazing upon Pompeii and remembering a lost civilization. 'You used to buy me horrible neck-laces from the local handicraft section for my birthday every year. Do you remember when that fancy Dublin magazine did a fashion shoot there?' She and Oona had hung about, trying to be discovered. 'What's that half-built mess to the side of it?'

'That's what ruined them.' Oona shrugged. 'Like the rest

of us, they thought the good times would last forever, so they started to build a boutique hotel. But then the crash came, so . . .'

The recession that had trampled like Godzilla over the world's economy had paused to give an extra stamp or two to Ireland. Times were tough; even an expat knew that.

Turning the corner, Asta expected to see the church, but instead she stopped short, saying, 'What's this?' A large car park was jammed with cars and coaches, an immense Christmas tree towering over them all, its branches dotted with tiny lit-up copies of the weeping statue.

'Duh! It's a *car park*. St Cath's gets so much traffic now, the church had to build a new one.' Coaches, vans and cars huddled in neat lines, vomiting out the faithful, who scurried to the church eagerly. It was a lively scene, noisy and festive. 'We're here.' Oona gestured to a striped souvenir kiosk sporting a 'closed' sign near the broad steps of the modernist church.

'This is your new venture?'

'These St Catherine groupies'll buy *anything*. I'm making a mint.' Oona inserted herself into the tiny interior, as if she was part of a Punch and Judy show. 'Jaysus, it's freezing in here today. Feckin' snow. Look!' She brandished a small rubber figurine. 'A bendy St Catherine! Isn't it gas?' She rearranged her holy curios, uprighting a sequinned Jesus who'd toppled over in the night. 'I'm expecting a big crowd today. St Catherine hasn't cried in a while, and a coachload of Japanese people booked in at the hotel yesterday.'

'Ooh, a *uniform*,' said Asta, suitably impressed, as Oona pulled on a striped overall under her jacket.

'I customized it.' Oona settled the neckline, which was

cut rather low for an overall. 'Can't deny the faithful a view of me knockers.'

'Anyhoo,' said Asta. 'Must dash.' She wanted to revisit her own special places.

'Dash? Where?' griped Oona. 'Oh, look!' She bounced on her Uggs, waving. 'There's Christiano!'

Across the car park a dark-haired man, swaddled in layers against the cold, raised a lazy hand in response.

'C'mere, Asta.' Oona, with the dexterity of a street magician, swapped places with her cousin and tied a money belt around her waist. Asta found herself, somehow, inside the booth looking out. 'I have unfinished business with that guy.'

'No! Hang on!' Marooned inside the kiosk, Asta watched Oona bustle across the car park to swipe the cigarette from Christiano's hand.

Giving up – nothing came between Oona and a hot holidaymaker – Asta watched her flirt with a gaggle of coach drivers.

She's like an animal, thought Asta fondly. A healthy, handsome brute of a thing. *Oona doesn't think, she acts.* Her eyes were bright and her coat was glossy. *I miss you*, thought Asta, aware that it was a ridiculous thought to have about a person standing twenty feet away.

Like foam, small drifts of melting snow collected on the steps of the church and frosted the tops of the neat hedges that lined the car park. It was half-hearted snow, not real Christmas-card weather; it would soon be gone.

A queue formed. Guesstimating prices, locating the pile of paper bags, Asta did her best. The money belt kept falling off. Her breath visible in front of her, she was stumped when a nice Italian lady asked if the Pope-Soap-on-a-Rope was organic. Shouts for help were met with a leisurely wave as Oona joshed with her hungry-eyed admirer.

'Erm, let's say eight euros.' Asta handed a St Catherine room freshener to a dainty Japanese customer. In the queue, brandishing their papal mouse mats and their Jesus mugs, were Americans, Swedes and Africans. Tobercree was a wonky United Nations.

Eventually the queue thinned enough for Asta to read Angie's emailed reply to the hasty lines she'd sent earlier.

To: a.looney@boulevardmagazine.com
From: angie507@hotmail.co.uk

Good God, woman! Stop moaning. So your evil mummy is making you stay at her house instead of a hotel – I'd LOVE to stay at my mother's house, God rest her soul. Do your job, sure, but let your hair down.
Have some Christmas sex!

The church bell tolled, slow in the frigid air. Far below, busy as worker ants, the crowd moved as one towards St Catherine's wide stone steps, leaving a lone customer at Asta's stall.

Russian, furious, he brandished a wind-up Baby Jesus. 'I'm sorry, I . . .' Asta couldn't understand his rant. As far as she could make out, he was comparing her wind-up Baby Jesus unfavourably to other wind-up Baby Jesuses on the market. When he threw it contemptuously on the counter and stomped off, Asta removed the hated money belt, acknowledging to herself that she was a dead loss as a novelty religious knick-knack vendor.

'Oi!' she shouted inelegantly to Oona. 'I'm off!'

'Really?' said a deep voice from a foot away. 'You're deserting your post?'

Six feet tall, with legs as long as . . . well, very long legs, the stranger was hard to miss, but Asta had managed it.

'Well, yes, I'm not really the kiosk . . .' She tailed off, uncertain of the job title. 'The kioskerette,' she finished with a mumble.

'I see.' The man nodded gravely. 'Shame. Because I can't live without this any longer.' He picked up a nun-shaped bottle of bubble bath. He half-smiled, gauging her reaction, checking that they shared a sense of humour.

That, Asta deduced much, much later, was the moment it all started. For good or ill, that barely-there smile from the corner of the stranger's generous mouth set the ball rolling.

She tingled. It was a subtle tingle, but then, she hadn't tingled at full throttle for many years.

'You're English.' Asta was abrupt, her manners killed by the tingle.

'I am,' agreed the man. His grey eyes reminded Asta of an indignant sea.

Asta swallowed. *Twenty seconds in, and I'm having poetic thoughts about his eyes.*

'I'm completely English,' he continued. 'Is that OK with you?' His tone was on just the right side of combative to be flirtatious. A smile unfurled lazily, in no hurry. It was a smile built for sunshine, and it warmed Asta despite the unrelenting chill of the air.

'Suppose.' Asta heard an answering flirty note in her own voice and was taken aback. Asta Looney didn't do flirting. Except, apparently, she *did*. 'Hang on, you must be the Englishman from the—'

'Big House,' he interrupted. 'It's actually called Tobercree Manor, but I've given up trying to get people to call it that. Yes, I'm the Englishman from the Big House and I apologize unreservedly for the many centuries of oppression, famine and inequality my kind has perpetrated upon your kind.'

'No problem. We didn't really mind.' His laugh was rumbling, throaty, like a tube train roaring by deep underground. 'These things happen.' Asta stared, actually stared, at the man's hair. Despite being close-cut, it struggled to move, twisting this way and that. The colour transfixed her. Pepper and salt, a tweedy mixture of the original black and a premature white, it was Asta's favourite hair colour. A girl could get lost in such hair . . .

Asta looked away. She hoped she wasn't drooling. Where, she wondered, was her true, man-proof personality? Perhaps it had frozen up, like her nose.

'You sound like a local,' said the Englishman, 'but I haven't seen you around.'

'I live in London these days.' Asta hesitated. 'My folks are here.'

'I'm from London.'

'Do you miss it?'

'Nope.' It was a fast nope, the nope burglars offer to policemen when asked if they're hiding anything under their jacket. 'Listen.' He leaned in. 'Do you ever go to Looney's Bar?'

'Sometimes.' Asta bit her lip literally, and her tongue metaphorically.

'They serve the best Guinness for miles.'

Phew, thought Asta.

'Although,' he went on, 'it's run by a madwoman.'

Not so phew.

'I'll probably pop in for a pint tomorrow night.' The man looked away, looked back. His eyes supplied the subtitles and Asta read his interest. 'So, if you happen to be passing, and if you happen to hanker after a small sweet sherry or whatever . . .' He punctuated his invitation with a broad smile, a riot of a smile, a party all on its own. 'I'm Jake, by the way.'

'I'm Asta.' Asta congratulated herself for recalling such intricate detail under such crazy pressure: Jake really was very sexy. *More sexy than handsome*, she realized, puzzled at how this could be.

'So do you think you might? Pass Looney's tomorrow night? And fancy a drink?' Jake seemed amused rather than irritated at how slow on the uptake the kioskerette was. 'With me?'

'Definitely!' *Too keen!* 'Well, probably not.' *Not keen at all. Plus stupid after the 'definitely'.* 'Yeah. Yes, I'll probably be passing. Why not?'

'I can't think of a single good reason.' Jake's accent, rough-edged in this soft-toned village, reeked of the London Asta had left; the real place, not a biscuit-tin version populated with Beefeaters. 'So. About eight?'

Out of the corner of her eye, Asta clocked her cousin's outline growing as she sped across the car park. Oona had abandoned Christiano in favour of the situation unfolding at the stall. Desperate to move Jake along before Whirlwind Oona hit, Asta garbled, 'Good. Yes. Bye.'

'Yessir!' Dismissed, Jake saluted and ambled away towards the main street.

'That's him!' hissed Oona in a stage whisper that could be heard in the hills. 'You know! *Him* him, the English fecker!'

'I've ascertained that,' said Asta coolly. Judging by his shaking shoulders, Jake was still in earshot.

'Was he chatting you up?' Squeezing into the tight space with Asta, Oona was avid, more animal than ever.

'Ow.' Asta budged up. 'Not really.'

'You're so bad at lying. Oh my God.' Oona seized Asta's arm. 'You've pulled the Englishman. *Everybody* fancies him! Even the lesbian from the butcher's. He's loaded. And he has a majestic arse. I'm so jealous. Wait 'till I tell everybody!'

'No!' Asta held up a stern forefinger. 'There's nothing to tell. It's just a drink.' The scuttlebutt would reach Kitty. Asta kept her romantic life, such as it was, from her daughter.

'Ach, you never change.' Oona rubbed her gloves in glee. 'It's not nothing; it's a date with the local heart-throb which will probably culminate in the most amazing shag in the history of amazing shagging.'

'I'm not here to shag, amazingly or otherwise, I'm here to –' Asta halted.

Oona smelt the misstep and narrowed her eyes. 'You're here to what? Spit it out.'

'I'm here to write an article.' Asta was relieved to confess. 'About the weeping statue.'

'So . . .' Oona took a step backwards, not easy in that confined space. Her words froze in the air between them. 'You didn't come to see us? Me?'

'I did!' Asta closed the gap, keen to explain herself. 'You more than anybody.' Surely Oona knew that? Did they all think Asta was made of iron? She'd trained herself to be self-sufficient only because she'd had no option. 'You must know how much I miss you.'

'How would I know that?' said Oona. 'You stay away as if we're contagious.'

71

'I *had* to stay away. You know how it was when I got pregnant.'

'I do . . .' Oona relented, then brightened, with a lightning change of mood, 'So, your article'll be in *Boulevard*? Cool!'

'That's the idea. Listen,' said Asta, feeling like a heel, 'don't tell Ma and Gerry, eh? They'll . . .'

'Go apeshit?' Oona understood.

'They think I'm here for them, which I am, *of course* I am, it's just that I—'

Ignoring the self-serving babble, Oona said, 'You should meet Dervla, the deaf girl who was cured.' She whipped out her mobile: with Oona the thought was the deed.

'Great.' Asta hid her excitement. Her first ever interview, just like that.

Conan would be mightily impressed.

Following the river as it edged past back gardens, some neurotically tidy, others berserk, Asta took her first deep breath of the past twenty-four hours as she reacquainted herself with her favourite walk. She was alone, with just the icy rushing water for company. She envied the tourists enjoying this pretty, modest place without the various albatrosses that flapped around her own neck.

A screech of girly laughter through an open window reminded her of Kitty. It was peculiar not to know where her daughter was; in London she kept tabs on Kitty with the efficiency of the FBI.

The bench was still there, waiting patiently. It had been a reliable sanctuary when Looney's Bar was too crowded and too hot. Asta brushed off the melted snow with her mitten and sat down.

Whoosh! Time-travelling again.

It was to be the most grandiose wedding Tobercree had ever seen. Asta's sister had been planning her big day ever since she'd first held a crayon and drawn a meringue dress; the table plan had been nailed down half an hour after Martin's proposal. Gerry had nabbed a local celebrity, and Tobercree's nose would be rubbed in her joy.

Radio presenter Martin Mayberry mixed MOR music with chat so inoffensive that his show was billed as 'the Mammies' favourite'. Curly of hair and suspiciously white of tooth, the Voice of Tobercree was exactly what the doctor would order as a son-in-law for Ma (assuming the doctor had absolutely no taste).

While the house shuddered at the approach of the wedding juggernaut, Asta was anxious. Etienne had gone home weeks before, and her anxiety was misinterpreted by the world at large as pining. Gerry's mood changed hourly. If the bad moods were tricky, the good moods were murder. She would grab Asta and whisper, tears standing on her lashes, 'Don't fret! One day all this will happen to you too!'

I hope not, Asta would think

The distress grew and grew until it buzzed like white noise in Asta's ears, drowning out the Were-Bride's roars and Oona's eulogies to her new crush – a boy who worked in the chemists and was, therefore, a sophisticate: *he knew about tampons.*

The urge to run to Ma with this grown-up version of a

skinned knee was powerful, but Asta knew this was one scrape her mother couldn't put right with a kiss and a Disney plaster. Ma was stretched in all directions. The news would shatter her, like the plaster St Catherine Asta had dropped when she was a child.

The white noise fizzed louder until Asta assumed that surely everybody else heard it, too. The dressmaker took out the seams on the magenta and pistachio bridesmaid dress for the third time. Much of the day, Asta was the same shade of pale green as her cummerbund.

'Once!' she raged to herself. 'I do it *once* and this happens!'

In the kitchen one morning, the white noise filled the silence as Asta watched her mother puzzle over a stack of wedding bills, eyes huge behind television-sized glasses held together with Sellotape.

I can't tell her, thought Asta. *I just can't.* The next moment she heard herself say, 'Ma, I'm pregnant.' Asta bowed her head and waited for the mushroom cloud to erupt over Tobercree.

What happened was much, much worse. Ma went quiet. And Ma was not a quiet woman.

'Ma?'

'We'll find that, what's his name, Etienne.' Ma took off her glasses and put them to one side. 'We'll find him and make him marry you.'

That didn't sound like a solution; how do you go about *making* somebody marry? 'I don't know where he lives,' sobbed Asta, spilling her first tears. 'I don't even have a phone number.'

Over the next couple of days, Asta caught Ma looking at her in a particular way, wondering and mistrustful, like a bus passenger who's noticed a suspicious package on a seat.

'It's time to tell Gerry,' said Ma one morning, her voice flat.

There were moments that day when Asta admitted a begrudging admiration for her big sister's stamina and creativity: her spectacular tantrum made all previous efforts look like rehearsals.

Effortlessly out-mad-ing Lady Macbeth, Gerry tore out her newly highlighted hair, snarling, 'I thought she was just getting fat!'

'Now, now,' said Ma.

'Don't *now now* me!' raged Gerry. 'It's my big day but everybody will be looking at Asta and thinking about the little Frenchy inside her!'

Breaking her silence, Asta said, 'Don't call my baby that.'

Gerry had the grace to look contrite. 'Sorry,' she muttered. 'Are you, you know, all right?'

'I suppose so,' answered Asta, taken unawares by the question. If she'd known that it was the only time any of them were to ask her, she might have given a more honest answer.

There was an unexpected ally in the shape of the groom-to-be. 'Don't be too hard on her,' said Martin, during a subdued family dinner. 'She's not a bad girl. Just silly, that's all.' He smiled benevolently, giving Asta the benefit of gleaming veneers. 'Just a silly, silly girl.'

Asta felt neither bad nor silly. She felt hopeless.

Once the news had reached Gerry, it was a hop, skip and a jump to their aunt. Peg declared herself 'disappointed'. On the hour, every hour.

There was the inevitable visit from a stern Father Dominic, his grey comb-over bristling with holy indignation.

Ma bristled too: she'd have preferred to keep it from Father Dominic, but she buttoned her lip and broke out the fruit cake.

'Adoption.' Father Dominic was adamant. 'It's the only way.'

The look Asta gave him said it all.

'Child,' he said to her, almost kindly, 'nobody expects you to bring up a bastard alone.'

Asta left the kitchen, and the house, and made her way to the bench by the river, where the water made her tears seem insignificant.

'Perhaps,' said Ma carefully, when Asta came home from the river and had pulled on her most comforting nightie, 'Father Dominic has a point.'

'Nobody's bringing up this child except me.'

'But the talk, Asta.' Maybe Ma read her daughter's face: she changed tack. 'Ask yourself, love, if you can offer the baby what a loving family could offer it?'

'Isn't this a loving family?' asked Asta, her heart a hollow scoop.

Ma recoiled, as if slapped. 'Don't twist my words, madam.' She pushed herself up from the table on red knuckles. 'Ah sure, we'll manage.'

One certainty towered above the situation, like a card rising out of the pack in a magic trick.

I can't bring a child into this atmosphere.

No pink little innocent should be welcomed with a dispirited 'we'll manage'. The baby's paternity, Asta realized, meant she could never live comfortably at home again.

From decision to slinking down the stairs, suitcase in

hand, was less than an hour. Asta had no intention of *managing*; she planned to *live*. As a sinner, her destination had to be the fabled capital city of her sort.

London.

The bar was busy that night, a regular's birthday. Asta crept down the private stairs, unseen and unheard. Her hand on the handle of the back door, she fought the urge to take one last look at the saloon. At her family.

Unable to face another scene, Asta knew it was better for everyone if she erased herself from the Looney family album as cleanly as possible.

Bye, all.

She wiped her wet face with her sleeve and was about to reach for the handle of the back door when it opened, and a blast of peat-scented night air delivered Gerry. She took in the suitcase, and drew a deep breath to fuel her shout . . . and then the sisters' eyes locked. Gerry closed her mouth, frowning. Finally she stood aside, nodding a permission at Asta.

Asta slunk out, and Gerry closed the door firmly behind her. From the bar, a snatch of an old song followed her up the high street.

At the present-day Looney's Bar, bowls of stew were being attacked by people whose dress sense and dentistry made it impossible for them to be Irish. Asta moved through a multi-language babble punctuated by laughter and the chink of cutlery.

Cantering out from the ladies' loo, Gerry roared, 'There you are at last!' She loved to imply that people were late.

Grabbing her sister by the shoulders, Gerry's size-nine stiletto kicked open the door marked PRIVATE. The clamour of the bar was snuffed out as the heavy door swung shut behind them both. 'Up the stairs with you,' said Gerry, patting Asta on the bottom as if training a frisky Shetland pony. 'Ma's about to carve. She hates to keep a priest waiting.' It was an ambush. Asta had hoped to prepare herself before meeting her old foe, Father Dominic.

The kitchen door opened on Ma revving an electric carving knife in Asta's direction. 'Asta! Come in, love! It's lamb! Your favourite!' The exclamation marks always came out when she entertained clergy. 'Look who's here! Isn't it only Father!' She revved the knife towards the priest seated at the table.

The man in black ducked with a muted yelp, then gathered himself and stood up, reaching across the table to take Asta's hand. 'It's a pleasure to meet you, Asta,' he said, in a low, cultured Dublin accent.

'And you.' Asta shook the offered hand. It wasn't Father Dominic's withered old paw. It belonged to a stranger, who presumably had dressed up as a priest for a bet. Surely nobody that handsome could manage to be celibate? 'Whoever you are,' she added, with a smile.

'Forgive me. I'm Father Rory.'

'Of course he's Father Rory.' Ma was irritated, as if Father Rory was instantly recognizable, like Elvis. 'Who else would he be?'

This new clergyman was an improvement on Father Dominic. True, the old priest hadn't set the bar very high, with his Rudolph-red nose, his dandruff and his dancing dentures.

'Nobody, and I mean nobody,' said Father Rory, with an easy smile, 'makes a roast dinner like Mrs Looney.'

'Ah, now, whisht!' Ma's blow-dried white curls shivered with pride as she hacked at the lamb like a psychopath who'd got through to the final of *Masterchef*.

The doling out of meat, gravy, roast potatoes, mashed potatoes, carrots, cabbage and mint sauce took an age. Just as it all seemed to be accomplished, an extra roast potato for luck was dropped onto Father Rory's plate. Taking a sip of his wine, Father Rory said, 'Very nice, Mrs L. Serpico Cabernet?'

'The 2007,' twittered Ma. 'Your favourite.'

Gerry nudged Asta. They'd been seated together, opposite the 'grown-ups'. 'Remember when the bar served two kinds of wine? Red and white?' Gerry had prominent front teeth, and threw herself about when she laughed. 'It's all posh, now. People expect it. Martin and me,' she said proudly, 'have wine with dinner. *Every night*.' Gerry leaned over to the old dresser, laden with crockery. 'Let's turn him up,' she said, twiddling the knob of what looked like a funky Roberts radio but was in fact an ancient one from the design's first time around.

'Turn who up?'

A mellifluous voice filled the kitchen, answering Asta's question: 'It's requests hour with me, Martin Mayberry, and all my lady-friends out there in radio-land. Let's get funky, girls!'

As 'Wombling Free' seeped out of the radio, Asta asked a tentative question. 'How's Father Dominic?'

'He's in good shape for his years.' Father Rory's neat dark hair had a spring to it, as if it took some taming to look so civilized. His brown eyes managed to be languid and sharp all at once. Add to that a jawline he'd borrowed from the young George Clooney and Rory was quite the Father What-a-Waste, as Oona had christened any half-presentable priest. 'He takes a back seat now, but believe me, that man knows everything that's going on.'

Wry, affectionate noises were made by Ma and Gerry, as if Father Dominic was some cuddly OAP and not the unutterable git Asta knew him to be. She added a darker, 'I bet he does.'

'More meat, Father?' Ma bobbed in her seat.

'Have mercy, Mrs Looney, I've only just started.' Father Rory admonished his hostess with a smile, and threw a complicit glance Asta's way.

'That was a lovely sermon on Sunday, Father.' Gerry turned to Asta. 'Very moving. All about, um, poor people or something. Are you going to mass this Sunday, sis?' Gerry smiled as she lobbed the grenade.

'Well, I . . .' The 'no' was ready on Asta's lips, but some ancient voodoo prevented her saying it in front of a priest.

'We'll be glad to see Asta if and when she chooses.' Father Rory saved her nimbly. 'I've heard all about Kitty. If she's half as marvellous as your mother makes out, she must be something very special.'

'I like her,' said Asta, 'but then I'm biased.' She wondered what Ma had found to say about the granddaughter she barely knew.

'Oh, listen! Listen!' Gerry flapped her hands in the direction of the radio.

'. . . all the way from London town.' Martin's voice lapped like an oil slick at the hem of the best tablecloth. 'She's a very special girlie, so Asta: this one's for you!'

The very special girlie stopped mid-chew.

'Andy Williams,' said Ma approvingly. 'Martin has such taste. Did I tell you he switched on the Tobercree Christmas lights this year?'

'What's with the face?' scowled Gerry. 'Andy Williams not good enough for you?'

'Andy Williams is fine. Great. I love Andy Williams and hope to have his children.' Asta didn't want to linger on Martin: she and Gerry would never see eye to eye about him.

Ma was bobbing again. 'Have you enough gravy, Father?' She eyed his plate suspiciously. 'Don't you like your carrots?'

'Wine, Father?' Gerry bobbed too. Asta remembered it well, this competitive bobbing around a man of the cloth. 'Is the radio too loud?'

'How long have you been in Tobercree, Father Rory?' asked Asta.

'Long enough to put on a stone, thanks to your mother,' smiled Father Rory. He patted a non-existent gut, prompting Asta to notice how well built he was. All that stuff about the one true God aside, you had to hand it to the Catholics: they recognized the power of good tailoring. Rory's impeccable black suit – a proper, raven's-wing black – was timeless. The dichotomy of severe tailoring with a whole lot of attractive yet chaste man was not lost on Asta.

Pull yourself together, she scolded herself. *You're not in* The Thorn Birds. She'd only been home for half a day, and already she'd run into two extraordinary men. *Pity one's a priest and the other one's . . .* There was no reason to rule out Jake, but she ruled him out anyway. *I'm not here to have what Angie would call Christmas sex!*

As a planet-sized strawberry pavlova was divided into huge and slightly less huge portions, Gerry regarded Father

Rory over the rim of her glass. 'Did you hear, Father,' she began, in an artful manner, 'about the Logans?' She paused, hugely enjoying herself. 'Trouble at t'mill, apparently.'

'Is that so?' Rory was blithe. 'Just a little slice for . . . Ah.' A hunk of meringue the size of a child's head landed on his plate with an audible *whump*.

Gerry warmed to her theme. 'Mrs Logan's a *leetle* too friendly with her neighbour, apparently. And her only married three years or so. Terrible shame.' A smile played on her lips.

Elbows on table, chin on hands, Rory said affably, 'I have a very comfortable bed of my own. Therefore I find it difficult to be interested in what goes on in anybody else's.'

'Of course, of course,' backtracked Gerry.

Fifteen–love to Father Rory, thought Asta. 'I can't wait to see the statue.' Time to don her secret-agent hat. Like her other hats, from bobble to straw, it didn't suit her.

Wiping a morsel of cream from the corner of his mouth with an heirloom napkin that only appeared when holy men were on the premises, Rory said, 'St Catherine's quite the celebrity.' He turned his intelligent gaze on Asta. 'Have you come all this way just to see her?'

'What? No.' Asta was rattled. Perhaps the pope trained his minions to read minds. 'But she's fascinating. Even if you don't . . .'

'Believe?' Rory supplied the word that Asta stumbled on.

'Yup. *Believe*.' Asta nodded and said, clearly, at last, in her mother's kitchen. 'I don't believe.'

'God bless us and save us,' muttered Ma.

'Typical,' said Gerry.

'I bet you do believe,' said Rory. His smile had warmth and sadness in it. 'In something. Or someone.'

'She believes in God,' said Ma primly.

Another complicit glance between Asta and the priest. 'I believe,' said Asta slowly, 'in people being kind.'

Gerry snorted.

'How about,' said Ma, all brightness and activity, 'a pot of tea in the parlour? Do you believe in *that*?'

The parlour was so clean that forensic scientists couldn't prove humans had ever entered it. Kept 'for best', it had stalled in the eighties. When the border that almost matched the wallpaper that almost matched the carpet had been pasted up, the Looneys had been flabbergasted by the modern wonder of it: now, the decor made Asta smile nostalgically. Christmas cards were pinned up above a vase of holly on the mantelpiece. Christmas had only a toehold in this austere room.

Already in an armchair, long legs outstretched, Rory said, 'Good thing Father Dominic's taking six o'clock mass. One needs time to recover from your mother's meals.' He waited until Asta had sunk a foot or so into the dam of multicoloured cushions along the sofa. 'Why *are* you here, Asta?'

That was none of Rory's business. Furthermore, it suggested there was more to her trip than met the eye. 'To see the family,' she said.

'I'm glad you're here,' said Rory. He was straightforward now, no-nonsense. He had one manner for Ma, quite another for Asta. 'Whatever the reason.'

'I'm glad you're glad.' The sparring note to her voice was one she'd honed with Conan. The thought of him brought her up sharply. *I wonder what he's doing now?* 'So,' she said, 'the statue.' Conan would be proud of her, jumping right in like that. 'Your brainchild, or Father Dominic's?'

'Brainchild?' laughed Rory. 'She's hardly that. Father

Dominic takes a back seat. I deal with the . . . issues St Catherine brings up.'

'And the money she's brought in.' In her efforts to avoid her mother's cringey politeness, Asta was rude.

'The money comes in handy. But it's not the point.' Rory leaned forward. 'The point is the stillness she brings. The calm.'

'It was anything but calm outside the church earlier.'

Rory laughed, a quick sudden *ha!* 'It gets a bit manic. Everybody,' he said, his tone wondering, 'wants a miracle, it seems.'

'I heard about a deaf girl being cured.'

'Yeees.' Rory drew the word out, giving it a dubious edge.

'Did you see it?' *Did you flick the switch marked 'Miracle'?*

'I was at a deathbed that night.' Rory made a steeple of his fingers and studied them. 'I heard the screams, though. The village went crazy.'

'Would you call it a miracle?'

For a while, Rory didn't answer. 'Come and see me tonight,' he said at last. 'Steal a moment with St Catherine without the coach parties.'

A personal invitation for a *tête à tête* with the saint: Conan couldn't ask for more. 'What time?'

'Ten. No, half past. The last worshippers will have left. It'll be peaceful.' Rory smiled. 'She might surprise you.'

To: a.looney@boulevardmagazine.com
From: c.orourke@boulevardmagazine.com

Got anything for me yet?
  Cx
  P.S. Who am I sleeping with?

To: c.orourke@boulevardmagazine.com
From: a.looney@boulevardmagazine.com

(a) I'VE ONLY JUST ARRIVED!
  (b) Helen – she's the rich blonde with the fake boobs.
Oh, hang on – they all are . . .

To: a.looney@boulevardmagazine.com
From: c.orourke@boulevardmagazine.com

(a) I know you've only just arrived. Hit the ground running!
  Cx
  P.S. and (b) I've just dumped Helen. Text is acceptable
these days, yes?

Dominating the village, even at night, St Catherine's was
floodlit. The crowds had left a post-party feel in the cold
air.

Stamping her numb feet in the porch, her face bathed
pink and blue and yellow by the giant Christmas-tree lights,
Asta peered through the glass doors. St Catherine's smelt
of polish and people, so unlike the unloved, dusty churches
of London weddings, buildings that were only woken up
to serve as atmospheric 'lifestyle' backdrops.

Like an elegant vampire, Father Rory materialized in
the gloom, his pale face visible before his dark suit grew
solid. 'You came.' He unlocked with a smile, as if he was
flattered.

Walking into the candlelit twilight, Asta felt her knees
bend involuntarily into the genuflection she'd been taught

in the womb. The roof soared above them, invisible, its timbered cat's cradle beyond the reach of the candle glow. Ahead of Asta, rows of neat modern pews advanced on the altar, which glinted with gilt and scarlet. It was a modern church, a practical building, not a setting for miracles.

Asta took a left turn to where she'd sat beneath St Catherine's statue every Sunday morning, with Oona at her side popping gum and her mother in front, belting out the hymns.

'St Catherine's been promoted,' whispered Rory, steering her towards the front of the church. 'She's taken St Patrick's place.'

'And where did poor Patrick go?' Asta was arch. 'Is he in a bedsit somewhere?'

'He's doing fine,' said Rory. 'I'll tell him you said hello.'

To the left of the altar was a large, domed niche, glowing with gold leaf. A low iron railing fanned out in front of a robed plaster figure. Shoes squeaking on the waxy floor, Asta made her way through the shadows.

Retreating, Rory said softly, 'I'll leave you two alone.'

St Catherine's pearly face swam into focus as the velvet bumper around the railing prodded Asta's knees and folded her into a kneeling position. Her arms dropped automatically onto the iron framework, and her hands fell gently together as if in prayer; then, finding that the pose felt too submissive, Asta groped behind her for the hard edge of a pine pew and slid backwards onto it.

'So, here we are,' she said conversationally to the saint. Made of solid plaster reinforced with wire, Catherine was, according to Asta's research, an 'indoor Lourdes model', three feet high and produced by a famous works in Cork City. Asta and the statue were about the same age, but, immune to fashion, Catherine had stuck to the same cream robe with golden sash throughout Asta's flirtations with leggings and shifts and ripped jeans and underwear-as-outerwear. Likewise, Catherine's golden halo had outlasted Asta's perms and bobs and streaks.

There were no lines on the saint's face, no evidence of financial worries or the strain of bringing up a child alone. It was bland, beautiful, serene. The downward slope of the eyebrows, the barely-there red crescent of the lips moved Asta. She blinked; how easy it was to be taken in! How could a statue *move* her?

As the cypresses shushed and laughed outside, Asta considered the cheap, mass-produced ornament. It seemed to sparkle. St Catherine was a luminous point in the dark, her expression an uncomplicated vision in a complicated world.

Closing her eyes – churches, like cinemas, made her drowsy – Asta thought about the long, long day that was drawing to an end. Some aspects of her homecoming had been exactly as imagined.

Ma's high blood pressure: tick.

Gerry's prickly sarcasm: tick.

Aunty Peg's lukewarm welcome: tick.

But much of it had been a surprise.

Kitty's delight in her 'homeland'.

Tobercree's modernity.

A fanciable Englishman.

A hottie priest.

Asta opened her eyes.

St Catherine looked straight down at her. Those eyes were still sad, but the light from the candles lent them a gleam that was . . . yes, thought Asta, *sympathetic*. How easy it would be to sit bathed by that gentle gaze all night . . .

I haven't come all this way just to fall for the trick! She leapt up, just as the main doors crashed open and a flood of small figures surged up the aisle.

'St Catherine!' Squealing children filled the church, clambering over pews, showing no respect whatsoever for the House of the Lord.

'Is she crying?' asked a girl with a missing front tooth.

'I love her dress,' said another shyly.

'You can see her boobs through it,' said a small boy with an unnervingly deep voice.

'Children, keep it down. It's very late.' Rory tried not to laugh as he brought up the rear. 'Sorry, Asta. The Sunday school's just back from a day trip and they asked to say good night to Catherine.'

The children burst into song, one of those faux-pop hymns Asta hated even more than the traditional ones. A freckled boy brought out a tambourine and bashed it perfectly out of time while the shrill voices floated up into the rafters.

'She's my favourite saint,' a black-haired scrap confided to Asta, taking her hand trustingly.

'Why do you like her so much?' The soft feel of the little girl's hand was like an early Christmas present.

'Because she's kind and pretty and . . .' The child shrugged. 'She's always here.'

The children were rounded up and Asta followed them, willing herself not to genuflect on the way out.

Father Rory was by the doors. Asta couldn't get out without talking to him.

'I'm disappointed,' she said breezily, walking past him out to the porch. 'Catherine didn't cry for me.'

'She's a saint of the Holy Roman Empire,' said Rory, dents in his cheek betraying a need to smile. 'Not an *X-Factor* finalist.'

'Couldn't you have pressed a button or pulled a lever?'

The joke fell flat. Rory's dimples disappeared. 'It's not about miracles,' he said. 'It's about you, Asta.'

Out on the steps of the church, the cold night air held a base note of the sea. Asta didn't want anything in Tobercree to be about her. 'Good night,' she said, looking up into a jet-black sky, the stars hanging in it like extravagant Christmas decorations.

'Shall we see you at the vigil tomorrow night?'

Asta remembered the vigils of her childhood, nights when the whole community came together to pray through the night, long after the church would normally be closed. They'd been dreamily exciting for a sleepy child, deadly dull for a press-ganged teenager. 'Perhaps.'

'Let me see you home.'

'No need,' said Asta. 'Save your legs.'

'We're not walking.' Rory took her arm, a firm gesture that brooked no argument, and led her to a gleaming motorbike. From a lidded pannier he retrieved a helmet and handed it to her. 'Put it on. Muss up your lovely hair.'

'This is yours?' The heavy helmet made Asta's head wobble.

'All mine.' Rory swung a leg over the beast. 'Hop on.'

Catholic porn, thought Asta, arms around Rory's waist as they roared up the main street.

The room was dark, the only noise the patient tick of the old clock. It was all so familiar. The weight of the slippery satin quilt. The raspy embrace of the stripy flannelette sheets.

'Ow.' From the floor, Kitty complained as a limb came into contact with a hard part of the camp bed. 'Doesn't Grandma own any duvets? This quilt thing keeps slithering off.'

'She's vehemently anti-duvet. Gerry told her you can choke to death on them.'

'Choking on a duvet . . .' Kitty was incredulous. 'Is this your old room?'

'Yeah. Same wallpaper. Same carpet.'

'Cool taste you had back then.' The floral wallpaper and the swirly carpet could induce fits if happened upon unexpectedly.

'This was back in the days before teenagers ruled the world, when we had to put up with what our mums decreed.'

'The accents are lovely,' said Kitty sleepily. 'And they all talk at once. Irish surround-sound.'

'Don't get too used to it. One week, remember?' Those days stretched ahead of Asta, each one longer than its allotted twenty-four hours.

'Aunty Gerry's larger than life, isn't she?'

'You could say that.' Asta kept the sardonic note out of her voice.

'What's she really like? When she's not acting?'

What an astute daughter I have. 'Gerry's a good person.' Some positive spin was needed: Asta was weary of warnings. 'Underneath.'

'I've always thought of us as a small family,' said Kitty wonderingly. 'But I've got loads of relatives.'

'Don't worry.' Asta yawned. 'Soon be just you and me again.'

'They're like you've always said. Nosy. Noisy.'

Did I say that? It didn't sound very . . . nice.

'You left out how friendly they are. My cousins took me to the cove. It was *so* cold, Mum. We skimmed stones in the sea.' Kitty sighed, a pretty, happy sound. 'Just like you and my dad.'

'Hmm.'

'Pity I never met my granddad. Grandma says he was a lovely man.'

'He was.' Asta had only a child's recollection of her father. To her, Da was a beard, a shouted laugh, a piggy-back. And a terrible long afternoon when he collapsed just shy of her tenth birthday and adults came and went and Aunty Peg kept her in the kitchen with her favourite fizzy pop and that was that. No more Da.

'Good night, musha.' Asta used the endearment from her own childhood that Kitty had outgrown.

'Good night, *Assumpta.*'

'Stop mocking your poor old mother and go to sleep,' laughed Asta, turning over, bedding in. She wondered if she'd dream of glamorous priests or flirtatious English chaps or anything at all. The best dream would be no dream.

'Asta! Asta!'

Over and over again, she hears her name shouted from the foot of the tree. The voice is angry. And familiar.

It's dark in the treehouse. She can sense Etienne but she can't see him. The voice rings in her ears.

Etienne steps out of the black. His hands are over his ears. He eludes her outstretched arms.

Eventually conceding that the dream she'd woken from had stolen any chance of getting back to sleep, Asta crept past her sleeping daughter. The kitchen was calling to her.

Still papered in 1970s chevrons of brown and beige, with a jumble of mismatched units and rugs criss-crossing the floor, the kitchen was the very opposite of lifestyle living.

'Oh.' Asta had expected the room to be deserted. 'Sorry, Ma. I'll . . .' She hesitated, taken aback at the sight of her mother leaning over the table, palms flat on the checkered cloth, tears dripping onto the scarred bread board.

'No, no. Come in.' Ma wiped her face and pulled her nylon dressing gown tighter. 'Don't mind me. I'm an old fool.'

Her eyes on her mother, Asta took a chair. 'Are you—'

'Cocoa?' Ma blew her nose vigorously. 'Or one of them Options yokes? Are you watching your weight?'

'No.'

'Oh.' Ma didn't hide her surprise.

The cocoa was warmed in a battered old pan. Right at the end, Ma dripped in some double cream. 'That's what makes the difference,' she confided. 'I bet you nobody puts cream in their cocoa in that London.'

Asta took the mug gratefully. They sat in silence, the room still and sleepy around them.

'Ma,' said Asta carefully. 'You were crying.'

'I'm just an old silly. Jaysus, I cry at anything.' This was untrue: legend had it that Ma had giggled when Bambi's mother died.

Asta let the silence lengthen, until Ma bent under the pressure and said, 'It's the sight of her, Asta. My own little granddaughter. My Kitty. Thank you, love.' She searched Asta's face. 'Thank you for bringing her home.'

December 17th

To: angie507@hotmail.co.uk
From: a.looney@boulevardmagazine.com

Why am I here? Why aren't I at home with you, admiring my tree, icing the cake, wondering why my white and gold table setting looks nothing like it does on the Martha Stewart website?

Instead I'm confused and all over the place. I should never have come back to Ireland.

Asta wondered whether or not to mention the handsome Englishman. *Better not.* She pressed send.
Ping! Angie's reply arrived almost immediately.

To: a.looney@boulevardmagazine.com
From: angie507@hotmail.co.uk

You've met someone!

Downstairs, a sausage, a rasher of bacon, two fried eggs, a Stonehenge of black pudding, a slice of fried bread and a mug of tea hot enough to maim awaited Asta at the breakfast table.

'Good morning, prodigal sister.' Gerry was there, despite the earliness of the hour.

'Oh, Mum, we normally just have granary toast, or some natural yoghurt.' Asta sat, defeated, at the plate.

'Is that so?' Ma nodded at the other side of the table, where Kitty was wiping her plate clean with the last fragment of fried bread.

'Natural yoghurt's awful bad for you.' Gerry was certain of her dubious factoids, gleaned from such scientific journals as *Chat* or *Pick Me Up*. 'Gives you piles.'

'You're up early, darling daughter.' Asta picked at a corner of her black pudding. It was earthy, bold, utterly Irish and highly un-Chelsea.

'I'm meeting the gang at nine.'

So they were already 'the gang'. 'Where are you all off to?'

'Around.'

Asta stopped nibbling. She'd nibbled almost the whole block of black pudding, but everybody knows there are no calories in a nibble. 'Around where?'

'God, Mum,' snorted Kitty.

'Around where?' Asta was patient, but relentless. She'd always been solely responsible for Kitty, and they'd both recognized this and played by the rules.

Before Kitty could snort again, in a different key to illustrate the subtle increase in exasperation, Ma shot-putted more black pudding onto Asta's plate and said, 'Sure, you used to roam all over. I never knew where you were.'

Gerry studied her fingernails. 'And look how well that turned out.'

'No harm can come to Kitty in Tobercree,' said Ma stolidly, with a wink at her granddaughter.

'Hmm.' Outgunned, Asta retreated. She couldn't shrug off her London sensibilities as easily as Kitty, but even Asta had to admit that Tobercree's streets were somewhat less mean.

A clatter of feet in the hall announced Oona, bed-headed in a tatty dressing gown. 'Any tea going, Aunty?' She toppled into a chair. Her pale face bore the marks of the pillow and her extensions were gone: possibly they'd escaped in the night. A perk of living next door to the bar was twenty-four-hour access to Ma's hospitality.

'You *still* have your breakfast here?' Asta was amazed.

'Every morning,' beamed Ma, who took immense pleasure in infantilizing adults.

'Me dad says hi.' Oona whipped cleanser from one towelling pocket and a fistful of cotton wool balls from the other, and began to remove last night's make-up. It wasn't a job for the faint-hearted.

When Asta's uncle had been deserted by his 'flighty piece' of a wife, Oona had vowed to stay at home and look after him, although anybody who'd witnessed the Guantanamo Bay treatment of Oona's childhood pets would challenge her ability to 'look after' anything. Now that his daughter was grown-up, Oona's father occasionally made meek noises about turning her room into 'the best damn model railway Tobercree's ever seen', but Oona maintained that he couldn't get by without her.

'No bacon today, ta.' Oona yawned. 'An extra egg, though, if there's one going.'

'Coming up, hen.' Ma swung into action, a samurai with a frying pan.

'Ma, sit down. I'll do that.' So long accustomed to preparing everything that passed her lips, Asta felt uncomfortable at the sight of overworked Ma slaving for this long-in-the-tooth brood.

'Sure it's no bother.' Ma cracked eggs with one hand and pricked a sausage with the other.

Watching her cousin trowel on that day's warpaint, Asta queried if she really needed three different shades of eyeshadow.

'I need four.' Oona pushed the brush around her lids, squinting at her psychedelic self in a tiny mirror as a Matterhorn of fried food landed in front of her. Managing to shovel sausage and apply sparkling highlighter at the same time, she said, 'Declan sends his love. He's getting right on my you-know-whats, I can tell you. That fella's going for a long walk on a short pier if he doesn't shape up.'

Ma tutted. 'Declan's a grand young lad. You hang on to him, miss. You're not getting any younger.'

'The voice of Irish feminism.' Asta raised her mug in a toast.

Harrumphing, Gerry sugared her tea. 'Beggars can't be choosers.'

'Hey,' Oona offered her profile. 'When'd you ever see a beggar this feckin' gorgeous?'

'Never,' smiled Asta, wishing for the umpty-fifth time that she had a fraction of Oona's chutzpah.

'The snow is heavier today,' said Ma, fiddling with the curtain. 'I heard that Kelliher's cows were dancing up in the top field. That means bad weather to come.'

'The BBC forecast disagrees with Kelliher's cows,' said

Asta, who had neurotically checked the website first thing. 'I think I know which one to trust.'

'Kelliher's cows,' said Ma and Gerry in unison.

Feet tucked beneath her on the parlour sofa, handwritten notes fanned out on the coffee table, Asta stared at the screen of her trusty little laptop as if it might suddenly come to life and write the article on its own. Getting what she wanted had proved dangerous; Asta's desire to get the piece just right cramped her ability to come up with even an opening paragraph.

Framed by tinsel, the sky beyond the window was a startling milky white. Asta stared, desperate for inspiration, but found there only the face of the man she'd be seeing tonight.

I have a date. Other women had dates; Asta had drunken endurance tests. Was Jake just another blank page waiting for her to mess it up?

Her fingers began to type.

To: angie507@hotmail.co.uk
From: a.looney@boulevardmagazine.com

You're a witch.

Yes, I have kind of met somebody, and kind of arranged a kind of date. But – like my own butt, it's a big one – he's a player, Angie. He was practised, confident, he had technique, for God's sake. He more or less picked me up. (And yes, I can hear you from here, I more or less let him.)

So, no go. I'm not a notch on a bedpost, even a bedpost with prematurely greying hair (if you see what I mean).

If I was there, I'd shake you. And when I shake people they stay shook!

It's a holiday romance. You're there for one week. Jump in with both feet. So what if your heart gets bruised? That might start it beating again!

Unwilling to dwell on Jake any longer, Asta put together a word picture of Father Rory, knowing Conan would soon be on her back for a progress report. She redrafted her paragraphs over and over, but the man was like wet knitting, impossible to pin down.

Despite having no income, Rory rode an expensive motorbike. The parish kids obviously adored him. He was too handsome for a cassock, and had a way of looking at her that suggested he could read her mind.

Asta had been prepared to battle Father Dominic: she knew his weaknesses. In no particular order they were drink, flattery and drink. In stark contrast, Rory seemed to be in complete charge of himself, with no chinks or foibles to exploit.

Where's the dirt on Father Scamalot? We need the dirt. Give me dirt, woman!

Cx

P.S. What am I allergic to?

To: c.orourke@boulevardmagazine.com
From: a.looney@boulevardmagazine.com

The list of your allergies is taped inside your bathroom cabinet, as it has been for thirteen years, but FYI you're allergic to coriander, shellfish and commitment.

I don't think there *is* any dirt on this priest.

To: a.looney@boulevardmagazine.com
From: c.orourke@boulevardmagazine.com

I'm also allergic to smart-alec women. There's always dirt on a priest, foolish girl.

Cx

P.S. This whole you-being-in-a-different-country thing . . . it's not working for me.

Asta stared at the last line of the last email for quite some time.

'Let me do that,' said Peg, impatient to get at the dough Ma was kneading.

'Get off, Peg.' Ma slapped her sister-in-law's arthritic hand away.

'You're doing it wrong.'

'I've been doing it like this for forty years.'

'Then you've been doing it wrong for forty years.'

Watching, amused, from her perch on a kitchen stool, Kitty said, 'I love Grandma's bread.'

Ma lifted her nose, triumphant, and Peg retreated. All in

black, as if she'd caught her dress sense from the priests who employed her, Peg was a crow of a woman. Tackling the washing-up, she greeted Asta with, 'Would it kill you to give your mother a hand?'

'And good afternoon to you too, Aunty Peg.' The old bag had a point, though; Asta noticed the bills and statements that overflowed from the dresser drawers. 'What if I look through these . . .' she began, reaching out a hand.

'No, thank you.' Ma was brisk, a martyr to her fingertips. 'Just stir the stew, will you, love?'

When Kitty was sent out to the corner shop to buy sugar – and went *without a single eye roll* – Peg sniffed and said, 'So, madam, tell me what you say to that child when she asks about her father? Hmm?'

Ma shrank within her twinset and redoubled her kneading. 'Ah, now, Peg . . .' she said.

Peg cut Ma off. 'It's an important question and I have a right to ask it of my own niece.'

Do you? Peg's niece wasn't so sure. 'I answer her honestly.' Which was, in itself, a dishonest answer. Asta felt the snake of her lies squeeze her ever more tightly. She was hot, despite the frost on the windows.

'A child needs two parents,' said Peg.

'To be fair . . .' said Asta, treading carefully. She'd never spoken back to her aunt before. 'You're not an authority on the subject, Aunty Peg. You've never had a child.' *You've never even felt a man's hand on your thigh.*

Ma made a strange noise in her throat as she slammed the bread into the oven.

'I've never climbed a mountain, either. But I know better than to attempt it in a bikini.' Peg turned to Ma. 'It's time the statue cried, don't you think? The village needs it.'

Ears pricking up, Asta said, 'Needs it how?'

'There's a wonderful atmosphere when St Catherine cries,' said Peg, her lined face glowing.

'It's like a party,' said Ma.

'Of course, you youngsters know nothing about the lives of the saints,' said Peg, drying each dish as if it was a sinner.

Happy to be a youngster in somebody's eyes, Asta said, 'I've never been in a situation where I thought, *if only I knew more about the lives of the saints.*'

'St Catherine was a radical,' said Peg, looking dreamily into the middle distance, like Asta did when she talked about cake. 'The powers-that-be wanted her to live as a recluse. Just because she was a woman.' Peg awarded St Catherine an admiring head wobble. 'But no! Brave Catherine refused. She spoke out.'

Returning with a bag of sugar, Kitty said, 'Cool! St Cath was a feminist.'

'One of them women's libbers that burned their brassieres?' Peg's imagination had stalled in the 1970s. 'Never!'

'I'm sure,' said Asta, her face carefully innocent, 'that St Catherine wore an underwired cotton-rich balconette at all times.' Peg's approval of speaking out surprised her; the scorn for feminism didn't.

'Are you going to the vigil?' Peg obviously expected a 'no'.

'Yes,' simpered Asta.

'Good,' said Peg half-heartedly, disappointed at having to retract her claws.

Any invading army worth its salt peppers the landscape with monuments to its victory. The scattered trainers, Coke cans and dead bodies made it clear that teenagers had conquered the parlour.

On second glance, the bodies weren't dead, just draped over the sofas with eyes fixed on Angelina Jolie, who was saving the world (in a sexy way, natch) on the TV screen.

'Time for the vigil, KitKat,' said Asta, provoking much harrumphing and grumbling. After a full day of pounding Tobercree's footpaths, talking to Tobercree folk and deleting every word she typed, Asta was just as reluctant as her daughter, but the vigil was important local colour.

Father Rory had confounded her further that afternoon. A minibus had slowed beside her on the high street, its side emblazoned with the words *St Catherine's Parish is on the Move!* Rory had waved from the driver's window, as children of various ages and with various disabilities waved gleefully from the back.

'We're off to soft play!' he'd shouted, looking very like a man having a whale of a time, and not at all like a man with an evil plan to defraud the gullible.

'Sweetie, you said you wanted to come,' coaxed Asta as Kitty's Doc Martens marched sullenly down the stairs behind her. 'Let's go out the back way,' she added, glancing anxiously at the door to the bar.

A couple of hours earlier, Asta had crept down those stairs alone. It had been almost eight, not that it mattered. *Jake's probably forgotten*, she'd told herself. She hadn't washed her hair just because of this date thing. No, not at all. Her hair had needed a wash. *Whether he turns up or not, it's no biggie*. It was barely a mediummie.

As she had descended one step at a time, the swell of hectic conversation had grown louder, like a tide washing up the stairs. Asta had been shaking. *I'm being absurd,* she'd thought. *I've walked into that bar countless times.* She would no doubt recognize half the faces there. Nerves were totally out of place in this situation.

So why had she turned, barging back up the stairs as if followed by the demons that populated Father Dominic's sermons? These were very personal demons, the ones that clambered all over Asta whenever she got close to a man, sinking their teeth into her soft parts, tripping her up, enjoying her fear. *I'm too busy to have a drink with him tonight*, she'd thought as she slammed her bedroom door. The demons had cackled. They'd known a lie when they heard one.

Now, with a moody teen in tow, Asta wondered if Jake was still sitting beyond that greige-painted bar door. *I'll never know*, she thought, pushing at the door to the patio instead.

The door resisted her.

The key was kept by the cash register. Asta had no choice but to shoulder her way through the buzzing bar, colliding with a man turning away from the counter as she did so.

'Sorry,' said Jake, then, recognizing her, 'Hello there.' He brandished his watch with a wry lift of his eyebrows. 'Better late then never, I guess. Our date was for three hours ago.' He leaned in. 'I have to admit I'm a tiny bit drunk.' He raised a pint, absolving her for her tardiness. 'But you're here now. What can I get you?'

'Sorry, there's been a misunderstanding,' said Asta, damning that patron saint of Hopeless Daters for letting her down again. She was very close to him; the scrum in the bar made sure of that. 'I've got to be somewhere. Somewhere else,' she elucidated doltishly. Behind Asta, Kitty had perked up and was relishing this tableau. Jake considered Asta, puzzling something out. 'So this is a brush-off, yeah?'

'No,' said Asta hastily. 'Not at all.' She coughed, her stomach in ferment. 'Well, maybe.' She had no idea what she was doing. She was in freefall. This man was not Conan and yet she wanted to tear off this man's clothes with her teeth.

'You're weird,' said Jake. He said it happily, as if weird women were his favourite sort. He stood to one side. 'You'd better get going. You have to be somewhere.'

Trotting after her mother as Asta pushed through the throng, Kitty hissed, 'What was all that about?'

'Nothing.'

'He's hot,' said Kitty appreciatively. 'But old. Really old, Mum. Even for you. He's got grey hair, for God's sake!'

'Premature.' Asta defended the man she'd stood up. 'Anyway, he's nobody, it's nothing.'

'Yeah, right,' said Kitty, delighted. 'Whatever, Mum.'

The cold assaulted them as they stepped outside. Snow-flakes, wet and feathery, flew into their mouths before they could muffle up in scarves and tug on their woollen hats. 'I'm getting together with the gang later,' said Kitty. 'We're having a bit of a party.'

'Who'll be at this bit of a party?' Asta, head down, barely noticed the glow of the outsized coloured lights strung along the shopfronts.

'Oh, the usual crowd . . .'

Asta recognized the inflection, as if Kitty was hesitating on a top step: her daughter wanted to tell her something. 'And . . . ?' she prompted.

'God, Mum, you're so nosy!' protested Kitty, adding, in a carefully neutral manner, 'And Finn.'

The name glimmered, begging to be noticed.

'Ah,' said Asta, 'Finn.' She had no idea who this boy was, but in Ireland one direct question to any local female would immediately elicit his age, reputation and inside leg. 'Is Finn, like, a special friend?'

'Mu-um!' Kitty turned hunchback with embarrassment as they trotted across the car park, joining the stream of churchgoers turning the powdery crystals underfoot into icy slop. '*Special friend!* He's a mate, that's all. Bloody hell.' She looked covertly at her mother. 'Sorry,' she mumbled.

Asta was drenched with love for this urban-raised girl apologizing for what was, in the grand scheme of things, a pretty feeble curse.

'I've heard worse, sweetie.'

Relieved, Kitty leaned in close as they passed Oona's shuttered kiosk and whispered, 'Grandma swears *all the time.* All the old women do over here. It's mad.'

'Grandma doesn't swear. I know the word you mean.' Asta hesitated, unsure how to explain. '*Feck* isn't what you think, it's not . . .'

'Fuck,' giggled Kitty.

A look told Kitty that Asta would only travel so far down the sweary road. 'There's a very old Gaelic word, spelled *f-e-i-c*, which is used as an all-purpose exclamation. It's not a euphemism for the F word. It's a totally Irish expression all of its own.'

'So I can say feck?'

'We-ell . . .' Asta laughed at Kitty's hopeful face, as if permission to say 'feck' would be a dream come true. 'I suppose.'

'Did you say feck when you were my age?'

'Can't remember,' lied Asta.

'When you were my age you left home.' Kitty sounded defiant, as if broaching a taboo subject. 'I've worked it out. You had me when you were seventeen, so you must have left Ireland when you were sixteen. So, Mum, it's not fair that you won't let *me* leave home. And I'd only move around the corner, not across a sea!'

'It's different.' *Thank God*. The idea of Kitty going through Asta's trials was unthinkable.

'How come you won't allow me the independence you had?'

That stung. Asta's independence had been thrust on her. 'I didn't do it for fun.' This was further than she'd ever gone before with Kitty.

They stood facing each other on the church steps, motionless like pebbles in a freezing river, people surging past them.

The girl's face was a map of her emotions, one that Asta had been reading since it was just a bloody smudge. Now Asta read curiosity and reticence there. She waited, willing to answer any questions Kitty might have, scared of what they might be.

'Mum, why didn't you run to my dad when you left Tobercree?'

'Oh, love . . .' Asta wished for eloquence as the wind bit deep into her face. For Kitty, Tobercree opened a tin of worms marked 'Absent Father'. She looked at her daughter, who was the shape of a young woman but was still a baby inside. 'It wasn't because I didn't want to. Your dad would have loved you.' She reached out impulsively to hold Kitty to her and they rocked together, tubby with layers.

'The snow's stopped,' said Kitty, disappointed.

Kissing the tip of her frozen nose, Asta said, 'Run back to the gang.' *To Finn*.

Keeping her relief just this side of good manners, Kitty darted off into the coal-coloured night.

It was standing room only in the incense-filled church. Asta had been on her feet at the side of the packed pews for an hour, when the bell high above them tolled midnight.

The bar was shut; Jake had presumably gone home; Kitty was with her gang; Conan would be settling the bill in some swanky dive. And Asta was deep in her own past, among a crowd of people hell-bent on Heaven.

Expecting to see Rory doing his thing from the altar, Asta had found instead a self-regulating event. From time to time the ageless rhythm of murmured prayer swept along a line like a Mexican wave. The teenage girl beside Asta received a text on her mobile: *where r u hun? xoxo*. A baby a few rows away squeaked like a creaky door.

But mostly it was silent. A warm, textured silence that Asta leaned back on. The barn-like building was suffused with a Christmas Eve feeling, the same trembling, fragile anticipation of magic. Sleepily Asta reminded herself to cast a journalistic eye over the congregation, and conjured up some clever descriptions that she'd forget the moment she opened her laptop. Every now and then she glanced at the little saint in her grotto, just in case any sacred waterworks kicked off.

'I see something!' hissed a voice from the back of the church.

The crowd leaned forward, like one creature with many heads. 'Nah,' a man muttered. 'She'll not cry tonight.'

Despite being the focus of all this intense scrutiny, St Catherine was as untroubled as ever, her bland blue eyes fixed, sightless, on the congregation. The girl with the mobile phone nudged Asta. 'Have you ever,' she whispered in a sugared-almond voice, 'seen her, you know, cry?'

Asta shook her head *no*.

'You have to look with this,' smiled the girl, tapping the centre of her forehead. 'Your third eye.' She tapped it again. 'Your soul.'

'I see.' Asta smiled, but fidgeted. She was a fraud, only here to expose another fraud. The girl was naive, yes, but she was also happy, and Asta had no intention of arguing with her. 'Thanks. I'll try.'

The line was jostled: newcomers joined the crush. Asta pressed tighter against the cushioned behind of the woman in front, and caught a glimpse of a face she knew right at the front of the congregation.

Kneeling at St Catherine's feet, her elbows on the wrought-iron surround, Gerry must have been one of the first to arrive. It felt wrong for Asta to witness her sister's face with that expression on it. There was none of Gerry's usual archness, just shining concentration, balanced between agony and sublimity. It looked like a quiet orgasm, and made a voyeur of Asta.

The newcomers pressed further into the church. Asta breathed in to let them pass. A whispered voice in Asta's ear sounded like a roar in the stockpiled silence.

'She's here every day.' Martin's civilian voice was indistinguishable from his radio one: both made Asta long to swing a mallet. 'A wonderfully devout woman, your sister.'

'Yeah,' said Asta, keen to move away, but hemmed in by holy people having virtuous thoughts.

'It's grand having you at home again, love.'

'Hmm.'

'After all the pain you caused, I'm glad you're finally doing the decent thing.' When Asta ignored him, Martin said, 'I met Kitty. What a darling girl.'

'Will you whisht!' A burly woman, buried under scarves, turned around, indignant. 'Oh!' She melted, visibly. 'Martin Mayberry! I'm your biggest fan! Aren't you even more handsome in the flesh!'

St Catherine suddenly had competition. People turned, gasping, leaning across to shake the blessed hand that had touched a Nolan Sister.

This muted brouhaha coincided with the natural end of the vigil. As if the crowd had a single brain, it stood, shook itself and made for the exits. Asta pushed, keen to put some space between herself and her brother-in-law.

'Hey!' His voice was at her shoulder halfway across the car park. Asta sped up, burrowing faster through the crowd.

'Oi, hang on!'

On second hearing, she realized the voice wasn't 'mellifluous', 'honey-coated' or 'drenched with Irish charm'. It was English, flat, with a whiff of sulphur. Asta turned, and went a particular shade of pink that a Dulux chart might dub 'Sweaty Schoolgirl'.

'Jake!' Some instinct prodded her not to recall his name so readily. 'Isn't it? Or is it something else?' Buffeted by a stream of spiritually satisfied humanity, Asta stepped out of the current to stand beside a motorhome with US plates.

'No, you were right the first time.' Jake's smile was a bright slit in the moonlight as he tucked himself in beside her. 'And you're Asti. Like the drink.'

'No, no, I'm Asta. Like the . . .' *Joke! Joke! Make a joke!* 'Like the, erm . . .'

The silence went on long enough to provoke thoughts

of suicide before Jake said, in a low, sandpaper voice that Asta really rather liked, 'Like *you*. You're just like you.'

'It's easy.'

'Can't be that easy.' Jake's eyes, grey earlier, were black. 'Or we'd all be doing it.' He herded her back into the mob with a tilt of his body and a sweep of his arm.

As they walked with the thinning crowd, Asta commented, 'Wouldn't have thought vigils were your thing.'

'Why? 'Cos I'm a heretic of an Englishman?'

'No. Well, yes.' Asta made an apologetic face, hoping it didn't give her too much of a double chin. She was, she realized, regressing to the kind of teenager she'd never really been: perhaps she had an alter ego. A really rubbish one, who fell to pieces around handsome men. 'OTT religious behaviour feels very Irish to me.'

'I go to mass every day. I find it very . . .' Jake passed a hand over his mouth. A long-fingered hand, with no rings and pleasingly short fingernails. 'I can't lie to you, Asta. I've never set foot in a church. I'm a bit drunk, and a bit cheesed off because this fabulous woman stood me up, so I was on my way to buy chips when I got caught up in this flood of people coming out of the church. I couldn't understand why the chippie was open so late, but now I get it.'

'*Chipper*.' Asta put him right. 'If you want to fit in, you must learn the lingo. Not *chippie*. It's *chipper*.' She attempted a look of haughty pedantry. 'The *er* is vital.' She was relieved to discover that Jake was a fellow cynic. And that he'd forgiven her for her no-show.

Without asking, Jake bought a bag of chips for Asta as well. Without asking, he led her to the bus stop and leaned against the angled plastic ledge, evidently expecting her to do the same.

Asta didn't like being second-guessed. She could be, as Angie wasn't shy of pointing out, 'a bit of a madam' at times. But this didn't seem to be one of those times. Jake's presumption was cosy rather than arrogant.

Besides, a chip's a chip.

An onlooker might theorize that Jake was just as tempting as the chips, but admitting this was problematical for a woman with Asta's history and hang-ups, so she smothered the thought with a chip. Her plan had been to rush home and write up the vigil; she imagined Conan waiting for her copy.

Such readiness to stray from the path surprised Asta. As did that metaphor – following it to its logical conclusion made Jake the big bad wolf.

'So,' said Jake, his eyes their cloudy grey again, thanks to the film-noir light of the street lamp. 'What's your story, Asta? You home for good?'

'No. God, no. No. Nonono.'

'OK.' Jake smiled, and his eyes creased playfully. The bright eyes and the silvered hair didn't seem to be the same vintage, a conundrum which intrigued Asta. 'That'll be a no, then.'

Asta giggled, shamefaced at her vehemence.

'Is there a Mr Asta?'

His bluntness startled her. There was only ever one reason why men asked women that question. 'No,' she said, careful not to be so emphatic this time. There was, after all, a Mr Asta-in-waiting. Kind of. 'There is a Ms, though. I have a daughter.'

'Is she teeny?'

'Not any more. She's sixteen.'

'I won't be smarmy and say you don't look old enough.'

'Good,' said Asta, gutted.

'Are you showing her off to the rellies?'

'I'm here to work.' Asta paused. 'I'm a writer,' she said, checking his face to see if he guffawed.

'Really?' Jake had a slow way of talking, of moving his hand through his hair. He wasn't an expostulator, nor a fidget. For a woman who came from a long line of expostulating fidgets, this was relaxing.

'Really. Well, no, not really.'

'Do you ever,' asked Jake, 'give a straight answer?'

'Yes. And no.'

This was fun, Asta realized with a jolt. She was having fun. Talking to a man. Whom she also fancied. Long accustomed to being wary of the opposite sex, she enjoyed letting down her defences. Perhaps it was because he listened intently, as if she interested him. *Big bad wolves tend not to do that.*

'Do you write books? Or short stories?'

Up to now, just shopping lists. 'Articles.'

'You're a journalist.'

'I suppose I am.' Asta didn't dare call herself that. Not yet. 'I'm working on a piece about the crying statue. I'm going to discover the trick, how they do it.'

'If it's a trick, it's a bloody good one.'

'If?' Asta pounced on the word. '*If* the man-made statue is crying?'

'OK, OK.' Jake waved a chip in surrender. 'It's clever, though. You have to admit that. Hardened journalists from all over the world have come to look at her and been . . .' He studied his chip as he searched for a word.

'Conned?'

'I was going to say *moved.*'

Feeling reprimanded, Asta stiffened. It was uncomfortable on her side of the argument, alongside the naysayers, the realists, the party poopers. 'Father Rory knows his stuff.'

'Brilliant at Wii tennis,' confided Jake. 'He comes up to my place now and again for a tournament.'

'In his robes?'

'Sometimes. Sometimes he's in normal clothes.'

'On his bike?'

'The Harley?' Jake shook his head fondly. 'Rory loves that beast.'

'Must have cost a fortune. I wonder how a priest would afford such a thing?'

Jake leaned back a little, his eyes suspicious. 'Are you pumping me for information?'

'Yes. Sorry.'

'Don't be.' Jake regarded Asta long enough to make her cough. 'Whatever you think of Rory, he's the best company in Tobercree.'

'He's charming, all right.'

'You say that as if it's a bad thing. Come on.' Jake stood, all activity and intent. 'I'll walk you home.'

Flustered, Asta hitched her slouchy bag over her shoulder. They hadn't finished their chips but he was walking her home, *ergo* she bored him. 'My mum's place is just up there.' She remembered one of the many and excellent reasons she ring-fenced her emotions: relying on a man's good opinion led to lacerating self-doubt. She clammed up, opening her mouth only to insert chips.

Her companion did the same. When they reached the bar, it was quiet and dark, as befitted the late hour.

'Ah . . .' said Jake, almost to himself. 'This is your mum's place?' He looked contrite, comically so.

'Yes. My mum's the madwoman who owns Looney's.'

'I'm an imbecile. Sorry.'

'Don't apologize. She's far madder than you realize. You also said she serves the best Guinness in Tobercree.'

'Which is true. Absolutely true. Best I've ever had.' Jake bit his knuckle contemplatively. 'I'm over-compensating, aren't I?'

'A little.'

Jake looked up at the sign. 'So that makes you a Looney?'

'Yes.' *Extra brownie points if you don't make a joke.*

'Asta Looney.' He regarded her with a slow-growing smile. 'I like it.'

'Anyway, good night,' said Asta, flustered by that smile. She could hear Angie's howls of frustration all the way from London. 'Thanks for the chips.' She reached into her bag for the key.

Jake scrunched up his chip paper and lobbed it at a bin a little way along the pavement. 'This is the moment we kiss,' he said. 'Don't you think?'

Asta made a small noise she hoped was covered by the sound effects of a very startled woman scrabbling around in a handbag.

'But,' said Jake, stepping back, 'it would taste of salt and vinegar, so let's leave it until next time.' He turned and aimed, 'Good night, Asta Looney,' over his departing shoulder.

'Good night!' she called, opening the door, darting in and pressing herself against the back of it. 'Good night,' she continued in a whisper, 'you big fat complication.'

Striding through the bar, barking her shins on shabby-chic stools, Asta let herself out to the flagstoned barbecue area, last resting place of many an economy sausage. The bluey, slush-spattered patio petered out into tamed grass, which in turn went feral and clambered up the hill to the woods. She raced to the point where the drenched lawn gave way to the damp, tussocky hillside and breathed in hungry lung-fuls of the biting night air. It was sweet, and sharp, and made her giddy.

Or, to be precise, *more* giddy.

The moon came out and outlined the frozen trees like a shadow theatre. A figure hurtled down the slope towards her, crowing with the sheer joy of being young and running too fast down a hill. Asta's pagan daughter tore past her and into the house.

The snowy woods were older than the church. They were the true Ireland, the one Asta could admit she missed.

The thoughts running through her mind would shock St Catherine, but Asta was marching to a different drum, with a beat far wilder than the little saint would approve of.

'Asta!'

Her name is bellowed now from the forest floor beneath the treehouse, but it's almost lost in the tumultuous noise of the wind whipping through the wood. The tiny animals are out of their hidey-holes, rampaging, tearing at each other with sharp teeth as the wind flattens the grass and batters the trees.

The treehouse tilts as a foot is placed on the rope ladder.

Asta pulls Etienne towards her, savagely kissing his face, her eyes shut tight, her ears full of her own name.

'Asta!'

December 18th

They were pretty snores, the kind a sleeping fairy might make. Kitty turned over on her camp bed and snuggled deeper as Asta pulled on an Aran and her jeans and crept out of the room.

'Yes, let her sleep,' agreed Ma, pouring tea in the kitchen. 'She wasn't home 'till the small hours. The young ones these days do have a great time. I was already working when I was her age.'

'And I was . . .' *Best not to dwell on what I was doing*, thought Asta, accepting the fried breakfast without demur. Resistance was futile.

'You loved an auld party when you were young.' Ma airbrushed history, carefully painting around the detail of the pesky unwanted pregnancy.

'I sure did.' Asta allowed nostalgia to colour her soviet memories. 'I was a bit of a loner, though.' She'd spent what her mother regarded as an unhealthy amount of time in her room, lying flat on the bed, legs up the wall, reading gluttonously. 'Oona always dragged me out.' She smiled at the memory of a testy teenager in leggings shouting up at Asta's window to *put down the book and come to the cove, s'il vous feckin' plait!* 'And there was always the gang knocking about. Up to something.' She'd been related to some of them, at school with all of them. They were a solid mass of good times. 'Where are they all?' said Asta, half to herself.

'Moved away, love,' said Ma, a mournfulness fluttering beneath the words. 'Not much work here any more. They got out, like you.' She looked at her hands as she chopped up meat for that day's avalanche of stew, and flexed her crabbed fingers. 'Well, not like you, not as . . .'

'Not as dramatically?' offered Asta, crunching into a slice of toast. 'Not as suddenly?'

'Not as cruelly,' said Ma quietly.

After a silence punctuated with chopping sounds and crunching sounds, Asta said, 'Kelliher's cows were wrong, Ma. The snow's stopped.'

Never one to let facts get in the way, Ma shook her head. 'They're never wrong,' she said. 'I'd trust those cows with my life.'

Tobercree was waking up. The newsagent's door stood open. The butcher swept his step. A burly man leapt off a lorry to roll barrels along the wet pavement towards the pub. The air was silvered by frost, the Christmas lights throbbing through a spectral fog.

Asta breathed in. The smell of peat was very Tobercree, as were whitewashed cottages, silver-painted railings, the croak of gulls and the vague feeling of having let down everybody you've ever cared about.

Climbing the gentle slope of the main street, boots stained

dark by puddles, Asta wondered if this Finn character had made an appearance at the party.

Five days, Asta reminded herself. *Just five more days and we'll both be safely home in our cosy nook.* If Asta stuck to the plan, deduced the scam, and scribbled diligently each night, she would have a finely crafted article all ready for Conan by the time flight E1179 to Heathrow took off at 12.05 next Wednesday. This Finn couldn't break Kitty's heart in such a short space of time.

Only five days to claim her kiss. Asta touched her mouth with her mitten, unable to quell the smile that creased her face. While it was still a sexy daydream, the kiss was wonderful. *But when I actually kiss men* . . . Well, for starters, Asta was usually plastered when lip-locking occurred. Perhaps it would be safer to keep Jake at arm's length, fantasize about the kiss and fly back to Conan after five chaste days.

Something was changing in Conan's attitude. She could feel a shift, a change of perspective, but Asta had waited so long for it to happen that she didn't trust her own judgement.

Perhaps I'll ask Kelliher's cows what they think.

At this early hour, as Asta had hoped, the echoing chapel was empty. Dust motes danced in the watery sunlight as she made her way to the sobbing superstar.

'Good morning, Catherine,' she whispered. 'Fancy crying today? Go on. Just a tear or two. For me.'

Ignoring her, St Catherine stood calmly at her post, eyes misty. If she noticed the discreet click of Asta's mobile phone, she didn't react.

'Smile.' Asta took a couple of shots to pore over later.

She glanced about her before throwing her leg over the wrought-iron semicircle that protected the statue.

It was quite a squeeze, saint and sinner in a niche built for one. St Catherine was a good head higher than her new friend, so Asta had to stand on tiptoe to examine the back of the statue's head. She saw only smooth plaster, white and bright. Asta put her arms around the statue, and looked the saint in the eye. A telltale scrape in the plaster would be invaluable.

'Ahem.'

'Jesus!' squawked Asta.

'Ahem again,' said Rory, standing a few feet beneath her, his hands behind his back.

'God. I mean, sorry. Sorry for the Jesus.' Asta wriggled out from behind St Catherine. 'And, actually, for the God.'

'And for spooning a saint?' Rory's expression was hard to read. He was grave, but Asta hoped she saw a *soupçon* of amusement in his eyes. 'You've barely been introduced.'

'Yes, sorry for that, too. For everything. Everything I've ever done. Truly.' Asta peeled herself from the statue, self-consciously hopping over the balustrade to stand beside the priest. 'You must think I'm mad.'

'I do,' he agreed. He had a patient air, not unlike St Catherine.

'You probably want an explanation.'

'You know me so well, to paraphrase Elaine Paige.'

This was all wrong. Priests were censorious and bigoted. They didn't make jokes about cheesy hits from the eighties. 'I was just . . .' There was no credible fib to explain the saintly dry-humping. *Besides*, thought Asta with a sudden realization, *all this lying makes me uncomfortable.* As if her bra was on back to front. (She knew what that felt like, and so can you if you're prepared to drink a whole bottle of tequila before bed.) 'I'll be frank with you.' Conan would be furious, but Asta felt an urge to tug her bra the right way round again, as it were. 'I'm writing an article for *Boulevard* magazine about the statue. About the church. The phenomenon. About . . . well, you.'

'Me?' Rory's brows mated suddenly. 'Who'd be interested in me?' He turned away, saying, 'Well, let me know if I can help, but try not to grope her again.' He walked briskly away towards the back of the church. 'She's precious, you know.'

Asta was conscious of disappointment; she had antici-pated a Mexican stand-off, not genial offers of help. It was difficult to feel like a hard-boiled investigative journo when scurrying after a man in a dress. 'Hang on, Father Rory; I need to examine her more closely. I need to –' She dashed out through the double doors after her priestly prey, but Rory was already halfway across the neurotically manicured lawn in front of the priests' house.

Her boots stalled at the lawn's edge. Asta didn't want to go any nearer to the low-built house, to hear the echoes of what had been said to her within its walls.

Rory had reached the black door that was never locked. Seeing Asta stranded on the other side of the grass, he asked, 'Did you want to come in?'

'Yes. I want to speak to my aunty.' Asta took the path, unable to trespass on the grass. 'Father Dominic's house looks exactly as I remember.' Asta tried to make that sound like a good thing. Somewhere, inside this modest 1930s red-brick house with its window boxes and its criss-cross paned windows, lurked her old tormentor. 'Right down to the doormat.'

'Technically, it's the church's house.' Rory held the door open, standing to one side with that impeccable politesse of his. 'There've been a few improvements.'

Asta, mute with surprise, stepped slowly over the threshold. Where was the psychedelic hall carpet, the turquoise paintwork, the faint smell of holy old people? She was in a white and glossy space-age cube, with a glass back wall and a floor of shiny marble.

'You approve?' Father Rory enjoyed her amazement.

'This is more Los Angeles than Tobercree, surely?' whispered Asta.

'Through here.' Father Rory, his outline inky in the polar surroundings, led her down a long white corridor. 'I hear you met our Jake Jones. Nice chap, don't you think?'

Impressed by his intelligence-gathering, Asta said, 'Oh, well, I, no, but, actually yes, hmm . . .'

Rory looked back at her. 'I see he's had his usual effect on the opposite sex.'

'No, not at all.' Asta untwisted her tongue to say, 'I barely spoke to the guy.'

'He speaks well of you.'

Asta twitched all over, relieved she hadn't blushed.

'You look a little pink, Asta,' said Rory solicitously as he pushed at the door to the kitchen. 'Are you feeling OK?'

'Aunty Peg!' Asta had never been so glad to see her spiky relative.

The vast, clinical kitchen dwarfed the defiantly dated woman in black energetically beating the bejaysus out of eggs and sugar in a bowl. Peg paused and wiped her hands on the chequered tea towel that lay over her shoulder like a dying cat. 'Will you have a little cappuccino?' she asked.

This was a step too far. This was madness. Irish priest

houses offer a choice of tea strong enough for a mouse to trot across it, or whisky. Nothing else. Ever.

'If it's no trouble,' said Asta.

'Marvellous.' Rory was all movement again, but escape was not that easy. 'Faa-ther,' called Peg, with a sweet voice she never wasted on her family. 'Will you be having my ham salad or my egg sandwich for your lunch?'

'Either. I'm sure both are excellent, Peg.' He was impatient, his eyes backlit by something other than the milk of human kindness. As Peg did battle with a milk nozzle, Asta asked, offhand, 'What *did* Jake say about me?'

Rory laughed, rubbing his chin. 'I couldn't possibly tell you. You'd blush even more.' He nodded a goodbye. 'Enough matchmaking. There are souls to save.' But before he could leave Asta had a question for him, one that made his face fall.

'You offered to help with the article. Could I take the statue away for an hour or two at some point? To examine her properly.'

'St Catherine's not a magic trick.' Rory's voice was almost a hiss. 'She was respected for her formidable intelligence and she died for what she believed in. I won't have her pawed for the sake of your career.'

'But—'

'No buts.' Rory had shrugged off his liberal modern trappings and reverted to the hardline language of his predecessor. 'The answer's no.' Mellowing only slightly, he said, 'It's not about science, Asta. It's about wonder. And hope.'

'And *you*,' said Asta. 'This is about you, Father.'

'What was all the whispering about?' Peg examined Asta's face after Rory left the room.

'Nothing.' Asta's airiness was designed to deflect

suspicion, never easy with a woman who made the KGB look like fumbling amateurs. She seated herself at the granite-topped table. 'Fab kitchen. I see you've got an electric steamer. And a plasma screen. And a glass-fronted fridge. And an ice-cream maker.' Asta grinned. 'What Da would have called *every modern inconvenience*.'

'I'm a very lucky woman,' said Peg bitterly, handing Asta a cup topped with a milky bouffant. She looked at the ice-cream maker as if she'd like to drop-kick it into the garden.

'They'll never replace you with a gadget.'

'And who suggested otherwise?' Peg brushed off empathy the way another woman might brush off a mugger. 'I've given my life to this house.'

And for what? 'When was the place refurbished?' Asta trod carefully; one whiff of suspicion, and Peg would clam up.

Deftly lining a cake tin, Peg poured in vanilla-scented batter. 'Just after the St Catherine circus took off.'

Twirling an imaginary moustache, Asta said, 'Circus? You sound as if you disapprove.'

'It's not up to me to approve or disapprove,' sniffed Peg, hesitating in front of the daunting bank of ovens before opening one and popping in the cake tin. 'I leave the thinking to the fathers.'

'Where's Father Dominic?' Asta peered cautiously around her, as if the old sod might leap out of a cupboard, waving a crucifix.

'Having a little nap.' Peg softened; it was like watching a bulldog fall in love. 'Sure, his tireless devotion to the church wears him out.'

Yes, thought Asta. *Shouting endlessly about Hell must*

take it out of a chap. 'Is that nice old lady who does the accounts still here?'

'Long dead,' said Peg happily. 'Father Rory looks after that side of things now. To save money. He's trained and everything. That man can do anything.' She sounded as proud as if she'd raised him from a pup.

'So I suppose he okayed the money for the house to be done up.'

'Suppose.' Peg was airy as she beheaded spring onions. 'After he bought a new minibus, and rebuilt the parish centre.' She scattered onion over a hard-boiled egg snug beneath a mayonnaise duvet. 'We do have grand Irish-dancing evenings in there.'

'I can imagine,' said Asta, who'd rather not. 'Did the parish buy him that motorbike?' She winced: the question was too bald. A pro like Peg would spot it a mile off.

'That death trap! I say a dozen Hail Marys every time he swings his leg over it. It's more suited to rock stars, like Des O'Connor.' Peg paused. 'What's it got to do with you, miss?'

'Nothing, nothing at all.' It was time to retreat to softer ground. 'Have you seen St Catherine cry, Aunty Peg?'

'Not yet. But I will.' Peg was complacent.

'So,' asked Asta, 'you believe in her powers?'

'Sure, isn't it always the women who step up when there's trouble?' Peg opened another oven and took out a circular loaf. She laid it in front of Asta, wholesome and majestic. 'And God knows this country needs some help, with the banks acting the maggot and the politicians letting us down.'

In Peg's opinion, St Catherine was just another belea-guered, time-strapped housewife mopping up a mess with a long-suffering roll of the eyes. Asta wondered if the fathers ever noticed how tired their housekeeper looked, how dark the circles under her eyes, how stooped her shoulders.

As if sensing pity, Peg snapped, 'Look at the time! Amn't I missing the start of me programme!' She pressed a button on a transistor radio, the only low-tech apparatus in the kitchen apart from herself. 'I always tune in to our family superstar.'

Over the dying strains of Boney M, Martin's voice said, 'Time for a phone-in, ladies.'

'Oh, I love his phone-ins!' Peg sounded almost girlish.

'Aunty, do you know a boy called Finn?'

'Whisht!' Peg turned up the radio to focus on Martin's voice.

'Today I want youse all to phone in and tell me the most romantic thing that ever happened to you. And if my wife's listening, don't call in, darling! Sure, you'll only embarrass me!'

'Romance!' Peg tutted. 'Men are only good for one thing.'

Surprised, Asta lifted her eyebrows, then lowered them again as her aunt elaborated, 'Moving wardrobes.'

'Finn, Aunty Peg?'

'Oh, yes. He's no good.'

'In what way?'

'He's a bad lot.'

'Could you be more specific?'

'Ladies, was it a red rose on your pillow? Or a box of choccies on Valentine's Day?'

Martin doesn't have much of an imagination, thought Asta.

'Finn,' said Peg, 'is a wee messer.'

Asta gave up.

'Ring in now and tell me the most romantic thing a man ever did for you.'

Taking half the loaf wrapped in a tea towel for Ma, Asta recalled her name spelled out in pebbles on the sand of the cove, with a wobbly heart drawn around it. 'Thanks, Aunty Peg. This smells divine.'

'Hmph.' Aunty Peg, uncomfortable with gratitude, was already prepping her next task. 'I have twenty nuns visiting this afternoon, and they're all mad for me tarts.'

She and her aunt made quite a pair, thought Asta as she left the kitchen. One woman whose most romantic moment happened seventeen years ago, and another whose most romantic moment was when a man moved a wardrobe for her.

To: a.looney@boulevardmagazine.com
From: c.orourke@boulevardmagazine.com

Thanks for your email, and about time.

Top marks for discovering that Rory used Catherine money to do up his house. Couldn't care less about nicey wicey details of disabled kids gallivanting about in minibuses. The motorbike sounds like his Achilles' heel. There can't be any justification for using church funds to buy it. Where's the interview with the cured deaf girl? And how does he make the statue cry? You only have a few days, Asta. Without the scam, this is just a slice of Irish whimsy.

Cx

P.S. The freezer's making a funny noise. Like this: wheep wheep wheep. What do I do? Do I have to move house?

'No. Fair's fair. I won't tell you Dervla's address until you tell me what went on with Jakey-Wakey, the King of Sex.'

'I'm late, Oona.' Asta waggled her watch as proof. 'I can't be late for my first interview.'

'Hang on.' Oona broke off to wrap a Holy Ghost dog chew for an American man. 'Does this top look all right on me?' she asked Asta after she'd sent her customer away with the wrong change.

'It looks very – hang on, that's my top,' said Asta.

'Now, Jake, tell. Leave nothing out.'

'There's nothing to tell. I didn't meet him.'

'Did you get a better offer?'

'I had to work.'

'What can I hurt you with?' Oona snatched up a musical crucifix and jabbed it in Asta's ear.

'Ow!'

'That's for dereliction of female duty. I'm ashamed of you, letting a quality item like Jake slip through your fingers.'

'So what?' Asta attempted nonchalance. 'I'm here to work.' She hugged herself. The snow might have stopped, but a frigid breeze was rolling in off the distant purple hills, making straight for the tiny booth.

'Next time you bump into him, you owe him an apology.'

'Yeah, right.' On the contrary, it was Jake who owed Asta. *He promised me a kiss.* The last email from Conan had betrayed not one whiff of tenderness. *Am I sacrificing myself for a lost cause?* She could claim her debt the next time she bumped into Jake. By the law of local averages, Asta should have bumped into him already; it was hard to avoid folk in a village the size of Tobercree. Maybe St Catherine was meddling, keeping them apart.

'What did you mean, Oona, when you said my family needed me?'

'You really have to ask?' Oona stared at her cousin. 'Your ma's running herself into the ground.' Oona put her hands on her hips, not easy in that confined space. 'Have you no eyes in your head?'

'Well, I can see she's short-staffed . . .'

'She does everything!' Oona bit her lip, then seemed to make a decision to go on. 'And something doesn't add up. The pub's packed every night since St Catherine started bringing in the crowds, yet your ma still can't afford extra staff. She does the books, but I don't think she's up to it. She's making mistakes. She's getting on, Asta.'

'Nooo,' said Asta, knowing how absurd she sounded. *Why should Ma be immune to the march of time?* 'Well, she's older, obviously, but not *old* old.'

'Your ma's coped without your da for more than twenty years, and she's running out of steam. She won't accept help. It's too much for her, but she won't admit it.'

So accustomed to being the problem of the family, Asta had taken her eye off her mother. 'I didn't notice,' she said.

'You weren't here.' Oona was matter-of-fact.

'What can I do? I can't imagine Ma retiring.'

'Your ma *is* Looney's Bar.'

'Exactly. Her sense of self is rooted in the bricks and mortar. It'll kill her if it fails. It's always thrived, the heart of the community.'

'And it's not just your ma who needs sorting out.' When Asta just looked dumb, Oona said, 'Surely you've noticed the change in Gerry? She was always an awful suck-up but she never used to be such a holy Joe. Mass every morning and evening? Something's wrong there.'

'But what can *I* do about any of this?' Asta felt overwhelmed. She thought back to a week ago when all she'd had to worry about was preparing for Christmas. 'I live on the other side of the sea!'

'You'll have to move back.' Oona smiled in a *job done* way.

'I can't do that.' Asta realized how naive she'd been to believe that her family had just jogged along, unchanging. 'If Da was still here,' she said wistfully.

'But he's not.'

'Give me Dervla's address,' said Asta, suddenly keen to be out of this tiny space, out in the bracing cold, striding along, achieving something, even if it was only putting some distance between herself and this unsettling knowledge.

Dervla's garden had been crowded with frogs. Not the living, croaking variety, but fakes. Jumping frogs. Lounging frogs. Leap-frogging frogs. One had worn a top hat out on the freezing barren lawn. Later, when Asta listened to the interview through her headphones as she walked to the post office, she winced at how much time she'd spent asking her interviewee about the frogs.

After a lifetime of deafness, Dervla had twisted some of her words, but she was bubbly and glad to talk. 'I won't talk to any of them auld newspapers,' she'd said. 'But you're different.'

Am I? I'm going to use your words to discredit the saint

who cured you, thought Asta as she fast-forwarded to find the exchange that had unnerved her.

Asta landed halfway through one of Dervla's sentences. '– big crystal tears running down St Catherine's face. They looked like stars in the candlelight. It was so beautiful. She looked sad, as if she knew what ailed each and every one of us and wanted to help.'

Asta pressed down the button. She didn't need to hear how a tourist had caught the tears and rubbed them on Dervla's ears. She landed bang in the middle of what she was after.

'– but the only drawback is that now, of course, I can't work at the deaf school because you have to be, well, deaf, and I'm not any more. I love those kids.'

Asta remembered the loss on Dervla's face. It was there again when she'd said her husband was delighted for her, really he was, 'but it's strange with me being able to hear and him still being deaf'.

St Catherine hadn't tied up all the loose ends. Asta had liked Dervla; she was game. And, so she said, 'saving up for a giant frog doing the splits'.

Oona caught up with Asta, puffing out frosty shapes. 'What *is* that you're carrying?' She pointed at the package in Asta's grasp.

'A barm brack.' said Asta. 'For Gerry, God help her.' Barm brack, a raisin-studded teacake of gargantuan proportions, is the speciality of many an Irish matron. In the right hands, it is a divine thing. Ma's hands were not the right hands: her barm brack could stop a bullet.

'Hel-*lo*!' A Nordic-looking man, the camera around his neck marking him out as a tourist, stepped back to let the women pass. 'Hi there, sexy,' grinned Oona, jutting out her bosom in a greeting that transcended language barriers.

'Control yourself,' said Asta. 'Think of Declan.'

'Declan can put up with a little low-level flirting.'

'Low-level?' Asta had heard about Oona drinking vodka from a Russian sailor's welly while Declan was at the vigil. 'Get the door for me, would you?'

The tinkle of the old-fashioned bell above the post-office door summoned Gerry from the back room. 'It's you,' she said flatly. 'I thought it was people.'

'A present from Ma.' The barm brack hit the counter like a corpse hitting a pavement. 'Why didn't you tell me the pub's going under?'

'If we told you everything, you wouldn't be a black sheep, would you?' Gerry manhandled the cake under a wooden counter crowded with chocolate bars and penny sweets: the post office did double duty as a corner shop.

Oona groaned. 'Drop the boxing gloves, you two. Play nice.'

'I always play nice,' smiled Gerry, displaying frosted peach lipstick on her prominent front teeth. 'Ma's fine. I'm fine. The pub gets by. Don't cause trouble the moment you arrive. Especially as you'll be fecking off again in five minutes.'

'I want to help.' Even as she said it, Asta felt her whole body clench. If helping meant staying, it would amount to martyrdom. Perhaps they'd erect a statue of her in the church.

'Bit late for that.' Gerry folded her arms. 'You wouldn't believe the atmosphere after you ran away. Ma blamed herself. It ruined my wedding.'

'You mean *I* ruined your wedding.'

'I suppose I do,' said Gerry, blinking at warp speed. She

blinked when flustered; Asta guessed that her sister was conflicted about heaping so much blame on her.

'I'm sorry.' Suddenly, Asta really was. Terribly sorry. She could imagine the atmosphere; the Looneys were good at them. Busy building her new life, she hadn't stopped to think about the effect on the ones left behind. 'Truly, I am.'

'Well, whatever.' Gerry was graceless at accepting compliments, presents and, it turned out, apologies. 'It's a long time ago.' She fussed with a display of plastic rain bonnets. 'Here's lover boy,' said Gerry, at the period ting of the bell.

The preparatory tingle in Asta's pants was shut down when she saw Declan's scrubbed pink face. 'Declan! It's been years!' she cried.

Those years had had little effect on Declan. His face was still boyishly round and his dress sense was still stuck in the 1950s. 'It's grand to see you back home, Assumpta.' He eyed Oona, who hadn't acknowledged his arrival by so much as a flicker of a false eyelash. 'No doubt Oona has told you of our relationship?'

'Yes, and I'm delighted.' Flummoxed, but delighted.

'Perhaps you can be a good influence on her.' Declan spoke sadly, as if discussing a naughty cat that repeatedly widdled on the lino. 'I despair, Assumpta, I really do.' He gestured at his beloved's chest. 'Oona, darlin', we talked about this.'

'You talked. I had me iPod in.' Oona zipped up her padded jacket. 'Happy?'

'Men are weak, Oona, and they will sin in their hearts at the sight of you.'

'To be accurate,' murmured Gerry, 'the sinning usually happens behind the bus stop.'

'She's wild, Asta,' said Declan.

'Perhaps,' ventured Asta, 'that's why you like her.'

'I don't *like* her!' Declan glared at Asta as if she'd insulted him. 'I love her.'

'Aw, Dec.' It was unexpected, this sweet honesty, from one so uptight. 'That's lovely.'

'It's not a bit lovely.' Declan sounded desperate. 'I have to share her with every eejit who blows into Tobercree. Take my advice, Assumpta. Do not fall in love.'

'OK,' said Asta. 'I promise.'

Gerry cut in. 'Shush, you eejits. Here comes a proper customer.'

'Charming.' Asta turned to take in the proper customer. 'Jake!' she said, approximately a thousand times louder and more breathlessly than she would have liked.

'Asta,' said Jake. His smile stiffened as he looked around him. 'Er, hello, everyone,' he said uncertainly, realizing he was the subject of keen scrutiny.

Oona regarded him hungrily, as if he was a free kebab; Declan was sniffy; Gerry wore an expression of dismayed shock.

'You two know each other?' she asked angrily, as if accusing them of something unspeakable.

'We've met,' said Jake easily, sending Asta an unmistakable cry for help with his eyes.

It was warming, that collusive glance, and Asta felt bold enough to ask, 'Is that allowed, sis?' She wondered if Jake remembered the promised kiss. A clinch in front of this audience was unlikely. *Besides*, she reminded herself primly, *I hardly know the man*. If he attempted to kiss her, she would rebuff him. She would. She really would. You could bet on that, and your money would be safe.

'Jake!' When Gerry regained the attention of her 'proper

customer' she asked, in a cut-glass accent straight from old black and white films, 'What, Jake, may I have the pleasure of doing for you, as it were, today, Jake?'

Asta caught Oona's eye and her cousin nodded, face crumpled in amusement. *Yes,* the nod said, *not only is your sister Jake-ing the poor man to death, but she uses her telephone voice on him.*

'Stamps, please,' said Jake woodenly, like a bad actor in an am dram.

'Ha!' laughed Declan bitterly. 'Stamps, is it?' He'd noticed his girlfriend's leer. 'Stamps!' he repeated, as if they were evidence of Jake's debauchery.

'Shut up, Declan,' said Oona, adding 'darlin'' for the sake of appearances. 'Shouldn't you be at work? Houses don't sell themselves.'

Declan treated Jake to a particularly dark look, saying to Oona, 'Don't forget. Mammy's place at eight. She's doing her famous faggots for you.'

Oona sighed. 'Her famous *poisoned* faggots, probably.'

'Eight o'clock. Don't forget.'

'Yes, yes, eight o'clock, faggots, lovely, can't wait, get out.' Oona shooed her fiancé out of the post office as if he was a trespassing goose.

His long back straight in his battered leather jacket, Jake paid for his stamps as behind him Oona mimed, with exaggerated facial gestures and a crouched posture worthy of a Maori war dance, *Talk to him!*

No! mimed Asta back, embroidering this simple message with throat slitting gestures.

Say something to him! Oona mimed punching Asta.

'Is it safe,' asked Jake, 'to turn around?'

One more throat-slitting, a venomous one this time, and Asta said breezily, 'Sure!'

Licking a stamp – Asta briefly envied the little sticky rectangle – Jake handed an envelope to Gerry, said 'Thank you,' and made for the door. 'See you around,' he said to Asta and Oona.

'Yeah,' said Asta, struggling not to look disappointed; where exactly was this *around* that men spoke of?

'Oh, and Asta,' he said, cornily thoughtful, one finger to his lip, 'I can't give you that little something I owe you right now. But I will.' He winked. 'Believe me, I will.'

When the bell had pinged again, Oona leaned back against the closed door. 'A little something?' she almost shouted. 'Jayzus, I'd like to little-something him. What's going on?'

Holding Jake's letter up to the light, Gerry murmured, 'You and Jake have a lot in common, Asta.' She put the letter to one side, on a pile that Asta suspected was her Steaming Open pile. 'You're both runaways.'

Asta knew that her sister was dying to be asked what she meant. *I won't give her the satisfaction*, she thought, just before saying, 'What do you mean?' in a wobbly voice.

A caricature of the classic gossip, Gerry looked both ways before leaning forward over the counter. 'How come a man of his age has all that money and no job? How come nobody writes to him?' She craned her head forward to hiss, 'Why did he have to leave London in such a hurry he only brought one small bag with him?'

Gerry knew why. And Gerry knew that Asta knew she knew why.

Asta had known there was something awry with Jake. His practised technique, that easy way he'd reeled her in, had struck a discordant note alongside the symphony of lust played by her heart and her loins. 'Men,' she said, lightly. 'Can't live with 'em, can't tie their wrists to their ankles and drop them down a well.'

'They can't all be my Martin.' Gerry turned up the radio. 'Not many wives can access their other half as easy as this!'

'Our phone-in today is about death.'

'Nice,' said Asta.

'You shush, you,' said Gerry.

'Not any old death, but the death of a pet. When our old pooch was put down I cried like a lady. This wonderful song might just sum up how you felt about Tiddles or Rover.'

Over the opening bars of 'Wind Beneath My Wings', Asta said 'I didn't know you had a—'

'We didn't.' Gerry cut her off. 'Artistic licence. Martin's allergic. Dogs. And cats.'

And taste.

Oona snorted, 'I don't believe this guff about Jake. You're just jealous, Gerry. Like everybody else in this village with a functioning set of lady bits, you fancy the pants off him, and you can't bear it that he fancies your sister.'

'I do *not* fancy Jake.' Gerry was outraged.

'You so do,' laughed Oona. 'But you made your bed and now you have to lie in it. With Martin. You went for Mr Goody-Two-Shoes, but Asta and Kitty have both gone for bad boys.'

'Kitty?' Gerry turned to Asta, rabid for news. 'What does she mean, bad boy?'

Reluctantly, Asta said, 'Seems like Kitty's keen on some boy called Finn.'

'Finn!' Gerry was a volatile mixture of appalled and delighted. 'She knows how to pick 'em.'

'Like me, then.' Asta beat her sister to it. 'So,' she asked, knowing she shouldn't, 'just how bad is this bad boy?'

'Bad enough.' Other People's Badness would be Gerry's subject on *Mastermind*. 'He sits on the wall outside the chemist most days. Swinging his legs,' she added darkly, as if leg-swinging was proof of moral decay. 'He used to have a motorbike. He had a drink taken, so they say, when he rode it into a wall.'

'Quite a catch, then.' Asta felt hot.

'Spends the whole of his holidays from uni just loafing about the village.'

'He's at university?' Asta brightened.

'Well, yes.' Gerry looked as if she could have kicked herself for offering up some hope. 'But God knows what he's studying.'

'Degree-level Wall Sitting, maybe,' suggested Asta. Gerry's photofit, designed to scare, had done its job. 'I just hope she doesn't get her heart broken.'

'Her heart!' Gerry snorted. 'That's not the part of Frenchy's anatomy Finn's interested in.'

Growing up with Gerry, Asta had held her tongue so often it had a groove in it.

'It'll be all over the village that Jake fancies you by, ooh, about now,' said Oona, as Asta walked her to the kiosk. 'Gerry'll be telephoning, sending telegrams, dusting off her homing pigeon to make sure everybody knows.'

Seeing Jake again had unsettled Asta. He wasn't the cool, elegant Englishman of books; he was real, and male, and unignorable. Nothing like Conan – who despite his status was cosily familiar to Asta – Jake was perhaps a little too much for her to handle. 'As of now, I'm evicting Jake from my thoughts. I don't have time for it.'

'Feck off,' said Oona heartily. 'Right now you're regretting running into him in those awful jeans.'

'I am not!' Asta's indignation was all the stronger because Oona was spot on.

'And you're wishing you'd put some mascara on because your eyelashes don't show up without it and your eyes look a bit piggy.'

'Please, no more compliments.' The cavalry arrived. 'Kitty! Over here!' shouted Asta, as her daughter dodged a Scandinavian tour group on the narrow pavement opposite. 'Don't mention Jake in front of Kitty,' she warned Oona with her best *I mean it* glower.

Oona mimed sewing up her lips, then locked arms with Kitty as the teenager reached them. 'So,' she said conspiratorially. 'I hear you've been clicking.'

'Clicking?' Kitty looked dubious, falling into step as the three of them carried on up the main street.

'You know,' encouraged Oona, leaning in. 'Pulling. Getting off.'

'Mu-uum,' said Kitty, with a headmistressy look. 'What have you been saying?'

'Get used to it, darlin',' said Oona. 'In Tobercree, gossip travels faster than light.' She nudged her. 'You've taste. If I was a few years younger, I'd go for Finn meself.'

'I haven't *gone* for him,' said Kitty, chin out.

'Worried your boyfriend at home'll find out, eh?' Oona couldn't imagine a world without sexual intrigue.

'There's no boyfriend at home.'

'Oh. Broken heart?'

'No. I've never had a boyfriend.'

Oona pulled away to goggle at this new life form. 'But you're sixteen!' she roared.

'Exactly.' Asta attempted the quelling tone patented by her mother. 'She's *only* sixteen.'

'Your ma,' said Oona confidentially, 'is expert at looking as if butter wouldn't melt in her mouth but a few minutes ago she was flirting with the sexiest guy for miles.'

'Mum?' yipped Kitty. 'Flirting with a guy?' She paused. '*My* mum, that one there?'

'That very one. Mind you,' Oona looked away, as if into the past. 'She always nabbed lookers. Your dad, for example. Bit wet, but a wonderful piece of machinery.'

'I have a photo,' said Kitty. 'He looks nice.'

'Your mum used to snog the face off him in that doorway there.' Oona pointed to the pet shop. 'And over there,' she pointed at the church hall, 'we had discos. We smuggled booze in, *of course.*'

Kitty was loving every word. Asta was not.

'Was my dad a good dancer?'

'He was keen,' said Oona diplomatically. 'But he and your mum didn't dance much, they were too busy—'

'Snogging!' sang Kitty. She looked at the pet-shop porch as if she could see Etienne there. 'Imagine if he came to find me,' she said. 'Imagine if he just turned up.' She shook herself. 'I'm off to Liam's to watch a DVD with the gang. See you later, *Ma*.' She roguishly underlined the Irish-ism.

The two women trudged in silence past the enormous Christmas tree in the car park, which had started to lean to the left.

'She really thinks . . .' began Oona.

'That somewhere out there Etienne's waiting with open arms and the desire to make up for sixteen lost years? Yup.'

'I stirred her up, didn't I?'

'Yup. We don't discuss it.'

'Why the hell not?' Oona was sharp.

'She doesn't ask. Or she didn't, until lately.'

'She shouldn't have to ask. It's only human to want to know this stuff. If Kitty wants to meet her dad, you have to help her do it.'

'I'll cross that bridge when I come to it.'

'You're at that bridge, you eejit. It's time you started being open. About Jake, for example. You're allowed to have a sex life, you know. Love isn't a crime.'

'Oona . . .' Asta halted suddenly and faced her. 'Shut up. Please.'

'And a teenager with no boyfriends?' Oona shook her head. 'You're handing your hang-ups to the next generation.' She stood still as Asta walked on, raising her voice to say, sad but sage, 'Cuz, what you need is a damn good seeing-to.'

'Mixers go down there. Not *there*. There!' Ma was handing over six bottles at a time to Asta, who was squatting behind the bar. 'Diet tonics on the left. Juices beside the pump.'

The bottles came thick and fast. Asta shoved them into position like glass soldiers awaiting the call to arms. 'Hang on, Ma!' she pleaded. Ma did everything briskly, but Asta was on a steep learning curve, one that smelt of old beer and crisps.

The prodigal daughter had decided there was no time like the present to turn over her new leaf and *notice* Ma. She set to cleaning the countertop with a striped rag.

'You missed a bit.' A finger tapped on the ghost of a ghost of a stain.

Looney's Bar had 'standards'. It wasn't, as Ma liked to repeat, 'any auld pub'. It was a pub where no germ would dare set foot. Ma herself, though, was untidy. The buttons on her Crimplene blouse were wrongly done up.

'We're out of cheese and onion,' said Asta.

'No, we can't be.' Ma scratched her head. 'Are we?' When she looked lost like that, she aged ten years.

'You're fine, by the way, Kitty,' said Asta, wiping her brow. 'Don't even think of giving us a hand.'

'OK,' said Kitty, without looking up from her magazine.

'Ah, sure, she's a growing girl,' clucked Ma. 'She needs her rest.'

'Grandma's right,' agreed Kitty, enjoying herself. 'I need a lot of rest, Ma.' She nodded gravely. 'A *lot*.'

Asta growled as the street door opened.

'We're closed!' cawed Ma, before swerving to quite another voice and saying, 'Father Rory! How lovely! Won't you come in! It's Father, girls, look!' Ma's hands fluttered to the curler in her fringe.

'I've popped in to pick up the tea urn you kindly offered to lend us for the parish meeting.' He turned to Asta. 'Ours is on the blink.'

'Can't run an Irish parish without tea,' smiled Asta.

'Heresy,' said Rory.

'What's the meeting about?' she asked, as Ma opened a cupboard in the hall and proceeded, with many a muted *feck it!*, to extract an urn. 'Buying another motorbike?'

A cloud passed over Rory's symmetrical features. 'It's rather more mundane than that,' he said evenly.

Asta had the bit between her teeth. 'More improvements to your house? A Jacuzzi?'

'There are no plans for a Jacuzzi.'

From her window seat, Kitty let out a heartfelt, 'Shame.'

'There you go, Father.' Ma struggled back with an enormous receptacle.

'Goodness, Mrs L, that's big.' Rory seemed afraid of the urn.

'Asta'll carry it down to St Catherine's for you,' said Ma.

Relishing the look on Asta's face, Rory said, 'I wouldn't dream of it. Besides, she has enough to do writing this article of hers.'

'Writing?' Ma looked puzzled. 'Sure, she doesn't write articles, do you, love?'

'Well . . .' Asta heard Kitty slink out of the door, like a cat that knows a storm is coming. 'Actually, Ma, I'm writing a feature for my boss's magazine.' She swallowed. It was about time, and she would feel better once she'd 'fessed up. 'About the statue's tears.'

'I don't understand.' Ma's face was carefully still. She could obviously smell something, but was clinging to the hope that it wasn't a rat.

'I'm trying to find out what the trick is.'

'You're going to write in a magazine that St Catherine's powers aren't real?' Ma covered her mouth. 'Why would you do that?'

'It's my job, Ma,' said Asta, a beseeching note in her voice. She didn't expect her mother to approve, but hoped she might understand.

'Ha!' barked Ma. 'Job, is it? Destroying something beautiful. Not what I'd call a job.' She seemed to have forgotten

143

that Rory was there; she never normally barked in front of men of the cloth.

'It's not beautiful,' said Asta, 'if it's a lie.' She didn't want to be at loggerheads; she could feel the repair work she'd done to her relationship with her mother beginning to flake.

'Tobercree has a spring in its step again,' said Ma, rubbing her temples. 'We've been on Yank news and everything.'

'You can be proud of Tobercree without St Catherine.'

'It'll break your sister's heart.' Ma polished a beer pump with real vitriol.

I'm steadily working my way through my family's hearts. 'How would exposing the statue hurt Gerry?'

'You know how,' said Ma.

Manhandling the urn, Rory broke in to say, 'I'd better be off. Sorry if I spoke out of turn.'

'You didn't, Father. You *couldn't*,' Ma reassured him.

Leaning towards Ma, Rory said gently, 'Remember, your daughter has a living to earn.'

Alone in 'her' room, Asta played through the sound bites she'd collected on the steps of St Catherine's. The breadth of accent and age was impressive, against a backdrop of muted carol singing from inside the church.

An elderly American lady had said, 'St Catherine is something pure in a dirty world.'

A tiny Japanese boy had shouted, 'St Catherine loves me!'

The ancient German couple, hand in spindly hand, had been clear. 'She gives us hope that somebody is listening, that somebody cares.'

On the tape, Asta heard herself mumble, 'That's beautiful.'

She'd been referring to the couple's rapport every bit as much as their comment. Asta had never envied film stars or pop idols, but she envied that old couple in their matching anoraks, carrying their lunch in a plastic bag. They were in love. It was obvious. They *liked* each other; that, too, was obvious.

That's what I want, she'd thought, with a sudden hunger.

Jake offered something explosive; something memorable, but transitory. He was an International Man of Mystery, and she had no time to unravel the clues.

Jake would give her a whirlwind of a night. No doubts on that front. But she was weary of whirlwind nights. She wanted a whirlwind life.

The door was flung open. 'Ma,' said Kitty, 'I'm off out.' Dressed up for Finn, Kitty was the same, but different.

'You look amazing,' said Asta, awed by her daughter's glow in the dimness of their shared room.

Pulling a brush through her hair, bent almost double, Kitty grimaced. 'No, I don't.'

'Oh, but you do.' Asta smiled indulgently as Kitty straightened up, dark hair exploding around her like a supernova. 'I know I'm biased, but all the same.' There was a curve to Kitty's cheek that wasn't Looney in any way. It was elegant, almost austere. She'd kept the best bits of her father. *Clever girl.*

'What if we . . .' began Kitty, as her hair settled down.

'If we what?' Asta wondered if Kitty had slept with Finn yet. *Would I be able to tell?* Back in 1998, Asta had been amazed that Ma couldn't read it on her face.

'What if we went to France?' Kitty was a child again,

unleashing that pleading look she'd used over the years for dolls that wet themselves, Lego kits, and more recently, an iPhone.

'Ooh,' said Asta. 'Well.'

'Not to look for my dad, or anything. Just to see where the other half of me is from.'

Asta knew a fib when she heard one. Any foray into France would be a mission to track down Etienne: Kitty had got her incontinent doll, her Lego and her iPhone. 'Maybe next year.'

'Yesss!' Kitty punched the air, bangles jangling.

Come next year, Asta would head her off at the pass yet again.

'There's a party starting downstairs. People are getting instruments out.'

'Friday night is hooley night at Looney's.'

'Hooley?' puzzled Kitty.

'It's an Irish party. More than a party. A party-plus. Hooleys,' she said, 'are *wild*.'

To: a.looney@boulevardmagazine.com
From: angie507@hotmail.co.uk

Are you emailing from Victorian times? Whaddyamean you're worried because Kitty's got a boyfriend and you haven't had the 'sex conversation'? Do you really think you have to tell that bright, clever young woman about safe sex? Hell, girlfriend, those girls could tell us a thing or two.

And so what if he's a bad boy? She'll slap him into line. If her heart gets broken, well, that's partly what they're for. A little love never hurt nobody.

Never mind all that. Your smokescreen is too obvious to work on ME. What about JAKE?

To: angie507@hotmail.co.uk
From: a.looney@boulevardmagazine.com

Jake?

He's still handsome, still tall, still broad-shouldered with dark hair that's going white. His grey eyes still change colour with the weather. His voice is still like silk on gravel.

And I'm still scared of him.

Please don't shout. Or use capital letters.

Jake's very male, which makes me feel very female. There's a huge sexual charge. I mean, huge. I'm surprised people don't point and shout. But you and I know how my sexual encounters turn out.

He's downstairs right now, below these floorboards under my feet, at the hooley.

I could sneak down. Take a peek. Like a child on Christmas Eve. But I won't.

There's something shady in his past. He's on the run. And there are other women's fingerprints all over him. He's too damn good at flirting.

You know what I'm looking for, Angie. Something fresh out of the box. Something just for me.

To: a.looney@boulevardmagazine.com
From: c.orourke@boulevardmagazine.com

Editor's getting anxious. Hurry up, kid.

Cx

P.S. Are you sure I'm not engaged to anybody? I have

this nagging feeling that I might be, as if I've gone out and left the gas on. Hope not. Sick of women. Why can't they all be more like, well, you?

An hour had passed since a few exploratory notes on a fiddle had drifted up the stairs to where Asta sat on her bed, staring at her notes. Now the fiddle soared, voices were raised in a jumble of old tunes, and dancing feet made a wild, inexpert clatter.

Concentrating, Asta reapplied herself to the squiggles on her page. She had forbidden herself to analyse Conan's comment. Wishing all women were more like Asta might simply mean he wished they paid his TV licence and made him coffee. Reading into his dashed-off postscripts was dangerous.

His imperative to 'find the dirt' worried her. In meeting Rory, Asta had discovered, late in life, that she could thoroughly disapprove of somebody and really rather like them at the same time.

The bare toes of her right foot tapped, just the once. She smothered them with the toes of her left foot and wrote 'Father Rory – motives' on the top of a new sheet of paper. Money was an obvious starting point. Fame was next on the list. 'Getting people to mass' was a limp number three.

Her left foot wiggled. Her pen rapped on her thigh. As she wrote '4 – rejuvenating the village', she heard a voice humming. It was her own voice. *One reel and I'm anybody's.* Jake was down there, possibly tapping his foot to the very same rhythm.

The door burst open. Oona stood in the doorway, a

Valkyrie in a micro-mini. 'Put down your stupid writing pad and join the craic.'

'I have thousands of words to write,' said Asta, a touch hopelessly. 'I have to concentrate.'

'This silly article's not the only reason you're here,' said Oona sulkily. 'You're here because you miss me and can't live without me. Remember?'

'Yes, I remember,' said Asta, with a conciliatory smile.

'So make the most of me and come downstairs! Jake's down there and *tempus* feckin' *fugit*, Asta. You're wasting precious shag time.'

'The poetry just tumbles out of you Irish women.'

'He wouldn't have to ask *me* twice.'

'But he hasn't,' Asta bent over her page again. 'Asked me, that is.'

'D'you need a gilt-edged invitation? He fancies the pants off you. You fancy the pants off him. Ipso facto. Et cetera, et cetera.'

It's not that simple. 'Sex and me, Oona, they don't mix. I can only do it when I'm out of my head. And then, that's the relationship stalled before it's even pulled away from the kerb. I don't have your attitude, Oona. I wish I did.' She giggled. 'Well, maybe a happy medium between me and you.'

'Are you saying that I is a tart?'

'I'm saying you are a liberated, open-minded, free-spirited . . . tart.' Asta and Oona guffawed together. 'And quite my favourite tart in the world, but I have to get this done, so please, Oona, feck off.'

Obediently fecking off, Oona grumbled her way down the stairs.

Back in London, Asta passed Irish-theme bars promising

'live music' and 'great craic'. The only time she'd ever encountered a spinning wheel was in just such a place. Craic, one of the few Gaelic words to cross the sea, couldn't be franchised; it was spontaneous. Craic erupted on an ordinary night, like a forest catching fire.

A Vesuvius of craic was building in the bar.

The rhythms seeping up through the old floorboards were heathen. They had nothing in common with the po-faced hymns sung at St Catherine's.

Surrendering, Asta tossed her pen aside and flew down the stairs in bare feet.

The first face she saw was Jake's, head and shoulders above the crowd. He was nodding in time to the bodhrán that Oona bashed as she perched on the piano, a mistletoe wreath on her head.

Asta loved the bodhrán. It looked like a giant tambourine, but had a meatier tone, befitting its history as the Celts' war drum. Despite WAG-ish nail extensions, Oona wielded her bodhrán masterfully.

Asta hadn't heard the bodhrán's idiosyncratic call since she'd left Tobercree. There was no Irish music on the sound system at home, and she listened now as if for the first time. It was a brazen yell, a warm and welcoming skirl. Her frame swung to its shape, pausing only momentarily when Asta realized that the ebullient fiddle music which had beguiled her down the stairs was Gerry's.

Quite a different Gerry to the post office/church/Ma's kitchen incarnation, this version's hair was out of its severe ponytail and falling over a face shiny with passion. Lost in the tune, Gerry was possessed, her elbow scissoring up and down.

'Go, girl,' murmured Asta, borrowing a favourite phrase

of Angie's. The Christmas tree jumped in time with feet slapping on floorboards, its lights dancing, its baubles swinging. The whole room seemed to bounce with energy as Asta peeked at Jake, feeling a shiver of illicit excitement at watching him without his knowledge.

He was chatting to a giggling elderly lady, leaning down to her level as she swatted him for being a naughty boy. He ignored the younger, tanned and buffed filly at his elbow who was obviously trying to catch his attention. *Perhaps*, thought Asta, her hips swaying, *I was wrong about Jake*. Just because he didn't talk like Prince Charles didn't make the man a Kray twin.

Then, as if sensing her scrutiny on his skin, Jake met her eye. His full mouth contracted into a pout and he winked.

Dipping her head, Asta launched herself into the melee. *I wasn't wrong about him*. Dangerously seductive, Jake would dance her down a crooked byway if she let him. Asta made for the wooden bulk of the bar counter, deciding to circle Jake for a while. *Let him wait*.

'Hi, lemonade, please,' she said to the part-timer Ma had roped in to help. If Asta was going to get kissed tonight – and she *was* going to get kissed tonight – she wanted to be sober and in the moment.

'There y'are at last, Asta, love!' said Ma delightedly, negotiating a full tray of empty glasses through the throng and banging them on the counter. She nudged her daughter. 'There's nowhere like Looney's for a hooley!'

'True,' laughed Asta, as Ma pulled eight pints without spilling a drop. 'Ma, you're in your element,' she shouted over the music.

'Am I? S'pose I am. Never thought about it.' Ma was

swept off for a jig by a serious twelve-year-old in a bow tie.

Asta watched her mother 'hopping and lepping'. The unfashionable nylon dress touched her heart, as did the rigid curls, so carefully tended. Ma had never thought about it, so she claimed: a devout daughter, wife, mother, she'd always done what was expected of her. And still found time to cultivate a personality larger than your average Saturday-night quiz-show host. Surely there was something heroic in that.

Across the room, Asta looked for Jake and found him at the same moment his gaze found her. He raised a glass this time and frowned slightly, cocking his head to entice her over. She smiled and waved her crisps. *Urgent crisp business is keeping me here*. There was more circling to be done: Jake shouldn't be too confident of his kiss.

A pause in the music allowed Oona to leap to a standing position on the piano and shout, 'Any requests? And keep them clean, Jurgen!'

'*Mein freches mädchen!*' roared a bulky blond gent, banging his fist on a table. Asta knew no German, but she guessed he wasn't complimenting Oona on her needlework: the distress on Declan's baby features as he lurked, Baby-cham in hand, suggested he'd come to the same conclusion.

'Come down from there, Oona,' he wheedled, his milk-pudding voice lost in the babble. 'Have you a drink taken?'

'I've a hundred drinks taken!' Oona reassured him before launching into 'The Siege of Ennis', a lively number requested by a woman tucked behind a table, nursing a cup of tea. Peg always asked for 'The Siege of Ennis'. The tapping of her brogues denoted wild abandon.

Circling expertly, carefully preserving the distance between herself and her prey, Asta passed through the crowd, surfing the tide of chatter. There is no still place in the whirl of Irish society.

An arm reached out and grabbed her. 'Mum!'

'KitKat!' Asta instinctively kissed her daughter and clocked what was in her glass.

'It's lemonade, Mum, *lemonade*.'

'Didn't cross my mind it could be anything else,' said Asta, chanting *vodka? Gin? Schnapps?* to herself in a berserk chorus. She glanced over her daughter's shoulder at a young man, beer to his lips, watching Oona sway and bounce above him. 'Is that . . . him?'

'God, all right,' groaned Kitty. '*Yes*, you can meet him. You're so *nosy*, Mum.'

'But I didn't say anything . . .' Asta tailed off.

'Finn.' Asta gestured to the boy as if he was Exhibit A. 'Mum.' She waved her glass at her mother for Finn's benefit.

'Nice to meet you,' said Asta.

'Hiya, Kitty's mammy.' Finn wasn't a boy at all. Not quite a man, either, he was a forest imp in a biker jacket.

Asta baulked at the term, but couldn't deny that her daughter's first boyfriend was hot. Chestnut hair fell over his tilted eyes. She was prepared to bet that his ears were pointed. 'Having a good time?' she asked banally, surreptitiously inspecting him for love-bites, lipstick marks, prison tattoos.

'Oh, yeah,' said Finn slowly, staying just this side of sarcastic.

Kitty laughed, and nudged him. Finn made a face, a parody of the henpecked hubby, and draped an arm around her shoulders. He draped it loosely, casually, but his eyes found Asta's as he did so, and her paranoia read ownership there.

'What are you up to during the holidays, Finn?' The question had to be repeated: Oona and Gerry had embarked on a raucous 'Whiskey in the Jar'.

'This and that,' smirked the boy.

Finn had, Asta noticed, very white, very small teeth, and lots of them, as befitted a mythical woodland creature. A born dissembler, Finn gave Asta nothing at all. Perhaps he knew she'd already made up her mind about him. *Or perhaps*, and Asta thought this far more likely, *he doesn't give a monkey's belch what I think of him.*

'See you later, kids.' Asta pushed off into the crowd, realizing exactly why her daughter was attracted to Finn. Suddenly she understood Kitty even better than she had before. Not all of this new understanding was welcome.

Marooned in the opposite corner to Jake, Asta plotted her route towards him. Past those French people, behind the half-asleep woman in a hat, through a swarm of Brits and she'd be there. *I'd better speed up.* Some women, orange ones with filled-to-capacity Wonderbras, had beaten her to him.

'Ow!' Asta felt a sharp nudge in her back.

Oona had reached down from her spot on the piano. 'Get on with it, you dim-witted slapper. He's being eaten alive over there.'

'I'm on me way.' Asta raised her eyebrows. 'On *my* way,' she corrected herself under her breath as she passed Declan, who was tugging at Oona's skirt and mewling.

'Coming through!' Ma forged a path through the giddy mass, a tray of steaming bowls held aloft.

Asta stepped back to let her pass and found herself

between Peg and Father Rory. *Damn.* The walls of Looney's Bar were like tar: everywhere she landed, she stuck.

Pulling out a hanky, Peg licked it and rubbed at Asta's cheek.

Wincing, Asta tolerated it, just as she had in childhood.

'There, that's better.' Peg put the hanky away, satisfied with her handiwork.

'Much better,' agreed Rory piously, avoiding Asta's eye.

Clicking shut her handbag, Peg said, 'I'm away home. *Some of* us have an early start in the morning.' Peg carved a path to the door with her old-lady superpowers. Ma halted and looked from Father Rory to Asta, smeared wine glasses adhering somehow to each fingertip. 'What have you done with Peg?' she asked, accusingly. Irish mothers love to accuse; it saves time.

'She's gone home to pray that Graham Norton finds the right girl and settles down.'

'Whisht, you and your cheek,' said Ma amiably. 'That woman's a saint.'

'St Peg of Tobercree,' said Rory, with an inflection that managed to please Ma and amuse Asta.

'Did Aunty Peg ever have, like, a boyfriend?' It felt vaguely salacious to ask such a question.

'Peg? Boyfriend?' Ma's eyebrows disappeared up into her lacquered fringe. 'Jesus, Mary and Joseph, no! Can you imagine . . . ?'

'No, I can't.' Rory's expression suggested he didn't much want to.

'So, she's a . . .' Asta couldn't say 'virgin' in front of the woman who'd borne her.

'Well, of course she is!' Ma's blood pressure almost blew

the roof off the pub. 'I saw you talking to that Finn fella. And?'

'And he seems OK.'

'You know about –'

'– the motorbike,' Asta said in unison with her, both their heads moving in a gesture that denoted deep Looney disapproval.

'Finn's a dreamer,' said Rory.

'He's a hooligan,' said Ma.

'Don't judge him before you know him,' suggested Rory, raising his voice to battle Oona's bodhrán solo. 'Tobercree's a small place; things get exaggerated. How bad can he be?'

'Always sitting on walls,' said Ma, damningly.

'Oh, well, in that case I take it all back,' said Rory. 'Hang him!'

'I'm not usually narrow-minded,' protested Asta. 'But she's my daughter. She's naive. What if she gets pregnant? Or he introduces her to drugs? I don't want her living on benefits with a drug problem and Finn's baby.'

'You remind me of somebody.' Rory narrowed his eyes and put a finger to his lips. 'Got it! *Peg.*' Rory pointed at Asta. 'You sound just like her.'

'I do not!' Asta's reaction was instinctive, as if he'd likened her to Charles Manson.

Ma was unmoved. 'We want to protect Kitty, Father. We don't want her to get into trouble.'

Like her mother did. Asta, fastidiously paranoid, supplied the unspoken postscript.

'Teenage sex,' said Rory, unleashing the phrase without warning and causing Ma to choke a little, 'is always with us. If we taught them how important sex is, how wonderful and mystical, then they might approach it with respect and love. Suspecting them of getting up to all sorts the moment our backs are turned makes sex a naughty box they have to tick. Kitty seems in touch with her feelings. She probably sees sex as the magical thing it truly is. Trust her, Asta.'

He was Angie in a cassock. 'I do,' she said. And she did. She really did. *It's the world I don't trust.*

'I've work to be getting on with.' Nothing put a rocket under Ma like the mention of sex. She set off into the crowd with an autocratic, 'Out of me way, youse eejits!' as Asta slipped past Rory and out through the back door into the frosty night.

Cool at last after the furnace of the bar, Asta looked up at the dark, glittering hills. With the noise of the hooley muted behind her, a word echoed in Asta's mind.

Rory had described sex as *mystical*. A celibate had a more profound understanding of sex than she did. Winded, Asta folded over, as various pigeons came home to roost all at once.

The drinking, the abandon, the heady rush of power over another person – none of this was mystical. And her sweaty, mechanical acrobatics were not wonderful to recall. She had twisted sex into a chore, something expected of her at the end of a night out. Asta remembered her dreams, those recurring visits to the treehouse that made her nervous about closing her eyes.

I've lost my way. Asta was thirty-three and had never had sex with any man more than once.

Time to stop circling. Asta pushed open the door and re-entered the pocket of light and life. *I won't rely on Dutch courage*, she promised herself. *And I won't waste time pussy-footing around.* She'd spent so long wanting Conan that now she didn't trust herself to read the signs with Jake.

She would claim her kiss. Her mystical kiss.

Charging out, Declan almost knocked Asta off her feet.

'Sorry, sorry,' he mumbled, head down as he blundered into the dark, a furious little bull. Once inside, Asta guessed the reason for his departure when she saw Oona on the lap of somebody who may have been a Jurgen, or possibly a Dieter, or even a Hans. It was neither a Paddy nor a Calum: they don't build them that blond in Tobercree. At some point, Asta would have a chat with Oona about her treatment of Declan. But not tonight. Tonight, Asta had other plans.

Her goal was across the room. Their ESP was failing: Jake didn't turn round when she zeroed in on the back of his head. Asta moved through the bodies around her as the party reached its zenith, the singing, caterwauling climax after which Ma would turf everybody out into the night. There was a kiss with Asta's name on it on the far side of the room, and she had to claim it before Ma rang the bell for last orders.

'Easy, Mum!' laughed Kitty, as her determined mother ploughed past her.

'Sorry, love, didn't see you.' Asta noted the black biker jacket hanging loosely on Kitty's narrow shoulders.

'Everyone's going to the cove after this. I can go, can't I?' Kitty's question was blank, a formality.

'Of course.' So many tiny lettings go. *Remember mystical, remember wonderful, remember trust*, Asta counselled herself as the crowd devoured her daughter. Jake had turned around, listening to a woman who Asta couldn't help wishing was wearing more clothes and blessed with less breast. Asta recognized her as Tara, part-time waitress and full-time flirt. Purposeful, Asta moved in as her prey, oblivious, joked with the people around him, his easy smile pushing his stubbly cheek into manly furrows. He handed a drink to Tara, and Asta stared.

All manner of alarm bells jangled. Asta replayed Jake's move in slow motion, like a World Cup goal. The way he handed Tara the glass was innocuous; no eye contact, no body brushing. *So why has it stopped me in my tracks?*

The alarm bells harmonized into one ugly note. The absence of eye contact, of touch, was exactly what was wrong. Jake handed the drink over casually, with no etiquette or interaction. They weren't just friends. Jake and Tara knew each other – in the biblical sense. The way the girl leaned back towards Jake, the ease with which he placed himself so closely to her. There was a language in that. The language, not of romance necessarily, but of sexual posses-sion. Asta swallowed, uncertain.

A cold blast of air was followed by a loud, 'Aww, would you look who it is!' The music stopped and the merrymakers turned to the open door.

'Good evening, lovely people!' The Voice of Tobercree accepted the smattering of applause graciously, the dim bar lights finding gloss on his dark hair.

'Give us a song!' shouted somebody from the back of the room, a cry taken up by the crowd.

'No,' muttered Asta under her breath. 'Do *not* give us a song. Please.'

'I'm in very poor voice tonight.' Martin patted his throat affectionately. 'I've been yakking all day, y'know.' He waited for the indulgent laughter to pass. 'But if my beautiful wife would like to accompany me, I'll attempt "The Mountains of Morne".'

Preliminary eye-dabbing began before Gerry had even

wrung the first note of the maudlin classic from her violin. An old man in a tweed cap was already sobbing like a new Miss World as Martin opened his mouth to sing.

Asta needed to escape to the cloistered security of her childhood room, to the certainty of her chewed pen and her scribbles.

'S'cuse – s'cuse me.' Asta parted the scrum as Martin's silky voice expounded the virtues of the mountains. He was a fine singer, if you liked cheese: Asta had had enough dairy product for one day.

A person making for the door might collide with a person heading for the gents' loo. Asta and Jake were doing just those things, and their trajectories crossed on the fringe of the spellbound crowd.

'Oh,' said Asta, not altogether happily as the human tide shoved her against Jake.

'At last.' Jake smiled down at the woman flattened to his chest.

Asta righted herself. 'Where's your little friend?' she asked.

'Who? You mean . . . ah, I get it.' Jake's brow lowered. His eyes were intent, and at this range very potent. 'So that's the reason for all the evils?'

'What evils?' Asta assumed a look of innocence, the look of a woman who could no more send an 'evil' than she could, say, swallow a postbox. 'May I?' She tried to push past.

'No,' said Jake, close to her ear. 'You may not.' He pulled back a little and contemplated her face for a moment, as if deciding something. 'OK,' he said finally. 'We may as well be grown-up about this stuff. Tara was a fling.'

Asta held his gaze, but said nothing. If he dared to try

and kiss her after this she'd shove him, hard, backwards into the gents'.

'Nothing more, nothing less. No bones broken. All over.'

'And you're telling me this why?'

'Because, woman, you've been avoiding me all night, and then I looked over to see daggers coming out of your eyes.' Jake laughed gently, intimately. 'Actual daggers. That's quite a skill.'

'I wasn't avoiding you. You can chat to your little *fling* all you like. It's none of my business.' If he bent down and tried to kiss her now, she'd bite him.

'You're right, it *is* none of your business.' Jake's drawl was slow and good-natured, belying his words. 'I just wanted to tell you, that's all.' He bent towards her.

Asta stiffened.

'Good night,' said Jake in her ear. 'Sleep tight.' And he turned to push open the door marked *Fir*.

Etienne tears his lips from Asta's. His face is angry in the eerie green half-light.

Below, the rope ladder creaks as the intruder climbs.

With one movement, Etienne snatches at Asta's flimsy dress and she's naked.

December 19th

The snow was a memory. It had snuck off without a goodbye, leaving Tobercree wet and shivering.

'I can hear the sea!' Angie shouted on the other end of the mobile. 'Is that a gull?'

'Yes.' Asta held the phone aloft so her friend could virtually share the still-pink morning at the cove. 'And the clouds are dissolving into cotton-wool streaks. It's going to be another freezing day. Hold the phone out the window for me, would you?'

'You sure?' laughed Angie.

'Lovely,' sighed Asta at the barrage of honking horns and the growl of an idling double-decker. 'Ooh, is that a siren?'

'Has Jake handed over that kiss yet?'

'Blimey, cut to the chase, why don't you?' There was silence on the other end of the phone; Asta wasn't getting off that easily. 'There was no kiss. I am kiss-less. Call me virgin-lips.'

'He broke a contract,' said Angie. 'Call your lawyers.'

'I don't want his silly old kiss,' said Asta. 'Turns out it's not an exclusive. I'd have to share him with half the strumpets in village.'

'Strumpets!' Angie hooted. 'Listen to you! You're only there until Wednesday, love, we're not talking the love of your life.' She paused. 'Or are we? Do you like this guy?'

'I barely know him. What I do know, I don't like much. He's a player, Ange.'

'Imagine if somebody who didn't know you like I do took a peek at your sexual history? You're not as pure as the driven snow yourself. Love 'em and leave 'em, that's your style.'

'That's because I'm twisted and scarred and not right in the head,' said Asta with perfect sincerity. 'There are reasons.' She half hoped that Angie would press her. Her head was full to bursting; letting some of her demons out might ease the pressure.

'Reasons, schmeasons,' scoffed Angie. 'We're all mess-ups. Perhaps this Jake has his *reasons*. Maybe he's looking for love in all the wrong places.'

'You're wasted in social work, Angie. You should be writing country and western songs. Jake's not looking for love, he's looking for a leg-over.'

'Sometimes,' reasoned Angie, who would never admit defeat in a debate until one of the debaters was dead, 'they arrive together. While the leg-over's happening, love sneaks in by the back door.'

'I've had enough leg-overs to last me a lifetime, thanks very much.'

'But you feel something for him, don't you? Beyond just fancying him?'

'I thought I did.' Jake had interested Asta. She'd stood up straighter around him, ready to spar, ready to *talk*. 'He looked like somebody I should get to know. But he's just a shagger.'

'You sound so disappointed. You need one of my hugs, girl.'

I need one of Jake's kisses.

To: a.looney@boulevardmagazine.com
From: c.orourke@boulevardmagazine.com

Offer the priest money to take the statue away for a couple of hours. £500 should do it. That amount would buy a ton of nutritious food for the orphans, or a fancy watch, depending on his mood.
   Cx
   P.S. I've run out of champagne. I'm scared. Come home and sort everything out.

As Asta picked her way over the stones of the cove, she thought of Conan. He was puppyish with her; to the women he dated, he was stand-offish and a touch sadistic. With his dashing looks and his man-about-town status, Conan was accustomed to being the Adored One in his relationships.

The tone of his emails, their plaintive edge, was nothing like his usual bruising style. *Have I*, thought Asta, *accidentally found the way to bring Conan to heel?* After years of heartache, all it took was going away for a few days. The idea of a big bear like Conan in her power was a sexy one.

Men are like buses, she thought. *They all come along at once.*

164

Back in what Asta thought of as 'her day', Tobercree's only hairdresser had been a mobile one who arrived in a van that smelt of peroxide and offered crew cuts or perms. Now there was Suki's Hair Designs, a palace of chrome and glass populated with terrifying assistants sporting asymmetric fringes and swooping eyeliner. The stylist seated Asta, her hair dripping, in front of a mirror, and pushed her fringe this way and that, evidently dismayed with what he found. 'What we need,' he said, 'is a totally new look!'

'No.' Asta was firm. 'What we need is the old look, but a weeny bit shorter.'

'But the old look is, well, *old*.' The hairdresser lowered his voice. 'It's very ageing.' Asta wanted to throw off her crinkly cape and smite him with his own straightening irons.

'I like it long. I like my fringe.' Asta eyed him sternly in the mirror. 'Just a centimetre or two. OK?'

'Don't you want to look fab for the fireworks tonight?' When Asta looked blank, he filled her in. 'For St Catherine. There's a big party planned.'

'I can enjoy the fireworks with long hair.'

'You're the boss. But I warn you, you're very last year.'

Asta was attached to her hair, in more than just the obvious physical way. She liked the way it sat, heavy, on the nape of her neck. She toyed with it while she read. She hid behind it. 'Like I said, a centimetre or two.' She'd stared down London hairdressers: a Tobercree native, even one in leather trousers, was a pushover.

Having been splashed and head-massaged and conditioned and asked if she was going anywhere nice tonight, Asta contemplated her nude face in the brashly lit mirror. She zoned out of the rumbling buzz of hairdryers and chat – 'She should chuck him, she should. He's never been right since he ran over that sheep'; 'How about a few highlights, Marion? Sure, you'd be the dead spit of that Jennifer Aniston!'; 'Did you hear about me poor mammy? Her legs are bad again. I put it down to all the Angel Delight she gets through'– and examined the pale oval in the glass.

It was tired, that face, and wary. Not a good look. She was beginning – oh, God! – to resemble Ma. Asta tried a few expressions to shake the ghost that settled over her features, but no, Ma was unmistakably there in the creases between her eyebrows and the sardonic dip at the ends of her mouth.

Wrinkles already, and never been kissed. Well, she'd been kissed *many* times. But she'd never known love, not the real warm feather bed of love. Lust; that was old news to Asta. There was no poetry to it on its own, but with love . . . that would be a different matter.

A question mark of water dribbled down her forehead. She dabbed at it with a dye-stained towel as two newcomers entered the salon.

'Told you it was her,' said the one in black.

'I didn't recognize her without her crowning glory,' said the one in the leather jacket.

'Hello, Father Rory!' called almost everybody in the shop.

'Hiya, Jake,' said a Nefertiti-eyed junior, trying to look provocative as she swept up hair with a broom.

Feck off! thought Asta with every fibre of her being. She was wet, wan and looking like her mother, her hands trapped in the folds of the hated cape.

'I hope you're not changing your hair,' said Rory, his hands proprietorially on the back of her chair. 'You've such lovely hair. Doesn't she, Jake?'

'She does.' Jake folded his arms and caught her eye in

the mirror. He seemed – damn him – to be enjoying her wriggling discomfort.

'Fancy a coffee, Jake?' A phalanx of women advanced on him. 'I do a smashing head massage.' *The man's catnip to the sluttier end of Tobercree*, thought Asta. As Jake dealt charmingly with his fans, she addressed Rory's reflection. 'I have a proposition for you, Father Rory.'

Erk, that came out wrong. Asta squirmed harder.

'Drop in to see me later.' Nobody made exact appointments in Tobercree. After lunch. Before dinner. Soonish. 'It's about the statue, I dare say?'

'Yup.' Asta tried to concentrate, tried to ignore Jake's growing harem.

'Still testing St Catherine? Still pushing?'

''Fraid so.' Asta watched a girl who'd been overdoing the half-price Botox attempt to smile at one of Jake's jokes. 'We're not all natural believers.'

'Indeed. But Gerry makes up for you.'

That troubles him, thought Asta, as a peal of synthetic, fuck-me laughter wrestled her focus back to Jake's coterie. He caught her eye in the mirror.

'Not the evils again!' Jake made a cross with his fingers, as if to ward her off.

This casting of her as grumpy, resentful, *older* displeased Asta. 'That's not evils,' she protested. 'That's my face.'

The two men laughed above her wet head.

'Guys, guys!' The stylist waved them out of his way. 'Let me get to my lady!' He tossed his Mohican and said to the disgruntled woman in the mirror, 'A centimetre, I promise.'

'Cut it all off,' snarled Asta.

To: angie507@hotmail.co.uk
From: a.looney@boulevardmagazine.com

I have short hair.
I. Have. Short. Hair.
Please send a head-sized brown paper bag. The fringe is swoopy but the rest is SHORT. I look like a wardress in a really hard prison. Or a little man. And the little man I look most like is my dead grandfather, who was not sexy.
WHY? WHY? WHY?

To: a.looney@boulevardmagazine.com
From: angie507@hotmail.co.uk

It looks good in the picture. It shows off your cheekbones.
As for why . . . OBVIOUSLY Jake is implicated.

To: angie507@hotmail.co.uk
From: a.looney@boulevardmagazine.com

I like him a lot but there's a mystery, something dark and messy, like a scribble over his lovely face.

Everybody had an opinion on Asta's new hair. As it was Tobercree, nobody felt obliged to keep that opinion to themselves: Asta's London life lacked this Irish version of a Greek chorus. In no particular order, the opinions were:
Oona – 'Jayzus! Hubba hubba! Wahoo!'

Ma – 'Jesus, Mary and Joseph. You've a real look of me father about you, God rest his soul.'

Kitty – 'No, it's nice. It is. It's nice, honest. It'll grow back.'

Gerry – 'I always loved your long hair.' (She had never previously mentioned it. Not once.)

Jake – well, Asta had no idea what Jake thought of it, because he'd left the hairdresser's mid-cut. And what's more, she told herself, as she pulled at her scant hair, *it doesn't bloody matter what bloody Jake bloody thinks.*

To: a.looney@boulevardmagazine.com
From: c.orourke@boulevardmagazine.com

What the hell are you up to over there, kid? How come you work so fast in London but take your foot off the gas the minute you hit Ireland? I need words, lady. Lots and lots of words.

Cx

P.S. I bet your hair is great.

'Well, yeah, I kind of knew about Tara,' said Oona as she gift-wrapped a St Catherine suedette pochette.

'Kind of?' pressed Asta.

'Well, all right, Mrs Picky, I *knew*.' Oona shrugged. 'The whole village knows. Tara's the sort who causes scenes and throws drinks over people.'

'Was Jake, you know, seeing her?' asked Asta. 'Or was it a one-night stand?'

'She reckoned she was going out with him. But then, she would, wouldn't she? I never saw them together.'

'And the others?'

'How'd you know about the others?'

'Well, I didn't, not for sure, until I just asked you.'

'Nice move.' Oona was impressed. 'You've all the makings of a top detective. Or a top suspicious old cow.'

'I knew Jake was a wrong 'un.'

'He's a man with needs.' Oona went into a little reverie. 'Mmm . . . Jake's needs,' she sighed.

'I had a lucky escape.' Asta nodded vehemently. 'I'd have been one in a long line.'

'Nah.' Oona snapped out of her mucky daydream. 'He looks at you all quare. Jake really likes you.'

'You're not helping,' sighed Asta.

'I'm not trying to help. I'm trying to shove you into his arms. So Jake has a past. So what? By our age, everybody has a past. Unless they're freaks. Do you want a freak?'

Asta shook her head: no, she didn't want a freak.

'Let down your hair, Rapunzel. Jake has the spunk to climb up it.'

'I cut my hair, remember?'

'Your metaphorical hair,' snapped Oona.

'How were Declan's mammy's faggots?'

'Very faggotty.' Oona's expression spoke evocatively of last night's dinner. 'And burnt. I didn't get there until after closing time. Jurgen gave me a lift.'

The dafter the better – a simple rule, and infallible when it comes to postcards. For Angie, Asta selected a picture of a donkey, inscrutable and hairy. Conan was easy: a soft-focus image of St Catherine.

The post-office queue was slow, with four or five shoppers between Asta and her sister behind the counter. Asta tuned out Gerry's loud small talk ('You can catch Alzheimer's from anti-perspirant, you know!') and hummed 'Away in a Manger', her favourite carol.

Another customer joined the queue, and Asta budged up politely. She absent-mindedly put her hand to her neck, where her hair used to be: this was a new habit.

A breath landed on her neck like a breeze, and a low voice said, 'Stop playing with your hair. It looks gorgeous.'

A ketchup tsunami claimed Asta's face and décolletage under her layered woollens.

Another whisper that only she could hear: 'Who knew the back of your neck was so sexy?'

Asta heard, a few feet away, Gerry ask a small man how his varicose veins were coming along. In her parallel universe, she spoke softly so only Jake could hear. 'On your own today? No lovely ladies hanging on your every word?'

'No. It's my afternoon off from ravishing the locals.'

He could claim that kiss by brushing his lips against her vulnerable neck. 'What are you buying?'

'Nothing. I saw you, and decided to follow you in and annoy you.'

'Gerry'll make you buy something. She doesn't welcome the casual browser who doesn't know what he wants.'

'I know exactly what I want.'

Asta waited a moment. She licked her lips and turned around, just as the antiquated bell above the shop door jingled.

There was nobody behind her.

According to the sweet-faced nun who'd answered the door, Father Rory would be back soon and Asta was welcome to wait in his study if she liked.

I like. Asta was alone in Scam HQ.

The study had survived the makeover and remained resiliently old-fashioned, with striped wallpaper and faded curtains. In Father Dominic's time the room had been in perpetual twilight. Now it was bright and sweet-smelling, and the desk's surface was orderly.

Asta had scruples. Lots of them. She was, if anything, overburdened with the little pests, but they all dissolved when she spotted a file marked 'St Catherine's Parish Accounts' sitting on the blotter.

Her heart banged in her chest. A quick flick through those pages could answer some vital questions. But Asta wasn't cut out to be a spy: she was paralysed by a vivid mental image of Rory walking in to find her knee-deep in his doings, until a second image – this time of Conan dancing a jig on her corpse – spurred her to action.

She rifled through the document greedily. Years of cooking Conan's books meant that she knew her way around accounts, and she easily found the lists of outgoings. She ran a shaking finger down the page. The roof, the central heating, the ludicrous kitchen, it was all there. And the new parish centre, the minibus, the overseas charity, the hardship payments to needy parishioners. But no motorbike. Asta checked the fixed assets section in case the cost was being spread over a number of years.

No. No motorbike.

So. *The parish doesn't own the motorbike.* Rory was permitted no personal money whatsoever, so he couldn't have paid for it. The fancy bike had fallen between the cracks of the accounts. Asta closed the book and nipped back to the far side of the room. She had her first solid nugget of evidence. She felt a little queasy. She was, she realized, disappointed, even though this revelation would make her job far easier.

The door opened, and in strode Rory in full regalia. On Father Dominic the vestments had resembled fancy dress, but in his green and gold embroidered get-up Rory looked as if he could be headlining at Vegas. 'Asta!' he said, pleased. 'What can I do you for?' He checked his watch, an expensive chrome chunk on his wrist. 'I'm taking mass in a couple of minutes, so . . .'

'I want you to reconsider, Father, and give me access to the statue.'

'I've made it perfectly clear how I feel.' Rory was firm without jettisoning politeness.

'I'd be happy to pay you.'

'Pay me?'

'Would five hundred pounds be enough? For a couple of hours?'

Rory shook his head, as if trying to dislodge something unpleasant from his ear. 'You think five hundred pounds is the price I put on St Catherine's dignity?'

'Um, not exactly.' Asta should have rehearsed, she realized. It had come out all wrong. *It's not as if he's averse to the odd backhander.* 'I didn't mean to insult her.'

'You look at St Catherine and see a plaster shape. I see something beautiful. I see something beyond the reach of a bribe, Asta.'

'But you could use the money to do good.' Asta felt her brain fold in on itself: she was debating ethics with a man who stole from the poor box.

'St Catherine's not for sale.' Rory sounded sad. 'Or *hire*.'

'OK. I won't ask again.' Asta made for the door.

'I guess you're looking for scandal about me?' Rory held the door for her. 'Let me state here and now that anything you hear about me and Mrs Huffington is idle gossip.' He was sober, troubled. 'Our relationship is purely platonic and always has been.'

'I'll keep that in mind.' Another lead. Just like that. *Mrs Huffington.*

'Could you run a quick errand for me? Deliver a note?'

'Father, haven't you heard of emails? Texting? And haven't you heard of grown women being too busy to *run errands*?' Asta had known she'd be revisiting her childhood by coming back to Tobercree, but she hadn't realized she'd regress. Despite Asta's age, her mother saw her as some barm brack-toting serf, ready to do her bidding without complaint. In the four days she'd been home, Asta had 'popped' to the butchers once, 'nipped' to the minimart four times and 'slipped' to the post office a host of times; she was all popped, nipped and slipped out.

'I've heard of emails, and even texts.' Rory's dimples were back, and doing their darnedest. 'But sometimes a note in human handwriting is the right way to do it. Some messages are too subtle for the dead hand of technology.'

This echoed Asta's own feelings, but Rory's expectation that she'd do his bidding smacked of old-style patrician priest-ing, à la Father Dominic. 'Father, I have work to do. And fireworks to *ooh* and *aah* at.'

Scribbling with a silver pen retrieved from a secret pocket

somewhere in his peacock robes, Rory said, without looking at her, 'It's for Jake.' Then he did look at her, and he seemed ready to be amused.

'Oh,' said Asta. 'I see.' She coughed. 'Well, it's on my way.'

Rory considered this. 'You've a strange grasp of geography.' He folded a small piece of paper fastidiously and handed it over. 'It's urgent.'

Once upon a time, the Big House had stood in arrogant isolation above Tobercree, but slowly the land in between had been developed and nowadays it sat where the village petered out, at the end of a lane dotted with more modern homesteads. Ireland's architects had turned, bafflingly, to Spain for inspiration during the taste-free 1970s, and the Big House's neighbours resembled haciendas, albeit ones called 'Shamrock Heights' or 'Pat'n'Sue'. The weather was immune to the Costa Brava vibe, and the wind howled around Asta's legs as she trotted up the lane.

The ornate iron gates stood open. Asta crossed the circular drive like a trespasser. Back when the abandoned Big House had served as Tobercree's answer to an adventure play-ground, she'd stood in the jungle of a garden and lobbed rocks at the rows of tall Georgian sash windows. Now order had been applied, but with a light hand. The house was freshly whitewashed, glowing in the gloom of the winter evening. The shrubs had been tamed, but not defeated. They loomed, bare and wintry, above Asta's head as she approached the resuscitated house.

The broad front door that had once hung off its hinges

was now snug in its setting, surrounded by refurbished stained glass. Years of perving over interiors magazines had given Asta an eye for architectural quality, and she could see that Jake had spent much of his misbegotten gains on this beautiful building. She pressed the old brass bell-push and heard a slow *ding-dong* on the other side of the door. As she waited, it struck her that if she had known earlier that she was about to find herself knocking at the door of the village's resident international man of mystery, she wouldn't have worn her prehistoric duffel coat.

No response. Nothing stirred.

And then a torrent of noise as an enormous dog rounded the side of the house, barking up a storm. It stopped, skidding on the gravel, when it saw the visitor backed up against the front door. It cocked its head.

To Asta, it seemed as if the dog was deciding whether or not to eat her. She liked dogs, but this creature hardly qualified as one: surely there was a touch of pony in its pedigree? It was an Irish wolfhound, a huge beast with a shaggy coat the colour of smoke. His large head tapered to a smile, albeit a smile furnished with a row of pointed teeth. He took Asta in, then turned and bounded away around the side of the house where he'd come from.

'Do you want me to . . .' Asta trailed off on realizing she was talking to a dog, and furthermore, a dog that wasn't there any more. She scuttled after it.

The gardens at the back of the house still belonged to the past. Beyond the stone terrace the grounds were wild and untended, home to a skip and an intriguing building that looked like a shrunken house fashioned entirely from driftwood.

Astride its roof sat Jake, tapping with a hammer. The

dog announced Asta with a gruff *woof*, and Jake looked down.

Asta smiled awkwardly.

Jake stared as if he couldn't place her for a moment. Then, 'Coffee?' he said.

He slid down from the roof and landed squarely a yard away from her. He wore a tattered jumper over jeans whose barely-there blue spoke of years of faithful service. He nodded at Asta, then turned with a low whistle for the dog, who tailed his master up broad stone steps into the house.

The lack of a proper greeting threw Asta. Jake didn't seem pleased to see her, and her confidence shrivelled. The kitchen was huge, stone-flagged and cream-walled, with chunky wooden units in lieu of the more predictable run of cabinets. The old fireplace was intact, and ornate enough to suggest that this had originally been a drawing room.

'How'd you take it?' asked Jake, leaning on a burnished worktop.

It took a second for Asta to realize he was talking about coffee. 'White, please. Two sugars.'

Perhaps, she thought, Jake kept his rakish charm on a hook in the hall and picked it up on his way out. 'Lovely room,' she said, sincerely but limply.

'Ta.' Jake flicked a switch on the kettle and busied himself assembling cups and taking milk from the funky free-standing fridge, an appliance which excited sudden and profound fridge envy in Asta.

The dog, after padding around with its nose hopefully to the stone floor in search of random crumbs, folded up with a wheeze by the modern glass doors.

'This is for you.' Asta held out the note.

'Thanks.' Jake reached out and took the piece of paper.

The forearm that showed between his battered watch and his rolled-up sleeve was just hairy enough to incite abrupt rude thoughts in his guest.

'It's from Father Rory,' she said.

'Yeah.' A smile spread over Jake's broad face as he scanned the message.

'Urgent, he said.' Watching him fold the note and poke it into the back pocket of his jeans, Asta sensed a wilful loosening-up. She'd been set up, she realized. By a priest.

'Nice duffel,' said Jake.

'It makes me look as if I live under a hedge.'

Jake shook his head in mock impatience. 'Take a compliment when it's offered, woman.'

There was an anti-magnetism between them which didn't exist down in the village. 'I like your dog,' she said.

'Setanta?' At the mention of his name, the hound sat up expectantly, desire for a biscuit written all over his soppy, moustachioed face. 'Setanta's my best buddy. He's a rescue dog. Can you imagine,' asked Jake, 'somebody mistreating a beautiful creature like him?' He seemed to catch himself at the end of the sentence, regretting it. 'Two sugars, did you say?'

'I did.' Asta moved away, taking in the rows of crockery on open shelves. She admired its creamy, thick contours. Jake had taste. 'You've been studying Irish folklore, then?' she asked, a tease somewhere in the question.

'You mean Setanta's name?' Jake looked doubtful. 'Have I got it right? Setanta was the original name of . . .' He hesitated. 'Cu . . . ?'

'Cuchulainn.' Asta helped him out. She knew how all those C's and H's tripped up the English.

'Yeah, him,' said Jake gratefully. 'Some mythical hero

who stood guard over a nobleman's baby after he slew the real guard dog by mistake.' He smiled conspiratorially. 'Note my use of *slew*. This place is having an effect on me.'

Asta giggled politely and took the mug he held out. The atmosphere was improving: her regret at doing Rory's bidding ebbed away. 'Careful. We'll have you believing in fairies before too long.'

'What do you mean *believe*? Do some people doubt them, then?'

'Great kitchen.' The fridge envy was only the start, and Asta now had worktop envy, range-cooker envy and subtle-paint-colour envy. 'Is that a blue or a grey on the walls?'

'Blue-grey. Or grey-blue, possibly.' Her praise seemed to please Jake, his smile slashing through day-old stubble. 'I built this kitchen myself.'

'No!' Asta was impressed. He had taste *and* skill. Maybe, she mused, he'd made his fortune building kitchens: *evil* kitchens. 'Who's that?' She pointed to a framed snapshot on a white-painted dresser. A blurred woman, middle-aged, with an ill-judged hat.

'Nobody.' Jake shoved the picture into a drawer with one swipe. 'I did the kitchen first,' he explained, ignoring Asta's quizzical half-smile at his treatment of the photo, 'because, you know, it's the heart of the home. If I got that right, I guessed the rest would follow.'

'I didn't think men used phrases like *heart of the home*,' teased Asta, her confidence growing as the coffee slid down and Jake inched nearer around the cabinets. 'Do you bake cupcakes too?'

'Where do you get your ideas about men?' Jake surfed on her teasing vibe. 'Vintage copies of *Woman's Own*?' He opened a drawer and drew out a large chopping board. 'I cook. I clean. I even discuss my feelings when the wind's in the right direction. This will astound you, but I'm about to make a sandwich without even looking up the recipe. Ham? Or tuna?'

'Oh, er, tuna.' Asta negotiated a stool. 'How far have you got with the rest of the house?'

Buttering bread – *posh* bread with bits in, Asta noted approvingly – Jake said, 'I've started on the big living room. Which was once the ballroom, I think.' He pulled a face, as if embarrassed to use such a term. 'And I've remodelled the master bedroom. Stuck in an en suite.'

Asta's eyelashes fluttered like epileptic moths at mention of the master bedroom. It reminded her that she was alone with the most sexually desirable man she'd ever encountered. It also reminded her that she was hopelessly juvenile and couldn't hear the aforementioned man say 'master bedroom' without – to use the technical term – going all funny.

As her eyelashes slowed down, Asta realized she'd ranked Jake above Conan in the 'sexually desirable' stakes without thinking.

'It's the first place I've refurbished. Starting from scratch with a ruin is very liberating.' Jake mixed tuna in a bowl with spring onions, seasoning and a modest tablespoon of mayonnaise. 'But scary, too. When you can do anything you want . . .' He stopped mixing for a moment. 'Sometimes it's hard to know what to do.'

'I'd have a few ideas on how to spend cash, trust me. They'd all be deadly dull,' laughed Asta. 'Paying bills. Getting a mortgage. Replacing my cooker.' She took in the chrome magnificence of Jake's range. 'Mind you, I'm a bit daunted by yours. So many knobs.'

'So little time,' murmured Jake, avoiding her eye and

suppressing a smile. 'Grub's up.' He plated the sandwiches and placed them on a tray, his large hands dainty.

Glancing through the window at the darkening sky, Asta caught sight of a silver shimmer in the grounds. 'You've got a lake. An actual lake!'

'Well, yes, but it's stagnant, and mossy and . . .' Jake gave up trying to downplay it. 'Yes,' he admitted, as if guilty of some misdemeanour. 'I've got a lake, Asta.' He gestured to a modern oak table and chairs. 'Is here OK?'

'That's odd . . .' Asta was still peering outside. 'I'd have thought you could see the village lights from here.'

'No, the house is side-on to the valley. Although,' Jake reconsidered, 'there is a vantage point that's high enough to see down to the main street.' He opened the back door, and the cosiness of the kitchen was invaded by a flurry of cold air. 'I'll show you.' He held out his hand.

Asta regarded it for a long moment, then took it. Jake's palm was warm and calloused, like his voice. He led her over to the structure on the terrace he'd been working on when she arrived. Then, without warning, he dropped her fingers and put two strong hands on her waist.

Asta let out a small 'Oh!' of surprise as Jake lifted her, seemingly without effort despite all those cooked breakfasts currently settling on her thighs, onto the top of the little wooden house.

'Ow,' she yelped. It was tricky to get comfortable on the apex of the roof but by the time Jake joined her, balancing the plate of sandwiches, she'd managed it. 'What are we sitting on? Is this a playhouse? A shed?'

'It's a kennel.' Jake pointed down to Setanta, who was wagging his tail and staring besottedly up at him. 'A big dog needs a big doghouse.'

'Does it have,' asked Asta, 'an en suite?'

Jake, seated beside her as if they were two kids on a climbing frame, stopped chewing to look at her closely and frankly. At this distance she could make out a darker, velvety stripe around the grey of his irises. 'No,' he said eventually. 'But it does have a mezzanine level.' He ignored Asta's laughter. 'Setanta hates sleeping on the ground. Don't know why I'm bothering, really. The lazy bastard will still insist on sharing my bed.'

'Must be a big bed,' said Asta, proud that she could contemplate the size of Jake's bed without losing the power of speech. This was progress.

'I could say something saucy there, but I won't.' Jake looked down at his feet. 'Something tells me you wouldn't like it.'

'The village looks so small from here.' Asta changed the subject. Tobercree was a constellation in the darkness, its street lamps and lit windows dots in the cold. 'And so calm.'

'We both know it's anything but.' Jake shook his head. 'You Irish are a wild bunch, aren't you? Even the buttoned-up ones like your sister. Once she gets that violin out . . .' He mimed Gerry's exuberant style, almost knocking the nibbled sandwich out of Asta's hand. 'And I've seen your mum break into a reel at the end of a night. What about you . . . do you have a crazy streak, Asta?'

You don't know the half of it. 'Nah,' she said, chin tilted, glancing sideways to see whether Jake bought this. 'Honest!' she said when he looked dubious. 'D'you like them crazy?' she ventured. 'Like Tara?'

Jake took a deep breath and said, much more seriously than Asta thought her light question warranted, 'Look, I don't much like this personality you've foisted on me. Can we drop it?'

'What personality?' How, Asta wondered, had they veered off suddenly into discord?

'The lad, the playboy, the serial swordsman.' Incongruously, he offered her the last sandwich. 'I have my moments, sure. I'm no angel, but I'm not the man you think I am.' He paused. 'I hope.'

Asta hoped so, too, even though the hint of danger was part of Jake's charm. It was the perfect moment to call a truce, but some feisty instinct to throw a spanner in the works made her say instead, 'Are the rumours wrong, then? You *haven't* slept with local girls?'

'The rumours,' said Jake, with long-suffering patience, 'are right. I've had a couple of relationships.' A quizzical look from Asta forced him to say, 'All right, all right, *relationships* might be dressing it up a bit. Short relationships.'

'Finished the morning after?'

'Not quite.' Jake paused and sniffed, collecting himself. 'I left a lot behind to come here.' He seemed uncomfortable but determined to carry on, to explain. 'I was, I suppose . . . yes, dammit, I was *lonely*.' He gave a comedy shudder. 'Hate that word. But it's the only one that covers it. I drank a bit too much; that made me feel better. Until it didn't. And the village ladies seemed to like me, so . . . I went with it.'

'Are you telling me they had their wicked way with you?'

'Nope. Nobody had their wicked way with anybody. It was a game of two halves. I didn't seduce anybody, I didn't make any promises, I didn't break any hearts.'

'Tara was keen on you, apparently.'

A look passed over Jake's face, an eloquent look that spoke of emotional late-night phone calls and stand-up rows in the street. 'Tara's a great girl,' he said carefully. If he noticed Asta bristle, he ignored it. 'We had a good time together.' More bristling, but he persisted. 'We just didn't click.'

This was a restrained account; according to Oona, Tara was not so much a 'great girl' as a 'nightmare girl'.

'It was fun, don't get me wrong,' continued Jake. 'But it had a short shelf life. And despite what you think of me, that's not what I'm looking for.'

'What *are* you looking for?'

'Something with a future. Something with *legs*.' He smiled. 'I've discovered I don't like being on my own.'

'You could go back to London,' suggested Asta, her newly toned sleuthing skills at work.

'Not an option. Listen,' he said, a frown darkening his face. 'I don't feel comfortable talking about all this Tara stuff with somebody like you.' He held her gaze, and amended that to, 'With *you*.'

'Think of me as Father Rory. Think of this as confession.'

'I could never,' Jake said, 'think of you as a priest. And I don't do confession. I'm a dirty Proddie, not one of your lot with your get-out clause in the confession box.'

'I'm not "one of my lot" any more,' said Asta.

'You can't just stop. It's not like joining like a gym.'

'I *have* stopped, though. I'm not bringing my daughter up with any of that nonsense.'

'Is that why you're gunning for St Catherine?'

'I don't like hypocrisy.'

'Very high-minded.'

Asta checked his expression to decide whether to be wounded or not: she decided against it. Those grey eyes were merry and provocative. Like his mouth. She coughed. 'Just doing my job.'

'How do you think they make her cry?'

'Not sure. Not yet.' Asta turned slightly, searching his face. 'So, you really don't believe in it? At all?'

'Of course I don't!' Jake sounded amused that she should doubt him. 'But it doesn't bother me that other people believe in it. It's Rory who puzzles me. He's so rational about everything else.'

Delighted to have found an ally, Asta bounced on the roof and almost toppled. 'If it stands to reason that the statue can't actually cry, then it stands to reason that somebody *makes* her cry. It also stands to reason that it's Rory. Which makes him a liar.'

'Ooh, big word.' Jake sucked in an exaggerated breath. 'Rory's a good bloke. Interesting. Funny. Not how I imagined a priest.'

'He's a liar,' repeated Asta. 'Sorry, Jake, but he is.' However fascinating a character Father Rory was, he'd engineered a mass fraud on her home village.

They sat in silence for a while.

'It gets dark so early around Christmas.' Jake gestured across the valley to where the night seemed to flatten the village roofs. 'But the sunrises make up for it. Sometimes, if I'm up early enough, I can see mist rising, like . . .'

'. . . like the dreams of all the people in the houses.'

'Just like that,' said Jake, before startling her by jumping down from their perch. He held out his arms. 'Come down. There's something I want to show you.'

Asta didn't really need to be helped down, but she acquiesced, landing toe to toe with Jake, their noses a few inches apart.

'In here,' he said, curtailing their proximity, preceding her to a stone workshop tucked away out of sight behind a dense screen of hawthorn.

Inside, he flicked a light switch and Asta flinched at the neon brightness.

'What do you think?' Jake nodded at a chest of drawers.

'You made it?' Asta was impressed. She ran her hand along the top of the piece. It was bumpy and unrefined, but beautiful.

'I did. With driftwood from out by the dunes. That's why it's got such texture. Should I plane out the irregularities?' His eyes were questioning. 'Or do you like them?'

'I like the irregularities,' said Asta. *Very much*, she added, at home to Mr Subtext. 'It's got soul,' she ventured.

'Really? I was afraid it looked amateurish.'

'Not at all.' Asta tried a drawer. It ran back and forth as if gliding through butter. 'Is this what you do? Did?' She stumbled. 'For a living, I mean.'

'I'm officially jobless,' said Jake, ignoring the opportunity to tell her what he used to do. 'What you see here is the result of a man having too much time on his hands.'

'You should be proud.' Asta sensed that he wasn't. 'It's a work of art.'

'Hardly.' He ducked his head and was outside again, as if fleeing the praise.

'I mean it.' Asta followed him out onto the terrace. 'That chest would fetch a fortune in some Chelsea boutique.' Jake was the only person in Tobercree – apart from Kitty – who knew the absurdity of London – a different brand from Tobercree's absurdity, one where money called the shots.

'Maybe.' He stuck his hands into his pockets and wheeled to face her. 'But I was serious, you know, about me being pointless. I'm no use to man nor beast. You should be aware of that.'

'Me? Why do *I* need to know?' Her contrariness kicked in, hot on the heels, as ever, of her libido.

'Come in here. Just for a minute.' Jake pulled Asta down by her elbows so that her knees bent, low enough for her to get through the door of Setanta's kennel. The canine tenant, who was inside and reclining on the unfinished mezzanine a foot off the floor, raised his unruly eyebrows.

Crouching beneath the low roof, the easiest option was to kneel. They faced each other, on their knees. Asta opened her mouth to say something.

'Shush.' Jake took her head between his hands and tilted it masterfully. 'You owe me something.' His mouth moved towards hers and just as a little groan escaped Asta, he kissed her.

Jake's lips were gentle. They touched her mouth fleetingly. His hands still cradling her head, he leaned back. 'OK?' he whispered.

'Very,' she murmured, closing her eyes in anticipation and moving towards him.

This kiss was longer, a statement of intent. Their mouths moved together, their breathing the only sound Asta could hear. Jake's hands moved from her hair down to her shoulders, and then bound her tightly to him as his tongue parted her teeth. With a soft, grateful moan he swayed against her and they wobbled slightly in their mutual hunger.

'Blimey,' said Asta eventually, as they reluctantly pulled apart, needing to breathe.

Jake brushed her new fringe tenderly out of her eyes. 'I'll see that blimey and raise you a bloody hell.' He hugged her enthusiastically, like a child might, wrapping his arms around her so that her face was tucked over his shoulder. 'Ooh, you taste good,' he said into her hair.

Setanta's eyes met Asta's. They were quizzical, as if trying to work out why humans would do something so undignified. She winked at the dog, before shivering at the kiss that Jake laid on her bare neck, beneath the collar of her hated coat. It was as if a dragonfly had landed on her skin: a dragonfly that knew what it was doing. Asta ducked to claim his mouth with her own, and they might have been kissing from that moment to this if a loud bang hadn't jolted them apart.

'Jayzus!' yelped Asta.

'Fireworks,' said Jake. They scrambled out of the kennel into a world transformed by the gold and fuchsia and orange stars blazing and dying over their heads. The house glowed with colour, and the ground seemed to quake at each bang as the sky fizzed with light and then darkened, only to erupt again.

'Up here.' Jake scaled Setanta's roof and helped Asta clamber up behind him. He laid an arm around her shoulders and, after a moment's caution, she leaned into his side. *Why do I feel as if I know him on such short acquaintance?*

There was an unfamiliar feeling in her chest, as if her duffel coat hid a bubble that was about to burst. She was, she realized, happy. That was all. *I'm happy.*

It was novel, this weightless joy: so novel that Asta shed a sudden tear for the fact that she'd managed to reach her thirties with so little experience of it.

'Hey!' Jake's breath was warm on her cheek. 'Crying is St Catherine's job.' He wiped the tear away with his forefinger, then tilted her chin to make her look at the fireworks.

He didn't ask why.

Asta was grateful.

'Asta!'

Etienne has gone, melted. As if he was never there.

'Asta!'

She clutches at her own body, pink and naked in the green murk of the treehouse. The intruder climbs relentlessly up, his weight on the ladder making the treehouse jolt and sway.

Asta rolls across the floorboards, her bare flesh catching on splinters and nails.

She can't stop him.

December 20th

Over breakfast, the questions came thick and fast. They were not subtle. They were not roundabout. They were rude.

Oona, mopping up fried egg with a toast crust, was insatiable. 'Jake's pretty damn hot without clothes, yeah? Is he a demon in bed? Kinky? Does he like to slap?'

'Jesus, Mary and Joseph!' honked Ma, juggling hot toast, one hand to her chest in a stricken gesture. 'Asta doesn't know what Jake looks like without clothes.' She gave her daughter a beady look, one that could turn a terrorist. 'Do you?'

'Of course I don't!' Much more of this, and Asta would develop a tick of some sort. 'Shut up, Oona.'

Kitty had a question, too. 'Are you going out with Jake, Mum?' Kitty was confounded by this idea, as if Asta had split an atom on the tablecloth. 'Is he, like, your boyfriend now?'

'No.' Asta spoke without thinking, accustomed to thinking of herself as a lone ranger. The clue was in the title; it's lonely being a lone ranger. She'd waited so long for Conan to make a move that this relative stranger had beaten him to it. She and Jake were two consenting adults – there was nothing to stop them getting closer. Conan had no rights over her heart. All he'd ever done was ignore it, after all. 'If he was, darling, would you mind?'

'It'd make me feel sick,' said Kitty, 'but I wouldn't mind.'

Oona butted in, her mouth full of black pudding, 'Just to be clear – you have, or have not, seen his willy?'

'I haven't, Oona!' shouted Asta. 'And in case you've forgotten, *that's my daughter sitting there.*' She bit off a corner of toast. 'And that's my mother having a hernia by the cooker.'

'Jake seems a decent fella,' pronounced Ma. 'But sure, you can't get too involved, love. You've only four days left.'

'Exactly.' Asta sighed. 'Exactly, Ma.'

'If we end up going on Wednesday,' said Kitty, looking at the ceiling.

'If?' Asta nudged her daughter. 'There's no if, KitKat.'

'Just saying.'

Ma chipped in. 'She's just saying. Plans change, sure.'

This had the feel of a heist. 'Plans can't change when Christmas is around the corner and you have a job and a home and a timetable and—'

'A stick up your bum,' sniggered Kitty.

'We have to get back, sweetie,' said Asta. 'I know you like Finn.' She withstood the tempest of *whatever*. 'And I . . . I like Jake,' she stammered. 'But we can't let men derail our plans. That's not how it works.'

'Not in Asta-land, anyway,' muttered Kitty, chin out, looking awfully like her father.

On the way to delivering a bacon bap to Oona's kiosk for elevenses, Asta's phone sang from her bag. She scrabbled for it, glad nobody was around to see her fervour.

Good morning, lovely woman. I can still taste your lips. I'm seeing you today, aren't I? About 5? Your place? God, it's handy dating a girl who lives in a pub. J x

A bacon bap can cushion life's disappointments. Oona might have felt let down by Asta's resistance on the nookie-with-Jake front, but there was solace in her snack – and in marvelling at Jake's many virtues. 'He cooked you an actual omelette in front of your eyes, like a feckin' Frenchman?'

'He did.' Asta was smug.

'With herbs in?'

'*Fresh* herbs.' Asta paused before delivering her killer blow. 'Which he'd grown himself.'

'Jayzus.'

'We listened to David Bowie. On a turntable. We played with the dog.'

'Did he walk you home?'

'Yup. To the door.'

'But nothing happened?'

'Loads happened,' said Asta patiently. 'We kissed. And believe me, the way Jake does it, that's plenty for the time being.' Asta was tingling again, and her legs were wobbling: she'd need a wheelchair if Jake kept up his present high standards. 'We might never get around to sex.'

'Come off it,' said Oona, ignoring a customer who was leaning over the massed banks of tinsel to reach the Virgin Mary napkin holders. Every new day brought another layer of Christmas decoration to the kiosk; Oona was almost obliterated by fake holly. 'You're queen of the one-night stands.'

Asta winced. 'Gosh, I've always hoped somebody would call me that one day.'

The kissing – and there had been much of it, in different locations – had been lusty but wholesome. Like eating a bowl of whipped cream, it was naughty but nice. Asta hadn't felt so keenly sexual yet so vanilla-clean since the early days of Etienne. Touching Jake was worlds apart from the booze-fuelled antics of London.

Licking her fingers and wiping them on her novelty mistletoe deely-boppers, Oona pointed across the drizzly car park. 'There's that Ukrainian I have me eye on. YOO-HOO! SEMEN!' she yelled.

It was an open goal, but Asta ignored it. 'If you *have your eye on* this Ukrainian, why don't you do the decent thing and cut Declan adrift?'

'He's my long-term bet,' said Oona, shaking out a Seven Deadly Sins tea towel. 'He's my stand-by. Safe option.'

'There must be some division of the love police I can report you to. Some women might think that way, I suppose, but I've never heard anybody admit to it.'

'That's why you love me.' Asta wondered how she'd feel about Oona if they'd just met. She suspected that, despite the swearing, the arrogance and the romantic double stand-ards, she'd love her just the same. 'Declan's no fool. What if your stand-by gets fed up waiting for you to get these bozos out of your system?'

'Not gonna happen.' Oona wrinkled her nose. 'I'm the most fun he's ever had. Without me, all he'd have is his mammy and his annual weekend at the Skibbereen Shire Horse Festival.' Oona relented, and the mask slipped slightly. 'Look, don't fret about Declan. I love the little bastard.'

'Ever the romantic.' But Asta felt appeased. This morning she wanted everybody to be in love.

'Oh, look, it's your Kitty. By the Christmas tree.'

'With Finn.' Asta gulped. 'Holding hands.'

'The wee sluts.' Oona clutched her heart. 'Avert your eyes, Mummykins. Your daughter's leaning in for a yuletide snog.'

'Aargh,' said Asta quietly, burying her face in her hands. 'Have they finished yet?'

'She's gone into Father Dominic's house.'

'Eh?' Asta's hands flew from her eyes. 'Why?'

'I've seen her pop in there a few times.'

Her maternal antennae twitching, Asta set off across the concourse.

'While you're in there,' yelled Oona, 'ask Father Rory if he fancies some marked-down shop-soiled Baby Jesus finger puppets.'

An altar boy, resplendent in scarlet and white, opened the front door and showed Asta to the study, where he pushed the door and said, 'Some woman for ya, Father.'

'Where have you hidden my daughter?' Best to be blunt, Asta reckoned.

'Hidden?' Rory looked perturbed. Prettily perturbed, like the lead in a US soap opera. 'Kitty's way too large to fold into a drawer.'

'I saw her come in,' said Asta, unamused. 'Where is she?' All those years of steering Kitty away from the hocus-pocus, only for Kitty to find her own way there.

'Hand on heart, I haven't seen Kitty. But I can make a guess where you'll find her.' Rory stood up. 'Follow me.'

A few steps down the hall he rapped on a door, and was answered by a croaked, 'Come in!'

The room they stepped into was a time capsule of chintz

and mahogany buried in the twenty-first-century cool of the house. Seated on an armchair, a tattered tartan rug over his bony knees, was Father Dominic. He looked decrepit and delicate, as if held together by dusty Sellotape. Much smaller than Asta remembered, he was a small, black-frocked creature with a nodding head that kept time like a withered metronome. It was as if Darth Vader had shrunk; as if Dracula, Prince of Darkness was sipping tea in an old folks' home. But when he raised his eyes, she saw that familiar spark of distaste. 'Assumpta,' he said.

'Father Dominic.' Asta nodded, her feet yelling *Run!* 'How are you?' she asked.

'I'm well enough, child.'

Asta glanced at Rory and read the truth in his face: Father Dominic was dying. 'I won't disturb you.' She ducked away, gesturing at the Scrabble board on a low table in front of him. 'You're in the middle of a game.'

'So you brought your daughter home.'

Asta's face hardened. Infirm or not, this man had no right to mention Kitty. 'I did,' said Asta; *the little bastard is a young woman*. 'But I doubt you and she will ever meet.' That was as far as she dare go with this diminished man, but it had to be said.

'Really?' Father Dominic wheezed with amusement. 'You know, Asta, it's never too late to ask forgiveness.'

'For?' bridled Asta.

'For your wee sin.' Father Dominic evidently believed he was being paternal, conciliatory.

'Kitty's not a sin,' said Asta, through teeth so gritted they might shatter. 'And I don't need to ask for your forgiveness.'

Quivering, Father Dominic strained forward in his seat to say, 'You always were—'

'My go, isn't it?' Kitty sidestepped her mother into the room, balancing two china cups on a tray. 'Hi, Mum. Have you come to watch me whip Father D at Scrabble? This game's in its third day.'

'Father D?' repeated Asta.

Kitty placed one of the cups carefully within the elderly priest's reach, and settled down to ponder her lettered tiles. 'C, R, A and P,' she said wonderingly to herself.

'Myself and Iseult are having a grand battle,' said Father Dominic.

Iseult? Asta thought for a second that the priest's mind was coming adrift, but she remembered the Irish myths she'd learned as a child and it made sense. Iseult had been a fabled warrior princess, kidnapped and carried away across the sea to England. 'So I see. I'll be having a word with *Iseult* later.' Asta's full-fat glare couldn't lift Kitty's head.

'See you at mass, Asta,' said Father Dominic, taking up his tea.

As the door closed on the cosy scene, Rory asked gently, 'Did you not know?'

'You know I didn't know!' hissed Asta. 'You know what everybody knows and doesn't know. You know everything.'

'Ah, some faith at last!' he smiled.

To: angie507@hotmail.co.uk
From: a.looney@boulevardmagazine.com

So, I've got to have the world's quickest love affair with Jake, who last night kissed me loads and loads. And loads. I still don't know how the statue cries, or how Jake made his

money, or why he can't go home. But what I do know is
that I gave birth to a freak – the only teenager in the
known world who wants to hang out with priests.

To: a.looney@boulevardmagazine.com
From: c.orourke@boulevardmagazine.com

I demand something to read today. The article should be
coming together by now. There's nothing else to do in
Tobercree, so come on, Asta, get on with it.
   I've been thinking – you won't have time to 'do'
Christmas properly when you get back. You and Kitty must
come here for the big day. I'll get caterers in. Paper hats
and turkey and Dom Perignon.
   Cx
   P.S. Do I still have my tonsils?

Asta had waited years for an invitation like this. Christmas
didn't happen in Conan's diary. He spent the twenty-fifth
of every December holed up in his master suite with a
double-barrelled airhead. This year, something had changed.
The 'yes' Asta wanted to type stuck to the ends of her
fingertips, the same fingertips that had explored the back
of Jake's neck just a few hours earlier.

Asta had a serious heart. She couldn't be flippant about
either Jake or Conan.

Conan's circling me. Asta had longed for this shift in
perspective, for her boss to realize that they could have
something, *build* something. She knew him inside out. She
knew his every habit, his every foible, all his well-hidden
virtues.

Whereas Jake, she could only glimpse. There was so much more, locked away, than what he offered her.

Conan was an open book. Albeit one with torn edges, and food smeared on the pages.

'Thank you for the invitation,' she wrote, unusually formal. 'We'd love to come to you for Christmas.'

According to that know-all Google, there was a shoe shop in Pollapolka called 'Huffingtons'. A chase from link to link unearthed a Facebook photo of the owner. Catherine Huffington was thirty-five years of age, a keen skier and about eight times as pretty as Asta would reasonably expect a shoe-shop owner to be. Her Facebook relationship status: 'It's complicated'.

A-ha. Asta whipped out her notepad.

The enclave of small modern houses tucked away from the main drag were, apparently, 'executive'. *Whatever that means,* thought Asta, ringing the doorbell of Number One. A life-size blow-up Santa Claus guarded the door. The whole estate was dressed up to the nines for Christmas, with cheery but tasteful lights winking around each front door, and each lawn dotted with sleighs and reindeer and 'Father Christmas Please Stop Here!' signs.

Gerry and Martin's house, like the others, was boxy and modern. It had an integral garage – a fact which regularly caused Ma to wake in the middle of the night, purring with pride – and many, many windows. At each window a cream blind was pulled to the exact same drop as all the other blinds. At one window was Gerry, who screamed when she spotted Asta in her porch, and disappeared.

Asta looked up at the tatty Irish sky, a patchy grey with clouds hanging heavy in it, as she heard the thunder of feet on stairs beyond the glazed front door. That sky looked far too common to hang over an executive spread such as this.

'Come in! Come in! Come in!' Gerry hauled Asta over the threshold. 'Fancy you coming all this way.'

'It's only five minutes' walk from the pub,' laughed Asta, delighted with her welcome. Perhaps Gerry was more manageable on home turf. 'I hear you're not well.' Gerry was pale, Asta noticed, following her through an archway edged with silver tinsel. In the powdery light of the twinkling Christmas tree there was a drawn aspect to Gerry's face that hadn't been there yesterday. 'Ma sent me with a care package.' Another errand.

'She never stops thinking about us,' said Gerry, her mask slipping, a real woman peeking out.

'Crikey, sis! What a kitchen!' Asta knew what was expected of her, but the awe was genuine.

'D'you like it?' Gerry seemed confident of the answer.

'It's massive. You could fit my whole flat in here.'

'It's zoned,' said Gerry, filling an electric kettle. 'For differing lifestyle needs. Eating, sitting, cooking, like.'

'Zoned,' repeated Asta, slightly baffled. 'It's so grand, Gerry. I'd be too scared to cook in here.' The granite, the chrome, the rows of winking crystal glasses were quite a contrast to her neat white galley back in Chelsea.

'You get used to it.' Gerry rubbed at a mark on the worktop with a tea towel. A poinsettia in a gold pot stood by the toaster, as if terrified to move.

'It's so *clean*.'

'I have a little woman, twice a week.' Gerry gestured to the sitting room. 'Like the portrait?'

'It's lovely,' lied Asta with complete conviction. Above a leather sofa hung a huge black and white studio shot of Gerry and Martin in close-up, laughing as if officially the happiest couple in the world.

'This was the show home for the estate,' Gerry explained. 'Martin insisted on them throwing in all the carpets, curtains and furniture. When he sees what he wants, he goes for it.'

And in this case, he'd gone for flavourless good taste that offended nobody but could never burrow into your heart. Asta thought of her little nook in London, with its patchy paint job and its scuffed furniture. *It's waiting for me.* She liked the thought. She accepted the coffee Gerry held out. '*You* wanted the fixtures and fittings as well, I hope?'

'Of course I did.' Gerry was touchy. 'We want the same things, Martin and I. Me. I.'

'Right down to curtain tiebacks?' Asta thought she'd said it lightly, but her sister's face told her different. 'May I have a tour?' she asked.

It was a shrewd move. 'Come through to the sitting zone.' More tinsel, more foil stars and more blinking lights. When it came to Christmas, Gerry had inherited Ma's heavy hand; Martin's beige style was overpowered once a year, apparently.

'That plasma screen is so huge we can see every blackhead on the newsreaders' noses. That's a log-effect fire. The peach leather armchairs recline. Aren't they gas?'

'They're very gas,' agreed Asta.

Once she had expressed deep admiration of and love for the utility room, it was time to see upstairs.

'SHOES OFF!' shrieked Gerry, as Asta's boot hovered

over the bottom stair. 'It's wall-to-wall oatmeal one hundred per cent wool twist up there.'

A phone rang in the depths of the kitchen. 'That'll be work.' Gerry clucked her disapproval. 'They can't sell a feckin' Snickers without ringing me. Go up and I'll follow you,' she said, turning and disappearing into the Shouting at your Work Colleagues zone.

Up, into a blizzard of magnolia, climbed Asta. The banal politeness of the house was giving her the creeps. She peeped into the master bedroom. A big, low room, it was a Sahara of oatmeal wool twist. The bed looked like a cushion sale: where, wondered Asta, did Gerry flop amidst all this perfection? The room was sterile, ready to be photographed rather than romped in.

Feeling vaguely intrusive, Asta opened the next door off the landing as she heard Gerry yelling, 'How many times, Nadia? NEVER STACK THE AIR FRESHENERS NEXT TO THE TIGHTS!'

The door opened onto colour and pattern. A butterfly mobile revolved slowly from the ceiling, and a mural of bluebirds swooped across the far wall. They clearly weren't part of the show-home trappings; Gerry had decorated this room herself.

A shaft of winter sun found its way through the cloud and lit the white cot so it dazzled.

Gerry had self-identified as a mother, even as a tiny child. She was maternal – not soft, no, never that, but maternal – with her dolls, with the family pets, with Asta. The village had confidently expected a Junior Voice of Tobercree nine months to the hour after the wedding reception ended.

Asta felt choked with emotion. This room was *real*. A whole lot of love awaited the baby that Gerry hadn't yet told her about. A cousin for Kitty, a niece or nephew for Asta, a grandchild for Ma. Gerry's little one would change everything for the better.

Groping in her bag, Asta found the package Ma had given her. Something for morning sickness? Inquisitively, she pulled at the cheap crinkly paper and saw a box of tampons.

The sun disappeared behind a cloud as if a switch had been thrown. Looking up, Asta saw the room as it really was: dusty, ignored. The butterflies were cobwebbed. No tinsel in here.

Asta gently closed the door and crept downstairs. Gerry was still on the phone. Asta crossed to the intimidating double doors of the fridge. She would cook something simple for her sister's lunch.

It wasn't much, but it was something.

A text arrived as Asta took the long way back to the pub, her feet slow despite the biting cold.

How are you? C x

Conan had never before asked her how she was.

The cast members of Asta's life weren't sticking to their scripts: Conan was treating her like a woman and not a sexless serf; Kitty had given up begging to move in with Maisie; Gerry had revealed a world of personal pain Asta had been unaware of.

Over lunch when Gerry had returned, like a broken record, to the topic of Asta's defection and its after-math, Asta hadn't defended herself against the charge that she'd been 'living it up in London'. The memory of the neglected nursery was too fresh in her mind.

There wasn't even a script for Jake; he strode all over her mental landscape, laying waste to whole cities of comfortable thought processes. She slowed as she conjured up his long legs, his truth-or-dare smile, the way he had of lowering his head and looking at her up through his lashes.

The conjuring up went too well; Jake had taken corporeal form, and was on a swing in the tiny playground opposite the church. Asta squinted. That couldn't be Jake, because grown men didn't have time to loll about on swings, legs braced, seat twirling. That was what teenagers did.

'Asta!' He cupped his hands and shouted her name. 'Over here!'

A snatch of her dream from the night before came back to her, but Asta stamped on it; Jake wasn't to know that hearing her name called like that, in an expecting-to-be-obeyed masculine voice, made her feel sick.

On the other swing stood Finn, with a booted foot planted on either side of Kitty's bottom. 'Mum! Jake knows Chelsea really well!' she called as Asta approached.

'He told me.' Asta would have liked to kiss Jake on his wide humorous mouth, on the end of his nose, on his mocking, sensual eyes. But she couldn't do that in front of the fruit of her loins, and she was grateful when Jake showed the same restraint.

'London, London, London,' scoffed Finn. 'What's so great about London?'

Kitty swivelled to look up at her beau. 'It's got everything.'

'Like?' asked Finn.

'Erm, like theatres, museums, clubs, palaces, history, nightlife, art, music—'

Finn cut her off. 'There's an ice rink eight miles away in Pollapolka.'

A look, a complicit *oh dear*, flashed between Kitty and Jake. 'Pollapolka is *not* London,' giggled Kitty.

'I know that.' Finn was uncomfortable, outflanked.

'It's an amazing city,' said Jake. 'But it's entirely possible to live your life without going to London.'

'According to Mum, London's the centre of the universe,' said Kitty, leaning back so that Finn had to leap off the swing. She flexed her legs and the swing started to climb.

Standing back to give her daughter room, Asta smiled. 'I'm a born-again Londoner.' She felt slightly awkward, unsure where to stand or how. Jake, happy on his swing, seemed to have more in common with the teenagers than he did with her right now: she was a woman with a remorseless schedule, whereas he had all the time in the world.

A remembered snatch of Gerry's gossip tugged at her like a riptide; *nobody writes to him*.

'Are you an only?' Asta asked Jake. When he looked blank, she said, 'Like Kitty. An only child. Or do you have brothers and sisters?'

'I did.'

Strange answer. Had they all been wiped out in one fell swoop? 'Do you want to talk about it?'

'Do I look like I want to talk about it?'

'No,' conceded Asta. To lighten the atmosphere she'd somehow caused, she said, 'You look exactly like a man who doesn't want to talk about it.'

'Spot on,' said Jake, accepting the olive branch, but not explaining himself.

Swinging higher and higher, Kitty shouted, 'I'm investigating, Mum, like you!'

'What are you investigating, sweetie?'

'I asked Father Dominic if he could remember the company that organized my dad's exchange trip. And he told me!'

Asta looked blank, not trusting any expression she might dig out in response.

'We can call them!' Kitty was radiant as she swung past, hair over her face. 'Dig up some info.'

'Maybe.' Asta felt Jake's eyes on her, but didn't turn to him. If he wasn't prepared to be frank with her, why should she discuss such intimate matters with him?

Jumping from the swing to land squarely on her feet, Kitty laughed. 'See that? I'm like a stuntwoman!'

And, thought Asta, full of love, *you're like an eleven-year-old*. As her daughter wound herself around her new flame, Asta said, carefully casual and therefore high-pitched and tense, 'What do you see in Father Dominic? I've never noticed you playing Scrabble with old folk back home.'

'I don't know any old folk. I've always wanted a granddad and Father D's friendly and sweet and a bit lonely. The only other person he sees is Aunty Peg, and she's rubbish at Scrabble.'

Nobody comes to see him because he's cruel and unmerciful and a wrecker of lives. It was tempting to tell Kitty what Father Dominic had called her when she was still in the womb.

'Mum, I don't have to like the people you like.' Kitty steered Finn out of the playground. 'You carry on muckraking about Father Rory and let me get on with my life, yeah?'

Watching her amble down the road, wondering how to

respond, Asta didn't hear Jake until he repeated, more loudly, 'Is that what you're doing? Muckraking?'

'I wouldn't call it that.'

'Rory's my friend, Asta,' said Jake, amusement notably absent from his tone.

Aware that they hadn't yet touched, and desperately wanting to, she said, 'Rory's in this statue nonsense right up to his neck.'

'Where's the harm?'

'The harm?' spluttered Asta. 'The harm is in the lie.'

'So you never lie?'

Jake couldn't have known how that arrow would fly straight to the core of Asta. 'I try not to,' she said feebly, abruptly defeated.

'Hey. Hey.' Tender now, Jake came closer and laid his hand on her cheek. 'Is this our first row?'

The feel of his gloved hand on her chilled face was wonderful. Asta relaxed into his offered embrace, noting happily that she was just the right height for him to kiss the top of her head. She cooed, actually cooed, at their perfect fit. 'I'm Irish,' she murmured against the ribbing of his corduroy jacket. 'If this was a row, you wouldn't have to ask.'

'You're pretty when you're annoyed.'

'Jake!' Asta swatted him. 'That is such a cliché. And it's sexist.'

'If you told me I was handsome when I was angry, I wouldn't mind.'

'That's because your gender hasn't been belittled and marginalized for generations. And stop kissing my nose when I'm trying to educate you about the history of feminism.' Asta was disappointed when he obeyed.

'Sorry, Ast, I'm not very reconstructed sometimes. I'm rougher than what you're used to.' Jake bit his lip. 'I have a terrible confession. I've called all my other girlfriends "babe". I keep going to say it to you, as well. I shouldn't, should I?'

'Not if you value your knackers.'

Jake protectively cupped the said body parts with one hand, and nodded meekly. Asta leaned against him, enjoying the warm solidity of his body. 'A little support would be nice.'

'One person's truth is another person's nonsense. Take your sister. She prays to St Catherine. If everything goes well, she'll credit good old Cath. If not, she'll think she didn't pray hard enough. Where's the harm?'

'Rory's giving my sister false hope.' Asta thought of the empty cot; Gerry's prayers hadn't filled it yet.

'Bollocks,' said Jake happily.

'You can afford to sit on the fence, but I have to provide for Kitty by writing this story.'

'What do you know about what I can and can't afford?' Jake was grim suddenly.

'Exactly.' Asta raised her voice. 'What *do* I know about you, Jake?'

A brittle silence separated them until Jake took Asta's chin in his hand and made her look at him. 'That saint brought us together. Don't laugh – she did. I've never prayed, but if I had to, I'd thank St Catherine for bringing you into my life.'

He kissed her, abruptly and hard, his teeth clashing with hers before their lips worked it out. 'I'd rather kiss than fight,' he murmured.

'Me too,' said Asta. 'Really, really, me t—'

Evidently, Jake would also rather kiss than talk. His ardour pushed her backwards until her back met the fence.

'Ow,' laughed Asta.

'Shut up,' said Jake, who wasn't done kissing.

They were only interrupted when a clutch of toddlers stormed the playground, putting an end to their fun. Jake rested his hands on Asta's shoulders. 'What do you say we agree to disagree? Let me take you out tonight. Maybe even venture beyond the edge of the village?' He made a frightened face.

'Sorry. I can't.' Asta's lips were glowing as if radioactive. 'I've masses of stuff to write up. And there's pondering to do.' *Not all of it about the statue.*

'But we only have a few days, and—'

'Jake, this is my job.' As his hands dropped away, Asta thought, *I knew this would happen*. Romance gets in the way; romance in *Ireland*, where all rules are off, gets in the way twice as much. 'I'm on a deadline.'

'Don't I know it.'

'Walk me home, though, yeah?' She squeezed his hand, trying to warm him up. 'Tell me something I don't know about you.' *Shouldn't be difficult; I know barely anything about you.*

Jake rubbed his chin. 'I like baked potatoes. I hate Monster Munch. I support Arsenal. I can burp the alphabet, but I won't, don't worry. What else? Surely that's enough?'

'Did you leave a girlfriend back in London?'

'I hope,' said Jake, amused, 'that your professional interviewing technique is more subtle than this. You really want to know?'

'Yes.'

Checking her to see how she took it, Jake said, 'I had a girlfriend for just over a year. It ended when I left London.'

'What happened?' asked Asta, with all the serenity of the Queen opening a garden fête. Beneath her placid question she was thinking *shit! Oh God! What if he's still in love with her? What if she turns up? Shit, shit, shit!*

'It wasn't right. She wasn't right. Or I wasn't.' Jake was tongue-tied. It made Asta warm to him. 'I didn't behave very well.' His grey eyes were on the ground. 'I'm not proud of it.'

'What did you do?' Asta wasn't sure she wanted to know.

The look Jake gave her was a definite warning. 'Let's just say I wasn't kind.' He put a finger to her lips. 'Don't interrogate me, Asta.'

Conan's wry face reared up in Asta's mind. Compared to this cryptic man, he was guile-free. 'Sorry. Subject closed.' She would try again later. *And he'll probably rebuff me again.* 'Do you know a Mrs Huffington? Friend of Rory's.'

'I've met her. Wouldn't say I *know* her.' Jake looked into the middle distance. 'She's a hard woman to know.'

'Where did you meet her?' This could be revealing.

'On Rory's bed.'

Asta suppressed a squeal. She hadn't expected it to be *that* revealing. 'On?' she pressed. 'Or in?'

'In, I suppose. She was sitting there. Very quietly. Mrs Huffington's very quiet.'

'In his bed . . .' Asta felt as if she should shout *hold the front page.*

'Hang on.' Jake raised a finger. 'Is this going in your article?'

'No. Well, it might.'

'Isn't Rory allowed to have friends?'

'Your chum Rory's a priest, Jake. He's supposed to be celibate, not cavorting with shoe-shop owners.'

'She owns a shoe shop? That *does* surprise me. Did I say they were cavorting? Great word, though.' Jake lowered his voice to a sexy burr. 'Fancy a bit of a cavort later?'

'Yes, obviously, Mr Jones, I fancy a bit of a cavort later.' A bloody good cavort, she thought, snuggling in closer to his side. 'But I can't.' She cited the work she had to do and her plan to help out in the bar, but that was only half the story, and Jake looked as if he was on to her.

I'll ruin things if we get naked, she thought miserably as he left her at her door. The rest of the world had sex as easily as they sneezed, but for Asta it was an obstacle course that left her with a hangover, bruises and an aching sense that she was profoundly out of step with the rest of the human race.

'What are you after?' Ma had asked, suspicious, as Asta loaded the massive dishwasher in the bar, cleared tables, and managed to smile at farmers in differing states of inebriation.

'I'm just helping, Ma,' said Asta.

'Get out of me way.' Ma ushered her from the bar. 'I have all the help I want.' She motioned at Kitty and Finn, ferrying loaded trays.

'Ma, they're underage,' hissed Asta. 'You could lose your licence.'

'That man Kitty's serving,' said Ma, 'is our Chief Super-intendent. I know a thing or two about him.' She lifted her nose. 'He won't be enforcing any auld laws in here, darlin'.'

Impressed by this mafioso streak in her mother, Asta retired upstairs to collate her notes and email Conan.

To: c.orourke@boulevardmagazine.com
From: a.looney@boulevardmagazine.com

Scoop alert!
    Stand by your (stupidly expensive designer) bed! There's a woman in the mix!

Conan hadn't emailed since his Christmas invitation. *He's already regretting it.* Her boss spent his life avoiding intimacy – engagements didn't count – and Asta imagined him biting his manicured fingernails to the quick at the thought of two real live women sitting at his festive table in paper hats, reading out jokes from crackers and eulogizing the Body Shop gift sets they'd just exchanged.

As evening turned Tobercree's roads slickly black, Asta had a visitor.

Once he'd endured Ma's relentless hospitality and had refused tea, cake and a fry-up, Rory said to Asta, 'I'm disturbing your work.'

'No, not at all.' Asta shuffled the pages on her lap, hoping he hadn't seen the one marked 'HUFFINGTON AND RORY AFFAIR???' in loud capitals.

'I've had a change of heart. You're right.'

'Am I? Good. About what?'

'About allowing you access to the statue. I've been secretive, when I should have been open. You can take her away and examine her.' Rory held up a hand, wincing as if a sudden migraine had struck. 'But, please, Asta, don't offer me money again.'

'I shouldn't have done that.' It had been Conan's idea; he thought money solved every problem. 'Thank you,' she said, feeling it to be an inadequate response. His about-turn astonished her. 'Thank you very much.'

'We're taking up floorboards in the church. A rat problem.' Rory shuddered. 'As you can imagine, it needs to be taken care of before Christmas. The church'll be closed for health and safety reasons. St Catherine will be all yours for two hours. Treat her with respect, won't you?'

'I promise.' Rory's devotion to a plaster statue was either touching or ridiculous: tonight, in the lamplight of Ma's parlour, it was touching.

'Good.' Rory stood up, brisk again, all action. 'I warn you. She's heavy. Collect her at lunchtime on Wednesday.'

'But . . . I'm going home on Wednesday morning.' *As you well know.*

'Of course you are. Sorry, Asta. Is there no way you could stay a little longer?'

'No way whatsoever.' The path ahead was straight and true, and Asta intended to stick to it. If she didn't get back to Conan soon, he'd have a beard down to his knees and be subsisting on witchetty grubs. 'Never mind,' she said, as disappointment surged through her.

'I want to help, really I do.'

'Then answer a question for me.'

'Anything.' Rory displayed his palms in a gesture of transparency. 'Shoot.'

'Your motorbike.' Asta saw his face change subtly, as if he'd trodden on something squishy. 'Does it belong to the parish?' When he didn't answer straight away, she asked, 'Or did you buy it yourself?'

'I couldn't buy something of that value,' said Rory quietly. 'I have no personal wealth.'

That was all he gave her before he left, saying he hoped he'd see her before she went back to London.

Rory's hypocrisy appalled Asta, yet she couldn't deny that she was drawn to him. It was a baffling combination. Perhaps, she mused, their failings were a good fit. *I'll miss him.*

A car horn outside blared. The tourists swarming towards the church often grew impatient to see the bawling saint. *Shush*, thought Asta. *Some of us are trying to work.* She added a more honest, *Some of us are trying to obsess over our love life.*

'Mum!' Kitty crashed into the parlour. 'Go to the window!'

'What? Why?' Asta was crabby at having her introspection disturbed.

Oona was suddenly there, too. 'Do what you're told for once!' She pushed aside Ma's whiter-than-white nets.

'Cool car,' breathed Kitty.

'Is it a Bentley?' Oona wasn't sure.

'It's a vintage chocolate-brown Bentley.' Asta, joining them at the window, was impressed.

'With your boyfriend in it,' noted Oona, pulling up the window so the cosy room was suddenly arctic.

'Come on!' Jake called up to them from the driver's window. 'Get in, woman!'

'Where are you going?' shouted Asta, a tickling feeling

in her body, as if somebody had substituted prosecco for blood in her veins.

'Does it matter?' Jake blared the horn again. Behind him, a coach-load of Asian pensioners stared up at Asta.

'I have work to do,' Asta called, 'and I—'

'*Get out!*' roared Oona, slamming down the window. 'Go!' She advanced on Asta, shoving her bag into her hands. 'Out! Now! Shoo! Vamoosh!'

'But . . . Kitty . . .'

'I'll be fine.' Kitty rolled her eyes and folded her arms and tapped her foot; the boxed set of Ma tics. 'Have a ball, Mum.'

'But I should change.'

'Your attitude, yes, but your outfit's fine.' Oona gave the fluffy white jumper over faded jeans her approval. 'You look virginal.' She cocked an eyebrow. 'And that's no mean feat.'

'But I have to research the—'

Oona pushed her out. 'Run! Before I strangle you, and ruin me new nails.'

Rushing through the bar, flinging a 'Ta-ra!' at Ma, Asta shed her doubts. *Even swots deserve a break.*

The car was roomy, the cracked old leather seats soft. Jake drove a little too fast down the main street, his tyres creating a tidal wave of slush, before passing the church and swinging out of the village.

Finally, he spoke. 'Good evening, beautiful.'

Asta beamed. Perhaps this man was as wicked as Gerry hinted, but hearing him call her 'beautiful' gave her a kick. 'Where are we going?' Even with her new short style, Asta still had bad hair days: today it had decided to look like a small, fluffy cat. She would have preferred notice of this spur-of-the-moment outing. She flattened her hair, poked it, re-fluffed it, and gave it a damn good telling off in her head. 'Are we off to Pollapolka?'

'Nope.' Jake, his eyes intent on the road, enjoyed the game. 'Try again.' He drove fast but sure, both hands on the wheel, presenting his finely sketched profile to his moll.

'Further?' said Asta warily. She had to be back: she'd planned cheese on toast with Kitty. She glanced out at the damp, cold scenery, at the crowding naked trees and the potholes. 'We're on the Dublin road.'

'Are we?' Jake sounded surprised. He swung the car on to a wider, well-kept stretch, right by a large blue signpost proclaiming DUBLIN in emphatic white capitals.

'We can't go to Dublin!' Asta had a dozen reasons why it was impossible. 'Kitty's cheese on toast . . . and my ma thinks I'm watching *Midsomer Murders* with her later . . . and my hair's gone stupid . . . and . . .'

'Shut up, sit back and enjoy the ride.'

A long, wet tongue flicked unexpectedly across Asta's cheek. 'Yarg!' she said.

'Down, Setanta!' laughed Jake. 'We've got a passenger. Hope you don't mind.'

Asta turned and met the shaggy eyebrows of her phantom snogger. Setanta was grinning, his tongue draped over his teeth. He was so much bigger than the average dog: it was like having a bloke covered in fun fur on the back seat. 'Of course I don't mind,' said Asta, feeling unaccountably shy now that they were out of Tobercree, now that Jake was in charge. 'I love your car.'

'She's a stunner, isn't she?' Jake was evidently proud of the vehicle. 'I know it's a cliché, but they really don't make them like this any more.' Jake liked items with history, with charm. And he liked her, which led to a conclusion Asta wasn't vain enough to admit.

'Shall we have some music?' She reached out and tinkered with the satisfyingly bulky radio controls built into the walnut dashboard.

As the needle ran up and down the stations, a mishmash of music and voices filled the car. Setanta gave an affronted grunt from the back. The clamour fell away and over a snatch of 'Copacabana' Martin's voice declared, 'And the lucky winner of this morning's quiz will get a thousand litres of prime manure. I'm too good to you people!'

Setanta howled like a banshee. Both Asta and Jake reached out, their fingers competing to change channels.

'Martin seems to be on all day and all night,' wailed Asta.

'I'd rather talk to you anyway,' said Jake.

'Bet you say that to all the girls.'

'No, I only say it to one girl. Woman, rather.' Jake half turned without taking his eyes off the road. ''Cos she's a woman, this one, isn't she, Setanta? We're on our best behaviour with her.'

'Are you, Setanta?' Asta swivelled to ask the dog, who was now licking himself with great care, as if his rump was a Ming vase. 'Why?'

'Tell her, Setanta. Tell her she's unusual. Tell her she's pretty. Tell her all that stuff I daren't say.'

'Why is he scared to say it?' Asta asked the dog, who had paused his *toilette* to stare, nonplussed, at her. 'Your master doesn't strike me as the shy, retiring sort.'

'Tell her, Setanta, that he's afraid to say it because part of her unusual-ness is that he's never sure whether she's going to simper daintily or hit him with her handbag.' Jake glanced into the footwell. 'And it's a very big handbag.'

'Tell him, Setanta, that a little healthy fear is good for a relationship.' Asta hesitated. She wanted to tell her hairy confidante that she liked Jake right back, but something stilled her tongue. Instead she turned back to face the windscreen and asked conversationally, 'Do you get up to Dublin much?'

'Now and then.' Jake put his foot down. The car responded, and the bedraggled hedgerow became a blur. 'When I need to clear my head. Tobercree can get a bit claustrophobic. Guess I don't need to tell you that.'

'There are people living there who've never been to Dublin. Hell, they've never been to the next village. And they're proud of it!' marvelled Asta.

'If they're happy,' said Jake, 'then fine. But I need a change now and then. Dublin is a quick fix of the big, bad world.' He half turned to her: they were alone on the wide grey road driving into the dark. 'What do you think of your capital city?'

Asta admitted, 'I've never been.'

'What?' Jake let out a loud *Ha!* 'So you're the same as the people you were just pooh-poohing.'

'I didn't pooh-pooh,' Asta said defensively. 'I bad-mouthed, maybe.'

'Nope. It was a classic pooh-pooh.' Jake slapped the wheel. 'I'm going to show an Irish girl Dublin!' He checked himself. 'Woman. An Irish *woman*.'

Cruising in on the N4 in a splendid old car, a noble dog on the back seat and a swashbuckling love interest beside her, Asta discovered her capital city.

'I love it!' she said giddily as they lapped St Stephen's Green, an elegant park *à la française* in the middle of town, circled by distinguished Georgian houses. 'The front doors,' she grinned. 'The famous Dublin front doors.' Each wide and solid Georgian door was perfectly glossed in blood-red, black or racing green.

Lit from within, a gigantic Christmas tree made of white glass balls cast electric white shapes onto the wet pavements of Grafton Street. The wide, busy road was crammed with shoppers, all of them transformed by the gigantic chandeliers and loops of diamond-bright lights strung above their heads. *Nollaig Shona Duit* was picked out in crystal bulbs.

'That means "happy Christmas",' said Asta.

'I guessed,' said Jake.

Like a compact London with added cosiness, Dublin's mixture of boho and luxe won itself a new fan. Asta was too enthralled to notice she was hungry until Jake posited 'Dinner?' with that sexy drawl of his, and suddenly she was ravenous.

'How about here?' suggested Jake. They were standing outside a chi-chi restaurant that could have been Parisian, were it not for the souvenir shop next door proffering battery-powered leprechauns.

'What about . . .' Asta inclined her head Setanta's way.

'Who could refuse that face?' Jake bent down and tickled Setanta's grizzled snout. 'Leave it to me.' He went inside, leaving woman and dog on the pavement.

There was no sign of snow in the capital. If there had been any, the relentless pace of city life had swept it away. All in all, despite Dublin's charm, Asta wouldn't swap it for Tobercree, which felt as if it had its own magical weather system. Snow was never out of the question in Tobercree.

In a minute or two Jake was back, ushering them both in. 'As long as Setanta lies under the table and doesn't draw attention to himself, we're fine.'

Beneath their corner table, Setanta was as good as Jake's word and lay across their feet, inert as a duvet, for the duration of the two very fine courses that were served above his head.

The wine list was waved away: Jake was driving and Asta was in romantic rehab, with no desire to invite her evil other self to the table. All the same, she felt tipsy, her knee jammed against Jake's and his quicksilver gaze alighting on her face and seeming to like what it saw.

'You weren't my only unexpected visitor today,' she remarked over coffee that came in delicate china cups. She told Jake about Rory's offer.

'Oh, no,' said Jake woodenly. 'But that would mean you'd have to stay for Christmas. What a calamity.' His look was roguish, as if he was daring her to jump from a great height.

'I can't,' said Asta.

'You *won't*,' said Jake.

She caught on. 'Wait a minute. Did you plan this with Father Rory?' She prodded him in the side and he curled up, laughing, defensive. 'Did you?' The two men had previous convictions to take into consideration; Asta might never discover what was written in the 'urgent' note she'd delivered, but she knew Rory had trumped it up to get her up the hill and into Jake's reach.

Leaning away to evade her accusing finger, Jake drew shapes on the tablecloth with his coffee spoon. 'I do have to come clean about something.' He cleared his throat. 'I should have told you before, but nobody knows, and it felt . . . wrong.'

Intrigued, apprehensive, Asta leaned in. Beneath the table, Setanta gurgled in his sleep.

'The Harley Davidson,' said Jake. 'I bought it.'

'You?' Asta had researched that bike: it cost at least ten thousand pounds. She sat back a little. Jake's wealth took on a new dimension. 'As a gift? For somebody you've only known a little while?'

'I admit, it was ostentatious.' Jake sounded ashamed, as if confessing to a seedy crime.

'No, I don't mean that.' Asta smiled. 'Silly. It's your money, you can do what you want with it. I'm just finding it hard to believe that you really did buy it.'

'I did. Rory's mad about bikes. But he has no money. I don't give a monkey about bikes, and I have far too much fucking money . . .' Jake trailed off.

'So you surprised him.' Asta was puzzled. Why did Jake look so guilty?

'Shall we get the bill?' Jake rose suddenly, prompting a sudden fart from Setanta. 'I appreciate you letting the dog stay,' he told the manageress as they left. 'Thanks for looking after us.'

'No problem.' The manageress smiled her thanks, and a promise that she'd look after Jake any old time.

Asta took Jake's arm, in a *Oi! He's mine, missus!* way.

Jake bent down and kissed her. 'You taste of garlic,' he murmured.

'Gee, thanks,' she giggled, their mouths still together.

'I love garlic,' said Jake, without removing his lips. He kissed her again. 'May I make a rule for the rest of tonight?'

'Anything.' Asta veered wildly out of character: those kisses were potent.

'No mentions of Rory, miracles, bikes or that sodding statue. Deal?'

'Deal.'

In a warren of quirkily individual shops, they came upon a tiny jewellery boutique.

'Oh, now this stuff is just my cup of tea.' Asta bent to examine the silver necklaces and lockets nestling in the fake snow of the window display. The price tags were discreetly turned face down, but Asta could tell they were too pricey for her purse. *Perhaps*, she thought, *I'll treat myself when* Boulevard *pays me*. *If* they paid her: would they even want an exposé with no revelation?

'Not a diamonds and rubies girl, then?' asked Jake.

'This small detailed work is what I like. Look!' Asta pointed excitedly at a tiny shamrock, enamelled in emerald green, dangling from a glinting chain. 'That's so lovely.'

'Too ethereal for me.' Jake tugged her arm to look at the neighbouring shop. 'Now *that*,' he said, nodding to underline his admiration, 'is a table.'

'Yes,' said Asta, deadpan. 'That *is* a table.'

'Oh, come on!' Jake was offended by her lack of enthusiasm. 'It's masterly. Look at the grain of the wood.' His eyes were shining, like Gerry's eyes when she knelt in front of St Catherine.

'It reminds me of that chest of drawers you're making.' Asta bent at the waist, peering in at the table. 'Same solid feel. Sturdy, but . . .' She hesitated over a marshmallowy word. 'Romantic.'

'You think so?' Jake looked flattered. 'Sturdy but

romantic . . .' He rubbed his chin, his fingers rasping on the smattering of black and white stubble flowering there. 'Is that how you see me?'

'Kind of.' Asta felt as if a spotlight was trained on her: she'd felt this way when she'd lost her travel card and the entire top deck of a number eleven bus had craned their necks to watch her ordeal at the hands of a sadistic ticket inspector.

'I think *you're* romantic, Asta. I think you're so romantic you're scared to show it, in case it all floods out and you lose control.'

'I'm not that interesting,' said Asta, uncomfortable.

'I disagree.' Jake took her hand. Temple Bar, Asta's favourite patch of the capital so far, hummed with life, its streets full of idiosyncratic bars jumping with Christmassy craic. She and Jake passed intriguing bookshops and stylish young people who could have sauntered out of a fashion shoot.

'Ireland's changed so much,' she said, wonderingly.

'If you stay away for years, things are bound to change.'

'Yeah. You can get *divorced* here now!'

'You soppy old thing,' said Jake. 'Already planning our divorce.' His arm was around her: it felt heavy and warm. And wonderful. 'If I marry you,' he said, his mouth curved into a playful smile, 'we won't get divorced, promise.'

Asta frowned. Just a small one, but Jake noticed it.

'No, no, no.' He smoothed out the space between her eyebrows with his thumb. 'Just joking. Don't get all high-horsey with me.'

'You're managing me, Jake.' Asta performed a contortion with her eyebrows to banish the frown. 'Like you managed the manageress of the restaurant.' She smiled. 'Don't, OK?'

'I'm not, Ast.' He was still smiling: he didn't seem rattled by this to-and-fro. 'I don't manage people, really I don't.'

'You do! You're ruthless, with your dimples and your salt-and-pepper hair and your crinkly eyes! You know the effect you have on the ladies, Jake, don't deny it.'

'It's the effect I have on you that interests me.'

'See!' Asta held up a forefinger between them, stopping his face closing in on hers. 'You're doing it again!'

'No, I'm just . . .' Jake wiped his face with one hand, the smile a tad strained. 'Can't you give me the benefit of the doubt now and then? I am what I am. A bit of a geezer, I suppose, but solid, remember?'

'You feel solid.' Emboldened by the night, by the lights splashed over the damp city, Asta nestled her face into his chest. 'It's just that this is new to me, this relationship stuff, and I'm so used to protecting myself . . .' She tailed off, hoping he'd understand, aware that, despite many opportunities, she'd never yet mentioned Conan's name.

'Trust me, Ast.' Jake's arms grew tighter around her, and they swayed together by the dirty ribbon of the Liffey.

Setanta made a small noise, somewhere between a sneeze and a snort.

'That translates as *feed me, you forgetful bastard.*' Jake unlatched himself from Asta, kissing the top of her head. 'Where shall we go? Who could feed a dog around here? Ah!' He pointed across the road. 'A five-star hotel! The obvious place.'

The bar of the Clarence Hotel was wood-panelled, the fire roaring in the grate defying the icy grip of Dublin in December. Seated in a leather bucket chair the colour of tobacco, Asta watched Setanta wolf down a bowl of *boeuf bourgignon* at her feet.

'Does Bono really own this place?' she asked Jake as he sat down with their Guinness: a pint for him, a dainty half for her.

'Apparently.' Jake looked around him. 'Plush, isn't it?'

Christmas was discreet at the Clarence, subtly referenced with red candles and an artful wreath. On the whole, Asta preferred her ma's 'if it stands still, cover it with fairy lights' approach. 'I feel a bit scruffy. I keep expecting somebody to discreetly ask me to go and untidy somebody else's establishment.'

'It's very laid-back here.' Jake took a sip, then hurriedly said, 'Oh, and, you don't look scruffy at all. Sorry. Missed my cue.'

'I still can't believe you managed to wheedle a dog portion of five-star food for Setanta.' Asta ruffled the dog's wiry back with her foot and he flashed her a dark-eyed, grateful glance.

'Must have *managed* the receptionist.' Jake resolutely ignored Asta's look and took a deep draught of his stout. 'Ah!' he gasped, content. 'That's what I call a drink.'

It was what Asta called burp-inducing treacle, but she was willing to go along with the spirit of the thing and sip at her half pint. She was keeping the clearest of clear heads.

The crackle of the fire filled the gaps as they sat quietly, both tired by their jaunt, only realizing now they'd sat down just how far they'd walked.

'S'pose we'd better make a move.' Jake slapped his leg.

'S'pose.' Asta looked at her watch and moved up a gear. 'How did it get to ten o'clock without me noticing?' She stood, scrabbling for her bag. 'Ma'll be worried . . . Kitty'll be wondering . . . Where's my phone?' She tailed him out through the bar, jabbing at digits on her mobile.

Jake slowed in the middle of reception. He licked his lips. Rubbed the side of his face. He locked eyes with Asta just as she was saying 'Hi? Ma? Listen, sorry . . .'

Jake jerked his head towards the reception desk. 'Or,' he

whispered, 'we could always . . .' His eyes finished his question.

'Just calling to let you know I won't be back tonight.'

They stood apart in the lift. They didn't touch. This was foreplay, Asta knew, and it was working.

'The penthouse,' said the pimply bell boy.

'You flash sod,' teased Asta, the moment they were alone.

'Come here,' replied Jake, and pulled her to his chest so abruptly that Setanta jumped.

These kisses were different. They were the kindling for a fire that had been a while in the building. Asta heard herself make a husky, animal sound as Jake's mouth moved on hers, his fingers entwined in her hair.

'You,' said Jake, 'are dangerous.'

Locked together and moving sideways like a crab of lust, they made it to a mint suede sofa and rolled onto it. 'Ooh!' said Asta, her nose pressed against Jake's, 'a spiral staircase!'

'Never mind the spiral staircase.' He moved down to paw at her jumper so he could kiss her shoulder, eating her with great warm gulps, his strong hands splayed across her back. Asta felt limp, swooning backwards as he lifted her to a sitting position, tugging her jumper off over her head. Acquiescing, she felt his five o'clock shadow graze the soft flesh above her strappy camisole.

A howl stilled them. Setanta sat on a deep crimson rug, head up, throat stretched, an ancient keening sound rolling out of his mouth.

Jake jumped up, shushing the dog, and Asta fell back

against the cushions with a soft thud. 'Sorry!' He turned back to her and held out his hands. 'Let's explore.'

As well as the spiral staircase, the penthouse suite housed a baby grand piano and a view of Dublin's rooftops. It was larger than most family homes and eighty times as chic. The sight of the gigantic bed made Asta feel happy but nauseous, as if she'd eaten too much birthday cake.

'I have to pop out.' Jake snatched up his jacket.

'Eh?' Asta felt blindsided. *Now?* 'Where?'

'Bit of business.' Jake winked. 'See a man about a dog.'

'No, seriously, where?' A cold feeling of abandonment crept around Asta, made her wrap her arms around herself. 'I mean, can't it wait?'

'Nope.' Jake was brisk, patting his pockets and heading for the door. Her expression stopped him. 'Don't look so forlorn, Ast! I'll be as quick as I can.'

'Where are you going? Why can't you just say?'

'It's nothing.'

'If it's nothing, then . . .' Asta was beginning to bore herself, but she had to ask him again. 'Then tell me.'

'I can't.' Jake frowned. His face looked different, older, without good humour to soften it. 'Why's it such a big deal? Why has the atmosphere changed? I'm popping out, OK? I'll be a little while. Then we can settle down, enjoy the view, have a nice evening.'

'Why be mysterious, Jake?' Asta felt light-headed, broaching a subject so vague and yet so vital. 'I know next to nothing about you, yet here we are . . .' *Yet here we are about to sleep together.*

'Look.' Jake's jaw was set. He ran a hand over his hair. 'Look,' he repeated, at a loss to explain. 'I'm building a new life here. From scratch.' He bit his lip. 'And you're the best thing in it. By a long way. But . . .'

'Ah,' she murmured. 'I hate buts.'

'*But*,' said Jake, 'I can't be everything you want just like that. I don't contrive to be mysterious. There are reasons.' He was uneasy, restless suddenly. He paced, circling Setanta. 'I can't tell you everything in one go, just like that. There are things I don't like about myself.' He looked at her, his grey eyes flinty and dark. 'Trust me?'

Asta unwrapped her arms. 'Do I have any choice?' She reminded herself wearily that Jake had no notion what he was asking of somebody with her history. 'Don't be long, though, yeah?'

Relief blossomed on his face. 'Oh, I won't,' he said with dark intent, and he was gone.

Asta flew into a frenzy of activity. She dashed to the bathroom, turned on the shower, paused a moment to admire the fixtures and fittings, then tore off her clothes.

Oh dear. A rosy rash wandered o'er her buttocks, courtesy of Ma's cheapo fabric conditioner. And those were *not* date knickers. And Jake had better have a thing for wobbly bits, or they were both in trouble.

Showered and cocooned in a fleecy white dressing gown, Asta felt better; but red-faced and piggy-eyed, she looked worse. Thanking whichever saint looked after Women about to Have Sex with a Gorgeous Man for the First Time, she found her make-up bag amongst the rubble in her tote. A little mascara woke up her eyes, a dab of blush revived her complexion. She tousled her hair – what there was of it. She sucked in her cheeks. She pulled in her tummy. She walked away from the mirror, then turned suddenly and looked provocatively over one shoulder.

Finally she groaned, let everything hang out and padded off to find the dog. Curling up beside Setanta on the rug, she confided in him.

'Setanta, I don't know how to do this. I've never done it this way before, all natural and organic. Well, not since Etienne. I usually take a running jump at it, drunk out of my head. What if he doesn't like me, Setanta, in *that* way?'

Setanta snuffled and licked her hand.

'That's lovely, but not terribly helpful.' Asta squeezed the dog hard, inducing a rumbly grunt. 'Trouble is, I feel so naked. In all ways.' If she added up all her one-night stands, it wouldn't compare to the shortest of romances. When she had twice the recommended weekly intake of dutch courage units inside her, Asta was a sexual virtuoso: sober, she was as naive as her Aunty Peg.

Maturity would be her watchword tonight, she decided as she flicked on the television and roamed, unseeing, through the channels. Tonight would be the gateway to adult sex, adult relationships. After a moment she switched the TV off again: it was too momentous an occasion for Judge Judy.

Crossing to the window, pressing her nose against the cold glass, she thought of Jake. Somewhere down there he was moving through the teeming Christmas streets, his secrets clutched tight against his chest. Robust, confident, ever so male, did he know that one of the chief emotions he inspired in Asta was compassion? He was, beneath the intrepid trappings, needful: she could almost believe that he was needful of *her*.

She pulled the velvet curtains shut: the penthouse shrank and became more intimate. Setanta had moved to the suede sofa, one dark eye on Asta, waiting for a reproof.

'You stay there, boy,' she whispered, wondering what on earth to do with herself until Jake returned.

December 21st

Asta awoke with a start.

Somebody was shining a bright, interrogating light in her eyes. She squinted and realized that there was no torturer, just a chink in the heavy drapes letting in a diamond of bright Dublin dawn.

She lifted her head, instantly regretting such recklessness. 'Ow.' Her teeth had been covered with grit. She coughed; somehow that managed to hurt every distant centimetre of her body. *I can't move my legs!*

With relief, she realized the paralysis was temporary; nine stone of Irish wolfhound lay snoring across her lower half. Twelve stone of Englishman lay a foot away, under the duvet, one naked shoulder the colour of honey breaking cover.

Across the room, the minibar hummed, its door gaping.

Jake's underpants were grey, jersey, and greatly enhanced by his bottom inside them. Asta, pretending to be asleep, covertly watched him pad to the bathroom. Under cover of running water, she sat up and took in the room properly. Miniature bottles were scattered, like Hansel and Gretel's breadcrumbs, all the way from the bed to the minibar. She leaned over, setting off a glockenspiel of horror in her head, and examined the nearest one. 'Christ,' she muttered, 'I even got as far as the advocaat.'

In the en suite, Jake sang loudly. *Terrible singing voice*, she noted fondly before catching sight of herself in the door of the mirrored wardrobe.

It seemed her hair had grown overnight: how else could it stick up a foot off her head? Her mascara was a raccoon fancy-dress mask, and there was a crisp stuck to her cheek.

Asta couldn't remember one moment of what had happened between herself and Jake. Had she ambushed him the moment he got back? Her alter ego liked to jump around the furniture; it liked to bite, and shriek; her alter ego was more or less a sexed-up chimp.

'Please, please, please,' she whispered, 'say I didn't do my Beyoncé dance.'

Showered and fragrant, Asta couldn't shake the sensation of being soiled and crumpled as she slumped in the Bentley's passenger seat. Eyes fixed on the tail end of the Dublin suburbs, she was grateful for Jake's silence. They'd barely spoken since she'd dragged herself out of bed: regret hung between like them fog.

Setanta filled the silence by chewing various parts of his own body with a relish Asta only applied to the entire Viennetta she sometimes consumed when Kitty was out.

The snow was back, and trying harder. Gusting down in

spirals, it had to be kept at bay by the windscreen wipers. Asta watched it fall, gauging its mood, as if it was an abusive husband she had to monitor in case he turned ugly.

The one silver lining to her hung-over cloud was the fact that she'd been too drunk to dream.

As silver linings went, it was flimsy. *I've cocked up again.* The fledgling affair was cut off at the knees before it had a chance to begin in earnest. How gross she must have looked to Jake as she frisked around the beautiful hotel room, a gyrating Hot Mama with a rash on her bum. God only knew what mental images were tormenting the poor man this morning. *No wonder he's not saying anything. He's too shocked to speak.* Nobody should be exposed to that much cellulite without prior warning.

Jake swerved, and braked abruptly to park across the entrance to a detached house. Asta braced herself. He would be kind, she knew, and that would make it worse.

'Look,' they said in unison.

Jake smiled at that: Asta was too tightly wound to do anything other than stare.

'Me first,' said Asta. 'I want to say I'm sorry. I'm not up to this, Jake. I'm unqualified when it comes to men. You might as well ask me to fly to the moon on Setanta's back as have a relationship. Can we draw a veil over last night?'

'Sure.' Jake nodded, looking intently at his own hands on the wheel.

'Thank you. We can walk away, get on with our lives, be civil. I understand, believe me, why you can't carry on with this, Jake, so don't feel bad.'

Jake's expression didn't change and he didn't look at her. 'You are the most . . .' He turned to her. 'I won't be civil,

Asta. I don't want to be civil. You're an idiot. Is that little speech because you're embarrassed? Is that it?'

'Well, yes, obviously. Partly.' Asta was flustered. Morning-after-the-night-before embarrassment was an old friend; an annoying old friend, who kept turning up even though she was never invited.

'I've seen drunk women before. I've even – don't tell anybody – been drunk myself. So what? You raided the minibar, got hammered and fell asleep. To be honest, you looked cute, out cold on the bed with Setanta beside you.'

'I was out cold?'

'Like a light. Mouth open. Dressing gown tightly done up. You were very sweet.'

'I was?' Asta didn't feel sweet. She reassessed the situation rapidly. 'So you don't mind that nothing happened? That we didn't . . . ?'

'I'm not Bluebeard. We can wait, Ast. I'm not rushing you. What happened with those other girls . . . that was about being new in town. And about being lonely, if I'm honest. And, if I'm even more honest, about ego. But you, Asta . . . I want you to be my girl.' Jake shrugged, half apologetic.

The silence returned, but this time it was silvery and delicate. It was a moment Asta would remember long after the snow had given way to sunshine, and she was back at her desk in London. She stared at Jake, looking at him properly, as if memorizing every angle of his face, every lash around his eyes.

Jake's honesty touched her deeply. This strong man, who flew solo through life, had made himself vulnerable in front of her. She reached out, kissed him, her relief converted to passion.

'When we do have sex,' began Jake, before pulling himself

up short. 'Sorry, make that *if*. If we have sex, it'll be special, Asta.'

How Asta yearned for special. She thought of Rory's belief that sex should be mystical. *I've forgotten magic. I even strip miracles of their sparkle.* She looked into Jake's eyes, and saw the potential for much magic in the way he looked back.

As they rejoined the road, Jake said, 'Look in the glove compartment.'

'What do you want? Map? Sunglasses?' Asta opened the walnut panel. 'Oh,' she said, at the sight of the small leather box. 'Is it . . . ?'

'Open it.'

It was a tiny gold shamrock, its leaves embellished with enamel the colour of grass.

'So that's what you were doing.' Asta turned the shamrock over, studied it. 'When you went to see a man about a dog.'

'It took longer than I thought. I knew the shop would be shut, but I found the owner's mobile number and tracked him down. With hindsight, I wish I'd stayed with you. It wasn't easy leaving mid-kiss. But they're lucky, aren't they? Shamrocks?'

This one is, thought Asta.

The snow was doing its best. Fluffy flakes hurtled down towards the church and the dead-eyed mill and the parade of shops, only to melt and die as they hit the ground.

The car slowed outside the bar. A curtain moved on the first floor.

'Thank you,' said Asta. *And not just for the famous hotel*

and the posh dinner. She was grateful to Jake for his compassion, the generosity that laughed off her foolishness and liked her better for it.

'Stay,' said Jake.

'I can't! Ma's waiting and I –' She caught up with his meaning. 'I can't,' she repeated, but not so flippantly. 'You always knew my plan, Jake.'

'Yeah, I did. I read the small print.' Jake shrugged. 'Just thought maybe we, us, you know, me and you, might have changed it.'

'It's not that kind of plan.'

Ma was shocked to the toes of her sensible slip-ons by Asta's refusal of a fried breakfast. She poked her head around the bedroom door and whispered, 'I know you're not hungry, but I brought you a cup of tea. And a tiny little almost-not-there bacon sandwich. With a fried egg.' Tiptoeing around the bed, she put down the tray and switched on the radio. 'It's awful quiet in here,' she added.

'That's because I'm working, Ma.' Cross-legged on her bed with an open computer on her lap, Asta looked like somebody working; in actual fact, she was riding out her headache and nausea and general feeling that somebody had replaced her brain with partying mice.

'Martin's on the radio!' As Ma retreated, she said, 'It's almost as good as having him in the room with you.'

'Don't wait too long for a hero, Ms Tyler!' advised Martin, his accent straddling Barack Obama and Westlife. 'They're pretty rare these days, love!'

Banging the radio to silence with the flat of her hand,

Asta parted the foggy curtains of her hangover and stared hard at the bones of her article.

Jake's admission that he'd bought the Harley Davidson had sparked a major rethink. Rory hadn't cooked the parish books to buy his precious bike. Furthermore, the priest had stayed schtum about its provenance in order to protect Jake.

One mystery is plenty for a growing girl. With two days left, Asta was no nearer to unravelling what St Catherine hid under her halo; and she was now also dizzy with curiosity about Jake's mystery millions. Although the dizziness could partly have been her hangover.

There's no intrinsic shame in having tons of money. It was a problem Asta would welcome with open arms. Yet Jake had owned up to buying the Harley Davidson as if confessing to a felony.

This train of thought disturbed Asta. It was foolish to let Gerry's remarks get to her, but her sister knew the truth and considered the money to be 'dirty'.

A text disturbed her even more.

It's not the same without you. Cx

The Tobercree minimart sold everything a reasonable human needed to get by: Scotch eggs, hair-removal cream, hay for gerbil cages. Asta stared at her mother's erratic handwriting on the back of an envelope.

'Wetting ponder?' she frowned.

'Washing powder.' Kitty threw a massive packet of Daz into the buckled trolley that only went one way – the opposite way to the way Asta wanted it to go.

'Oggs?'

'Eggs.'

'Ah. I can read this one. Chops.'

'Chips.'

Asta persuaded an oven-ready chicken into the trolley. 'That's for Aunty Peg,' she said, adding a murmured, 'And I hope they'll be very happy together.'

'My own mother,' said Kitty, heaving the trolley round the wheezing freezer cabinet. 'Staying out all night.'

'It was all very innocent,' said Asta.

'Then why have you gone red?'

'Because . . .' *Because I hate discussing this with my daughter.* 'Because it's hot in here.'

'I bet it was hot when—'

'No. Stop. Enough.' Asta held up a forefinger. 'I don't tease you about Finn. Please don't tease me about Jake.'

'Finn and me, Mum, we're not . . . up to anything.' Kitty looked at her mother anxiously over a box of cornflakes.

'I know you're sensible about these things.' Asta had assumed they were at it like rabbits.

'Do you think,' said Kitty, browsing the Pop-Tarts, 'we'll ever be able to say the word "sex" without you doing that face?'

'What face? I don't do a face.'

'You're doing it right now.'

'Really?' Asta was dismayed: sexual repression had banjaxed her own development, and she'd hoped she was bringing her daughter up differently. 'Sorry, KitKat. I try, you know.'

'I know,' said Kitty, insouciant, empress of her feelings as ever. 'You missed a great night in the bar.' She clapped her hand to her mouth. 'Mum, you won't have heard the big news! The statue cried.'

'No!' shouted Asta.

'Grandma saw it. Aunty Gerry wasn't there. She was fuming. But loads of people saw it. Real tears, rolled right down to her sandals, apparently.'

'Damn.'

'The bar had such a strange atmosphere afterwards. Dreamlike. As if something important had just happened.'

An outbreak of female politeness behind the minimart counter announced Father Rory.

'What can I do for you, Father?'

'A Mars Bar, Father? Or a nice little Crunchie? Ah, go on!'

'You're looking very well, Father.'

And so he was. Tall and inappropriately elegant in his black ensemble, Rory's glamour was at odds with the strip-lit shop.

'Just the newspaper, please,' he said, with a disarming smile that made the pensioner behind the till drop the change.

'So,' Asta remarked across the serried ranks of convenience foods, 'St Catherine sobs the moment I leave town?'

Rory leaned against the biscuit section. 'Catherine runs to her own schedule. I don't tell her what to do.' He cocked his head to one side, answering her teasing attitude with his own. 'And how would I know when you're out of Tobercree?'

'You know everything.'

'If only,' he smiled. 'How was Dublin?'

'See!'

After a two-hour stint behind the bar, Asta poured a small sherry for Gerry – it was pleasing when people rhymed with their drinks – and said, 'Right, Ma, that's me done for tonight.'

'Thanks, darlin',' said Ma, appreciative. 'I don't know

what I'd have done without you when that tour party of Italians came in.'

'I helped!' said Oona, affronted, from a banquette by the window.

'That wasn't the sort of help Ma meant,' said Asta, folding a tea towel. She'd felt sorry for poor Lorenzo; he'd left the premises dazed, with his trousers on back to front.

Asta hadn't told Oona the entire truth about what happened in Dublin, leaving it at a hazy *Oh, it was amazing,* despite her cousin's pleas for detail. 'Hey, you!' Asta tilted her head at Gerry, who looked surprised to be addressed so assertively by her little sister. 'Get your bum this side of the counter and give Ma a hand.'

'I can't. I'm in me good jeans.'

'All your jeans are good.' Gerry dressed as if expecting to be called to a mail-order catalogue photo shoot at any minute. 'Come on. Martin's not here. You might as well be doing something.'

'Martin's not avoiding you, you know,' said Gerry, as she tied an apron around her middle.

'That's, um, nice.' *I'm avoiding him, though.* Asta selected two cold bottles from the glass-fronted fridge and tucked them beneath her arm.

'Wrap up warm,' said Ma, handing over two jumpers and a fleece. 'That sky's full of snow.'

'He's not avoiding Frenchy, either.'

The look Asta sent Gerry careered off her sister's lacquered hair and landed among the salted peanuts.

Bumping into Kitty out in the street, safe in the midst of her gang, Asta whispered, 'I might not be home tonight, love.'

Kitty nodded. 'Good,' she said.

It was neither the time nor the place to be suffused with

love for her little girl, but Asta was grateful for Kitty's compassion and composure. Another girl might throw a strop, pull rank, but Kitty understood.

'See you, Mum!' And all of it done with a light touch. Kitty Looney was a class act.

Turning, Asta lowered her head against the onslaught of icy flakes scurrying through the iron-grey night, and strode up the street away from the village. Mighty, fearless, she was possessed by the pagan spirits of ancient Irish heroines, her courage growing with each booted step as she left the twinkling main street and climbed the hilly lane to the Big House.

'You look . . . different.' Jake peered at her dubiously, fondly, when he opened the front door. In his Aran, he looked the essence of Christmas cheer. 'What's going on?' He staggered back slightly as his guest foisted two bottles on him. 'Elderflower cordial? We're having a quiet night, then?'

'Not on your life.' Stepping into the house so their toes touched, Asta shook her head. 'I believe you and I have some unfinished business, Jake Jones.' She reached her hand to his neck and pulled him towards her, as her right foot reached back and kicked the heavy old Georgian door deftly shut.

A minute later, the door re-opened. Setanta loped out.

'Sorry, doggie – you know I love you, and all that,' said Asta. 'But you're far too young to witness what's about to happen to your master.'

To: angie507@hotmail.co.uk
From: a.looney@boulevardmagazine.com

I did it!

I finally did it!

I HAD SOBER SEX.

In fact, I had brilliant sex. Quiet sex. Quickie sex. Slow sex. Sex on a table. Sex instead of dinner.

HAPPY SEX!

To: a.looney@boulevardmagazine.com
From: angie507@hotmail.co.uk

Firstly, that's way TMI.

Secondly, that sounds like it was quite a night! You go, girl!

To: angie507@hotmail.co.uk
From: a.looney@boulevardmagazine.com

Correction: it IS quite a night. Oh hang on – my BOYFRIEND'S shouting my name. I think he might want more SEX!

The Aran she'd picked up from the floor of the bedroom reached to Asta's thighs. She folded back the cuffs, enjoying the frisson of the wool against her bare skin as she padded downstairs in the moonlight.

'In you come, Setanta.' The dog's claws tapped on the kitchen's stone floor like a hairy Fred Astaire.

The Big House was enigmatic in the moonlight, its corners obscure and its detail dark. Snow, waiting in the wings, made a fuzzy blanket of the sky.

Asta found a pot of cream in the fridge and upended it into a small copper pan. The kitchen slumbered around her as she made hot chocolate to her mother's recipe.

Stirring idly in slow motion, Asta's limbs were heavy. Yet

her body felt alive, as if new skin had been stretched over it. She sighed, a voluptuous sound she'd never made before.

After thirty-three years and countless lovers, Asta Looney had finally lost her virginity.

The logistics of making love with Jake were the same as in her other encounters, but the understanding between them made it more than the sum of its parts. Asta was elevated, improved, *changed* by the tenderness they'd shared.

The dimensions of the house echoed the space in her thoughts. She had room to expand and unfurl, like a young tree throwing out new branches, despite the depths of winter outside the door. Her skin was more receptive, her senses more acute. She loved everything she saw: the pot of chocolate; the gentle, hissing flame beneath it; Setanta.

'Good boy,' she whispered in a baby voice as she ruffled his flopping ears. 'Good, good, perfect boy.'

The real world, and her ongoing statue problem, felt very far away. As for Conan . . . Asta assumed it was part of sex's magic spell, that this daze would clear and she would have to compare/contrast the two men; but for now, life had shrunk to a bed with Jake in it.

Even so, the regimented piles of mail on the worktop intrigued her. She tiptoed across the ladder-rungs of cold moonlight on the floor.

Gerry said nobody ever writes to Jake.

There were a couple of hundred envelopes of differing sizes sorted into four wobbling columns. Some were air-mail blue, others pastel or white or brown. Each envelope had been opened, and its contents stowed back inside. More overflowed from a slumped mail sack on the floor, all of them addressed to a street in North London. This was forwarded mail. *That must be what Gerry meant; none of these correspondents knows Jake's real address.*

Setanta watched as Asta reached out a tentative hand. She picked up an envelope addressed in shaky lettering to Mr J. Jones, Esq. There was a felt-tipped tick in the right-hand corner. She looked at the others. They'd all been ticked.

Asta tapped a brown A4 rectangle ruminatively against the palm of her hand. The envelope throbbed with information about her new lover. It was tempting. 'What do you think these are, boy?' She supplied Setanta's answer in a gruff, kindly voice tailored to his personality. '*It's post, Asta my dear.*'

The overhead light clicked on just as the cream boiled over.

Jake said, 'To be precise, it's *Jake's* post, Asta my dear.'

The treehouse is still. The wind has died completely. Asta's naked body is criss-crossed with scratches.

The voice still calls. It's tireless. It'll call her forever, with that sour note in it, making her name sound ugly.

'Asta!'

A hand pokes through the window, stabbing at her soft bruises, prodding her cuts.

Asta woke up.

Even here? She looked around the bedroom, at the beautiful furniture Jake had made himself. Beside her, he stirred, rearranged his limbs, fell back into sleep.

If the dream could follow her into this room, it could follow her anywhere.

December 22nd

Prising away Jake's arms, Asta forbade him to walk her home.

'I need to come down before I re-enter Looney world,' she told him. He was ardent, strong; Asta liked how she really had to shove to separate them. 'Laters,' she said gently, reading his face and seeing doubt there; their disagreement had rattled them both. 'Really, we're good,' she added.

For a while, in the dip of the night, they hadn't been good at all. Jake's anger, all the worse for being dryly contained behind tight lips, had shocked Asta.

'I didn't read it!' she'd said, over and over.

'What if I hadn't walked in?' Jake had avoided her eyes, turning a shoulder towards her on the giant bed where they'd romped an hour before. 'I wouldn't come round to your house and go through your post.'

'I wasn't going through it!' Asta had slammed down her mug, spilling chocolate on the bedside table. *I'm sick of being blamed for stuff*, she thought hotly.

He must have sensed he'd gone too far. 'Christ, listen to me.' Jake had bounded up and put his hands on her shoulders. 'Of course you weren't. I just freaked out. Seeing you looking at it . . .'

Asta had been glad of the thaw, applying herself to his chest as if he was a grazed knee and she was a plaster.

Tobercree, rinsed clean by rainfall in the night, looked like a newly opened Christmas present as Asta dawdled on the bridge. She noticed the tumbling cold water, she noticed the stones in the clear depths, she noticed *everything*. The love that she and Jake had made as dawn came up had left her feeling inside out, part of everything, in love with it all.

Neither Jake's clever footwork in avoiding her direct questions, nor her own careful discretion about her feelings for Conan could spoil this high.

Below the pink sky, the village's wet streets shone. The famed Tobercree Christmas lights switched off with an audible pop as Asta passed beneath them. *They're much better than the Oxford Street lights in London.*

Asta's fellow early risers were all gorgeous, handsome, beautiful beings; even the matted gargoyle of a cat outside the church received the tickle under the chin it was so clearly gagging for.

As Asta bent over the diseased creature, she sensed rather than saw a couple leaving the church just as the bell pealed six. The couple parted ways, and the taller figure came towards Asta. She groaned to herself as she turned to greet him.

'Good morning, Martin.'

'Aren't we the early birds? Me and wifey were just having a quick auld pray before the day gets going,' said Martin heartily, rubbing his hands together.

'That's nice,' said Asta, thinking, *That's weird*. She wondered why Martin addressed everybody as if they were an audience and not just people.

'I don't have to ask what you've been up to. It's written all over your face.'

The repellent cat retched.

Asta's mood evaporated with a tiny *pfff!* She looked at Martin properly for the first time since she'd come home, taking in the thinning, dyed hair, the varnished skin and the pastel tie. Refusing to show him that he'd unsettled her, Asta said, 'I do enjoy our little chats,' and turned away.

'Funny, how life works out!' Martin called after Asta as she hurried away. 'Gerry praying for a baby and you popping one out just like that!'

Looney's Bar was already awake. Ma, rollers in, dressing gown savagely belted, was taking chairs down from tables in the bar.

'I've had a brainwave!' Ma was fizzing.

'Aren't you going to ask where I was?'

'No. Sure, you're a grown woman.' Asta looked around for hidden cameras; surely this was somebody dressed up as her mother.

'And besides,' hissed Ma. 'I know where you feckin' were!'

In the post office, holding up a lengthy queue, Ma outlined her plan to Gerry. 'A Christmas get-together for the whole clan!'

'But today?' Gerry grimaced. 'Why the rush?'

'Because it's Asta's last day.'

The countdown had begun. A giant, tinsel-covered clock was ticking loudly enough to deafen Asta. As she listened to Ma get Gerry on-side, she wondered how she'd cram everything she needed to do into her remaining twenty-four hours. The scam. The article. The man she could still smell on her own skin.

'Where is this so-called party?'

Asta didn't take Gerry's bored sarcasm personally. Her family had never been able to pull together. Asta longed to knit together the raggedy fabric before she flew away.

'In the castle.'

Asta and Gerry were as one, suddenly. 'The *castle*?'

Ma was full of the pros: plenty of space; atmosphere; somewhere that meant a lot to all of them. 'Remember your da used to take youse there for picnics?'

'In the summer!' Asta was appalled.

'So, we dig out all the blankets we can muster. I'll send Kitty and the gang up to build a little bonfire. We'll bake potatoes. We'll have a sing-song.'

And we'll freeze our little Irish asses off. 'Ma, seriously—' began Asta.

'It'll be *grand*.' Ma was done listening. 'Gerry,' she snapped. 'You're coming. We're all coming. And we're going to really, really enjoy ourselves.' She eyed both her daughters. 'Or we'll fecking die trying.'

'I can't promise anything, Ma,' said Gerry as her mother left the shop. She turned to Asta. 'How's your little essay going?'

'Don't panic. Your saint is still officially miraculous.'

The bell above the door tinkled, and Martin was among them: he managed to enter the scruffy little shop as if it

246

were the stage of the London Palladium. 'Well, look who it isn't, my favourite gals!'

The door opened again, as members of the queue gave up and another customer entered.

'Father!' beamed Gerry.

'Father!' Martin grabbed Rory's hand and wrung it, as if murdering a small mammal. 'You're looking well. Isn't Father looking well, Ger?'

'He's looking really, really well,' agreed Gerry, lips pulled right back, signifying her great satisfaction at how well Rory was looking.

'That's . . . nice. Do you have any, what are they called, highlighter pens in stock?' asked Rory, trying to ignore Martin's rapturous gaze.

'Oh, yes!' Gerry was eager to impress with her in-depth highlighter expertise. 'We have neon, fine-line, thick-line, and ones shaped like cats.'

'The cheapest ones, please.' Rory cracked and turned to Martin. 'Heard your show the other day.'

'Why, thank you,' said Martin, alarming Rory with a hug. 'That means a lot to me.' He nudged the priest. 'Have you heard about my sis-in-law's holiday romance?' He leered. 'Come on, Asta. Spill the beans.'

'There's very little to tell.' Confronted with Martin's stratospheric chumminess, Asta became robotic: he'd always made her feel as if she had ants in her medium-control pants even before their strange exchange that morning.

'Not what I hear!'

From her position of power behind the counter, Gerry cut in gnomically. 'A man with secrets is a dangerous thing.' She assumed a look of maidenly innocence as she dusted a row of plastic combs wrapped in discoloured cellophane. 'A man who did something he's ashamed of.'

'Me, I'm an open book!' beamed Martin, ramming his hands into the pockets of what looked suspiciously like golfing trousers. 'No secrets for the Voice of Tobercree.'

Asta reserved a special dislike for people who referred to themselves in the third person, believing it was just the sort of thing Hitler would do.

'Everybody's entitled to a secret or two.' Rory's voice was a deep, liquid counterpoint to Martin's high-pitched flute. 'Aren't they, Asta?'

Did he wink? *Are we*, wondered Asta, *in cahoots against Martin?* 'They are, Father Rory, sir.' Asta mimicked Gerry's schmaltzy deference.

'Jake, if that's who we're talking about,' said Rory, 'is a complex man who confronted an unsettling situation the best way he knew how. I don't judge him. That's not my job.'

'Of course, I didn't mean . . .' Gerry backtracked, eyes down. 'Just saying, Father. I don't really know the chap.'

Yes, you do! thought Asta. *You intercept his letters.*

'Jake needs what we all need.' Rory dug in his pocket for coins. 'He needs love.'

Martin took Gerry's hand over the counter. 'He needs what I have. The love of a good woman.'

'From what I hear, he's had the love of quite a few good women,' said Gerry. 'Plus a few who aren't so good.'

Resisting the dangled bait, Asta said, 'Rory, what do you think of Ma's notion to get all the Looneys together today?'

'I think that's splendid,' said Rory, smoothly.

'Hear that, Gerry? Father gives it his approval.' Asta had

turned Gerry's Weapon of Mass Destruction on her. 'So you'll come?'

'Yahum.' Gerry coined a new word that meant both *of course* and *if I had a stick I'd beat you to death*.

At the other end of the line, Jake said, 'Brilliant! A winter picnic.'

Grateful for his enthusiasm – Kitty had greeted the idea as if it were a dead toad in her lap; Oona had feigned a stroke – Asta had to say, hesitantly, 'Jake, it's family only.'

'Even better. I get a chance to spend some time with them. Particularly Kitty.' Jake paused. 'I mean, if we're having a thing, I should get to know her, shouldn't I? We *are* having a thing, aren't we? You're not just using me for my body?'

Wondering where 'a thing' stood in the hierarchy of relationships, Asta stalled. Was it above a fling? Below an affair? She imagined telling Conan she'd had *a thing* in Ireland. It was certainly an improvement on a one-night stand. 'Yes,' she admitted solemnly, 'you and I are having a thing.' She smiled. 'A lovely thing.'

'That's settled, then. I'm invited.'

'You're invited.' Asta enjoyed giving in to Jake. He made a game of everything.

The stone floors of Tobercree Castle had long been devoured by time. Only the gable wall still stood, tapering to point at the sky, cocking a Gothic snook at St Catherine's spire in the valley below.

An isolated circular staircase stopped abruptly, going

nowhere. Here and there was the bottom half of an ancient window, or a mottled step slippy with frost. Snowflakes pirouetted from a darkening sky, dancing over the feast Ma had conjured up.

'Wow,' breathed Asta, tears coming to her eyes at the beauty of the scene, at the effort her ageing mother had made, at the feel of Jake's gloved hand in her own as they hurried towards it.

'Welcome!' shouted Ma, all bundled up in her good coat and a fake-fur hat that looked like a dead teddy. She'd commandeered what was almost a room: two walls, crumbling but intact, and a roof that was gradually giving up the ghost. 'Who's for a mini sausage?' she yelled, exhibiting dangerous signs of over-excitement.

A small fire crackled and danced in the middle of the space. As Kitty and Finn fed it sticks of kindling, Ma draped rugs and blankets all around. Asta sank to the carpeted floor, grateful for its insulating properties beneath her bottom, and leaned back on a bank of cushions.

'It took ages to light all the lanterns,' said Kitty, her mouth full of sausage roll.

'It was worth it,' said Asta, taking it all in. Tea lights stood in jagged niches, on low boulders and on the buffet table, which was home to a sausage-roll mountain, a ham-sandwich slalom and a Scotch-egg stadium. On the back wall hung a gigantic foil star. Asta hailed it as an old friend. It had been part of Looney Christmases ever since she could remember, and she was glad it was still around.

The flickering flames were magnetic, pulling everybody close and creating a golden circle, a Christmas bauble in the midst of the barren winter landscape. Peg's picnic chair was pulled up close. Gerry posed awkwardly on an outsized cushion. Oona was cross-legged, trying to persuade a baked potato out of the fire.

The fire's glow warmed their faces. *These are my people*, thought Asta, emotion welling up inside her: the countdown was getting to her. This would be a happy memory, but just that – a memory – when she wrapped herself up in her London life again. *It's all there, waiting. The flat. The job. Conan.*

Asta glanced guiltily at Jake, as if he might read her thoughts. *Is it unfaithful to think about Conan?* Jake and Conan were impossible to compare. She found it hard to see past Jake; their recent closeness had seen him grow in her mind, so his outline blocked out all other men.

Soon she'd be back in the metropolis, answering Conan's phone, bossing him about – and clinking glasses with him over the most important meal of the year.

Accepting a mug of tea with a suspicious whiff of whisky about it, Asta wondered, *Who am I if I'm not true to Conan after wanting him for so long?* She watched Jake charm her mother, admiring the horrific hat, praising the trifle that had somehow survived the journey intact. *He's doing that for me.*

They were two adults, both free, both single; Jake offered Asta something that Conan had long withheld. *Conan won't be jealous; he'll just take the mickey out of me for having an affair with a guy I know so little about.*

'Usually,' said Oona, moving to sit next to Asta, 'I wear me most revealing gear to parties.' She pulled down her bobble hat. 'We're all in feckin' coats and scarves!'

'There's nobody for you to flirt with, so it doesn't matter. Where's Declan? I texted him. Is he coming lat –' Asta stopped and peered closer at Oona, whose lively, lovely face had closed up. 'What's happened?' she said, with panic-stricken intonation she'd learned from Ma.

'You might as well know. In fact . . .' Oona stood up, threw the remains of her beer down her throat. 'I have an announcement, everybody. As of an hour ago, I'm a free woman. Declan and me are no more. I thank you.' She bowed low, her hat falling off onto a rug.

Peg sniffed. 'Sure, you're better off without him.'

'Tru dat, Aunty Peg.' Oona saluted her scowling relative. 'There's plenty more fish in the whatever.'

The worm had turned; Declan had finally had enough. Asta stood to hug her cousin. 'I'm sorry,' she said, in an undertone. She knew what Declan meant to Oona, under all the bluster and blarney.

'I'm not!' Oona shrugged, and a hair extension fell in the fire. 'He's no fun.'

'Maybe if you give him a day or two,' said Gerry, 'he'll come round.'

Ma endorsed this suggestion. 'The man loves you, Oona. Anybody can see that.'

'But I don't love *him*!' Oona's blue eyes were damp, like rock pools. 'Not a bit. Not a teeny, tiny bit. See that?' She pointed to a speck of snow that had landed on her beer bottle. 'I love Declan less than that.'

'Perhaps,' said Peg, selecting a sandwich the size of a house brick, 'this'll help you mend your ways.' Her lips pursed even further, until they were a pretty good facsimile of a hen's bum.

'I'll never change,' snarled Oona. 'Not for that Mary-Ann, not for any fella.'

'I don't want you to change,' said Asta loyally. 'But I do want you to be happy.'

'I am!' beamed Oona. 'I'm deliriously happy! I can do what I like, when I like, without Declan whining in me ear.' Oona did a perfect impression of her ex. '*Oona, it's time to go home. Oona, you've work tomorrow. Oona, put down that African man. Oona, you're breaking me heart. Oona, I can't do this any longer. Oona . . .*' The impression ran out of steam.

'Oh, musha.' Asta touched Oona's arm.

Oona jumped. 'No sympathy!' she hissed.

Gerry had a plan. 'Dress more conservatively, and you might win him back. A little less, you know, *chest*.'

Martin said, 'Sure, you'll find somebody else. It's not too late. Women of all ages find love these days. Don't,' he said, head on one side like a sensitive terrier, 'think you're on the scrap heap, Oona, just because you're that bit older, that bit fatter. Men like a bit of meat on a woman's bones.'

'You should be an agony uncle,' said Asta, so admiringly that Ma thought she meant it.

'Thanks for your concern, Martin,' said Oona. 'But I won't be alone for long. I'm a slapper. And men like slappers. Don't they, Jake?'

'Oh, well . . .' Jake, trying to get comfortable on a rock with a sheepskin over it, looked as if he was well aware there was no right answer to that question.

'I'm gonna pull. I'm gonna pull like I've never pulled before.'

Ma put her hands over Peg's ears as Martin said, in mock terror, 'Watch out, fellas!'

'*You're* perfectly safe,' said Oona.

'You don't need a man,' said Asta. 'You've got me.'

'I haven't got you.' Oona's unhappiness made her blunt. More blunt than usual. Which was very blunt. 'You're about to sod off and leave me again. I don't want a *man*, Asta. I want *men*. Plural.'

'Quavers!' shouted Ma suddenly, her primal fear of her family starving to death reasserting itself. She lobbed a packet at Asta.

'Mum, is it official now?' Kitty, who'd crept nearer to hear Oona's proclamation, stood by the fire, her head back, her eyes challenging and amused.

'Is what official now?' Asta's mind was only half on her daughter's question, the rest of it lingering on the contours of Jake's bottom as he leaned over for a spork.

'You and Jake.' Kitty couldn't keep the giggle out of her voice. She'd been charged with a special energy all day, a turbo-happiness: Asta could tell it was because the family were all together, and wondered how her daughter had managed without this fuel back in London. 'Are you in love?'

Everybody leaned in. Then everybody seemed to realize they'd leaned in too obviously, and leaned out again.

'Um,' said Asta. 'Well.' She paused. 'Hmm.'

'No, really, Mum, are you?'

Gerry joined in. 'Or are youse just good friends, as the saying goes?'

Oona murmured, 'Or are you shagging each other's brains out?'

Peg crossed and uncrossed her legs very swiftly.

Martin said, 'Come on, Jakey. What's the story with you and our Asta?'

Not at all lost for words, as if he'd been waiting for somebody to ask him, Jake said, 'She's my bird.' He smiled. 'And I'm her bloke.'

'Oh, the romance of it!' trilled Gerry, raising an eyebrow.

Jake's bird went bright red and buried her face in a hard-boiled egg (not easy to do), wondering whether or not to protest. *I've never been anybody's bird.* It was a demeaning term: patronizing, sexist, trivial. Then she looked up and caught her bloke's wink. *Yeah,* she thought happily. *I'm his bird.*

The fire had been banked up twice as darkness claimed the castle. Draped like casualties of a battle, the picnickers were full.

Kitty groaned, 'Why did I do it? I don't even like quiche.' Finn put a consoling arm around her, but his face was a bored mask.

With Jake's head in her lap, Asta found her mind wandering. She tried to tug it back, but it was wayward and kept returning to the article. The *unwritten* article. The unsolved scam. And a disappointed Conan.

'Aunty Peg,' she said, interrupting the older woman's long rant on why Kylie Minogue's hotpants were the work of the devil. 'Do you know a Mrs Huffington?'

'But of course.' Peg frowned. 'What about her? Is she going in that silly magazine of yours?' She tittered, an unusual noise that sounded like chicks being crushed to death.

'She and Father Rory . . .' Asta couldn't believe Peg was being so upfront, and she trod carefully. 'They're very close, aren't they?'

'He sleeps with her most nights.'

Nobody else reacted, but Asta's world tilted on its axis. 'And . . . you approve?'

'He's entitled to a little company. That man works tirelessly for the Lord.' Peg smiled. 'I do wash her nightie now and then.'

Asta looked at her aunt for a full minute.

'Told you,' whispered Jake. 'Everybody likes Mrs H.'

It was getting darker by the second. The huddle of Looneys moved closer to the fire, but nobody suggested leaving the enchanted ruin. It was, against all the odds, cosy and comfortable. Asta thought of her laptop waiting for her back at the bar. She thought of how she'd have to cobble together a feature without the most pertinent facts. *Maybe I can engineer a meeting with this Huffington woman before my plane leaves*. She hadn't even packed yet; the laid-back air of Tobercree had infected even sensible, be-prepared Asta.

'I have an idea.' Jake's stubble tickled her ear as he whispered.

'Mmm?' Asta answered, responsive.

'Let's take a leaf out of your daughter's book.'

Asta looked across to where Kitty had been a moment before.

Jake carried on. 'She's snuck off for a cuddle. I vote we do the same.' He started to disengage from her, bending down to whisper as he did so, 'See you in that wood in five minutes, where I shall cuddle you to within an inch of your life.'

Five minutes later Asta stood, straining every nerve in an attempt to be casual.

'Off after your fancy man, are you?' Peg emanated disapproval.

'Oh, go and jump his bones.' Oona's face was disconsolate above her Fair Isle scarf. 'At least one of us is getting some action.' A storm of tuts followed Asta to the trees that encroached on the ruin. The wood was quiet, like an empty church, with only an insipid moon to light her way. Her feet crunched on the cold earth and the fallen frosted twigs.

'Jake?' Her voice was pitched between a whisper and a call. The wood was still, and she felt obliged to be respectful.

'Gotcha!'

Two strong arms reached out and twirled her like a top. Jake's mouth was on hers, greedy and playful.

Asta pulled back, giggling. 'Hang on, just—'

He kissed her again, impatiently, and she relaxed in his grip enough for him to loosen his hold. Then Asta was away, leaping like a deer through the trees.

'What . . . !' Jake took off after her.

Panting, Asta had to pump her legs hard to keep ahead. For some reason it felt crucial that she outrun him. Jake could catch her only when she allowed him to.

Shouting formless, childlike whoops, they plunged deeper into the woods, deeper into the cold darkness. In the pounding of her feet, Asta heard ancient drums. Bounding over a fallen tree, she found herself in a clearing. The moon made an effort and suddenly she could see clearly, as if the copse was lit by a million cold bulbs.

Asta halted so abruptly that Jake almost crashed into her.

'Careful!' he laughed, bent double, hands on knees, gasping. 'Asta. Hey! What are you staring at?'

The treehouse hung among the leafless trees, as askance and unlikely as it had been seventeen years ago; as it had been last night in her dream.

Jake straightened and squinted up at the branches. 'A treehouse! Cool.'

'My da built it,' mumbled Asta.

'Let's climb up!' Jake sounded energized after hours spent on his behind, pandering to Ma.

'*No.*' It came out very vehemently.

'OK.' Jake reached out to pull Asta to him.

'Get off me, Jake.' Asta pushed at him, hating his hands on her.

'What?' Jake teetered somewhere between surprise and annoyance.

'Leave me alone.' Asta was unravelling. She felt exposed and unsafe. Against Jake's chest was just where she wanted to be, yet she was all elbows, her own worst enemy.

'I don't get it. What's happening?'

'Let's get back to the others.' Asta lowered her head, turned away.

'Hang on a minute.' Jake was sharp, perturbed. 'I don't like this, Asta.'

'You don't like *what*?' Asta knew she was perilously close to taking out her feelings on an innocent bystander.

'This sudden mood. Did I do something? 'Cos you're making me feel like I have.' Jake exhaled, and his breath hung like smoke in the air between them.

'It's—'

'Do *not* say it's nothing.' He bent to peer at her face. 'Is it the treehouse?' He clocked the tiny frown Asta couldn't control. 'Does it . . .' He softened. 'Does it remind you of *him*?'

Asta guessed that Jake remembered Etienne's name, but didn't want to say it.

'Yes,' she said quietly. 'It reminds me of him.' She

swallowed hard. 'Bloody bastarding *him*.' Asta strode out of the clearing, back into the calm gloom of the woods. She tripped on roots, almost skidding on frozen patches in her haste to put some space between herself and that wretched shack.

'But, Asta, he didn't know about Kitty.' Jake kept pace with her. 'You said so yourself. If you didn't tell the guy, how—'

'Can we please *not* talk about this?' said Asta, as if filming an instructional DVD entitled *How To Alienate a New Boyfriend*. The scratchy voice, the waspish attitude: if Asta were Jake, she'd walk away.

But Jake wasn't Asta. 'Come on,' he said fondly, throwing a long arm over her shoulders. 'Let's get back to the soap opera you call your family.'

'Are they driving you mad?' Grateful for the change of subject, Asta was apologetic.

'I like them. Oona's a riot. Kitty's got a good head on her shoulders, although she expects more from that Finn kid than he can give her. Best to gloss over Martin. Gerry, I can't work out, but she's not happy. Aunty Peg scares the crap out of me, and that's exactly how she likes it. Your mum . . .' Jake searched for the *bon mot*.

Asta would have suggested *crazy* or *neurotic* a week ago, but neither word was appropriate now. *Powerhouse*, she thought. *Force to be reckoned with*. Ma had summoned up this whole extraordinary picnic in the blink of an eye, like a magician producing a white rabbit from a hat. Ma moved at one hundred miles per hour from the moment she stuffed her bunions into her slippers first thing in the morning until she fell into bed. She hadn't broken step when Da died; it hadn't occurred to her to sell the bar. At an age when most women were slowing down, Ma ran a pub and made it look easy. *How come I never noticed any of that before?*

'Your mum,' said Jake, 'is like many women compressed into one tiny package. Loads of energy. You're never quite sure what she's going to say next. A bit like . . .' He grew nervous even as he said it. 'You,' he ended on a gulp.

'No, she's not.' Asta swatted him, and he grabbed her wrist and kissed her hard.

'Ma wouldn't let you do that,' she murmured.

'With all due respect, I wouldn't attempt it.'

'Can we . . .' Asta bit her lip. 'Here?'

They'd reached another part of the woods, out of reach of the others. Ancient oaks crowded around, creating a private dell; discreet and romantic.

Catching her drift, Jake seemed keen. Very keen. 'Bit nippy.'

'I really don't care.' Asta pulled up his jacket and undid his belt.

When Jake hoisted her against a tree trunk, Asta forgot the treehouse, the article, Conan. For a moment, towards the end, she forgot her name.

'Wow,' he said, breathing hard, coming down from their mutual high, his arms still around her, her legs still around him. When he let her down, they clung together, neither wanting to let go.

'I wish,' said Jake, so close to her ear it felt as if he was inside her head, 'you trusted me enough to talk about the treehouse.'

'It's not about trust.'

'What, then?'

Asta began to disentangle herself, to do up buttons, to

pick up the scarf that had fallen to the barren ground. 'You're better at asking questions than answering them.'

'Touché.' Jake held out his hand. 'Ready?'

'Ready.' Asta took the hand, savouring the warmth of it in the midst of this big, cold wood. She felt close to him and she clung to the feeling, knowing it to be a bubble, knowing that real life was just along the path.

'You're not really going tomorrow, are you?'

Asta stopped dead. 'You know I am.' She registered how he looked away, how his face hardened. 'Jake, that was always the plan.'

'*Your* plan,' said Jake. 'I don't have a plan.'

He was sullen. The bubble had burst. And no wonder; the undergrowth was full of thorns.

'This isn't a holiday,' said Asta. 'It's a working trip. And tomorrow it's over. My boss is expecting me . . .' There had been no right time to tell Jake about Conan, and besides, what would she say? *Oh, and by the way, my boss treats me like a sexless younger sister but I've always loved him, and now he might,* might, *actually have missed me a bit, so . . .*

Jake dropped her hand. 'We're out of step.'

'That's inevitable,' said Asta, mourning the loss of that strong hand. 'One of us is a wage slave and the other seems to have grown a money tree. You don't have commitments, Jake, but I do. I have them coming out of my ears. I can't hang around the swings all day, or make two-storey dog boudoirs. I need to work. Why do I have to defend that?'

'You don't.' Jake stopped, sighed and rubbed his nose as if he wanted to whittle it to a point. He took up her hand again and gave it a squeeze. 'It's not my brain talking. It's my heart. And, you know,' he raised his eyebrows, 'my trousers. I don't want you to go.'

'There's this modern invention called a *plane*.' When Jake smiled, Asta said, 'London's not that far. You should know.'

'And *you* should know,' said Jake, 'that London is a million miles away from this wood.'

He was right, but Asta couldn't afford to agree. *I'll get home, see how the land lies.* Conan was an emotional loose end, and Asta had always tried to keep her emotions tidy.

She didn't want to step back from Jake. But she had to.

It took a while to retrace their steps. The bonfire was dying. Oona sat staring into the embers, while Ma filled Tupperware boxes with leftovers. Gerry hopped about on one leg, complaining of pins and needles.

Stacking cushions, Peg scrutinized Asta's face as she approached. 'You look quare, Asta.'

'Do I?' Asta quailed, worrying that her aunt could detect recent sexual activity in her eyes.

'You're upset.' Peg dropped the cushions and leaned towards her niece.

'She's fine, Peg,' said Ma, forcing a pork pie and half a pasty into an arranged marriage in a plastic lidded box.

'Your face is full of feeling.' Peg was adamant, taking Asta's chin in her hand. 'Since you were a wee one, I've always known when you're upset. Your eyes go misty. And you have a misty look about you now.' She turned to Jake. 'Did you upset her?'

Laughing, Jake held up his hands, and Asta answered for him, embarrassed. 'Of course he didn't, Aunty Peg.'

'Somebody did.' Peg's eyes were like lasers. 'Somebody did,' she repeated, more contemplatively.

'Come on, ladies.' Martin kicked dirt over the fire. 'Chop-chop.'

'Who put you in charge?' Oona rose up, slightly unsteady on her feet, whether from beer or melancholy, Asta couldn't tell.

Gerry, still hopping, said, 'My Martin's the man of the family since Da died.'

As Jake winced and bowed his head, as if expecting an explosion from her direction, Asta said demurely, 'I don't remember seeing that position advertised, Martin.'

'You've only been here ten minutes.' Gerry finally stood still. 'You don't know the half of it. You want everything to be like it was when you left.'

'Believe me,' said Asta, as vehemently as she could without raising the temperature too high, 'I don't, Gerry. I truly don't. Why do we even need a man of the family? It's the twenty-first century. Kitty and I get along all right.'

'Yeah!' Kitty backed her up.

Asta avoided Martin's velociraptor eye. 'Ma's the head of this family.'

'Me?' squawked Ma, in hand-to-hand combat with a leaning tower of Tupperware.

'Yes, you, Ma. You're at retirement age, yet here you are running a pub, on your feet all day, making stew 24/7, doing the books, serving the customers, opening up in the morning, locking up at night. You're the heart and soul of this family. It doesn't need a man for the job, it's got you.'

'Well . . .' Ma was rendered speechless, something only ever achieved by bereavement or mention of sex. She put her hand to her throat and stared at her younger daughter as if seeing her for the first time.

The speech had surprised Asta every bit as much as it

surprised Ma. Over the years of separation, Ma's personality had hardened into a patchwork of her faults. *I forgot her virtues.* Another mother and daughter might have hugged at this point, but the Looneys let the moment pass, both of them feeling it deeply but quietly.

'So,' said Martin, drifting past Kitty, not deigning to help with the clearing up, 'it's *down with men*, is it?'

'If anything,' said Asta, 'it's *up with women*. Equality.'

'Women's lib!' chuckled Martin, shaking his head at the ladies' funny ways. He punched the air. 'Who needs men anyways?'

'Isn't he just absolutely hilarious?' asked Gerry, eyes creased.

'It's a crime he's not on the telly!' said Ma.

'I don't think,' began Peg, with a look that could skin a rabbit, 'that my niece's life is a subject for humour.'

Kitty had unfolded herself from Finn. 'They don't call it women's lib any more,' she told Martin. 'Mum's not a women's libber, she's just a modern woman.'

'Doing her best,' said Peg, carefully not looking at Asta. 'Like she always has.'

Nobody had ever dared kiss Peg without written permission, but Asta felt like doing just that. The support was so out of the blue that it prompted a tear. She brushed at her eyes and opted out of the debate by handing Finn a pile of folded blankets to carry.

The boy took it without comment. His handsome face was impassive; it was a face to be admired, then forgotten. Asta wondered whether Kitty had seen through Tobercree's rebel without a cause yet.

'Ignore Martin, Mum.' Kitty's voice, as gentle as rain, sounded in Asta's ear. 'He's a Neanderthal.'

'Martin doesn't worry me.' Asta kissed Kitty's cheek. It was ice-cream cold, with a talcum softness Asta remembered from her daughter's babyhood.

'It makes me go a bit funny imagining you with any man, but if you *have* to be with somebody, then Jake's cool.'

High praise indeed. 'And Finn's cool, too,' said Asta encouragingly.

'God, Mum,' said Kitty, 'you're such a crap liar.'

'Oi, madam!' Ma, stooping over picnic carnage, was outraged. 'That's not a word I want to hear in your mouth.'

'Sorry, Grandma.'

'That's better, love.' Ma was returned to smiling content. 'Here, Asta, make yourself useful.' She held out a bulging black plastic bag. 'Take this to the bin over by the high wall.' Asta stepped to her and reached for the bag, but Ma didn't let it go. 'Are you really leaving tomorrow?' she said in a hasty whisper, as if they were spies passing sensitive information.

'Well, yes.' Asta tried to smile, but it died a death on her lips. 'I have to, Ma.'

'Yes, you do.' Ma nodded, blinked, smiled. 'Ignore me, pet.'

They both held onto the slippery plastic. The most banal situations can throw up the most extraordinary revelations. *I've missed you so much*, thought Asta, the realization blinding. *That's one of the reasons that I hold Kitty so close she suffocates.*

Her way to the bin was pitch-black. *Only Looneys would picnic in the dark*, thought Asta with an indulgent anti-pride that was new to her. The woods were still, as if the trees had died.

The bin liner split. Softly cursing Ma's love of own-brand

bargains, Asta placed the odds and ends in the bin one by one.

'Is he *the one*, d'you think?' Martin was right behind her.

'*What*?' Asta tumbled in empty cans with a clatter, refusing to look up.

'Jake. Is he Mr Right?'

'I don't think in those terms.' Asta was curt, as if each word cost her money.

'A nice new daddy for little KitKat.'

Asta gritted her teeth. Martin had a forked tongue: on paper his words were inane, but his tone added a pinch of mockery. 'Kitty's not little any more, and she's doing fine without a daddy.' Asta hated how her voice shook. That damn treehouse had unnerved her.

'We all need a daddy,' said Martin softly, as if he pitied Asta. He watched her stuff paper plates into the bin, 'Shame about you and Gerry. You just don't get on, do you? She's stuck in the past. She finds it hard to forgive you.'

'Don't explain my sister to me.' Asta clung to haughtiness as armour. She turned and faced him. 'Gerry knows I love her, and I know she loves me.' *I hope*.

'It's this longing for a child.' Martin shook his head. 'It's messed her up.'

'This is a conversation I should have with Gerry.'

'I reckon St Catherine must be laughing in her face,' said Martin, hands in pockets, rocking to and fro on his feet. 'There's poor Gerry, begging, praying for a child, yet she never has sex with her husband. Doesn't make a bit of sense, does it?'

'You surely don't expect me to answer that,' snapped Asta.

'You've never liked me, darlin', have you?' Martin's smile was neon.

'Martin, don't you think this conversation's a touch heavy for a picnic?'

'Brush me off, go ahead. But –' Martin leaned towards her. His voice dropped, but kept its sugar coating. 'I know what you are, Miss High and Mighty.'

And there it was, the reason she'd fled: unforgiving, finger-pointing morality.

'Martin,' said Asta, 'you don't know me at all. And I don't want to know you.'

Upending the torn bag, she heard him chuckle as he walked away.

Walking home in the dark was an adventure. Ma and Peg muttered 'Jesus, Mary and Joseph' each time their wide-fit shoes encountered a pothole. The teens flitted around and about, like ghosts.

'Thank God it's not snowing,' said Gerry, falling into step beside Asta. Jake had been requisitioned by Ma and Peg, each of them taking an arm as they inched towards the winking Christmas lights of the village.

'I like snow,' said Asta. Another reversal, in a week of them. She'd been fearful of being snowed in; now she appreciated its lacy beauty.

The sisters were silent, Asta digesting Gerry's hope for her own virgin birth and Gerry evidently screwing up her courage, because she suddenly said, 'I owe you an apology, Asta.'

'Do you?' Asta laughed. 'For what? It's a long list, Ger.

Telling me Santa was just Da in a cotton-wool beard? Squealing on me when I got detention?'

'For letting you leave.' Gerry spoke low, in a rush. 'That night, when you ran.'

'You couldn't have stopped me.'

'I could have tried,' said Gerry. 'But I let you walk out into the dark on your own and you're me little sister and I could have told Ma and she would have raced after you and . . .' Gerry shook her head. 'Things might be very different now.'

'Things are good, Gerry. Things are fine.'

'No, they're not. I'm sorry, OK. Let me say I'm sorry.'

Asta knew better than to smile at the fact that only Gerry could apologize so irritably. 'I accept your apology,' she said.

'Funny, isn't it,' said Gerry, 'you having a baby nobody wanted, when so many women are desperate for a child.'

One step forward, thought Asta, *then two steps back*.

Any magazine article has padding – paragraphs that don't add much, but are prettily written. The document on Asta's screen was *all* padding.

The opening sentences set the scene, describing Tobercree and its people. The section that outlined the effects of the Irish recession on Ireland's rural communities was informative and passionate. The sound bites were pithy. The interview with Dervla was moving.

Like a birthday party without a cake, the article screamed out for a reveal at the end – but Asta still had no idea how Rory made the statue cry.

The countdown had marched relentlessly on, as

countdowns tend to do. Just over sixteen hours left of her stay in Tobercree.

I've let Conan down. The article, however elegantly written, was incomplete and could never be published. It wasn't much of a Christmas present.

To: a.looney@boulevardmagazine.com
From: c.orourke@boulevardmagazine.com

I have four parties to go to tonight. And a gallery opening. But I can't be bothered. I'll just make up my column. People say the same things at every party anyway.

I'm going to assume you've found out the secret and you're keeping it from me as a big, sparkly Christmas surprise. Am I right? You've found out, yes?

I have a surprise for you too. It's big. I hope it's sparkly. But that's up to you.

See you tomorrow. I'll send a car to the airport. Come straight here!

Cx

P.S. Where's the phone number for the limo firm?

P.P.S. Actually, could you ring them?

To: angie507@hotmail.co.uk
From: a.looney@boulevardmagazine.com

No need to meet us at the airport in your trusty banger. Conan's having us picked up.

But that's not really why I'm emailing. I have a confession to make. Please try and understand why I've kept this from you for a very long time. It's something I should have shared, because you could have helped, like you always do.

And because we share everything.

Ange, I have feelings for Conan. Strong feelings. I've been calling them 'love' when I dared.

I kept them to myself because they weren't reciprocated. For years, all I had to nourish me was hope. I hugged the feelings to myself and just hung on, thinking they would blow over, like flu, but they never did.

I've been crazy about Conan for more years than I can easily admit, even to you.

And now there's Jake.

At first he was a wild crush. A fantasy. But things have changed. We've moved fast, by-passing a few of the usual stages of a relationship. (I suppose! Never really had one . . .) Perhaps it's because of Christmas, or the snow, or because we're both a bit battered by life and are amazed that we've met somebody who feels like home. It's not like we're teenagers – we're both mature and single and searching and blown away by what's happened.

Whatever the reason, the fantasy is now alarmingly real and I'm about to leave the pub to walk to Jake's place for our 'last night'.

But, oh God, Angie, Conan seems to have turned towards me at last. As if he's suddenly seeing me in colour, instead of black and white. What if there's a chance for us? What if, after all my longing for Conan, we might have something?

I'm so confused. I don't want to hurt anybody. I don't want to lose these riches I've only just found.

If only you were here. If only you could tell me what to do.

Ma wouldn't hear of it. 'No, Asta, *no*.' She propelled her towards the door. 'Scoot! Run off to your young man.'

Her last night in Tobercree was surprisingly mild. No cruel wind chucked Asta's cheeks, no snowflakes skied down her nose. She walked slowly, idling almost, past the great dark hole of the abandoned mill. It was the only murky stretch of the high street, flooded with people on foot and in cars, streaming away from the church.

The shops had gone up a gear as Christmas approached. The hairdressers offered 'last-minute Crimbo appointments!' in a riot of fairy lights. The butcher had placed a jaunty elf's hat on a pig's head. In the window of the newsagent's Asta saw a selection box of chocolate bars, her heart's desire when she was seven.

Her older heart had more complicated desires.

'Asta!'

Spinning, startled – that recurring dream lent her own name menace – she saw Rory.

'I suppose we should say goodbye.' He came towards her, speeding up across the tarmac of the car park, to take both her hands in a quaintly old-fashioned gesture. His gloves, she noticed, were finest-quality leather. His coat was undoubtedly cashmere. 'Have you finished what you came here to do?'

'Almost. There's just one pesky detail missing.'

'How the evil priest pulls it off? It's a broader subject than you thought, eh? You started off writing about a common or garden hoax, but found you were dealing with the biggie – the power of love.'

'*Love?*' Asta queried.

'St Catherine is loved. And all love requires a leap of faith.'

'Not a *blind* leap, though?'

'What other sort is there?'

Rory began to walk, and Asta fell into step with him, feeling small beside the tall figure in black. 'Take this fella you're seeing tonight, for example,' he said.

'I could be going anywhere! Why assume I'm going to see Jake?'

'Where *are* you going, if you don't mind me asking?'

She punched him lightly on the arm, briefly wondering if God would strike her dead for such blasphemy. 'Shut up,' she said.

'Jake *needs* your faith. It's a long time since anybody believed in him. Have faith in him, Asta, and it'll work miracles, you'll see.'

'You're asking me to change the habit of a lifetime.' Even though Rory was lying to the entire village, she felt able to talk freely to him. 'I'm as judgemental as Ma in my own way, even without two thousand years of theology to back me up. I've always been so careful, you see, because I have to be strong to protect Kitty. I can't invite anything in that might harm us.' Asta was accustomed to spotting a bad 'un, but she'd never before met a baffling mix of chilli and honey like Jake Jones.

'Have you even noticed you're at a crossroads?'

Asta looked about her.

'No, not literally,' said Rory gently. 'Kitty's about to take flight. You've done a grand job with her. She's going to be fine. Isn't it time the tiger mother thought about herself? Go with your instincts about Jake, Asta. Aim for hope, if you can't quite stretch to faith.' Perhaps perceiving that

Asta had reached her limit of priestly talk, Rory looked up at the sky. 'It's going to snow,' he said.

'I knew you'd come.' Jake opened the door as Asta's boots crunched across the cold gravel. 'No,' he corrected himself as she dashed to him and threw herself into his open arms. 'I *hoped* you'd come.' He kissed her, already aroused, already drunk on Asta, and whispered, 'I never take anything for granted with you.'

Asta is naked, but more than naked, if that's possible. She feels as if her soul is on view along with her body.

The treehouse is still. It's a precarious stillness. It balances on a branch that can't bear the weight.

She realizes the voice has stopped calling her name. The forest is quiet, but not with the layered silence of nature. It's as if somebody has turned the sound off.

Asta waits.

She hears her own blood roaring in her ears.

Down to the kitchen raced Asta, her bare feet making the smallest of sounds, as if a mouse was falling down the grand staircase.

The dream had suffocated her, jolting her awake to take a great gasp of air. Jake, a dark range of hills under the bedding, had said, 'Wassamatter?' in a voice furred with sleep.

She'd kissed his head for an answer and slipped out of the bed. She was on the run, possessed, not asking questions. *I must get outside.* Asta needed to bury her face in the night air, to wash off the traces of the dream.

She flung open the back door, to a world completely changed.

Snow, great white handfuls, teemed from the sky.

Asta held out a hand, and it was drenched immediately. A gusting white curtain billowed between the Big House and Tobercree. Nothing moved or scurried or squeaked; the snow had anaesthetized the countryside.

The terrace was carpeted with the softest, thickest pile, leaving Asta no option but to run out onto it and leave dancing footprints.

Jayzus, that's freezing! she thought, a little late, in the enchanted downpour. The sky above her head, a strange glowing grey, was full of snow. Enough snow to bury Tobercree.

A window flew up on the first floor.

'No plane can fly in this!' shouted Jake.

December 23rd

After a slow ride home in Jake's Land Rover, Asta had no time to collect her thoughts. Ma tied an apron around her daughter and pushed a tray into her hands. 'Table by the corner,' she said, turning back to the kitchen, where endless quantities of sausages were meeting their end on the griddle. 'This snow's a miracle,' she called after Asta's disappearing back. 'St Catherine's keeping you and Kitty here with me!'

Always the hub of the village, that morning Looney's felt more like a refugee centre than a bar. Extra tables and chairs had been drafted in to accommodate the many bottoms. Some homes in the village were without power, and Ma prescribed a full Irish breakfast for everybody.

The chatter was all of blocked roads and fallen telegraph poles and cows being rescued from ditches. It was an emergency of the prettiest kind, with the snow already banking against the window panes.

I'm in limbo.

Asta was suspended in thin air, not really here and unable to reach there. Around her, the village was in limbo too – the inhabitants as charmed as children with the sudden snowfall, looking about them in wonder at the magic trick nature had pulled while they slept. Overnight, their humble streets had shrugged on swanky new clothes to emerge as a ski resort. A holiday feel hung in the air, as if anything could happen.

Briskly, the Looney females fed the multitudes – and told off the multitudes, and ordered the multitudes to finish everything on their plates. Peg was in charge of seating newcomers; Oona was in charge of *double entendres*; Gerry was in charge of making women feel bad about their choice of coat.

Hemmed in by a toothless old lady on one side, and a man who kept pigs on the other, Jake accepted the fried this and the fried that and the fried the other and said, 'Women save the day, yet again, in Tobercree.'

Gerry held out the bar's massive cordless phone to Asta. 'It's for you! Don't be hours yakking. There's work to do.'

'Hello?' Asta reddened at the sound of Conan on the other end of the phone, as if he were her illicit lover and not her boss. The old Asta had split into two women and, incredibly, they were both getting what they wanted after years of nothing much.

Heading outside to the patio, a white, frostbitten square, she said, 'Did you get my email?'

'I did, and I don't believe a word.' Conan was raspy and irritable. Asta imagined a privately educated lovely lying unconscious beside him. 'There must be *some* way you can get back.'

'I can't change the weather.' Asta heard his incredulous huff; *as if I'm not trying hard enough*. 'The airport's closed. The ports are shut. And I left my magic broomstick in Chelsea.'

'You always think of something. Surely you can just—'

'Conan, seriously. I'm stuck here, so you'll have to wipe your own botty for the next few days. There's an upside. I'll have time to examine the statue. I'll nose out the secret and finish the article.'

'Screw the article!'

'Actally, no, Conan, *don't* screw the article.' Conan had so much, and it all came so easily that he forgot what life was like for the little people. 'The article's very important to me. Forecasts are saying the bad weather will lift on the twenty-seventh.'

'What? You won't be home for Christmas?'

'Nope.' Asta thought wistfully of the wrapped presents lurking in the bottom of her wardrobe, her themed tree slowly shedding all its needles.

'But I need you here, kid.'

'No you don't.' Asta held her breath, wondering what he'd say.

'I'll have to pull my own cracker.'

'There's a rude joke in there somewhere if we look hard enough.'

'No. No jokes. This article better be damn good, Asta.' *Click*.

Asta held the phone to her chest. Beyond the patio, the garden sloped upwards until the white foreground merged with the milky sky. Tobercree was covered, like a Christmas cake, with the purest white icing. *I'm trapped in one of the old tales*, thought Asta, her ears still warm from Conan's voice. Ireland was mythical, supernatural, a whitewashed world where strange things – like love and lust and crying statues – were everyday; London was normality and sanity.

Slipping back into the bar, Asta saw Jake smiling politely

at his toothless tablemate's repartee. *Jake's no myth; he's flesh and blood.*

There was a connection between them, even in this jam-packed room. Jake felt her eyes on him and looked up. Asta was warmed to her marrow by his small smile. That was what sex had done for them, created a special, private line of communication.

'Stop daydreaming!' A tea towel flicked across Asta's behind. 'Clear those tables,' said Ma, firing on all cylinders.

Gathering up plates so clean their pattern was missing, it struck Asta that Ma had never commented on Jake. *Odd.* Ma was a seasoned commenter. She commented on people's hair; their shoes; the way they walked; their philosophy of life; how they felt about Lulu. Therefore, her lack of comment on Jake had to be deliberate. It would be contravening all sorts of unwritten family laws to ask Ma why, but recent events had proved to Asta that doors can be kicked down, castles taken.

'Mum,' began Asta, gathering her nerve as her mother cracked an egg into foaming fat. 'What do you think of Jake? Of me and Jake?'

'He's a grand fella,' said Ma. 'Lovely manners. Nice short hair.' Ma had waged a ferocious campaign against long-haired men for decades. 'But, sure, what does my opinion matter? You've always done your own thing.'

What does that mean? 'Ma . . . are you disappointed in me?'

'Jayzus, are you kidding me?' said Ma, leaning so far back she was almost horizontal. 'You and Peg, youse have the right idea. Doing what you want, without a man getting in the way. That woman papers her parlour once every ten years in the wallpaper of her choice. And she has enough saved to bury herself.'

That didn't, on the face of it, sound like such a marvellous life to Asta, but evidently Ma had different criteria.

'Mind you, when there's a baby in the picture . . . it might have been nice if you'd done things the right way round.'

Bizarrely, Asta felt comforted by the conservatism: a leopard like Ma shouldn't entirely change her spots. 'Yeah, well,' smiled Asta, with a light touch for the first time on this subject. 'You wouldn't be without Kitty now, would you?'

'Indeed I would *not*.' Ma was smug, as if her beloved granddaughter was all her own work. 'That girl is the apple of my eye.' She flipped the egg expertly. 'When I think of what might have happened . . .' Ma looked at the egg, sizzling, but didn't seem to see it. 'She might be in some other family now. I was brought up to care so much what other people thought, Asta. I was brought up to put being respectable before *everything*.' She snapped back into the present. 'Thank God,' she said, 'you fought me. Thank God you were different.'

The words fell like confetti around Asta, each one beautiful. She'd never expected to hear such a sentiment from Ma.

'I suppose you'll be taking her away from me as soon as the snow melts.'

Asta nodded, eyes down. She hated disappointing Ma; she'd had her fill of it.

'In that case, I hope it snows forever.' Ma turned up the radio.

'Here's one for my snow maidens,' said Martin. 'Working

279

hard at Looney's bar, keeping the home fires burning so us chaps can go out and change the world!'

'How did Martin get to the studio?'

'Sure, he has a home studio in his garage. Nothing stops the Voice of Tobercree from getting on air!'

Every silver cloud has a mucky lining, thought Asta, escaping the kitchen and her brother-in-law's cobra hiss. She would have liked a moment to relive Ma's comments, but was almost knocked over by Gerry stampeding in to shout, 'Ma! The Fathers are in!'

'Jayzus.' Ma broke a yolk and dashed out. 'Hello, hello!' she beamed, like a quiz-show host. 'Asta! Say hello!' she snapped, as if Asta were a feral child she'd found in the woods.

'Hello, Fathers,' said Asta, in a super-sweet way that only Rory recognized as fake. She leaned closer to say discreetly, 'Is it still possible for me to examine St Catherine today?'

'Absolutely.' Rory seemed very relaxed for a man about to be rumbled.

'Where's my Iseult?' Father Dominic lowered himself slowly and painfully into the chair Peg set out for him. The tourist who'd been tipped out of the chair stood to one side with his bacon sandwich, a hurt look on his face.

'*Kitty*'s somewhere around, if that's who you mean,' said Asta. The old man's use of 'my' had set her teeth on edge.

'Explain to Jake who Iseult is,' said Ma, fussing with the cushion at Father Dominic's back.

'And me,' said Oona, joining them. 'Didn't she win the Eurovision one year?' She put an arm around Asta, as if she knew her cousin might need support.

'Please, miss! I know, miss!' said Jake. 'Iseult was an

ancient Irish princess who was kidnapped and taken to England. Yeah?'

'Fancy an Englishman knowing that,' said Ma, full of admiration.

'Only Kitty isn't a princess, is she, Father Dominic?' Asta's voice quavered. She hadn't rehearsed, but the words insisted on coming out. She stared levelly at the priest. 'My Kitty's a bastard, remember?'

The word detonated, forcing a strangled noise from Ma and prompting Peg to come up with an entirely new facial expression

'There's no call for that language.' Peg found her voice.

'It's not my language.' Asta glared at Father Dominic, whose face had turned brick-red. 'It's his.'

'You always did have a filthy mouth.' The old priest batted away Ma's attempts to calm him down. ''Tis a pity you'd rather write stupid stories about your betters than emulate your mother and sister. You're a cuckoo in the nest, Asta Looney.' When Father Dominic saw how this barb hit home – Asta shrank at the accusation, so close to her fears about her standing in the family – he half-rose from his chair. 'Try and be more like them! Wonderful examples of Irish womanhood.'

Oona squeezed Asta and said, 'Come on, we all know Gerry overcharges for Um Bongo.' She ignored Gerry's panicked coughing fit. '*And* she removes one segment from every Terry's Chocolate Orange.'

As Oona steered her away, Asta whispered, 'I went too far, didn't I?' Too late, she'd noticed how the cassock hung on Father Dominic's skeletal frame, how his withered hands shook. Part of her felt she *couldn't* go too far; Father

Dominic had sneered at her when she'd needed compassion. But . . . 'He's an old man, Oona. I should have let it lie.'

'All right, maybe you did go too far; but hang on. I'm not finished.' Qona led her to the window. 'Father Dominic isn't some apple-cheeked old codger. He held this village in a vice for years on end, lording it over us all with his own brand of cruel religion. If it hadn't been for him, your ma might have dealt with you getting pregnant. He could have helped, but he chose to make it worse. So what you said was true.'

Asta wasn't sure how to take this Oona. Sincere and philosophical, she was unrecognizable, as if she'd taken off her make-up and shown her naked self.

'*You*,' said Oona, impassioned, 'are a warrior princess, Asta.' Leaving no time for icky hugs or thank-yous, she pulled the curtain aside and said, 'Would you look at that!'

'What am I looking at?'

Still the snow came down, determined and delicate, on the heads of the faithful. They tramped through the white carpet, churning it grey with their boots.

'We're looking at that temptress, that hussy, that *nympho-maniac*.'

Asta followed Oona's pointed finger, and saw a plump woman in a cagoule.

Joining them at the window, laying a hand across the back of Asta's neck so that she shivered happily from her tailbone to her frontal lobe, Jake said, 'Who is she?'

'Is she . . .' Asta groped for the name. 'It's Emily!' A classmate of theirs, Emily had been a shy girl who stuck posters of the pope on her bedroom walls. 'She hasn't changed a bit.'

Oona swiped a glass from the nearest punter and raised it. 'A toast! To Declan and his new lady love!'

'Already?' Asta was shocked. 'He wouldn't.'

'He would,' snarled Oona. 'And he has.'

'What's Emily like?' asked Jake, mildly.

'Very, very, very, very, very nice.' Oona curled her lip. 'So nice, it makes your eyes water. Doesn't swear. Doesn't drink. Probably doesn't do poos.'

'Language!' shouted Ma from behind the bar.

'She's untouched by human hand.' Oona had an audience, as people turned to listen. 'She time-travels to the eighties to buy her pleated skirts. She swore only once in her life, when a horse trod on her foot, and she refers to that afternoon as her "misspent youth".'

'She sounds like a riot,' said Jake.

As the oblivious woman picked her way past in the snow, Asta said, 'Hang on, doesn't she look just like—'

'Declan's mammy? Yes.'

'Poor Declan.' Asta foresaw a life lived under female thumbs.

'Poor Declan, me arse!' Oona was furious. Her congregation cheered her on, enjoying themselves enormously. 'Didn't he dump me? Didn't he leave me by the side of the road to rot? Didn't he besmirch me in front of the community?'

'Declan's gone up in my estimation,' said Asta. 'I didn't realize he was up to actual besmirching.'

'It's not funny.'

'I know,' said Asta. 'But if you really want Declan back, perhaps you should go easy on the Kenyans and the Japanese and the Swedes and the—'

'You sound like Gerry, advising me to wear higher necklines. Who said,' glowered Oona, 'that I want him back?'

'With respect,' said Asta gently, '*you* did. Nobody makes that much fuss about a man they don't love.'

The drinkers looked at each other and shrugged in a *she's right* way.

'The truth is,' said Oona, 'I shouldn't love him. But I do.'

If Jake hadn't been there, Asta would have said *I know just how you feel.*

The Big House was as cold and still as if it had been placed in an icebox. From its tall windows the view was an expanse of pristine white; inside, a roaring fire blazed defiantly, warming the plaster saint lying on the threadbare chaise longue. Pale, radiant, St Catherine's periwinkle eyes were trained on the broken moulding of the work-in-progress ceiling. Setanta, sniffing the new arrival, gave her bare feet a lick.

'She giggled.' Jake pointed. 'Hallelujah! It's another miracle!' He regarded the prostrate saint warily. 'Where do we start?'

'Let me see . . .' said Asta, reluctant to lay hands on Catherine. Lying there, she looked vulnerable: like any woman about to be examined. Like Asta on the gurney as they'd sped her towards the delivery room sixteen years ago. She felt a kinship with the figure – which was odd, seeing as how the figure was made of plaster. 'I suppose I should examine the base.'

'Or maybe I should examine *you*.' Jake lunged and dipped Asta into a Fred and Ginger pose, his arms dangling her almost full-length. He kissed her, his lips strong and masterful.

'No – gerroff!' Asta wriggled so hard Jake almost dropped her. Inelegantly he pulled her to her feet.

'What?' he asked, crestfallen. 'You don't like the kissing, all of a sudden?' He scratched his head. ''Cos me, I like the kissing.'

'I do like the kissing.' The kissing was Asta's favourite hobby. 'But not in front of you-know-who.' Asta patted her hair and straightened her jumper. 'Doesn't seem right.'

Jake guffawed. 'Once a Catholic, always a Catholic.' He shook his head. 'Cath doesn't mind. Do you, love?' he asked the prone saint. 'In fact, I think she's got a saucy side.' He bent and pecked the statue on her cherry-red lips.

It seemed to Asta that the painted mouth curved ever so slightly. She shook herself. There was work to do. 'Let's find out if she's hollow.' She tapped St Catherine's feet. 'Damn! She's solid. That ruins my favourite theory, the old sponge-in-the-head trick.'

'Unless,' suggested Jake, 'our devious Rory hollowed out a space, buried the sponge and then filled in the hole.' He bowed, waiting for praise.

'You're *good*,' said Asta. 'Ah! But how would they moisten the sponge?'

Jake considered this. 'What if they made a small hole and pushed a tiny tube through?'

'You should debunk miracles for a living.' Asta peered at St Catherine's veil. 'The hole would be in the head, I guess. S'cuse me, miss.' She gingerly lifted the statue to examine the back of the head. 'Nothing,' she concluded, puzzled.

She checked every fold in the gown, the crooks of the

arms, the links of the rosary beads. By the time she'd finished, she knew St Catherine's body better than she knew her own. 'I can't find a single thing out of place.' Asta knelt and studied the saint's eyes, but St Catherine refused to look back; her gaze was firmly on the heavens. Flat, painted, her blue eyes lost their lustre close up. 'The glaze is intact. No holes anywhere.' Asta sighed. 'This statue is perfect, Jake. There's no modification on her whole body.' She shook her head slowly. 'It can't be. It just *can't* be.'

Fate had given her this chance; she mustn't waste it. *I have to bring something home to lay at Conan's feet.* She glanced at Jake guiltily, as if he might read Conan's name on her face. 'The truth is here somewhere.' Like a cat scrabbling under the sofa for a toy mouse, Asta felt the answer was out of her sight but within her reach. 'I'll examine her again.'

Another inch-by-inch exploration. Jake sank into the sofa opposite, a reconditioned Georgian beauty he'd covered in heather-coloured linen. 'Anything?' he asked.

'Nothing!' There *had* to be a clue on St Catherine's body. The only alternative was that the statue really did cry. Which was no alternative at all. 'This was supposed to be the day I solved the mystery. Conan's expecting a big *ta-daa!*'

'It's a setback, that's all.' Jake held out his arms and folded her into an origami embrace. 'Not all mysteries have to be solved. People need secrets. Sometimes they're the only things holding them together.'

This was the perfect moment to ask Jake about his own secrets. Fear held Asta back. Fear of what she might hear, and fear of what she might think of him afterwards. She realized she'd rather remain ignorant than risk hearing something that would compel her to walk away.

Jake got there first with an unexpected question of his own. 'Is there something you're not telling me, Asta? A secret you're keeping from me?'

'Everybody knows my sins all too well.' Asta disliked how easily she skated over the truth. She had more than one secret; she wanted to keep them that way.

Jake looked searchingly at her. 'You look lovely in this snowy light. A real colleen.'

'Nah, mate, I'm a proper Londoner, innit.'

'Never. You're my Irish colleen.' Jake's voice was low. 'And I have plans for you, O freckled one. Setanta, keep an eye on our visitor while I take the fair Princess Assumpta upstairs to have my wicked –' he smiled, slowly – 'my *very* wicked way with her.'

'But we can't . . . it wouldn't be decent.' One of Peg's favourite expressions popped out of Asta's mouth. 'Not with a saint in the house.'

Jake looked at her, held her gaze with the unwavering intensity that was second nature to him. Asta swallowed. This was a straight fight between the old order and the new. Her mouth dry, she asked, 'How wicked, exactly?'

If Asta sat up in Jake's bed she could see fields rolling off into the distance, white and sparkling like Narnia. But she didn't want to sit up. She wanted to play with Jake's chest hair and kiss his shoulders. As pastimes went, it beat crochet.

When Jake's phone jumped, he moved out of her reach. Asta pouted as she heard him say, 'No worries. I'll come and get you.' The bed was the world, as long as they stayed in it. Under the big duvet, fluffy as a marooned cloud, it was as white as everywhere else but a lot more cosy.

'Come on.' Jake threw back the covers and leapt into his underpants, like a fireman. A sexy fireman. 'Rory needs rescuing.'

The truck, one of a selection of knackered utilitarian vehicles that lived in the outbuildings, gripped the deserted road as best it could. People had elected to stay in, next to their fires, dosing themselves with tea.

According to Angie, it had snowed in London; by now the capital would be ankle deep in ugly slush. Here, the snow sat perfect and glittering, turning familiar scenery into an otherworldly landscape. All was calm, as if the clocks had given in.

In limbo, all bets were off; Asta could be somebody else entirely.

'Promise me,' said Jake, eyes narrowed as they negotiated the slippery incline, 'that you won't upset Mrs Huffington with too many questions.'

'*She's* with Rory?'

'Apparently she always goes with him to help hand out Christmas presents at the children's hospital. Only Rory would honour that obligation in weather like this.' Jake looked sideways at Asta. 'The gifts are bigger and better this year, thanks to St Catherine's money-making magic.'

Unhearing, Asta patted her pockets for the audio recorder. 'This is a scoop, Jake!'

'There he is.' In a lay-by, the bike rested on its side, a weary metal horse. Rory was dressed as Father Christmas, his outfit a red splash in the snow. In Asta's recollection, her childhood Santas hadn't been quite so tall or well-built, with motorbike leathers beneath their capes. He trudged towards them, a sack over his shoulder. 'The bike just couldn't cope with the snow. This is so good of you both.' He smiled at Asta, then seemed to notice her expression. 'Are you all right?'

'I'm wondering where you've hidden her.' Asta was hard-nosed. And red-nosed. 'She can come out, Father. I know all about her.'

'You do?' Rory played for time, looking to Jake for help, but Jake had already jumped down from his side of the truck and was squatting by the bike.

'I just want to have a few words with her. Get Mrs Huffington's side of the story.' Asta hesitated. 'I know you're very close.'

'We are,' agreed Rory reluctantly.

'Where's she hiding?' Asta peered around at the white bumps that used to be hedgerows.

'She's right here.' Rory reached into his sack and brought out Mrs Huffington. She'd seen better days; one of her eyes had been replaced with a button.

The sound Asta could hear was Jake's laughter.

'She's a teddy,' said Asta, stating the bleeding obvious.

'But Rory does sleep with her!' shouted Jake. 'That bit was true!'

To: c.orourke@boulevardmagazine.com
From: a.looney@boulevardmagazine.com

Conan!

This is my third email today. Why aren't you replying?

Are you angry 'cos I couldn't crack the secret even with St C in my hot little hands? Or have you keeled over, unable to get the childproof lid off the aspirin bottle? This isn't like you. Please let me know what's going on.

If you look in your oven – I hid them there as I know you never open it – you'll find my Christmas present to you. I knitted you some gloves. They're not cashmere. They're not an elegant shade of taupe. They're rainbow striped and one of the thumbs is a bit (very) long but they'll keep you warm.

To: angie507@hotmail.co.uk
From: a.looney@boulevardmagazine.com

Traditionally, this is the day we take the girls to see the Regent Street lights. It's the first time I've missed it since we met. Since you changed my life with your kindness.

Distance has given me perspective.

I can imagine you and Maisie gazing up at the lights, moaning it's not as good as last year, then having a pizza somewhere. Then you'll stop off at Sainsbury's and haul home the veggies for Christmas Day.

God, I love your roasties, Ange.

You know I don't believe in signs and symbols but maybe, just maybe, things do happen for a reason. The snow forced me to stay, but deep down I wanted to stay, even though I couldn't say it out loud and wouldn't even consider changing my tickets.

When did I get so hard, Angie?

The snow gave me no choice. Is it giving me and Jake a chance? A chance I wouldn't/couldn't give us both?

Conan's little-boy helplessness, beneath all the sophisticated bullshit, touches my heart. And so does Jake's loneliness. I feel like I could help him with his loneliness and his shame, if he'd only share whatever strange truth is right at the heart of him.

And, no, I'm not attributing the snow to St Catherine. Tobercree hasn't addled my brain.

Yet.

The bar's Christmas tree had lost some of its shiny balls. Asta knew how it felt, but, like the tree, she kept calm and carried on.

Kitty passed her mother, a tray in each hand. *The same girl*, thought Asta, as she took orders for stew, stew and more stew, *who won't clear our tiny table after dinner back in London.*

'Where's Finn tonight, love?' called Asta.

'Get off my back, Mother,' called Kitty.

Bashing out carols at the piano, Oona winked at Asta, who winked back. It was easy to bask in the atmosphere, drink in the tinsel-drenched bonhomie. The pub had settled into its new role as relief centre, mainly thanks to Ma's tireless cooking. It felt . . . Asta fumbled for the right word, and came up with *Christmassy.*

Yes, it was Christmassy, with everybody cooped up together, the log-burner churning out heat, food and drink on tap, and that special shimmering sense of Christmas Day drawing nearer and nearer after a whole year of anticipation.

There were rumours of yet more snow on the way. Asta couldn't pin down how that made her feel; fear and joy were now twins. Among the clientele, there was much agitated talk of how the village might be cut off, have to fend for itself.

'Sure, we'll manage,' Ma said over and over. The wording resonated with Asta; that was the very phrase that had tipped her over the edge and sent her off into the night with Kitty warm inside her womb. *Did I misinterpret Ma?* It didn't sound like grim despair; it sounded determined and strong.

Stopping off by the wooden bench where Jake bent over a book, Guinness in hand, Asta said, 'Can I get you anything, kind sir?'

'You could sit on my lap, wench.'

'Too busy, sir. And that constitutes sexual harassment, by the way.' Asta leaned down and kissed him, without even checking that Kitty wasn't watching. 'They're saying we'll be snowed in.'

'Fine by me,' murmured Jake, watching her lips as she spoke.

Isolation, thought Asta, as she wiped the table top, *is why Jake came here in the first place.* 'There'll be no post if we're cut off.'

Jake went back to his pint, his face clouded. 'True,' he said, with a briskness that ended the saucy banter between the kind sir and the wench.

Out in the kitchen, Asta gave Ma the orders – basically *a gazillion stews, please* – and checked her phone. *Are you sulking, Conan?* She bent to empty the dishwasher, puzzling over his silence and wondering what it could mean, when

Oona came in behind her, setting down yet more smeared glasses.

Straightening up, Asta told her cousin of the big bloke sitting by the back doors who was undressing her with his eyes. 'Admittedly, you've already done most of the work for him.'

'Is he built like a wardrobe? That'll be Afanasy. He keeps blowing me kisses.' Oona was inert, tired, her usual glow dimmed. 'I'll write *feck off* in the foam on his Guinness. I'm not in the mood.'

'He has the look of a wardrobe in love.'

'I want my little Dec back.' Oona blurted it out, as if the words had been welling up inside her.

Asta melted with compassion. 'Oh, Oona.'

Her voice faltering, Oona said, 'Seeing him with Emily is driving me nuts. Gallivanting about, wearing matching Fair Isles, shopping for his mammy's surgical stockings together. He looks so . . .'

'Happy?' suggested Asta, ducking in case Asta lashed out.

'Exactly!' Oona was outraged. 'Who gave Declan permission to be happy without me?'

'It's just a rebound thing. You'll win him back.'

'How?'

'First, and most crucially, I suggest you stop having sex with random foreigners.'

'Spoilsport.'

'And maybe stop wearing high heels, low tops and short skirts all at once. Just wear one at a time.'

'You sound like Gerry. That was her suggestion.'

Asta feared she sounded like a 1950s women's magazine: *wear a pretty frock to reel in Mr Right.* She took a loaded tray back out to the bar, uncertain why anybody should trust her on the subject of love. Then she caught sight of Jake, and his smile that was just for her, despite their hiccup. The thread between them was still taut.

The door opened, and polka dots of snow gusted in with Rory. Asta found him a seat and wiped the table in front of him, grateful he was alone. She dreaded Father Dominic more than ever since her outburst, as if the old man was a mirror for all her failings. 'Is St Catherine happy to be home again?'

'Of course. But I think she enjoyed herself with you and Jake. She's a gregarious girl.'

'I found her a little tight-lipped.' Asta put her hands on her hips and looked down at Rory. 'We found nothing. Your secret's safe.'

Whispering so that Asta had to bend down to hear, Rory said, 'What if the secret is, there is no secret?' He smiled. 'What if you're the secret?'

'Me?' Asta jumped and hoped he didn't notice. *Why is everybody talking about* my *secrets all of a sudden?* 'St Catherine's nothing to do with me.'

'We're all connected,' said Rory. 'And we all have secrets.' He held her gaze, obviously aware that she was thinking *especially you.* 'How we handle them, who we share them with – these things make all the difference.'

There was no time for further priestly philosophy, because Oona emerged from the kitchen, shouting, 'Is this outfit conservative enough, Asta?'

The whole bar clapped and roared as Oona, dressed as a nun, leapt to her habitual position on top of the piano and gave them all a twirl. 'Who could resist me?' she yelled, showing a great deal of nunnish leg as Asta bent double, hooting with laughter.

'I love that girl!' she cried.

'Me too,' said Rory, slapping the table.

The door flew open, slamming back on its hinges. Like a gunfighter in a Western movie, the newcomer had the bar's complete attention. Even Oona stopped can-canning.

A man filled the door frame, wrapped up against the tempest. Snow crusted his eyebrows, his nose was raw and when he said 'Is this Looney's?' it was in an American accent.

'Conan!' Asta heard herself squeal, and the bar came to life again as Conan kicked the door shut and crossed the room in two paces, crushing her in his freezing arms and kissing the top of her head. Letting her down but not letting go, he said, 'Never, *ever* go away again.'

Pressed tightly against Conan, Asta could just see Jake regarding them both with a look of intense concentration, trying to work out what he was seeing, like an explorer confronted with a Yeti or similarly inexplicable phenomenon.

As Conan gathered her up again and swung her around, she saw Jake drain his glass and bang it down on the table.

The whole of Looney's was watching the newcomer, but the women were watching especially hard. Ma hovered; Oona ripped off her wimple and applied lipstick; Gerry fluttered up to gossip heaven; Peg emerged from the kitchen, ready to be outraged.

'You must be the famous Ma!' Conan ignored the outstretched hand and hugged Ma until she squeaked. 'I see where your daughter gets the twinkle in her eye.'

Asta felt as if the world had tilted. Conan couldn't be here, and yet here he was. Her two realities had collided. She looked around wildly for Jake, not sure whether her heart was hammering because of Conan's arrival or with trepidation at what Jake must be thinking. *Probably both*, she thought. *As I'm now officially two people.*

Drinkers crowded Conan as if he were a celebrity; his demeanour demanded it. Conan now owned Looney's. As he unwrapped himself from tweed and cashmere, even Peg seemed won over by the corn-fed handsome looks that emerged. He pumped her hand, and her posture softened. He slapped men on the back. He kissed Oona full on the lips. He even petted a dog.

Asta, a hapless First Lady at his side, looked about for Jake. 'How did you get here?' she asked Conan incredulously, as somebody handed him a pint. 'The snow . . .' It was impossible. 'There are *no planes*.'

'I called in a favour from a chum.' Conan broke off to shout 'Cheers!' and the pub, as one, shouted *Cheers!* right back. 'A chum with a boat. He didn't want to brave the waters, but I have some pretty dirty dirt on him which he wants kept out of the media, so I twisted his arm. Then I hired this beast of a four-wheel drive in Dublin and threw money at a driver until he took the job, and here I am!'

Appearing at Asta's shoulder, Jake said, 'That sounds like a risky journey in this weather.'

'I had to get here, bro. Simple as that.'

Conan put his arm around Asta, and the irony almost floored her. *He chooses this moment to finally get touchy-feely?*

Conan beamed at Jake. 'Christmas wouldn't be Christmas without this gal.'

'What if other people felt the same way?' Jake was low and deliberate, a contrast to the party frothing around him.

Conan didn't seem to catch on; he remained jubilant. 'I'd tell them I have a prior claim!'

As Jake turned away, pushing through the crowd, Asta shook off Conan's arm and followed him. 'Wait,' she said. 'Hang on, Jake, please.' She sounded desperate; she felt it.

'I'm gonna shoot off,' said Jake, turning a serene and untroubled face to her. His eyes were cold, as if somebody had run around inside him switching off lights.

'He's not . . . This isn't . . .'

'Why not call me when you have your story straight, yeah?'

One cold waft of snowy air, and he was gone.

Conan stood back as Asta did her Personal Assistant thang.

'You're sure this is your best room? My boss has had a long journey, and he needs the best available amenities.'

Mrs Hannigan looked at Asta quizzically. 'As you know, it's me only room, love.' Bessie Hannigan's B&B was famed far and wide (well, to the outer fringes of the village) for the flammable qualities of its bedding, but it was the only berth for miles around thanks to the double whammy of St Catherine and the snowstorm.

'Does it have en suite facilities?' Asta was businesslike.

'What's them? Oh, I see what you mean. Yes, indeed,' said Mrs Hannigan proudly. 'Well, not exactly en suite. But he only has to share them with little old me.' She looked coquettish; she'd put her teeth in especially.

As Asta showed Conan to his attic room, pointing out the portion of it in which he could stand up, she said, 'I know this isn't what you're used to. If you'd given me some notice, I could have—'

'But giving you notice would have spoiled everything.' Conan frowned, his butch cherub face discombobulated. 'Although,' he said, lowering his voice (they both knew Mrs Hannigan was crouched outside the bedroom door), 'something already seems to have spoiled everything. Asta?' he pushed, when she said nothing. 'I thought you'd be pleased.'

'I am. I *am*.' She was. A week ago, Conan's appearance would have thrilled Asta to her core. She would have wondered, *is this it? Has he fallen at last?*

Up until this moment, Conan and Jake had been safely tucked into different boxes. Side by side, they were a bit much. As if she'd been given too many Christmas presents.

Asta wouldn't have believed such a thing was possible.

Scowling, Conan put a hand through his jaunty black hair. 'You're different here, Asta.' He sighed, the energy leaving his body. 'I'm whacked. Remind me why I can't crash at your ma's? She offered me the spare room.'

'She's overtired. She forgot there's already somebody staying in it.'

'I can tell when you're lying.'

'No, you can't,' laughed Asta. 'I lie to you on a daily basis. I lie that I've put two shots of whisky in your glass when I've only put one. I lie that I've sent off your column to your editor when actually I'm still correcting all the spelling mistakes. I lie that it's ten o'clock when it's only nine o'clock in order to get you out of bed. I lie—'

'OK, OK.' Conan put his hands to his head, warding her off. 'I get it. But I knew all those times that you were lying.'

'Now *you're* lying.' Asta giggled. This easy nonsense took her back to a place where she could be happy with Conan.

She gazed covertly at him as he sank onto the narrow bed, pulling at his shoes and socks like a circus bear.

'Good night.' Asta heard Mrs Hannigan trip over her own slippers as the landlady scuttled away.

'I didn't pack any, um, underwear.' Conan rooted in the butter-soft suede bag he'd brought on his odyssey. 'Or toothpaste. Or a toothbrush, come to that, so I guess the toothpaste doesn't matter.' He looked up, his face pouchy with exhaustion in the orange light thrown by Mrs Hannigan's nylon lampshade. 'See? I'm lost without you.'

'Conan . . .' Asta could cross the shabby room, nuzzle into him, start something she'd fantasized about for years. She was capable of sober sex; Asta was in charge of her desires.

That's why I'll walk away. There was thinking to do. 'Come back to the pub for breakfast, yeah?'

'And we'll talk,' said Conan. It wasn't a question. He was the boss.

Asta ran home, soles crunching on the new snow that settled on the thick ridges of the old, covering all Tobercree's blemishes.

She had her phone in her hand, waiting for it to buzz, but Jake was leaving her message dangling. *Let me explain*, she'd begged the indifferent ear of his answerphone.

Outside the silent, sleeping pub, she was at a cold crossroads. If she ran, she could be at Jake's door in ten minutes. If he wouldn't let her in, she could shout through the letterbox. What she'd shout, she wasn't sure, but she hoped for divine inspiration.

No. Asta pushed at the door and slipped across the bar

and up the stairs. Snappy, eyes on the floor, Kitty had been semaphoring her distress all evening. Her daughter needed her, and that trumped everything.

Kitty sat up in the dark of their room as Asta entered. 'Mum?'

Asta knelt by the camp bed. 'Yes, sweetie?'

'Oh, Mum!' Kitty flung herself at her mother, weeping, gabbling, almost knocking her backwards.

'Ssh, ssh, darling.' Asta clambered in beside her, holding her gently as the storm of tears, echoing the white squall outside the square of window, ran its course.

'I can't . . . get Finn . . . on the phone.' Kitty hiccuped out her woes; a story as old as the hills. Hearing her daughter reach the milestone discovery that men could be cruel made Asta feel ancient herself. 'He . . . won't answer my . . . messages.'

I know how you feel.

'Somebody . . . saw him . . .' Kitty clung harder, cried harder. 'He was with a girl. How could he? I thought he liked me.'

'He did, does, like you.' Asta pushed Kitty's hair away from her face. 'If he doesn't realize how special you are, he's a fool, KitKat.'

'He likes her better than me.'

'That's not it, sweetie. Finn's unreliable.' If only Asta could bottle all she'd learned and hand it to Kitty in one easy dose. These painful hurdles were how the girl would learn, but it was hard to watch. 'He's not worth your tears.'

It took a while to cry it all out. As they lay, comfortably entwined, Kitty's damp face wiped and her nose blown and her power of coherent speech returned, Kitty said, 'I do have one reason to thank Finn the fink.'

This was his new nickname; Asta was proud of the alliteration. 'What's that?' Her leg had gone to sleep, but she didn't want to disturb Kitty by moving it.

'He found a letter from one of the French foreign exchange students in his mum's stuff. Jean-Paul something. I'm going to write to him. I'm going to track down my dad.'

Asta stared at the snow's eerie shadows on the bedroom wall.

Kitty went on, 'You'll help me, won't you, Mum? This is, like, the biggest thing in my life.'

'There's stuff you don't know, Kitty.'

'Because you won't tell me!' Her outrage made Kitty yawn; it had been a long day for all of them. She settled down, kneading Asta as if she was a pillow. 'If you were me,' she said, sounding like the little Kitty she used to be, 'you'd want to know your dad, wouldn't you?'

'I would, sweetheart.'

Asta resisted the drooping of her eyelids. Tonight, of all nights, the dream would surely pounce.

The voice calls her name again. It's amplified, as if every tree in the forest has a mouth, all of them screaming 'Asta!' There is accusation in the sound, and threat.

The treehouse jolts violently and then drops like a stone, with nothing to impede its progress as it falls.

When it lands, it will break open, dumping Asta on the gritty ground, naked, for all to see.

December 24th

The breakfast table was cluttered with both food and people. Ma sliced bread as if competing in the bread-slicing Olympics; Gerry chuntered on about how St Catherine had almost cried – or, to put it another way, hadn't cried at all. Oona reached over Asta for the butter: dairy products, she claimed, were good for a broken heart.

'Give it here, then.' Kitty accepted the clucks and sighs. Even though the girl was suffering her first real heartache, she vibrated with energy, and not just because of the sparkling atmosphere of Christmas Eve.

She's excited about finding her dad. Asta, the Queen of Christmas, felt thwarted that she couldn't just enjoy the charged character of the day before the Big Day. The sight of that glittery twenty-four on the advent calendar – broken heart or no, Kitty had beaten her to the chocolate – made Asta long to pull on her elf costume and tap dance.

I've begun to thaw just as the snow settles. After days of exposure to her clan's clumsy togetherness, Asta could admit that she'd been trying for years to recreate this effortless family feeling with Kitty in their flat. Suddenly cut off from the family home as a teenager, she'd never had the opportunity to outgrow it.

'There's a rumour,' said Ma, 'that the statue will cry at Christmas.'

'Who started the rumour?' asked Asta.

'Me,' said Ma.

'That Conan fella,' said Gerry pointedly, looking at Asta. 'Now, *there's* a catch. If you nab him, Asta, you'll be set for life. You could even buy a house like mine.'

There was no need to point out that Conan could buy Gerry's entire housing estate with his loose change.

'He went through hell and high water to get here,' continued Gerry. 'If I was you, I'd dump that Jake and slap the handcuffs on Conan.'

As usual, Conan had thrown money at his problems. There was always somebody standing by to help smooth the way in return for pounds and pence. *I've been one of those people*, thought Asta.

'Lovely hair,' said Ma, approvingly. 'Lovely coat. Lovely manners. Lovely speaking voice. And an Irish name!'

'Is he coming here for Christmas lunch?' asked Oona. No *phwoar*! No theories about what he'd be like in bed. *Plus she's wearing a polo neck*. Asta barely recognized her cousin.

'I don't know.'

'Of course he is!' Ma was scandalized. 'Where else would he go?' She glanced at the turkey awaiting a good stuffing on the worktop. It could feed the entire village and still have enough left over for the mandatory sandwiches.

I haven't made plans with Jake for tomorrow. Asta checked her phone. No texts from Jake since last night. She pecked at the digits.

Come to lunch here tomorrow?! x

An answer landed immediately.

Conan the Barbarian's probably taken my seat.

Asta couldn't think of a reply, other than *Apparently your phone's been stolen by a sixth former. Called Daphne.*

I should be peeling potatoes. Planning gravy. Circling the programmes we're going to watch in the Radio Times. Instead Asta was on her childhood bed, reworking the article yet again. She slapped the words around, trying to disguise the lack of hard facts, until the story fell apart in her lap. Conan might have disowned the project, but Asta hadn't.

When Ma asked for help with the lunchtime rush, Asta was glad of the distraction.

Kitty looked adorable in a frilly apron over her skinny jeans, expertly taking orders. '*Oui*,' she said, to a table of four. 'Le beef is definitely organic, monsieur.'

Asta shuddered at the mongrel French. The only Christmas present Kitty wanted from her mother was the green light for her Find-A-Daddy quest. Popping her head into the kitchen, Asta's eyes widened.

Breaking a rule of a lifetime, Ma had put a man to work.

Conan's lily-white hands were wielding kitchen utensils for the very first time. Chopping carrots with an outstretched arm, as if they might fight back, he let out a feminine scream when the pot of potatoes boiled over.

Rescuing him, Asta popped him behind the bar, where she taught him how to pull a pint. They got up close for this, her hand over his as he grasped the pump. He was solid, bulky. *However flighty Conan is, he's been my rock for years*, thought Asta.

Assistants were ten a penny in London. Conan had stuck with his untrained PA, paid her more than she asked and welcomed her grubby-fingered tot into his high-end home. His need for Asta had helped her feel relevant in a new country; he'd supplied a feeling of home when she felt like an orphan.

The entire bar applauded when Conan pulled a perfect pint, amiably forgetting the five he'd thrown down the plug hole. Conan punched the air and downed the pint in one, holding Asta to him as his fans cheered.

This closeness was the stuff of Asta's fairy tales. Conan's joke of the previous night was correct; he *did* have a prior claim on her. *Yet here I am neurotically checking my phone every three minutes.*

Conan, big beautiful Conan, was the Christmas gift Asta had yearned for, dropping hints to Santa all year round. But now that she'd unwrapped her present, she had no idea what to do with it.

Her mobile buzzed and Asta jumped.

Fancy a drink? Or are you busy?

The response was rewritten more than the article.

Christmas has a way of distorting things. In its flattering light – all candles and crystals – everything looks great. What if her affair with Jake looked different when the fairy lights fizzled out? Asta wondered what she'd be left with when she went back to London: a photo or two, and the memory of Jake's mouth on her body? She could be passing up a future with Conan for a man she didn't really know.

I don't need a drink, but I do need to talk.

The silence was deafening. Both the statue and Jake were

holding out on Asta. Only Rory knew their secrets. But Jake . . . Asta realized she had a mole. *As we professional reporters say.*

At the post office, Gerry celebrated Christmas Eve with earrings that lit up, and by saying 'Merry Christmas!' in a tone that somehow undermined her customers.

Asta ushered out a small farmer, a quiet man who was rumoured to be embroiled in a love triangle with two of his prettier sheep, and turned the sign on the door to 'Closed'.

'Hey!' Gerry was incensed. She loved being incensed.

'I don't have long; Ma's snowed under. Literally. I need your help.'

'Huh. You? You never needed anybody's help, Asta.'

Shrinking, Asta felt embarrassed for her sister's lack of compassion. What did Gerry think she'd been doing in London for all these years? Skipping down Carnaby Street with the Beatles?

'You know it all, Asta. Always have done.' Gerry stared her down.

Perhaps, thought Asta, *it's not lack of compassion. Perhaps it's a failure of imagination.* Seen through Gerry's eyes, Asta was the sister who ran away to the glittering metropolis, who seldom called and never visited.

Gerry hadn't even moved out of the village. Her horizons had – quite literally – remained the same; the sun sank beneath the same hills every night for Gerry. How could she understand the compulsion to flee that had propelled Asta across the sea?

'We need to cut through the bullshit, Ger. Shrug off the past and talk to me like a woman. This is just you and me. No Martin. No Ma. I *do* need your help.' She hesitated, unsure how frank to be; Gerry might use it against her at some point. 'For the record, I've always needed my big sis.'

Gerry sniffed.

'Tell me, Gerry. What is Jake running from?'

There was silence. Gerry didn't bother bleating that she'd never tamper with the mail.

'It's like this,' she began.

Turning the sign to 'Open', Gerry joined her sister on the step. 'So now you know.' She fussed with Asta's scarf and pulled her knitted hat tighter down around her ears.

'Yup.' Asta turned to go, but Gerry grasped Asta's arm. The siblings rarely touched; Gerry's fingers were thin and strong, made to the same design as Ma's. 'I'm sorry, Asta. About calling Kitty Frenchy.'

Asta wanted to cheer. *Another miracle in Tobercree!*

'When she tackled me about it and explained how it made her feel, I felt just *awful.*'

'*Kitty* tackled you?' gulped Asta.

'She was right. She told me I'm the only aunt she's got and I should be on her side.'

Talking truth to Gerry took guts. Asta's daughter had sorted out her problem in a mature and measured manner, without roping in Mummy to help.

The sisters parted. The street, white and bright and incandescent, was like a scene in a snow globe shaken by some giant hand. The whitewash of the Big House served as camouflage; screened by falling snow, it might not be there at all. Somewhere in its faded rooms was Jake. Asta's new knowledge burned inside her, but another foot of snow had fallen. The lane was impassable on foot. She couldn't reach Jake if she wanted to; he may as well be a hundred miles away.

Looney's pulsated with warmth and cheer. And mild drunkenness.

Peg had brought Father Dominic in for a quick pre-mass stew. Asta, still in her outdoor gear, took the bowl from Ma's hands and laid it in front of the old priest.

It was a time for truces; bridges are built, not burned, at Christmas. Father Dominic thanked her politely. Nothing more than that. But it was enough.

In a holly-patterned pinny, Conan had been promoted from barman to head waiter. Ma whispered to Asta that he'd been downing a drink for every one he sold. Spotting Asta as he handed out menus, he grinned his dazzling grin. Work was a novelty for Conan. *That's him taken care of*, thought Asta. Conan could only concentrate on one thing at a time.

'Men!' said Oona at Asta's elbow. 'I have none. You have two. Yet we both have a face like a slapped bum.'

'To be accurate, you have more men than me.' Half the menfolk in the bar had Oona's teethmarks on them, like branded cattle.

'I don't want them, though. You know that nauseous feeling at the end of Christmas day when you've eaten all the Quality Street? That's how I feel, but about men.' She pointed at the wardrobe-shaped chap who was still making goo-goo eyes at her. 'He's a Green Triangle. Me favourite. But I'm *full*.'

'What's Declan in this analogy?'

'I can't reduce the love of my life to Christmas confectionery.' Oona looked affronted. 'Maybe I should get meself down to St Catherine and pray for him to dump Emily.' She poached a paper hat from a nearby head and placed it on her own ginger curls. 'I wish I had your problems.'

'No, you don't. Whatever I do, somebody gets hurt.'

'That,' said Oona, 'is life.'

The Big House was fading up on its ridge.

When Oona turned away from the window, she almost collided with the ramrod figure of her aunt.

'If you're going to stand there staring like a wet nelly,' said Peg, 'you might as well go and see him.' She tutted; Peg tutted twice as much over Christmas.

'I want to, more than anything.' Asta didn't care that her aunt would mock such lovesick baloney. 'But the snow's too deep to go on foot.'

'Then drive, you silly girl.' When Peg heard that her niece had never learned this basic skill, she turned and prodded a burly man at an adjacent table who was just about to put a dumpling in his mouth.

'You. Jimmy McGuire. Give me the keys to your vehicle.' When he hesitated, she snapped, 'Church business!' and, meekly, he handed them over.

'Come on, you.' Peg led Asta outside.

The wind slashing at her cheeks, Asta waddled through the banked snow. Above, the sky was already dark.

'Jump in!' Peg hauled herself up into the driving seat of

a tractor whose monster tyres stood higher than Asta's head. 'Get a move on,' she tutted.

Peg tutted all the way up the main street as the tractor trundled over the snow, unleashing a special tut for the darkened mill shop, more noticeable than ever in the bright Christmas Eve frenzy of last-chance shoppers. 'Crying shame,' she said under her breath.

Like its driver, the tractor took no nonsense, and smaller vehicles careered out of their way. Blessing herself as they passed the church, Peg turned the enormous wheels onto the lane.

'Now, listen. If this Jake fella hurts you, you tell him he has me to contend with.'

Nodding, Asta realized that in a contest between Jake and her aged aunt, she'd bet on Peg. Thinking back past the endless scolding and the constant lectures, Asta allowed other memories to surface. Aunty Peg saving Asta the choicest slice of apple pie, taking her side against Gerry in sibling battles, holding her small hot hand on the way home from mass.

I was always your favourite.

There was so much Asta could say to her aunt's profile, a stern outline never muddied with make-up or serum or anti-ageing potions. If she crossed a line by gushing, Aunty Peg would recoil, favourite niece or not. 'I didn't know you could drive,' was all she said.

'I can't.' The tractor clipped a signpost. 'Oops,' said Aunty Peg, the end of her long nose so red with cold it looked like a poker.

'Look!' Asta saw a figure take shape in the headlights. It was male, labouring through the deep white drifts as if wading in the sea, waving its arms to be noticed.

'It's a bad night to be out on foot. Ah, I recognize him.' Peg applied the squealing brake. 'Finn!' she shouted, as the tractor idled, breathing heavily like a dragon under her spell. 'D'you need a lift, son?'

Finn beamed, turning creakily in the snow towards them.

Keeping schtum, Asta bowed her head. Her aunt was a Christian lady, a good Samaritan. Picking up Finn on such a night was the right and proper thing to do. *Even if the little so-and-so trashed my daughter's heart.*

Peg pushed at the creaky window and leaned out as Finn laboured towards them, gratitude all over his face in place of the more usual boredom.

'Thanks very—'

A snowball landed squarely in his face, knocking him backwards to lie spread-eagled in the snow.

'*That's* for our Kitty!' Peg gunned the engine, leaving Finn on his back, staring after them.

When Asta had finished laughing – it felt good to guffaw after all her soul-searching – she said, 'So Kitty told you about Finn leaving her high and dry?'

'Indeed she did.' Peg squinted through the filthy windscreen. 'Poor scrap. She's too good for the likes of that waster.' The tractor slowed. 'Out you hop, young one.'

They'd reached the high iron gates. Asta landed on the compacted snow, turning to make a short speech, one that did justice to this extraordinary woman.

'You can get yourself home. I'm not a taxi service.'

The tractor reversed at insane speed. Tough love. Asta expected nothing less from her aunt.

The only source of light in the drawing room was the skittering amber flame in the marble fireplace. Jake had closed the shutters on the ethereal, white night.

'It must have been exciting,' said Asta, from the velvet armchair where she nursed a glass of wine. Stuffing had burst through the seams, and the fabric was worn.

Standing by the grate, his clean features jumping in the firelight, Jake said, 'Maybe that's why I'm blasé about miracles. One happened to me.' He stoked the logs. 'But then everything began to unravel. There was nobody to talk to about it. I didn't know anybody who'd been through the same thing.'

'People fantasize about it.' Asta was one of those people.

'Not me.' Jake threw himself into an even more knackered armchair opposite Asta's. 'I've never fantasized about winning the lottery.'

'Tell me about it.' By tacit agreement, Conan had been moved to the back burner until they discussed Gerry's revelation. Asta settled back, and a metal spring poked through the velvet into her bottom. 'I'm all ears.'

'OK.' Jake leaned forward, into the sacred circle of the firelight. 'I had a job. A normal job, a proper one. I was – am, I dunno – an IT consultant.'

'Sexy,' said Asta, before mouthing *sorry* and letting him carry on. The wine had gone to her head.

'I had a flat. A decent car.' Jake scratched his head, as if struggling to find anything of interest to say. 'I come from an ordinary family. I was hopeless at school. Dad buggered off when I was tiny, left me and Mum to it. Not so much as a birthday card.'

Jake paused, seeming to remember some fresh detail. 'When I was at college I got myself into a mess with my rent. I needed a hundred quid. I rang my dad and he said "no". Just like that. Fair enough, I suppose, but it hurt.'

'I'm not surprised.' Asta was on Jake's side. So far.

'I left home as soon as I could. My stepdad . . .' Jake ruminated and finally said, 'He's not the nicest man in the world.'

'Is he a sod?'

'He's a sod,' nodded Jake.

'So. There you are with your job, your flat, your car.'

'And a girlfriend. Karen.'

Asta had never liked Karens.

'I met her through a mate and she was well fit.' Jake stopped dead. 'If you like that sort of thing.'

'Which you obviously do. Which is fine. Even the International Court of Mental Girlfriends allows you to have prior relationships.'

'Karen and me . . .' Jake grimaced, as if trying to get his head around the subject. 'We got on well enough, but it was a dead end, and we both knew it. I wasn't sure about her and she really wasn't sure about me.

Nuh nuh ni nuh nuh, Karen! sang the idiot child inside Asta's head.

'One week, my mum made me buy a lottery ticket. For a laugh. I used family birthdays to choose the numbers. Suddenly, it was a tradition, and my mum gave me grief if I didn't get one. Mum'd watch the results show and I'd go, every week, *Calm down, Mum, I'm not going to win.* Until one Saturday . . .'

'You won,' said Asta.

'Karen and I were in a Chinese, having one of our very boring arguments. She wasn't good at rows like you are.'

'Why, thank you.'

'Karen was pissed off with me as usual, shooting me dirty looks and playing with her hair. My phone went and it was my mum, screaming that my numbers had come up. Karen told the whole restaurant, and suddenly the whole place was cheering, there was a bottle of dreadful champagne on the table and Karen was madly in love with me.'

'Really?'

'She was looking at me like she was planning to blow-job me to death.'

'Nice.'

'Sorry. Sometimes I forget you're a girl.'

'Again – nice.' Asta asked, tentatively, 'How much did you win?'

'I can't tell you without wetting myself,' said Jake. 'A lot. Double whatever you're thinking. So much that I immediately gave half to charities. Cancer, 'cos my granddad died of it. The NSPCC. The RSPCA. All anonymously. Which is harder than you'd imagine.'

'Why anonymously?'

'I didn't want any fuss. The money was a stroke of dumb luck. I didn't need to be thanked.'

'Not everybody would feel that way.'

'Well, I did. I gave all my friends a hundred grand.'

Asta tried to imagine somebody plonking a hundred thousand pounds in her lap.

Allowing himself a smile, Jake said, 'That was the last really good . . .' He stopped, collected his thoughts. 'The complaints began. Relatives took me to one side, saying blood is thicker than water, why didn't they get more than my mates. One bloke told me he'd been a better friend than anybody else and deserved an extra nought. Somebody else pointed out that if I could see my way clear to another fifty

K, he could get his hands on a Porsche. My aunt even kicked off about the amount I'd given to charity. "Charity begins at home", she said. And ends there, according to her.'

'I'm shocked.'

'So was I. My dad turned up. I remember throwing my arms around him. I'd waited so long and there he was. My *dad*.'

'Hmm,' said Asta.

'*Hmm* is right. Before he'd even said hello he was pontificating about his "rights", wanting more money than my mates because he was my dad. I wanted him to hang around, I wanted to get to know him. So I wrote him a huge cheque.'

'And?' Asta winced in anticipation.

'He buggered off again.'

'*No!*'

'Don't worry. He came back. Asking for more each time. And each time I gave in.'

'Why?'

'Because the money wasn't really mine. I hadn't earned it.' Jake's mouth twisted with the effort of making himself understood. 'And by then . . . it felt like dirty money. It had a weird effect on people, as if I was seeing them in a fairground mirror, all distorted. I tell you, if you want to see the human race at its worst, don't travel to a war zone. Just win the lottery.'

'And Karen . . . ?'

'Hanging on my every word,' laughed Jake. 'Head to toe in Prada, drinking Moët like it was Tizer. I wouldn't have bought that huge house in Hampstead if it wasn't for Karen. She almost had an orgasm when she realized it had a gym.'

'Why did you buy a house you didn't like?' Asta thought of Jake's attachment to the room they sat in.

'Because I could.' Jake looked sardonic. 'On a whim. Crazy behaviour. Having so much dosh overnight was like being drunk. My judgement was shot to bits. I could afford almost anything. I was like Elton John. But with hair. And straight. And taller. And—'

'I get it,' said Asta.

'I'd always made furniture, in my shed. But it looked all wrong in my rock-star mansion.'

'Please tell me,' said Asta, 'that *some* people behaved decently.'

'My oldest mate, Steve, was a diamond. He said I should have kept it quiet. And he was right.' Jake ran his lean fingers over his face. 'If I went out for a curry with mates, it seemed absurd not to put my hand in my pocket when everybody knew about my riches. Don't get me wrong; I was happy to pay and I left tips that made waiters try to kiss me. But it's the principle, isn't it? I felt like a mug. Everything was out of whack. And Karen . . . blimey. She was a robot version of the old Karen. Nicey-nice, round the clock. I started to miss the stupid rows. She hired an interior designer to redo an immaculate house. She commissioned a giant fish tank in the kitchen floor. The worst bit was the slowing down when we passed jewellers.' Jake looked into the past, still disbelieving. 'She acted like she was madly in love with me, but we both knew she'd been treading water, waiting for a better offer.'

'Then, hey presto, *you* were the better offer.'

'Exactly. Wealth is poisonous. It makes people lose their heads. I imagined it glowing in the bank vault, like nuclear waste.' Jake put his head on one side. 'This drivel must be so boring for you.'

'Are you kidding?' *We haven't reached the bit you're*

ashamed of yet. If Asta and Jake were to stand a chance, if he was to finally outrun Conan, he had to share everything with her. A puritanical voice deep inside asked Asta if she was willing to do the same; but if she concentrated hard on Jake's story, she couldn't quite hear the puritanical voice.

'Steve and I still went out for a drink now and then, but conversation was tricky. After years of ending each other's sentences, Steve was careful with me. As if he didn't believe I could be interested in his working day because I'd packed in my own job. Having more money than everybody in your office building put together is a motivation killer, but what Steve didn't realize was that I *missed* having a reason to get up.' Jake heaved a long sigh. 'When Steve's building firm let him go, he was devastated. But it took him ages to tell me, in case I thought he was on the scrounge.'

The pause for thought lengthened until Asta prompted Jake with, 'And then?'

'And then . . .' Jake exhaled, his cheeks plumped. 'The begging letters began. The lottery people had warned me, but nothing really prepares you for . . . Apparently most of them are false. Even so,' said Jake, in a defeated voice, 'they made me cry. There's so much sadness in the world, Asta! Tragedy, illness, bereavement all flooded through my letterbox every morning. I answered each one with a cheque. Then I noticed certain addresses cropping up again, but with a different story. Trying to sort out the genuine letters from the spongers took hours out of every day. But I felt . . .' Jake closed his eyes. 'I felt like I had a duty to help. But reading all those tales . . .' His smile was wan. 'It made me feel hopeless. I had nobody to talk to about it.' Jake looked at Asta with defenceless honesty. '*You* weren't there,' he said.

'No,' agreed Asta softly. 'I wasn't. Naughty me.'

'I came up with a system to stop myself going mad. Now I just send everybody a cheque for the same amount. Which means the spongers get paid for lying and people who genuinely need more don't get it . . . it's not easy doing good!' Jake stood abruptly and refilled his glass with brandy.

Here comes the nitty gritty. Asta wanted to hold him, but she stayed in her decaying armchair, wary of distracting him.

'The money isolated me. I was a different person, a man with no job who slept in every day, with hangers-on for friends and human misery mounting up on his posh doormat. Then my dad turned up again. "You're no son of mine if you won't write me a cheque."' Jake took a swig of brandy, and pulled a face as it burned. 'All through my childhood I'd told myself that deep down my real dad loved me, that he'd come home one day, rescue me and we'd be happy again. I just wanted to kick a ball around the park with him, you know?'

Missing dads; Asta bent her head. She thought of Kitty and she made a decision, there and then, in the moment before Jake picked up his story again.

'I gave him twice the amount he wanted, and left the house. I jumped in the fuck-off-fabulous Mercedes parked outside my front door. I drove to the airport. I saw the Aer Lingus desk. I thought *hmm, I've never been to Ireland* – and I bought a ticket.'

'Why not somewhere hot?' Asta was quietly impressed that Mr Moneybags had opted for rainy old Erin.

'I didn't want a holiday,' said Jake. 'I wanted sanctuary.'

'And you told nobody where you went.' They were at the black heart of the story.

'I ran away. Nobody knows where I am, not even my mum. My poor mum . . .' Jake put his hand over his eyes.

Asta recalled the photograph so hastily stuffed in a drawer the first time she'd been in this house.

'Steve, Karen, I dumped them all. They didn't deserve it. I should have ended things with Karen. I should have cried on Steve's shoulder. But I couldn't take that stupid life any longer. I *fled.*'

'But the begging letters followed you.' The mystery of the envelope mountain in Jake's kitchen was solved.

'I left a forwarding address with the post office. Ironic, isn't it? I discarded my loved ones but I invited all those strangers along for the ride.'

'It's called a conscience. It's nothing to be ashamed of.'

Jake didn't seem convinced.

'Anyway, I got off the plane, jumped in a cab, told the driver to take me somewhere quiet – and he dropped me here. This was pre-statue, when it *was* quiet. I stayed at Mrs Hannigan's for a week.' He nodded at Asta's *eew*. 'Which was a week too long. Then I found this place. Love at first sight. That was the one time I felt truly good about the dosh. I wrote a cheque on the spot and this piece of history, this gorgeous pile of bricks, was mine.' Jake looked around the shadowy room as if he couldn't quite believe it.

'You could have clicked your fingers and summoned a team of builders to refurbish it.'

'I needed something to do! I needed something to be proud of. Something I could point at and say *I did that*, rather than *I bought that*. That's why I'm taking it room by room. And making furniture.' He looked sheepish. 'That's when I'm really happy, if you want to know the truth. When

I'm planing wood, or carving the joint of a drawer. That's when I feel normal.'

'I've got news for you, Jake. You *are* normal.'

'I'm a normal coward. A normal liar. I wake up every morning and it hits me. The mess I left behind. Every day takes me a step further on this road and makes the mess worse, yet I can't turn back. I can't face it.' More brandy. Another scowl. 'That's how fucked up I am. The fact that my crime gets worse every day I stay away, actually *makes* me stay away another day.'

'Crime?' Asta shook her head. 'Don't be so hard on yourself. You panicked. You ran. Nobody's dead. The people who love you . . . they'll understand.' *Am I talking to Jake? Or the younger me?*

In that solid house, insulated by the snow, Asta felt things loosening deep within her. Knots were coming undone. *Life is so much simpler than we make it,* she thought as she rose, and led Jake by the hand to the kitchen, where she made, in his opinion, 'the best cheese and tomato sandwich the world has yet witnessed'.

'Admit it,' said Asta. 'You didn't want to tell me about the lottery money in case I got greedy.'

Jake was devouring his sandwich as if he hadn't eaten in weeks. 'I've seen first-hand what money does to people. It bends them out of shape.'

'Not Steve.' Asta liked the sound of this Steve she'd never met. 'And not me. I've always paid for myself and I like it that way. Honest.'

'I know that now,' said Jake, putting down his food. 'When we met, I thought *there's something about this woman*.' He hesitated, looking down at Setanta, who looked doltishly back and was no help whatsoever. 'I wanted to pursue it, see where it went, without the money looming over us.'

When we met. Jake made it sound as if that had been months, not days, ago. Two damaged souls, they'd found a richness that some couples take years to achieve.

'You aways call it *the* money. Not *my* money.'

'I keep it at arm's length. I don't want to get any dirt on me.'

'Rory knows?'

'He's been brilliant. The motorbike was my way of saying thank you. For listening. For telling me I'm not a dead loss. Actually,' said Jake, looking at Asta wonderingly, 'he says much the same stuff as you.' He looked away. 'It means more, coming from you. So, tell me, Ast. What's the verdict on your runaway boyf?'

'I don't have a verdict,' said Asta. 'I don't have the right to judge you.' *Particularly as I'm guilty of a similar 'crime'*. 'I do have a prescription.'

Intrigued, relieved, Jake said, 'Go on, Doctor Looney.'

It had come to Asta in a flash. Just like all the female elders of her clan in times of crisis, she had the answer.

'What you've done resonates with me. I ran away too. I didn't look back for *years*, Jake, and I'm telling you from the heart that time passes quicker than you could ever imagine. You'll turn around and it'll be a decade since you were in touch. Your mother will grow old while you're licking your wounds.' Asta thought of Ma's white hair, so defiantly curled. 'Your friends – your real friends – will need you, but you won't be around. I understand, too, how staying away makes it easier to, well, *stay away*. It has a momentum all of its own. You have to turn around. Face your past. Own it.' Asta wondered where the tears in her eyes had sprung from. 'Or it'll chase you forever.' Asta took his hand. It was dry and warm, and it immediately clasped around her own. 'Isn't it time we forgave ourselves and got on with life?'

She gathered herself until she could speak again. Jake respected her silence, just like she knew he would.

'Right, mister. Tonight you call your mum. You call Steve. You even call poor old Karen, who's probably redecorated your mansion with pink diamanté. As of *now*, you stop being preoccupied by the stupid money. Employ somebody to deal with the begging letters in a businesslike way. Oona'll do it, once the miracles dry up and nobody wants to buy her doodahs.'

Jake seemed about to speak, but Asta trundled over him like Peg in her tractor. 'And starting tomorrow . . .' She reconsidered. Tomorrow was Christmas Day. 'Starting the day after tomorrow, you need a job. Apply yourself to something *real* and reconnect with the world. There are good people out there, I promise. Be one of them.' She drew breath, suddenly aware of how bossy she'd been. 'Do you agree with that plan?'

'One hundred per cent.'

'These days,' laughed Asta, 'that's not enough. On reality shows, the bare minimum is one hundred and ten per cent.'

This is the oddest Christmas Eve ever, thought Asta, looking out from the truck's passenger window at the refrigerated trees, each one a ghostly mound in the dark. *This year Christmas is almost an irrelevance.* Usually, at this time on this day, she'd be helping herself to a sherry, singing along to carols on the radio and remembering the one vital ingredient she'd forgotten to buy for whichever Nigella showstopper she'd decided to attempt.

'Go on, Jake.' Asta leaned towards him at the wheel. 'How much did you win?'

Jake named an amount.

Asta didn't speak for a whole minute. 'Jesus,' she said eventually. 'I can see why you thought I'd get pound signs in my eyes.'

'What *do* I see in your eyes?' Jake was in earnest. "Cos I look into them a lot, and I see *something*. What is it, Asta? This thing that's happening between us?'

Asta wanted to use *that* word, the four-letter chappie that best summed it up. It wouldn't come out, though; it was shy.

The truck was noisy in the muffled landscape. Jake said, over its wheezing, 'I don't know what's gone on with that Conan guy . . .' He peered straight ahead, into the white shape carved by the headlights. 'But you have to sort it out. I'll make my calls, and you do whatever it is you need to do. I don't have any expectations and I won't ask questions, or argue. This bit's up to you.'

The shops were long closed, their fairy lights left on to cheer up the quiet snowscape. The truck idled outside the bar.

'You're right, Jake,' said Asta, as she undid her seat belt. 'I have something to sort out, and when I do . . . we'll talk again, yeah?'

'Good luck with it.' Jake gazed at Asta as she stood on the frigid pavement, as if committing her to memory.

'And you.' Asta waved him off. *You have no idea*, she

thought, *what my secret is*. If Jake knew what she was about to do to 'sort it out', he would try to stop her.

The porthole in the door of the bar showed Asta a room throbbing with warmth. Mouths were opened in song, heads thrown back with laughter, all illuminated by the kind light of the tree. Gerry fiddled hard as Oona pounded the piano.

In the midst of it all was Conan, one arm around Ma as he joined in with some rousing folk song.

Asta could hear different music. The music in her blood, the old rhythm of the woods. Making her way around the side of the pub, she began to climb, sinking in the fresh snow that had fallen on the hill.

Thank you, moon. Without its help, the forest would be impenetrable, just a luminous tangle. The snow seeped into Asta's boots and turned her jeans to wet rags as she delved into the woods, into Ireland's pagan history and her own past.

It had always seemed to Asta that the world held its breath on Christmas Eve, waiting for the annual miracle. The woods were expectant, even though miracles were now ten-a-penny in Tobercree, thanks to Rory.

I'm going to work a miracle of my own.

Although Asta's watch said six o'clock, it felt like midnight. Thanks to the snow, the silence was spookily complete. Hearing her own pulse in her ears brought her dreams to mind, and she quailed as she staggered deeper into the trees.

If she could exorcise the dream, perhaps she could apply herself to love. As if she was a bird watching from above, Asta saw the long path that had brought her here. *I've been too full of fear to allow love in*.

She was in a clearing. *The* clearing. Forgetting her icy toes and frozen nose, she placed her foot on the bottom rung of the rope ladder. The creak of the rope, the freewheeling moment when it span before it steadied, was familiar, as if all the years between now and the last time she'd climbed the ladder were just a cough.

With each rung, her certainty about her plan diminished. It wasn't just the dream that frightened her; the reality had been the stuff of nightmares, too.

Inside the treehouse, it was clean in that way that places left to themselves can be. Perhaps only humans make places dirty. Hardly any snow had found its way inside, and the pearly night air was still.

In that lopsided cube, Asta was both the adult Asta and the virgin who'd climbed the ladder seventeen years ago. Willing herself to do it, Asta conjured up Etienne. She could see, like a snowy spectre, his slender boy's body, with his concave chest and his head poised at an angle, watching her. She smiled at the dream Etienne, a creature of sunshine and summer.

The beat of the ancient forest died away. The treehouse was just an abandoned plaything. The silent trees held no monsters.

On with the exorcism. Asta closed her eyes, resisting the images of her dreams to recall instead what had really happened.

They'd kissed. Awkwardly. All Etienne's French aplomb had evaporated. Ever so carefully, as if she might explode, he'd peeled off her silky white tee. She'd kissed him again. He pulled her by the waist, a rapid movement that sped up the pace.

Their desire made them a creature with one mind. Asta and Etienne, mouths locked, breath short, were taken over by a mad urgency. As if the treehouse were on fire. As if they had moments to live.

She'd never taken off her bra in front of a boy before. Etienne's clumsy awe made the moment as special as she needed it to be. She tore away his shirt. She was afraid, and it was wonderful.

Passionate, greedy, unskilled, the teenagers giggled and grappled like two birds flapping about the treehouse.

Their skin was like new cotton sheets. Etienne was giddy, grabbing at Asta with his long, strong, skinny arms. He let out a thin, high, very French giggle, as if they were about to step onto a rollercoaster.

Toe to toe, their noses touching, his breath sweet on her face, Etienne hooked a thumb in either side of Asta's pants. The question in his eyes was answered by a vehement *Yes!* in her face.

The voice called her name.

Asta hugged herself in the here and now, recalling their shock as they'd heard, 'Asta! Is that you up there? Asta!'

Boy and girl sprang apart as if electrocuted.

The treehouse pitched. They realized the owner of the voice was on the ladder.

Asta's skimpy clothes, kicked into a corner, were out of reach, and Etienne rushed to cover her with his body, his long back arched towards the door.

Martin clambered in, grass stains on his slacks. His professional grin disappeared as he did a double take at what he saw.

'You feckin' savages!' Martin craned his neck, trying to get a proper look at Asta's nakedness. Etienne shuffled, covering her up.

Only twenty-five at the time, Martin had all the outrage of an old maid.

'Butt out, man,' said Etienne. 'We don't do anyzing wrong. I really like zis girl.'

'You can butt out back to France, sonny Jim,' bawled Martin, who was unrecognizable in this state. A state it had taken only a second or two to attain.

Etienne let rip with some molten French, and lashed out with his bare foot.

Martin leapt back. 'Oi!' he yelled. 'I'm here to protect this girl. I'm her brother-in-law.'

'Not yet you're not,' said Asta tartly, peeping over Etienne's shoulder, enfeebled by her nakedness.

'You be quiet, you.' Martin pointed at Asta, then turned his attention back to Etienne. 'Do you have any idea of the trouble you're in, Pepe le Pew? What'll your teachers say? And her parents? This'll be all over town in ten minutes.'

Etienne wilted slightly. He looked at the floor.

'Hop it,' said Martin, calmer, standing by the shoddy door. 'I'll make sure Asta gets home safely. And count yourself lucky I'm feeling lenient.'

Etienne looked into Asta's eyes. She nodded. He winced, shook his head, his mouth a downturned line. But she nodded again, and prodded him to go. As he pulled away from her, Asta put her arms across her chest and turned away from Martin. Etienne scuttled across the treehouse and grabbed his clothes, scooping up Asta's underwear. He stood between her and Martin while she pushed her arms through the straps.

'I go?' he whispered, uncomfortable.

'You go,' said Asta, in what she hoped was a reassuring manner.

When Etienne ducked out of the door, Martin turned to Asta. 'Tears, is it, you little slut?'

'I'm not a slut.'

'You have everybody fooled, bookish little Assumpta. Wait 'till your ma hears what you do in the woods.'

'Don't tell, please.' Ma took a week to recover if she overheard somebody say 'erection'. Asta would never be able to explain her feelings for Etienne. 'Please, Martin, please, you don't have to tell them!'

From Asta's viewpoint in the here and now, it seemed impossible that the girl she used to be didn't know what was coming. *Heaven help me, I was so naive.*

'I have to tell, you know that.' Martin put his hands to his head, as if he regretted such fuss and bother. 'Dear God, your Aunty Peg won't be able to look at you.' He said, more gently, 'You didn't mean to hurt anybody, did you?'

'No!' Asta scrabbled gratefully at this straw. 'I didn't mean any harm.'

'You're just an old silly, aren't you?' Martin stepped towards Asta, and put his arms around her.

Cringing, Asta cried harder as a penny dropped.

'There, there.' Martin stroked Asta's hair. His ring caught in a tangle, and hurt her. 'Let's keep this between ourselves.' He licked Asta's sunburnt shoulder.

Repulsed, finally realizing the danger she was in, Asta bucked, pressing her hand up under Martin's chin, but he caught her by the wrists and stared frankly down at her body. 'You don't know how sexy you are.'

'You're Gerry's fiancé,' shouted Asta. She was spitting. Crying.

In the cold present, older, wiser Asta pressed her hands into her eyes.

She remembered pulling away from Martin. She remembered his strength as he tightened his grip on her wrists.

Asta shook as she squared up to the worst aspect of the whole sad and terrible story. *I didn't struggle hard enough.* She hadn't really struggled at all.

Thirty-three-year-old Asta knew why. She could rationalize. Adult Asta didn't let anybody take liberties with her, but the tear-streaked sixteen-year-old had been raised to agree with the names Martin called her. Replaying it didn't change what had happened, but Asta longed for her younger self to knee him in the balls.

'Let me help you.' Martin's eyes were large, like a pup on a schmaltzy greetings card. 'It would be awful if the family turned against you, Asta. I don't *have* to tell.'

Asta knew a pact when she heard one. All the fight left her. Her skin felt like cockroaches.

'That's it, you big silly,' smiled Martin.

It didn't hurt as much as I thought it would.

Martin wasn't rough. He was cold. As he zipped up his flies he said, rattling it off as if dictating a memo, 'Tell nobody. I'll deny it. And they'll believe me.'

'I hate you,' said Asta.

'And as for you.' Martin looked her up and down where she sat on the floor, knees up to her chin. 'I won't be troubling you again, darling. You're a two out of ten, at best.'

Etienne went home the next day. Asta stayed indoors, so there could be no goodbyes.

A cloud drifted across the moon. Asta was so engrossed by her sunny, sinister past she was confused for a moment, to be standing in the chilly treehouse in the dark.

'Asta!'

She jumped, her hand flying to her throat.

'Asta!' *I'm imagining it.*

'Asta!' She'd somehow brought her past to life.

The treehouse lurched as somebody climbed the rope ladder.

'There you are!' said Martin cheerfully, one foot slapping on the boarded floor, head bowed to clamber through the child-sized door. 'What're you doing up here, you big silly?'

It took a second for Asta to realize she wasn't naked, that it wasn't like the last time.

'Get out, Martin.'

Martin, bulky in a padded coat, was wary, on edge, a little frayed. 'Reliving the good old days, are we?'

The disgust that flooded her was as strong as her fear. 'I'm not a teenager any more, Martin. If you come near me I'll—'

'You don't like me, do you?' Martin put his head to one side, pulled off his tweed cap. 'Funny, that, 'cos you were nice to me once. Very nice. Right here.' He smiled, pointing at the floor.

'You assaulted me.' That was the first time Asta had called it that; the word rang in her ears.

'Sure, there's no need to assault the likes of you. I just took the frog's place.' Martin dipped his head, trained his brown eyes on her. They were beautiful eyes, the colour of coffee, but Martin's sly expression made them ugly. 'I didn't have to lay a finger on you. You opened your legs of your own accord.'

They circled each other.

'You used my shame as a weapon.' Asta saw how uncomfortable the truth made him. 'You were ruthless about getting what you wanted.'

And you damn near ruined my life.

Asta didn't need a psychotherapist to explain why she had a horror of being manipulated, why she drank heavily before making love. All the anger she carried in her bones weighed her down. *Why have I fixated on the fact I didn't fight back?* That was an emotional red herring; it made no difference to the fact that this man had brutalized her.

When Martin took a step forward, Asta said, 'Touch me and I'll kill you.' She meant it, too, even though she'd never raised her hand in violence.

I come from a long line of strong women.

'Such drama!' Martin applauded sardonically. But he came no closer. 'Nobody's going to kill anybody. We're going to rekindle our relationship. It's so romantic, isn't it, the snow?' He sighed playfully. 'Strange how things turn out, Asta. Thanks to that sister of yours praying her head off for a baby, Tobercree thinks I'm shooting blanks.'

Asta was ready to spring, prepared for a sudden change of pace.

Still chatty, still suave, Martin said, 'None of them know she's been in the spare room for years.'

Asta thought of the enormous bed in the show house. The perfect marriage hid a well of pain; *and I wasn't here to support her.*

'The punchline is that you and I both know I'm already a proud daddy!'

'No, Martin. You're Kitty's father. You're not her daddy.'

'You look so cold.' Martin stuck out his lower lip. 'Poor Asta. I could warm you up.' He looked at his watch. 'We haven't got long. I have to get home for my show.' He kept himself carefully between Asta and the door. 'Whaddyasay?' He was all good cheer. 'Or shall I have a word with your ma? Tell her a home truth or two. Your sister would love to know our little secret.' He paused, and they both knew what he was going to say next. 'Perhaps it's time I had a chat with our darling daughter?'

The moon came out, its milky brightness amplified by the snow. It illuminated one basic fact Asta had missed. Repressing the vile memories, she'd never reassessed what had happened to her younger self with the wisdom of an adult.

Martin had more to lose than she did. The secret would end his marriage, sully his whiter-than-white public persona. The shame was all Martin's. *I did nothing wrong.*

If Asta had told her family at the time, they'd have believed her, not Martin. They weren't ogres, just people trying to get by. Hell, Aunty Peg would have flattened him with a borrowed tractor. There was no reason on earth to be frightened of this puny, odious man.

'Let's have some Christmas Eve fun.' Martin took a step closer, his confidence growing in the silence. 'Or do I go back to the village and tell them all our little secret?'

Backed up against the wooden slats, Asta felt the chill of *déjà vu*. But she was no longer sixteen. This wasn't a dream.

'There's no secret, Martin.' Asta was calm. 'I'm going to tell them. Me. I'm going to tell everybody what you did.'

Stepping back into shadow, Martin sounded confused. 'You can't. Your mother . . . Peg . . . they'll disown you.'

'Of course they won't. They love me. Besides, I have truth on my side.'

'And Kitty? Ah . . . that hit home. If you tell her, I'll fight you for custody.'

'This is no time for comedy, Martin.'

'Look,' said Martin, with the air of a man about to haggle. 'I won't touch you again if—'

'Damn right you won't,' interrupted Asta.

'But you *can't* tell them.' Martin stepped to the right and to the left as Asta tried to pass him. 'Revenge against me will hurt poor little Kitty.'

'There's nothing poor about Kitty, and what I do is none of your business. Let me get past, Martin.'

'Not until you promise—'

The mistake he made was to put out his hands to stop her. Asta shoved Martin with all the might coiled up in her body and he sprawled, landing in the corner like a doll.

His composure shattered, Martin looked up at Asta wild-eyed: he hadn't expected the mouse to roar.

Flinging herself down the ladder, Asta missed every second rung and landed hard in the snow.

Over her muttered curse as she limped speedily away, Asta heard the voice again.

'Asta!'

It was just a noise now. Asta wasn't afraid of it. She didn't want revenge; this was justice.

A snowflake was born high in the velvet sky. It whirled towards Earth with its companions, and wheeled over the tilted roof of St Catherine's as Asta scurried across the car park.

Cold, anxious and shivering with adrenalin, she turned for the church to lodge there for a moment and get her breath back.

The church was practically empty. Most people – lucky, lucky people – were at home wrapping presents, overeating and watching *Only Fools and Horses* for the fiftieth time.

How she envied them. This Christmas Eve would be memorable for all the wrong reasons; it would be the year Kitty heard life-changing news. Asta saw Rory genuflect towards the altar, then rise and turn to walk down the centre aisle, his heels loud in the hush. Everything fell away. The bravado she'd felt in the treehouse melted in the warmth of the church.

Noticing her, Rory acknowledged Asta with a nod. He looked again, more searchingly.

Asta realized why she'd come inside. It wasn't to do with warming up, it wasn't to do with gathering her wits. She was going to tell Rory. He marched towards her, big, dark and clear-cut. As he grew, he seemed to be a buttress against the messy pain of her past.

'In here,' he said as he neared Asta, motioning her into a small anteroom where flowers were arranged and collection money counted. It was a white, sterile room, livened up by a bunch of blousy roses lying across a table.

'Sit. Talk.'

Rory listened to the whole sorry saga.

'How do I tell Kitty?' Asta blinked back the tears; there was no time for such luxuries. 'She'll hate me. I just don't have the words to explain or describe . . .'

'Asta,' said Rory, his hand on hers. 'I'm so sorry you had to endure this. It's a terrible thing. You're blameless and you've taken back the power from that evil man. But this story isn't just yours. It's Kitty's. She deserves the truth about herself, however brutal. If she hears it from her mother, who loves her, it'll help. You can control the language, soften the blow a little. But she should know. You can help Kitty take it in, now and in the years to come.' He paused. 'Kitty will need time to absorb it. To grieve. To heal. She'll need her mother.'

'I can't tell her.' Asta was choked, her voice bald and unvarnished.

'You can,' said Rory. 'I'm only echoing the voice that tolls like a bell deep inside you. We always know what we should do. Go and find her and tell her. It's time.' Rory smiled, sadly. 'The truth is always the best way, even if it's not the easiest way.'

'Really?' Asta was weary. Christmas Eve had asked a lot of her, and it wasn't finished yet. 'So why won't you tell the truth about the statue?'

Taken aback by this right hook, Rory said, 'But you know the truth about the statue, Asta. You always have.' He stood up. 'Sit in the church for a while, before you look for Kitty. It might help.'

'I'm not one for praying, remember?' Asta tried to whistle up their customary sparring tone. It fell flat.

'Just focus. Meditate, if you want to call it that. Pull your thoughts down, back into yourself. The words you need for Kitty will come to you.' Rory waited for Asta to heave herself up from the chair and led her over to St Catherine. 'The words will come,' he whispered. 'Because they're already there.'

Alone, Asta slumped in front of St Catherine. Her thoughts ran amok, tripping over themselves. *Focus!* She sank forward onto the padded kneeler. This was the spot where her sister prayed so conspicuously every morning for a child she craved, yet did nothing to conceive.

Focus! Asta let the silence enter her. Not just the silence of an empty church, but the magical silence of the snow that held Tobercree in icy seclusion.

Way above her head, the snowflake flirted with the spire but didn't land, eddying by the stained-glass windows.

Focus! Asta felt her mind begin to yield. Her panic lost its electricity. She leaned forward, her hands clasped, her head bowed as she fell into a deep place inside herself. It wasn't dangerous there, it held no monsters. It was calm.

A splash landed on her outstretched fingers. Then another. Asta opened her eyes and looked up at the statue. Its face was wet.

As Asta watched, a fat tear formed in the very corner of Catherine's porcelain blue eye, slid down her creamy plaster cheek, dropped onto the pale gown and followed a fold all the way down to her bare feet. The tear dripped off the saint's dainty toe onto Asta's splayed fingers.

Asta stared deep into the saint's eyes. She felt flooded with light and courage. She stood up, her petrol tank full once again.

I know how it's done!

An arctic blast of air carried the snowflake above the closed shops, and the war-weary mill, and a woman dashing up the street.

The snow was like sand beneath Asta's feet as she ran. The speech she would make to Kitty played out in her head as if Asta had been rehearsing it since she'd first held her in her arms.

Racing around to the back door, Asta avoided the bar, which was still humming with music and joy. In the kitchen her mother was engaged in hand-to-hand combat with a turkey bigger than the average ten-year-old. The fowl wasn't going down without a fight; Ma's hair stood on end.

'There y'are, love,' said Ma, relieved to see some troops. 'Grab a potato and get peeling.'

'Where's Kitty?' Asta ignored the tottering tower of King Edwards. *I'll help later*, she promised herself guiltily. *First things first.*

'What's wrong?' Ma turned, frowning.

'Ma! Where is she?'

'Priest's house.' Recognizing an emergency, Ma wasted no words.

It was impossible to walk away without checking up on Conan.

Peeping into the bar, she saw him behind the counter, serving what looked like suspiciously generous measures. His good cheer warmed the room. At some point, Asta would have to speak to him. Not now. Later. *While I peel the potatoes?* Things to do later were piling up.

Up the lane scuttled the snowflake, scooting over tractor tracks. Ignoring the bungalows, it took a shine to the Big House. A handy gust of wind spirited it across the circular gravel drive, and it did a jig above the porch.

Out of breath from her jog back up the main street, Asta didn't expect to find Gerry in Peg's kitchen. Her heart contorted: she could actually feel it.

'Ah,' Gerry said, putting her cup down deliberately. '*You.*'

'Yes,' agreed Asta meekly. 'Me.'

A radio sat on the table, Martin's voice oozing from it.

Gerry said, 'I had a text from my darling hubby about you, just before he went on air. Something about a lie, and to talk to him first.' She exchanged a complicit glance with

Peg, who was beating a steak with a meat mallet and enjoying it rather too much. 'What,' said Gerry, 'have you done *now*?'

'Not now, Ger.' She turned to Peg. 'Where's Kitty?'

'She's with Father Dominic,' said Peg. She tilted her head back, half-closed her clever eyes. 'What's going on?'

'Merry Christmas Eve, Tobercree!' chortled Martin over the airwaves. 'I hope you're all snug and safe with your families on this special night. Because family is the most important thing in the world. Am I right?'

'Are you running away again?' laughed Gerry, as she broke off another hunk of fruit cake.

Asta had turned for the door, but she paused, and turned back. 'Gerry, do you want the truth?' She saw that her gravity had registered with her sister, who'd stopped the brack en route to her lips. 'Or do you want to look down on me for the rest of our lives?'

When her sister didn't answer, Asta returned to the table and sat opposite her. 'It's time you knew,' she said.

Wasting no words, Asta gave Gerry a potted version of what had happened in the treehouse in 1998.

The snowflake hung, almost immobile, on a frigid current above the Big House. When the glossy black door opened, it was caught up in the disturbed air as an untidy dog rushed out.

'In the truck, Setanta.' Jake jumped in beside him. 'Let's go and find our girl.'

The snowflake was sucked along in the wake of man and dog as they set off towards the village.

Wiping her eyes ferociously with her sleeve, Asta rapped on Father Dominic's door. She was hollowed out by her sister's face. When she'd left Gerry and Aunty Peg they'd both been stock still, as if posing for a macabre portrait, Peg's features distorted in disgust and the mallet hanging limp in her hands.

She wasn't able to look at me. Asta guessed she was no longer the favourite niece.

Stepping into the cosy parlour without waiting for a response, Asta said, 'I need my daughter. Now.'

'Mu-um!' said Kitty, eyes wide at such misbehaviour.

Father Dominic met Asta's grim expression with a questioning look. 'Your mother needs you, Iseult,' he said, raising himself up on his stick. 'I'll leave you be.'

Kitty helped the elderly priest to the door, then closed it so they were alone in the peaceful room. 'Mum, that was so rude! Poor Father Dom—'

'I have something to tell you,' began Asta, her eyes stopping the ever-ready mum-criticism in its tracks.

Kitty pulled in her chin. 'Mum, you're scaring me.'

I'm scaring myself, thought Asta. She opened her mouth and the words came. One after another. Like a river. Like a flood.

Asta told her daughter the truth.

The snowflake whirled through the door of the pub after the man and the dog. A creature of ice and frost, it began to change in the warmth. It began to lose its shape, its structure.

Asta was apologizing. 'I should have told you . . .'

Kitty said nothing. She cried, then stopped, then cried again. She inched into her mother's arms and held on tight.

Above her head, Asta closed her eyes in silent thanks. *She wants me close.* It could have gone either way. The facts of Kitty's conception were sordid, even after Asta had toned down the tale as best she could. *I said what I said with love.* That had made all the difference.

Lifting her head, Kitty was shell-shocked, her skin the colour of porridge. 'Don't worry, Mum,' she said.

That broke Asta. She remembered Kitty saying that when she was tiny and Asta was down in the dumps about a red bill, or another knife fight in the stairwell. 'Darling,' she said, messily, through her tears, 'how did I make such a kind human being?'

Not just kind. Kitty was strong. In that moment, as Kitty pulled her mother to her, saying a gentle 'shush shush', Asta realized her daughter really would be all right.

'We'll be fine,' said Kitty. 'We have each other.'

Smiling gamely, like soldiers who've survived a fierce battle, Asta and Kitty walked, entwined, back down the corridor.

A voice, confident and self-satisfied, drifted through the open kitchen door. Asta and Kitty shivered as if somebody had opened a door and let in the snow.

'Today's phone-in is about marriage problems. I have a local lady on the line who doesn't wish to give us her name. Go ahead, my love. You're among friends.'

Jake sat in front of a bowl of stew, as a snowflake died on his hair.

'You have to like stew if you live in Tobercree,' he whispered to Setanta, whose snout was on his master's knee. 'Really, *really* like stew.'

The musicians were on a break; the radio was whacked up to full volume as Ma, sage and onion in her hair and a whiff of turkey's backside about her, pulled pint after perfect pint.

'No sign of Conan,' said Jake to Setanta. 'Which is good. But . . .' He massaged the dog's ears. 'No sign of Asta either.' He bent down to his animal. 'Let's not think about what that might mean, eh?'

'Go ahead, my love,' said Martin, as clearly as if he was in the bar. 'You're among friends.'

'This is me son-in-law on the radio!' Ma enunciated carefully to an Egyptian man who knew no English beyond, 'Could you show me the way to the men's conveniences?' Ma tutted and huffed at the phone-in caller's disclosures.

'My husband's a very bad kisser, Martin,' said the caller. 'He doesn't help in the house. He's unfaithful. Not just once or twice, either. He thinks I don't know, but he's not very good at covering his tracks.'

'Dear, dear me.' Martin was only half listening.

Jake looked up from his dumplings and met Ma's eye, as both of them recognized the caller's voice.

'To be honest,' said the woman, 'I've put up with the marriage for the sake of respectability. The love is long gone. The bastard's all I've got. But the marriage is a failure. I'm a failure.'

'Aw, shame,' said Martin, as if they were discussing a dropped ice cream.

Ma turned the radio up even louder, her face creased with concentration.

'Is there somebody there with you, dear?' asked Martin.

An older voice came on the line, hoarse with rage.

'She's no failure. Sure, I never had a man and I never needed one. She's a saint to have put up with that snotty-nosed little feck of a husband for so long.'

'Ohhhhh, dear,' whispered Ma.

Jake put down his spoon.

'What my niece was trying to say, Martin Mayberry, is that you're not to come home tonight. We know everything, yes, *everything*, so she's changing the locks, and if you come within a hundred yards of her or her sister, I'll get out me scissors and I'll separate you from your tiny—'

A commercial for fertilizer cut Peg off.

In the kitchen of the priests' house, Asta and Kitty watched Peg fling the mobile phone across the room.

'There!' nodded the old woman, with an air of finality.

Gerry's head was on the table as Father Dominic hobbled in. 'Peg! Something very strange just happened on your lovely nephew's show!'

The radio belched out Martin's damage control. 'A little bit of humour for you there, folks,' he stammered.

Peg grabbed the radio, lifted the meat mallet and placed them both in front of Gerry.

Asta looked at Kitty. Kitty looked at Asta. Father Dominic looked at everybody. Nobody looked at Father Dominic.

'GAAAAAAH!' screamed Gerry as she brought the hammer down on the radio.

They all applauded. Except Father Dominic.

Jake hurried behind the bar and caught Ma just as she swooned.

Setanta, back at the table, heard angels sing in his hairy ears as he witnessed his very own Christmas miracle; an untended bowl of stew.

Three gulps, and it was gone.

A gaggle of Looneys toiled through the blizzard, heads down. Gerry was lost in a painful new world of her own, but she didn't repulse the hand Asta held out to her as they walked with Kitty back to the pub.

'Mum, why'd you make up all that stuff about me being French?' Kitty looked bereft. 'I feel as if I've lost Etienne. God knows what my mates will say. I'm always banging on about being half French.'

'I didn't think it through.' Asta squeezed her daughter's shoulder as they walked. 'There was no way I could tell you the truth. Everybody assumed poor Etienne was your father. It seemed to help, at first, when you were little. But then it snowballed . . .' Asta had been trapped in her fiction, but the facts were worse. 'It's the only lie I've ever told you.'

'Apart from Father Christmas. It wasn't until I saw Conan in that stupid red coat that I realized you'd been been making a fool of me for years.'

Conan. Asta knew she had to seek him out. This was by far the most exhausting Christmas Eve she'd ever experienced – including the one she'd spent running, screaming, from toy shop to toy shop looking for a Bratz Movie Starz doll.

'I forgive you about Santa,' said Kitty. 'And it's cool about Etienne. Well, not *cool*.' She shrugged. Her emotions were way ahead of her vocabulary. 'I'll have to get my head around . . . *him*.' None of them were able to call the Voice of Tobercree by his name. 'I know you did your best.'

'You. Are. Beautiful.' Asta kissed the top of Kitty's head, almost knocking them both off balance into the snow. Kitty could have made a scene, turned her back, but instead she'd been gracious and thoughtful. 'I'm a lucky mum.'

'I'm always telling you that!'

As they reached the squares of golden light thrown onto the white pavement by the bar windows, Asta contemplated how falling pregnant with Kitty had altered the course of her life. Their relationship was profound and unique. They'd climbed mountains together, with the promise of plenty more hiking to come.

Sorry, Father Dominic, but the little bastard didn't ruin my life; she made it.

Inside the bar, Kitty asked if she could go to their room.

'Shall I come with?'

'No, Mum. I need to be on my own. Just for a bit.'

'Okey-dokey, sweetheart.'

'Are you going out later?' asked Kitty.

'I'll be within shouting distance all night.' Asta read Kitty's mind. 'If you need me, holler.'

Ma beckoned above the drinkers' heads. Asta didn't notice

Jake watching her from a corner table as she followed Gerry into the kitchen.

No tea was offered. Ma's mood was beyond even the power of tea. She pointed a spatula at Gerry. 'Have I got it wrong, madam, or did you just dump your husband live on the feckin' radio?'

Gerry's eyes were on the floor, as if she were being upbraided in the headmaster's study for smoking behind the bike sheds.

'And why? For what?' Ma's voice leapfrogged up the scale until it was shrill.

'This has been coming for a long time,' said Gerry.

'And there's you praying for a babby every day,' snapped Ma, throwing up her arms. 'Jayzus, I don't understand your generation at all.' She stalked out of the kitchen, leaving the sisters with each other and the epic turkey.

'So this is what it feels like, sis.' Gerry slumped onto a wooden chair. 'Being misunderstood when you're trying to do the right thing.'

Such empathy from Gerry was rarer than unicorn droppings. Asta felt a bat-squeak of hope for their moth-eaten sibling rapport.

'Asta,' said Gerry, shaking her head as if dazed, her voice thick. 'I'm sorry. For what happened. In the treehouse.'

'You can't apologize for somebody else. It was *his* fault. Nothing to do with you. He's good at being bad, and nobody suspected a thing.' Asta laid a hand, tentatively, on Gerry's shoulder. 'I've carried the can for Martin long enough. No need for you to pick it up.'

'I didn't know about what Martin had done. You do believe that?'

'Of course you didn't.'

'But . . . but I was pleased when you left,' said Gerry. 'Because I knew Martin fancied you.' She gurned, as if she'd swallowed a fly. 'I'm a right bitch.'

'Sometimes,' agreed Asta. 'But you're a brave bitch to admit it.' She was gratified by Gerry's tired snort of laughter. 'Listen, seventeen years of marriage to Martin is punishment enough for an axe murderer, never mind an occasional bitch.'

'I'll never have a baby now,' said Gerry quietly.

'There are plenty of other men waiting out there,' Asta consoled her, thinking *but you'll have to sleep with one if you want a baby*. 'Let's take it one step at a time. Are you serious, really serious, about leaving Martin?'

'What,' asked Gerry, with a dry look, 'do you think?'

Asta smiled. 'Divorce isn't easy in this neck of the woods.'

'I don't care how long it takes,' said Gerry. 'I'm keeping the house, obviously,' she added, her ebullient consumerism emerging even in the midst of a crisis. 'I'll stay here until Boxing Day, give him a chance to pack up and get out.' She stood up. 'I'm going to find Ma. Put her straight on one or two points about her darling son-in-law. I'm not telling her *everything*. Not just yet. I like this, Asta.' Gerry smiled wanly. 'You and me being nice to each other. Shall we do more of it?'

'Why not? I think we could get good at it.'

Asking after Conan, Asta learned from Ma that she'd sent him back to Mrs Hannigan's 'for a lie down. He was a little *tipsy*.' She laughed indulgently, as if Conan was a puppy and not fourteen stone of pissed bloke. 'Your other fella's over in the corner.'

'My other . . .' Asta saw Jake, and crossed the maze of tables to join him.

'Ast!' smiled Jake. Then, 'Ast?' when he took in the look on her face. He jumped up. 'What is it?'

The concern made Asta buckle. 'We need to talk,' she said, through a monsoon of unexpected tears.

'No, no, we don't.' Jake struggled out from behind the table, knocking over his Guinness, to take her in his arms. 'You need to sit and cry and eat crisps.'

Moving away from the frank interest of strangers, Jake took her out to the glacial patio, where the chairs all bore heaped cushions of snow. Setanta loped behind them, ever vigilant for a dropped crisp. Setanta *loved* pubs.

'Assume the position.' Jake directed her head to his chest. 'Before you get on with it, is anybody dead? Is Kitty all right?'

Asta shook her head, then nodded it, as well as she could while clamped to him.

'Good. Then let it out.' Jake tightened his grip. On the trellis tacked to the walls, real icicles competed with plastic lights shaped like icicles. 'You looked like a raincloud full of rain back there. As if you've changed somehow.'

'Oh, Jake,' sobbed Asta into the comforting creaky leather of his jacket. When she lifted her head, her eyes like golf-balls, she accepted the tissue he gave her and said, 'I know how it's done, Jake. I know how Rory gets the statue to cry. He—'

Jake shook his head. 'Nah. Don't tell me.'

'What?' Asta gaped, blowing her nose, remembering too

347

late she'd vowed never to blow her nose in front of Jake. She sounded like an elephant imploding.

'I don't want to know.' Jake pushed back her new fringe. 'Instead, if you want to, tell me what made you cry.'

She spoke, and he listened. When she stopped, he said, 'I want to knock him down.'

'I already did that.'

'Good girl!' Jake kissed Asta's brow, in a chaste and protective way that sent a torrent of simple happiness through her.

'I've handled it so badly, for years and years. I just hope I haven't messed Kitty up.'

'You did the rightest thing in a situation where there was no right thing. Martin's the only one who should be soul-searching. You were the victim here, Asta.'

'I don't like that word.'

'Past tense. At sixteen, in that treehouse, you were the victim. Now you're *you*,' said Jake. 'And you're good at it.'

'I do my best.' Asta shook herself. She could cry later, but for now she needed to salvage Christmas Eve. 'Enough about me. How did your calls home go?'

'That can wait.' Jake held her near again. 'Come home with me. Let me look after you.' Asta imagined a bath, soft sheets, love being made while falling snow made patterns on the wall.

'Tonight, first and foremost, I'm Kitty's mum, Jake. Can you understand that?'

'You know I can.' Jake put his head on one side.

'I have to be here. She's coping amazingly well but she'll falter at some point and when she does . . .'

'You'll be there.' Jake sounded proud. A little disappointed for his own reasons, but proud.

Asta yawned. 'Besides, Conan's dead drunk and I need
to—'

'You haven't dealt with that yet?' Jake held her at arm's
length.

'Dealt with it?' Asta laughed. 'He's a person, not a blocked
drain.'

Jake stared at her. So hard that Asta's eyes started to
flicker around and about. 'I want to ask if you'll stay. Here.
With me, in this village. But I daren't.' He left a silence that
Asta chose not to fill.

Jake's hug, as he left, was brotherly.

'Out! Get out, you herd of heathens!' Ma steered the grumbling clientele into the street. 'Away to Midnight Mass with
youse all.'

The village had been given a facelift. Everything was new
and white and sparkling clean. The postbox was a mysterious monolith; the streetlamps wore crisp white crowns. Asta
joined the crowd trudging through it all, calling out greetings, breaking into song, on their way to a church tradition
even the pagans like her could get behind. Midnight Mass
was a party with all the best-loved carols sung at full throttle,
by the pious at the front and the hiccupping lushes down
the back.

As a snowball thudded past her ear, Asta thought of her
atheist lover up in the Big House. This was a holy night,
but one tinged with devilry, when all the little children stayed
up and made mischief in the way that only sleep-deprived
kids can. Humming with humanity, the familiar main street
was a twinkly grotto, a place of possibilities and of history.

Leading the lesser Looneys were Peg and Ma in their best coats, huge handbags on their arms, hats rammed onto their heads. Between them, Kitty was linked to them both, their arms through hers. It looked as if she was being arrested, but Asta knew she was being protected.

Ma's reaction to the whole sorry saga had been immediate and emphatic. She'd called her daughters together, and her daughter's daughter, and held them all to her. 'He'll never hurt one of youse again,' she'd vowed.

Asta had recognized the tone. She and her mother shared a determination that Martin's callous cruelty wouldn't win. The Looneys would go on. They would heal. They would triumph by leading ordinary lives.

There had been tears, those strange, happy-sad tears that verge on hysteria. Now that the truth was out, it had lost some of its ghastly power. They had no secrets. They truly knew each other.

Entirely absent was any note of rebuke or blame for Asta. Ma had clarity; no superstition or fear of what the neighbours might say clouded her view. There was one villain in this tale and, as she put it, he should keep one hand over his crown jewels if she ever laid eyes on him again. A phone call had been made to the owner of the radio station, an individual often seen enjoying one of Ma's lock-ins. Without spilling anything too intimate, Ma implied that the 'no scandal' clause in Martin's contract might soon be tested and – hey presto – the Voice of Tobercree was suddenly a Voice in the Wilderness, his contract terminated as of that minute.

As they made the familiar expedition to the church, Peg called over her shoulder, 'Girls!' just like she used to when

Asta and Gerry were small. It had the same effect; they chorused, 'Yes, Aunty Peg' together.

'Me and your mother have been talking.' Peg turned, her narrow face as pale as the snow. 'Gerry, if you want to adopt or have an I.O.U. baby, we'll help. Sure, it'd be grand having a little nipper about.'

That was quite some Christmas present. Gerry blinked back tears. 'Thank you,' she managed to say.

Asta nudged her. 'I.O.U.!' she whispered and took Gerry's hand. 'Me too,' she added. 'I'll help.'

'From London?' Gerry seemed to catch herself. 'Sorry. I've a way to go before I can stop being a bitch. I meant *thanks*.'

A shout in the darkness and Oona was upon them, jumping both sisters, yelling 'Happy Christmas, you old tarts!'

Asta was relieved. Like a missing jigsaw piece, Oona's absence had niggled at the edges of her mind. 'I've got so much to tell you, Oona.'

'Snap!' Oona stuck out an arm and yanked a figure towards them.

Declan, pink as a piglet, blurted out, 'We're engaged!'

Asta stopped dead, causing a pile-up of mass-goers. 'What?'

'Yeah, it's impetuous, but we thought, why wait?' Oona kissed Declan a little too enthusiastically for public consumption. 'When you know, you know!'

'Congratulations!' squealed Asta. Christmas was looking up. Something told her this union would endure forever, like a broken supermarket trolley that trundles on and on.

'Have you set a date?' asked Peg, managing to be both

approving and disapproving without even turning her head to look at the couple.

'Twenty-seventh of December,' said Declan.

When Asta and Gerry both spluttered, he added, 'Next year.'

The atmosphere in the candlelit church made Asta think of a stadium gig, one with a higher than usual proportion of old biddies in the audience. Her crew slid along a varnished pew, flicking through the order of service to see if their favourite carols were there.

'Silent Night' was present and correct, so Asta relaxed, feeling the fortress of her family around her. Lined up along the bench in order of age and scariness were Peg, Ma, Gerry, Oona and Kitty. St Catherine loomed over them, kind and serene and a big fat fake. Asta was mass-phobic, but would use the hour to sit quietly and possibly take a disco nap.

'Budge up.'

Asta jolted awake as a large figure sat down heavily beside her and took her hand.

'You stink of whisky.' Taking her hand was cheeky of him, but she let it happen. Conan's grip was snug, warm. Having waited so long to feel it, Asta allowed herself to enjoy it just a little.

'Why's everybody standing up?' Conan looked bemused as everybody leapt up around them.

'It's starting.' Asta registered the look Peg had lobbed down the pew. 'And shush!'

As Father Dominic spoke the ancient words in a faltering voice, and the congregation responded, Conan leaned towards Asta and said out of the corner of his mouth, 'There's so much I need to say to you.'

'Quiet!' For all sorts of reasons, Asta needed him to stop. She tried to withdraw her hand; it felt like a contract. Conan kept hold.

'I feel like I've left it too late.'

'You have.' That came out too harshly. 'Why now, Conan?'

'You went away, and I thought *what if she never comes back?* I realized my life would be . . . it wouldn't be a life.'

'Don't say that!'

Tuts heated up in the pew behind.

Grateful for the start of 'We Three Kings' to cover their hissed conversation, Asta said, 'I'm still here. I'm still me. If I hadn't met Jake, we'd . . .' *We'd be in Mrs Hannigan's right now*. Rolling about and setting the nylon sheets on fire.

'I can change, Asta. Give me a chance.'

'But why should you change?' Asta couldn't imagine Conan living any other way than in swashbuckling chaos. 'People shouldn't have to change.'

'I'd do it for the love of a good woman. That's you, by the way.' He winked.

Asta felt like throwing her prayer book into the air. She was a sucker for Conan's winks – as he well knew. 'Stop it. Stop flirting. This is a *church*. My Aunty Peg will strangle you with the strap of her handbag.'

Everybody sat again, Conan a beat late. As Father Dominic said what sounded like *muzzle wuzzle Christmas* – he'd never quite got the hang of the microphone – Conan whispered, 'For a long time, I've suspected you of being crazy about me. Was I wrong?'

'I wouldn't say crazy . . .' Asta nudged him with the sharp elbow she'd inherited from Ma. 'If you've thought it for a long time, why didn't you do anything about it?' She didn't let him reply. 'Because you've had it all your own way, and that's how you like it. Me yearning for you every day, and fresh totty in your bed every night.'

'You know me better than anybody else does. You know that deep down in this sad sack of a man, there's a decent human being trying to get out.'

'He's not trying very hard,' grumbled Asta. Her hand remained in his.

'I'll look after you, kid. I'll take you and Kitty around the world. We'll do what we want, live where you please. You won't have to work. I'll get some other assistant.'

Asta felt a pang; *she* was the only assistant for Conan.

'Please.' Conan forgot to whisper, and a battalion of headscarves turned to glare. He lowered his voice. 'That jerk is just some guy you met. A holiday romance. We go back years.'

'Would you ever have spoken up if I hadn't gone away? If Jake hadn't happened?'

'Of course!' Conan was doing his 'convincing' face, but Asta was not convinced. 'Let's do Christmas somewhere amazing.' He leaned in, and she recognized the seductive intonation from countless phone calls she'd overheard. 'We'll quit this joint, find a five-star castle, and then in the new year we'll go shopping. A diamond for every year I didn't tell you what you mean to me.'

Squirming, Asta felt sorry for him for getting it so wrong. The Conan she loved was the accident-prone, funny, sweet man who managed to be constant despite his fast-and-loose life. 'Do you know me *at all*, Conan? Why lead with your money?' Jake had hidden his wealth; she knew which approach she preferred. 'It was *you* I wanted, Conan, not your money.'

'Wanted?' Conan tensed, grasped her fingers harder. '*Wanted?* You have to give me a chance. You can't just—'

'WHISHT!' Peg had spoken, and even Conan shut the hell up.

Asta got nothing from the prayers, from the chants and tricks; but the solidarity of her community around her, swollen with people from all over the world, was a warm pillow.

And if Conan insisted on holding her hand, well, that was fine by her, too.

The crowd left slowly, people greeting friends and leaning across bodies to shake hands and bid each other a merry Christmas. Asta found herself leaning on Conan as they inched along, held fast in a sardine tin of humanity.

Outside, they stood apart, hand in hand. She savoured the sensation, knowing it was a brief window into what might have been. 'You're offering me a fairy tale, Conan. I don't believe in them. No, let me finish.' She held up a finger, and he bowed his head. 'In your fairy tale nobody works, everybody sleeps late, and other people pick up the pieces. I come from . . . well, *here*.' She gestured at the packed car park, buzzing and chatting beneath the huge blinking tree. 'I'm from working stock, where everybody pitches in. I don't want to be your partner in laziness and entitlement. I want to *make* my life.' She paused, watching how the words thudded home on his dear, familiar face. 'I do love you, Conan.' She dodged the immediate kiss he tried to plant on her; he had extraordinary powers of recovery. From lovelorn little boy to seducer in a heartbeat. 'Stop it! Conan, I don't love you *like that*. I love you as a friend. I value you. I can't do without you. But I don't love you like I love Jake.' *How peculiar*, thought Asta, *that I use that tiny, powerful word about Jake, not to him.*

'The tragedy is,' said Conan, 'I know you so well that I know I can't talk you round.'

'Nope.' Asta shook her head. They were out of step with the excitable, holiday mood. She looked at Conan, his cheeks cherry-red in the biting wind. 'I'm sorry.'

'Just once.' Conan leaned down, his eyes on her mouth. 'For what might have been.'

She should have pulled away. *Pull away*, she thought, very, very quietly. Asta deserved this one kiss, a kiss she'd imagined over and over and tried not to imagine over and over.

Conan didn't try to hold her. It was a goodbye kiss.

It was a damn fine goodbye kiss. Asta was a little dazed when his lips left hers and he dropped her hand. Her trance dissolved when she saw Jake leaning against his truck, hands in pockets, eyes like coals.

'Jake!' Asta shouted, threw up her hand, but by the time she'd pushed through the crowd that moved like lava across her path, the truck was a pair of red lights in the distance. She watched them until they were just dots, telling herself this was a silly misunderstanding, something that breaks up awkward teens, not mature adults.

Except it wasn't a misunderstanding. Asta's conscience was happy to put her right. *You kissed another man, and you enjoyed it.*

Conan had to elbow his way to her side. The hordes of people weren't moving on. The beacon of the church kept them in its thrall, as they stamped their booted feet and their laughter made misty patterns in the air. 'Did lover boy spot us?'

Asta wished she could be like the people around her. They were sparky, jumpy, anticipating the best and brightest day of their year. The snow that had kept her here and kick-started a revolution for Asta's family was just a sprinkling of fairy dust for everybody else in this wide-awake village sunk deep in sleeping hills.

'Well?' said Conan.

Asta didn't want to discuss Jake with Conan. Behind them, a small girl whimpered and asked her mummy why St Catherine hadn't cried for Christmas.

'Conan, I know how they make the statue cry,' said Asta. 'I looked into her eyes and I knew.'

'None of that matters now.'

'It matters a great deal to me, Conan. It's my big break.'

'Everything you want just takes you further away from me.' Snow was alighting on Conan's exuberant hair; it wilted, like the rest of him.

'Not everything can be about you.' From the corner of her eye, Asta saw a huddle of her relatives watching them from the church steps. Kitty was frowning, rocking on her heels. 'I love looking after you, but I have needs of my own. You don't know what it's like to be responsible for somebody.'

'So I'm just a selfish, greedy egomaniac? That's what I get for loving you?'

This glimpse of Conan-the-boyfriend was unsettling. The phrase *be careful what you wish for* sprang to Asta's mind.

She preferred the bumbling oaf she'd worshipped from afar. 'I'm going to write a damn good piece, and you're going to get it published. A deal, Conan, is a deal.' She glanced up at the hillside and saw lights come on in the Big House. *That's where I should be.* The revelation was sudden, complete; Asta cursed herself for kissing Conan.

Looking to the steps, Asta saw that her family had moved. She saw a flash of Kitty's bobble hat in the crowd, and realized that the atmosphere had altered.

There were mutterings, a random shout. A woman ran to and fro, as if caught in a trap.

'Mum!' Kitty found her and grabbed Asta's arm. 'Oh, Mum, it's terrible!'

'Look!' shouted a voice, and obediently everybody turned to where a man dragged himself up the main street, running as if on his last legs. Bent, hands on knees, he gasped out, 'She's not at home.'

Head and shoulders above the rest, Rory was pointing, marshalling, throwing the keys of the minibus to a hardy little nun.

'What's happening?' Asta looked up at Rory the way Gerry looked at the statue.

'Little Patsy Gallagher's missing. She's six.' Rory was as calm as St Catherine, but the straight line of his brows hinted at fear. 'Her ma thought she was with her da, and vice versa. She's been gone for hours.'

As if the congregation had one mind, they all wanted to help. Search parties formed as efficiently as if they'd been standing around waiting for just such an emergency. The main street was noisy with bands of men and women setting off in every direction, brandishing torches against the brutal dark and calling 'Patsy!'

'I'll take the woods,' said Rory. 'Where's Jake?'

'At home.'

'Damn.' Rory tore off his dog collar as if it was constricting his breathing. 'Come on!' he yelled, like a soldier going over the top. 'Let's find Patsy!'

Ma retreated into the church with the older people, rosary beads out and ready to pray hard. Peg, more practically, took charge of the missing child's parents and ushered them to the priests' house where, Asta knew, they'd receive strong hot tea and Peg's unique brand of steely support.

'Rory!' She shot out a hand as he took off. 'What can I do?'

'Take this.' Father Rory pressed a torch into Asta's hands. 'Round up a couple of people and go to the bridge. Don't go alone,' he added, looking into her eyes, making sure it registered.

'Do you think we'll find her?'

'Of course.' Rory bent to say into her ear, 'This mob has to keep positive.'

An elderly lady, her gaunt face stricken, pulled at his sleeve. 'Father, I heard somebody say Patsy was taken.'

'Not at all, Bridie. Patsy wandered off, that's all.'

Another old lady – Tobercree had an inexhaustible supply – said, loudly, 'There's nobody in this village would do something like that. Sure, aren't we all friends and neighbours?'

'How do we know,' said a man in a tweed cap, 'one of these newcomers hasn't grabbed little Patsy?'

Anxious folk clustered around Rory like bees around a pot of honey. Like bees, they buzzed. Asta tasted fear in the air; fear that was next to anger.

Oona and Declan had headed off with the first search

parties. 'Conan!' Asta called the slouching man to heel, and he followed. Their personal gripe was eclipsed by the thought of a child on her own – or worse, with somebody who meant her harm – out in the gloom beyond the fairy lights of the main street.

'What does this little Patsy look like?' Conan bashed his torch, trying to make it work.

'Like a six-year-old, Conan. The first six-year-old we come across on her own will be Patsy.' She snatched the torch and it lit up.

The bridge was only a few hundred yards away, but out there, with the snow banked all around, the village behind them was on mute. The icy, dashing water, once so scenic, now seemed sinister.

'We should, you know, check down there.' Asta played the beam of the torch over the river bank. 'In case . . .' There had been no time to acclimatize to this turn of affairs; Asta felt full, as if she needed to bawl. Controlling her imagination was proving difficult. Anything could have happened to the vulnerable child; Asta was empathizing when she needed to be effective.

'OK,' said Conan, uncertainly. He picked his way down the icy slope, his Savile Row shoes sliding on the frozen earth. 'What was that?' He jerked his head around to Asta.

'Just a . . .' Asta didn't know what had made the slithering, rustling noise. She overtook Conan, careering down the slight incline. Her flashlight exposed only stones and water. 'Damn.' Her feet were soaked. It felt trivial to care.

Conan put out a hand to haul her up as a knot of people rounded the road and approached them, their boots crunching in the snow.

'Nothing!' called out a man in front, in a European accent of some sort.

'She's just vanished!' said another voice.

'Into thin air,' added another, as they huddled, teeth chattering, on the hump of the bridge.

Bringing up the rear, Kitty materialized. She flew to Asta. *Patsy's somebody's daughter*, thought Asta, holding Kitty to her.

A police car, its lovesick siren howling, flew past, going much too fast for the snow-covered road.

'Should we go back to the church?' Asta suggested. 'Regroup?'

'Look!' A teenager pointed up the hill. 'Shit! What's that all about?'

Flames licked at the sky, the only hot colours in the freezing landscape.

'That's the Big House,' shouted a woman.

'No, no, it's not.' Asta was an expert on that view. 'It's near it. In its garden. But it's not the house.'

'What the devil's he up to?' a man wanted to know. 'What do we really know about that English fella?' He addressed the jaded pack, animated by his theory. 'Where is he? Why isn't he searching with us?'

Speaking up, Asta said, 'He went home before the news broke. He doesn't even know the child's missing.'

'I say we get up there and get some answers.'

The desperate pilgrims had cast Jake as a suspect. Asta's shouts of 'I know him! He's a good person!' were lost.

'Hey!' Conan could bellow when he needed to. 'Guys, calm the fuck down.' The swearing and the Yankee accent won their attention. 'We're here to find Patsy, not race around the countryside like Starsky and Hutch. I say we go back to Father what's-his-name and see if there's been any news. And then, if Patsy's still missing, we can drive up to investigate this mysterious fire. Are you with me?'

They were with him. For now.

Thank you, mouthed Asta as they all charged back along the road. Conan punched her chin playfully, like he used to.

The main street was a study in confusion. Men, women and children darted in all directions at once, with the occasional person being buttonholed by a Garda officer with a clipboard. A dog in a fluorescent harness trotted at the side of a burly policeman. Front doors stood open. The Christmas trees in windows looked sarcastic.

The neighbourhood was pulling together in its panic and fear. Nothing to do with Twitter or Facebook, Tobercree's community spirit was based on the tight-knit fabric of people who saw each other every day on the streets and in the shops. They didn't necessarily like each other, but they pulled together all the same.

'I need to see St Catherine,' cried a woman, as Asta hurried past her. 'She'll know what to do.'

Rolling her eyes, Asta went in search of a more reliable leader. Rory was besieged, one arm around a woman of about Asta's age. *The mother*, she thought, her heart aching for Patsy's mum, whose face was a numb mask of pain. Alongside, a police officer murmured discreetly into the radio on his lapel.

From the church doors, Father Dominic waved his stick. 'We must pray!' he croaked.

'We can pray *and* search, Father,' said Rory.

'I want to go in,' whimpered the woman cleaved to Rory's side.

Asta joined the sober herd, silent and weary, who filed in after Patsy's mother. Eager to demonstrate their solidarity, villagers and foreigners surrounded her. Conan, just behind Asta, laid his hands on her shoulders as they shuffled in, and it felt comforting.

A shout broke the respectful, unhappy silence. 'She's crying!'

The crowd surged forward. Rory had to hold Patsy's mother up as she drooped against him.

'She is!' yelled a child. 'St Catherine's crying!'

All the hair on Asta's body stood on end as she craned her neck to see glistening tears roll down the statue's face. With her melancholy eyes and her outstretched white palms, St Catherine seemed to channel all the anguish in the air, and turn it into something beautiful and unexpected.

'Your Rory,' said Conan, 'is nowhere near the broad.'

Indeed, Rory seemed as full of wonder as everybody else.

'What does it mean?' wailed Patsy's mother, a rag doll in Rory's arms. 'Is she dead? Is she found?'

Nobody had an answer. They all held their breath.

Even though Asta knew the scam, even though she knew those tears were tap water, she couldn't tear her eyes away from St Catherine's wistful face. Like the missing girl's frantic mother, she needed the tears to mean something.

The double doors at the back of the church flew open, kicked by a heavy-duty boot.

Asta swivelled, along with every other soul in the place, to see a gigantic wolfhound padding in, head down, ears back.

Behind Setanta came his master. In Jake's arms was a little girl, her face streaked with tears, just like the statue's.

The sirens had been switched off. The cops were guzzling Peg's tea. Father Dominic had fallen asleep at the kitchen table, on which stood Patsy Gallagher, laughing and dancing and apparently recovered.

Her mother was laughing too, as if drunk on relief. 'Get down from there, Patsy!' she said, without meaning a word of it. Patsy could do exactly what she wanted for the next few days; this Christmas she'd be spoiled and indulged by the whole of Tobercree.

Jake, rubbing his nose as if it was a magic lamp that might get him out of here, seemed dismayed by all the attention. His hand had been wrung by every resident and every tourist. He'd posed for photographs. A journalist had interviewed him. Father Dominic had clapped him on the back. Rory had given him a manly hug. Patsy's dad, recognizable as one of Ma's most faithful customers, had almost felled him with his beer breath as he thanked him over and over.

Asta sat in Peg's rocking chair in the corner, Kitty on her lap. Far too old to be on a lap, Kitty had insisted and her weight pinned Asta down, helped her feel calm again.

'I can't compete with that bastard,' said Conan bitterly. *If you'd used your thirteen-year head start, you wouldn't have to*, thought Asta.

'The nice man saved me from the spooks.' Patsy told her story for the umpteenth time, enjoying herself. *Patsy's a bit of a handful,* thought Asta wryly.

'I was hiding for a laugh,' she went on. 'I runned into the dark place.' Patsy had been curled up in the dead interior of the old mill, the only 'dark place' in Tobercree's illuminated strip. 'I was doing hide and seek and then it was scary and I was frightened and I was very fweezing and I thought I'd get in awful trouble with me ma. Lots of people were shouting my name out.'

Asta sympathized; for years she'd been chilled by hearing her own name, night after night in her sleep.

'That man bent down and said "hello you".' Patsy pointed at Jake, who gave her a waggly fingered wave. 'The dog was sooo sniffy.' Patsy giggled; it was like music.

'Setanta found her, not me,' said Jake.

Fond tutting, and Peg's 'Would you listen to his auld rubbish? The man's a hero,' obliterated Jake's plea to be relegated from 'hero' to 'lucky passer-by whose dog heard tiny cries inside ruined building'.

'I didn't even know Patsy was missing. I'd come down to . . .' Jake sighed. 'To find somebody else.'

Me. Asta looked away, choked with happiness, and saw through the kitchen blinds that the sooty sky was streaked with vivid pink. It was tomorrow. 'Happy Christmas, everyone!' she said.

December 25th

Bells rang as the truck inched up the hill.

'This is the weirdest Christmas morning ever.' And the best. Asta felt as if she was having all her Christmas goodies at once, sitting beside Jake in this jalopy, looking out at the sugar-coated trees and breathing in the clean, cold air of her birthplace.

'It *is*. It's been so odd that . . .' Jake pulled a face. 'I haven't bought you a present.'

'Who cares?' It was time to be free and easy with this man, to let him know her defences were truly down, that he had no rivals. 'You're the only present I want.'

'In that case,' Jake's smile was as bright as the early sun on the dazzling snow, 'we'll improvise when we get in.'

Christmas sex. *The best sex of all*, thought Asta, who'd never had Christmas sex.

'The statue stopped crying when you appeared with Patsy in your arms,' she said, as they neared the Big House. 'Should I put the disappearance in the article?'

'If her parents are cool with it.'

'How does it feel to be a hero?'

Jake scowled. 'It was dumb luck.'

From the back seat, Setanta let out a yawn-yowl hybrid as if to remind them who'd done all the work.

'Exactly, Setanta!' laughed Jake.

Asta was only half listening; the sight of his hands on the steering wheel, turning it lightly but expertly with those long fingers, was riveting. Never before had the suggestion of hair at a man's cuff aroused such rude thoughts in her.

'This mutt kept refusing to pass the mill. Whining. Looking in. Ears cocked. So I let him have his way. It wasn't hard to clamber in through a gap in a boarded-up window.'

Trying to concentrate, Asta said, 'The mill was the first place they searched.'

'The silly little thing hid from them,' smiled Jake. He and Patsy were chums now. She'd told him all about it, her curly head tucked in against his chest as he'd strode up the main street. 'She said running away had felt like a giggle but after a while she got lonely and frightened. But when people came looking, she thought they'd give her a good telling off so she stayed hidden.' Jake's attempt not to smile was doomed. 'Does that story remind you of anybody you know?'

'It reminds me of two people I know,' said Asta. The landscape was still frozen, but within the truck there'd been a thaw.

'Conan . . .' began Jake.

Or maybe not. 'Conan,' Asta repeated, trying to put no expression whatsoever into the name.

'I've been so angry, Asta.'

'Yeah.'

'It was the first lie, Asta. It made me think I'd got you all wrong. After all, I've only known you for a few days. Perhaps I'd built this character for you, of a woman I could trust. I felt like I'd needed somebody like you so much, I'd overlooked the parts that didn't fit my idealized version.' He hit the brake. The vehicle slid to a stop before the Big House gates. 'When Conan arrived, it was written all over your face. You had strong feelings for a man you'd only ever mentioned in a jokey, he's-an-idiot-but-you-gotta-love-him way.'

Written all over my face? And there was Asta thinking she was as cool as a cucumber. 'I never talked about it to anybody. Not a soul. I didn't tell you because we, you and me, all happened in such a rush. You blotted him out.'

'So you never thought of Conan when you were with me?'

Honesty, although the best policy, can be a bit of a bastard at times. 'I can't say I never thought of him.' Asta sat forward at Jake's growl. 'At times it held me back, stopped me saying what sprang to my lips.'

'*He* sprang to your lips last night.' Jake stared grimly through the windscreen. 'That was no work colleagues' peck I saw outside the church.'

'I can't believe that you of all people witnessed the only time Conan and I ever kissed.' Asta knew how she'd feel in Jake's place; she'd be in no mood to listen to explanations. 'He was cheeky to try. But, yes, I kissed him back.' Honesty again, poking its self-righteous little nose in. 'He was unattainable for years and I'd just *wanted* him for so long and suddenly there he was, on a Christmas platter.' Asta spread her hands, appealing to Jake. 'I kissed him to do justice to the old me, the woman I was before I met you. But the truth is . . . it was Conan's unattainability that kept me hooked. I do feel a lot for him. I feel protective; I feel responsible; I feel exasperated; I even feel love of a kind. But it's the love that comes with familiarity. It's a family love. It's nothing like the love I feel for you.'

Jake turned to her. Even Setanta seemed to prick up his shaggy ears. 'You love me, Asta?'

'I love you, Jake.'

He smiled with his whole body. He went limp, head back over the seat, barking out a loud laugh. 'That's that, then!' he crowed. 'Everything's going to be OK.' He sat up straight, all action. 'If you love me, Asta, you'll stay!'

'If you love me, Jake, you'll come back with me.'

Jake said nothing, but put the truck into gear. It rattled through the gates and onto the drive.

To the right of the house was a dull, glowing heap. The bonfire was dying. Jake opened the passenger door and helped Asta down, keeping hold of her hand as they wandered towards the embers.

'It's the treehouse,' whispered Asta. Her arms shot around Jake's middle. 'Thank you,' she said.

For one day, and one day only, Looney's Bar was closed. The occasional tap at the door and woebegone face at the window was ignored as Christmas lunch raged.

That was the only word that came close; the Looneys' Christmas table raged like a forest fire.

Tables crammed together were covered with red checkered cloths and laid with the best glasses and crockery, bracing themselves for the endless Irish *smorgasbord*. There was turkey, of course, a giant beast that would fuel sandwiches for days to come. There was ham. There were roast potatoes and carrots and peas and stuffing and little sausages all dressed up in bacon coats. There was a gravy ocean, and a sea of white sauce.

Asta had been eating for half an hour without making any impact on the amount of food on her plate. She prodded Jake, who seemed dazed. By the food, probably. Or possibly by the commotion.

'Why are they all talking at once?' he asked in a little-boy mew.

'Because that's what passes as conversation in this house.' Asta couldn't get enough of the noise. She'd be glad to get back to her zen flat, but for now, she was basking in the hubbub. 'More gravy?'

Jake looked at her as if she was mad.

Ma called from the head of the table, 'Don't forget to save space for me pudding, Jake!'

Across from Asta, Kitty pulled a cracker with Oona. There'd been no mention of the F-word; Finn's betrayal had been drowned in the deluge that had broken over mother and daughter in the past twenty-four hours.

Having won the cracker tussle, Oona roared out the joke. 'Why should you never invite footballers for Christmas lunch? Because they're always dribbling!' She picked up her wine glass. 'I tell you, I wouldn't boot that Beckham fella out of bed for dribbling!'

At her side, Declan cleared his throat – a stray sprout, perhaps – and Oona backtracked.

'Not that he'd be in me bed 'cos Declan'd be in it.' Oona winked at Asta, who knew her cousin was doing her best to reform her ways. It would take time. Asta had stood over her as she deleted all the Svens and Giorgios from her phone.

'No, no, honestly, *no*.' Rory almost had to get physical with Peg; she was forcing roast potatoes on him in a way that could get her arrested. He and Asta had shared many ironic looks as Peg and Ma lived up to the Irish matriarchal stereotypes; in another world, without his cassock, without Jake, it wouldn't be out of the question for Asta and Rory to . . . Asta stopped right there. *Too much prosecco!* One look at glowering Father Dominic, complaining that turkey got stuck in his dentures, doused any priest-based sexy daydreams.

Oona's father, rarely spotted, had joined them. A beefy man of few words, he got on with the serious business of eating without contributing to the chatter which ranged from the baby Jesus (Ma was very conscious of dog collars at her table) to whether Gerry should sell her house.

'I could move to LA,' said Gerry. 'Or Paris.'

No matter how hard Asta tried, she couldn't imagine her sister in either of those places. She couldn't imagine her outside Tobercree. Even the next village would be like Vegas to Gerry.

Peg muttered, 'I didn't do enough gravy.'

Jake drew lazy squiggles on Asta's thigh beneath the table as, above the table, her face went happily pink. Each detail reminded her of the sixteen other Christmases she'd spent at tables pushed together in the bar with these people, eating this food, vowing never to eat again, already fantasizing about Ma's eight p.m. buffet.

One detail had been left out. Just as Asta was mourning its loss, Ma stood up and said, 'A toast!'

Relieved, Asta held up her glass as she and the others rushed to stand, spilling wine and water in the process. Ma hadn't forgotten. Ma never forgot.

'To my man, the girls' da.' Ma put her head back, as she always did when rebuffing tears. 'To my James.'

'To James.' *Clink. Clink.*

'Do you think he'd have liked me?' whispered Jake, as chairs scraped back into position again and bottoms were gratefully lowered.

'He'd love you.'

They were standing up again, Peg tutting, Father Dominic almost toppling into his lunch, as Conan boomed 'Another toast! To Asta.' He towered over them all. 'And Jake!'

'To Asta and Jake,' mumbled everybody in a perfunctory way. Only Da ever got toasted at the table, and besides, there was turkey to eat.

The post-lunch lull split the mismatched colony. Elders snored on sofas. Kitty went for a walk with her friends. Asta cleared up the bar, with the help of Jake and Rory.

Job done, she brewed coffee for her helpers. Conan held out a cup.

'You didn't help.'

'I did; I stayed out of the way.'

'Nice toast.'

'I didn't mean it,' said Conan. 'I only did it so you'd think I was a great guy and leave Jake and run away with me.'

'My running-away days are over,' said Asta, handing him a coffee made just the way he liked it. 'And I know that's why you did it.' *I also know you meant it.* She took off her apron and threw it down. 'You chaps can snooze, or wrestle naked, or whatever. I'm going upstairs to finish this article once and for all.' She paused by Rory, slumped on a banquette looking as if he felt the very special pain only far too much turkey can induce. She handed him a steaming cup. 'Bear up. It only happens once a year.'

'I have to visit a dying man this evening,' said Rory. 'That always brings perspective.'

'I'm sure you'll bring him some comfort.' Asta knew that he would, with his light touch and his compassion. 'Rory, I need to tell you . . . I know.'

'You know? What do you know?' Asta watched him toy for a moment with pretending to misunderstand. 'I see,' he nodded. He seemed disappointed rather than startled. 'I look forward to reading the article.'

To: angie507@hotmail.co.uk
From: a.looney@boulevardmagazine.com

HAPPY CHRISTMAS, BESTIE!

Still lots of snow here, so still no planes. When I do get back, you'd better buy an Everest of wine boxes, cancel your plans and lock all the doors – I have so much to tell you!

It can all wait except this.

Kitty and Mum just ambushed me with their cunning scheme. They've been cooking it up together, and what could I do but agree? The upshot is, Kitty's staying here in Tobercree, helping Ma with the bar until she decides what she really wants to do.

It means Ma will have the support she needs and Kitty will have a proper job (even with an indulgent grandma, running a pub is tough). I feel as if my outer layer of skin has been ripped off. But you're only a baby, I wanted to shout. I gave it my blessing, because what else could I do? What else can we do but encourage them?

A rap at her door interrupted Asta's typing. 'Hello, sweetie pie.'

'Mum, there was something I couldn't say in front of Grandma. She'd get upset.'

'Go on.' Asta turned away from her computer, giving Kitty her full attention.

'When you were talking about the drawbacks of me staying, when you were trying to make me change my mind and come home with you, you mentioned Martin.'

The name landed with a bang. 'Like I said, darling, we don't know what Martin's going to do. Gerry thinks he'll move away, but she could be wrong. What if you run into him? Worse, what if he pesters you?'

'I did run into him. Today.'

'No!'

'I didn't go for a walk after lunch, I went up to that stupid show house. I told Martin to stay away. I told him I'm not interested in anything he has to say.'

Asta gaped.

'He got the message, Mum. I was very clear. I told him I have all the parents I need, thank you very much.' Kitty smiled. 'I'm a Looney woman, Mum. Relax. Martin can't hurt me, 'cos I won't let him.'

Kitty was no fluffy chick needing protection from the momma bird. *She's a ninja chick, flying the nest with all guns blazing.*

By the fire in the bar, Conan looked different wearing his glasses – older, and more intelligent. He finished reading, took them off, and *voila!* – he was Asta's big daft bear again. 'Hmm,' he said.

'You don't like it.' Asta stopped pacing. She'd sweated blood over that piece.

'I love it.'

'Yay!' She clapped, then realized she was applauding herself and stopped. 'But?'

'I need to know before I send it that you're sure you want to do this.' Conan gestured about him. 'I mean, you come here looking for a secret. You find tons of 'em.' He slapped the pages in his hand. 'Is this definitely what you want to print? Are you being fair to this town?'

'It's the truth.'

'OK, Mother Superior.' Conan stood up, stretched. 'Say goodbye to your mother for me. I don't like farewells.'

'Where are you going?' Asta's alarm took her by surprise. 'Stay, Conan. I want you to stay.'

'I have a guy outside ready to drive me to Dublin in an off-road vehicle that looks too Mad Max for my liking, but hey, I can't pull that private boat stunt twice in a week. Besides,' he said, shrugging on his coat, 'I don't have the motivation this time.' He held Asta at arm's length. 'Is that a tear I see? That's *too* cute, Looney. You don't need me here, getting in the way. Jake looks at me like he's a guard dog and I'm a guy with a crowbar.' Conan looked at his feet. 'I can't watch what's happening between you and him, knowing I squandered it all those years. Because that's *my* truth, you know?' He wandered over to the door. They both knew he wouldn't kiss her goodbye. 'That I had a chance with you, but I missed it. Over and over.' He opened the door, and Asta shuddered at the blast of freezing air. 'And over.'

Asta didn't just love Jake. She also loved his dog. And his house. Trailing her fingers over the stripped panelling, she accepted that she was in that initial glorious stage of a romance, where everything about your man thrills you – *Oh, I adore the way you snort when you laugh!* – and that it would morph over years into something quite different – *I'm divorcing you because of the way you snort when you laugh!* – but this was her first real love affair, so she gave in to it.

'Would you rather have sex with the house than me?' Jake returned to the grand sitting room they'd managed to make cosy, and lingered by the door. 'I can leave you two alone if you'd prefer.'

'How'd it go?' Asta wasn't letting him off the hook; she wanted to hear all about his call to Steve.

'It went . . . interestingly.'

Jake bounded onto the sofa, stretching out in his jeans and bare feet, opening his arms for her to join him. Welding herself to him, Asta savoured the sensation of the burning log fire keeping them toasty enough to be barefoot as snow fell pitilessly beyond the bare window.

Jake's mum had broken down when she heard his voice. She told him she understood. Plans were afoot for her to fly over to Ireland as soon as the weather stopped showing off.

Karen had been cold, then furious, finally begging him to marry her. When he told her that might be tricky, she'd spat that she was shagging one of his friends.

'She sounds nice,' Asta had said, glad that Karen had agreed to move out of Jake's house, pending a financial settlement.

With Steve, the first phone call had been sticky. Hurt, he'd been unable to accept Jake's reasons for going – and staying – away. 'I thought you'd topped yourself, mate,' he'd said.

'So,' said Asta, wiggling into position half on top of, half beside Jake. 'Did Steve like my idea?'

'You mean *my* idea?' Jake raised his eyebrows. 'OK, *our* idea.' He let out an exasperated huff of breath, enjoying the pretence of annoyance. After the naked fun earlier that evening, neither of them could be remotely angry with the other. Asta could have machine-gunned the village and Jake would have patted her on the head and pronounced her mass murder 'adorable'.

Whoever's idea it was, the second phone call had done the trick. Steve was on board.

It was simple. Jake was a man who needed something to do, something creative and engrossing that made him feel relevant. Steve was a man with building skills who was living on benefits. Both of them were miserable with their lot, but one of them had a stupid amount of money.

Together, pooling their resources, they could buy historic buildings in need of renovation and coax them back to life. Ruins would be revived to their former glory, not just patched up and stuck together. The buildings would breathe once more and Jake could stand back, look them up and down, and think *I did that*.

'I barely finished describing the plan, you know, working with councils on listed buildings and turning grand old mansions into affordable homes, before Steve was butting in with more schemes. We're in business, Asta. It's happening.'

Down in the village the church bells pealed. The jubilant sound matched Asta's mood completely.

'Happy Christmas, Jake,' she said.

December 26th

Staying up all night was 'hardcore Irish', according to Jake.

'I never do this, though.' Asta yawned extravagantly. 'I'm an early to bed, early to rise girl, me.' They'd talked and canoodled and watched the flames until now the room was brightening again.

'Listen.' Jake opened one of the French windows, cocked his ear.

'Brrr, that's cold.' Asta tiptoed over, already hearing the siren song of the big old bed. 'What am I listening to?'

A small but insistent noise, like silver beads rattling, grew until Asta could hear nothing else.

'The thaw's started.'

While they'd been by the fire, Tobercree had done an abrupt about-turn. Snow was melting, swelling the river. Roofs were dripping. Trees were shrugging off their Siberian furs.

Asta wanted to shout *no!* It was too soon. She hadn't had enough Jake yet. She wasn't ready.

'There's something else me and Steve agreed last night,' said Jake, watching her watch the melting world. 'The first project for our new company . . .'

Asta guessed. 'The mill?'

'You have to admit it's perfect. Imagine it renovated. Imagine the jobs. I'd be giving something back.'

'Yeah. It's perfect.' Asta felt as if the thaw had reached inside her and turned her heart to a cold, dripping thing.

'The planes will probably fly today.'

'Probably.'

'Asta . . .' said Jake. 'Stay.'

'Jake . . .' said Asta. 'Come.'

December 27th

'Not dancing?' Rory took the chair beside Asta.

'This gets in the way.' Asta pointed to the bump straining the lines of her new red dress.

They sat, silent, looking out at the cold outlines of the fields. Unlike the year before, there was no snow, but Ireland's bitter winter temperatures turned the panorama into a frosted masterpiece.

The new conservatory built onto the back of the refurbished Mill Hotel was warm, despite its glass walls and stone floors. The glass box was as chic as the rest of the hotel; Jake and Steve had turned out to be good at their new vocation. When Asta had flown out of Ireland, one year ago exactly, she'd been knotted with anxiety about how she and Jake would maintain their love long-distance. She needn't have panicked; Jake turned out to be adept at jumping on planes and surprising her. The love, so quickly grown, was maintained just fine.

'How long now?'

'One month to go.' Asta looked down at her swollen belly, proud of it, amazed by it.

'I've never asked,' said Rory, still gazing outwards, 'why you did it.'

'The article, you mean?'

'I couldn't believe my eyes when I got my hands on a copy of *Boulevard*. Why did you leave out the secret of how the statue cried?'

'The story didn't need it.' Asta shifted. The baby had moved; it was tap-dancing on her bladder. 'You were right. Annoyingly.' They shared a complicit glance in the lantern light. 'It *was* a story about hope. About believing things will get better. Tobercree was knocked sideways by the recession, but everybody pulled together, believed in the future, and came through. Then that little girl went missing, only to turn up, well, *here*,' Asta looked around her. 'It was a perfect illustration of how the village could take its destiny into its own hands. St Catherine might have shed a tear, but it was a real live man who found Patsy.'

'*Your* real live man.'

'I didn't name-check him in the magazine. He would've throttled me.'

'I have a pet theory. That you left out the secret in order to thank St Catherine.' Rory heard Asta's scoff and said, 'She helped you find the words to tell Kitty about the tree-house.'

'No.' Asta was adamant. '*You* did that. If anything,' she said gruffly, 'I was thanking *you*.'

'It all feels like a long time ago. No coach parties now.' Rory sounded relieved. 'We've lost them to St Philomena in Ballymahooley. She dances, apparently.'

Asta giggled. 'Brazen slut.'

'I don't think she twerks,' said Rory. 'More of a shuffle.'

'Sounds like me.'

Behind them, the hum of the party in the hotel function room was contained, the music a low pulse.

'How did you rumble me?' Rory was wry, curious.

'It was when I knelt in front of St Catherine on Christmas Eve. I'd just left Martin in the treehouse. All the plates I'd been spinning were smashing on the floor. And I tried to meditate, just like you advised. To clear my mind. Let the inspiration in. She looked directly into my eyes. And I knew.'

'What did you know?' This was the only truthful conversation about the statue Rory had ever had.

'I knew it wasn't the same statue as the one I examined. You gave me a different one, you trickster.'

Rory said nothing.

'I bet that face has been getting you out of trouble since you were a child,' laughed Asta. 'St Catherine, so tender, so compassionate, looked *down* into my eyes. The eyes of the statue I examined looked *up*.'

As if kicking himself, Rory shook his head.

'When I realized that, I concentrated and I saw it. Just a sliver of paint, a tiny arc, missing from the corner of one blue eye.'

'Where I drilled the hole,' said Rory.

'I nipped over the brass surround and peered at the back of her head. I saw the teeny hole where you poured the water in. And I saw the mark where you'd re-plastered over the sponge you put inside her head.' Asta could sympathize with the saint; some days, pregnancy made Asta feel as if she had a sponge inside her head, too.

'I couldn't control the crying.' Rory seemed keen that she know this. 'I just filled her head with water – yes, that *is* an odd sentence,' he agreed, when Asta giggled. 'Sometimes it would dry up and there was nothing. Sometimes she'd cry immediately. Other times . . .' He regarded her, levelly. 'On Christmas Eve, those tears were as much a surprise to me as they were to you. Maybe there was a divine hand behind it.'

'You're saying that to make yourself feel better. Why did you do it, Rory?' Asta didn't want to offend this man, her friend. 'Priests aren't supposed to lie.'

'Are you? Are any of us? But we do.' Rory sighed. 'You're right, of course. I'm just wriggling out of it. I did it because . . . the banks had gone bust. Our mill had closed. Shops were failing. I wanted to fight the misery, the sensation that we were in a downward spiral, that the recession was going to choke us. I did it,' he said, eyebrows raised at the simplicity of it, 'to cheer us all up!'

'It certainly worked.'

'It took off in a way I'd never envisaged. I never thought the story would go round the world like that. Everything snowballed. The huge amounts of money worried me. We bought a minibus, built a crèche, donated to the hospital. The tears brought nothing but happiness, but then it went too far and I couldn't step back. The miracles started. Dervla's cure took me by surprise. Like all the other miracles, it had to be a coincidence, but what could I say? One impetuous decision, and I was locked in.' He looked at Asta. 'Sound familiar?'

'A little.'

'Everybody yearned for the statue to cry. I found myself creeping into the church like a burglar, filling up that damn sponge. But after Patsy was found, I stopped. Then St Philomena started getting down with her bad self, so that was that.'

'You look much happier.'

'So do you,' said Rory. 'And so does Jake. When he's not looking completely exhausted.'

'Refurbishing this place was even more demanding than he thought. Has he told you he's bought two properties in London? One's an old hospital he's turning into affordable flats. The other's going to be our house.' Their forever house.

'Yes, we're losing him. Tobercree's loss is your gain.'

'Rory?'

'Yes?'

'Thank you.'

Rory smiled his film-star smile. 'No, Asta, thank *you*.'

Indoors again, the music a sonic boom after the quiet of the conservatory, Asta found a chair by a dishevelled table scattered with bottles and cake.

Weaving across the dance floor, Jake brought Asta a glass of water. His tie undone, his shirt coming out of his waistband, he had achieved Phase Three of wedding drunkenness. The 'I Love the Entire World' phase.

'You were busting some smooth moves out there, Jakey.'

'Did you like my robot?'

'That was the best bit,' said Asta, wondering which part of Jake's strange and very long solo had been his robot.

'I like you pregnant,' he said, looking at her the way Asta looked at Magnums. He bent to rest his head on her bump; the baby had tapped into a vein of super-soppiness deep inside Jake. 'I know it's a girl,' he slurred. 'When you're asleep, me and the baby chat and she told me she's a girl. She's going to be really clever and kind and very good at things and pretty and she won't take any shit at all.'

'I can't wait to meet her.'

'She'll be a bloody fantashtic footballer. And poetry! Oh, the poetry she'll write!'

384

Disentangling herself from a jiving local, Angie joined them, downing Asta's water in one. 'I'm danced *out*.' A London peacock in her blue and silver dress, Angie radiated good vibes. 'This place is a credit to you, Jake.' She looked around at the rafters and exposed brick. 'It's every bit as funky as some gaff in Chelsea.' Dancing on the spot, just about able to resist the lure of the music, she said, 'No snow, though! I'm disappointed. Maisie and I want to be snowed in up here.'

Oona teetered over in her platforms, her chignon just starting to rebel against the hairpins, her wedding dress verging on tasteful.

'Girl, you're *thin*,' said Angie, not altogether admiringly.

'I know!' Oona took it as a compliment. 'I'm a size eight.' She explained how she'd followed the Atkins Diet, and the 5:2 diet, with a little bit of Weight Watchers thrown in. 'Basically, I only ate half a sausage every other Wednesday.'

'The hard bit,' said Angie, with some satisfaction, 'is keeping it off.'

'Stuff that. I can't wait to put every single pound back on. Starting tomorrow I'm having Mars Bars for breakfast.' She blew a kiss to her own torso. 'Goodbye, waist, I'm going to miss you. But you're not half as much fun as a takeaway.' She turned to Declan, who had waddled up in his new suit. 'Get us a drink, there's a pet. And a sandwich. And a slice of Christmas pud. Ta.'

Jake had released himself back into the wild. Normally a man who never even tapped his foot, suddenly he just had to dance. A circle cleared around him; Asta knew that in his poor, drunken head Jake would think they were admirers, not people terrified of being kicked in the head.

'Jayzus,' said Oona, snatching a vol-au-vent out of a

passing guest's hand. 'That is one serious piece of machinery you found for yourself.'

'He's a handsome swine,' agreed Asta. And strong as steel, and soft as butter.

'With a bum you'd sell your granny for. Whereas Declan's bum . . .' Oona's expression suggested that her new husband's machinery wasn't quite as serious as Jake's.

On the dance floor, Jake and Kitty had hijacked Ma, who was now conga-ing self-consciously. They'd had to take a tray forcibly out of her hand, reminding her that she wasn't on duty.

The village had reeled the day Ma sold the pub. Old men wept on the pavement. Dogs cocked their legs at half-mast. Asta and Kitty had assumed she'd refuse to contemplate such heresy, but she'd agreed that it was time. 'I'm tired,' she'd said.

But not, it had turned out, too tired to run the new hotel for the first year or two. With Kitty at her side – they worked instinctively well together – plus more naps and a new hairdo, Ma was now Queen of the Old Mill.

As promised, the venture had created jobs and drawn a new strain of tourist to Tobercree, ones who demanded the local organic produce that Kitty sourced for the cafe. The cutting-edge style of the venture wasn't quite to Ma's usual taste; she'd had to be restrained from dotting the Japanese garden with gnomes, and she condemned the discreet Christmas decorations as 'half-arsed'.

Oona stretched luxuriously. 'Just think. This time tomorrow, I'll be ordering room service and watching a Tuscan sunset.' She prodded Asta. 'It's still OK to visit on the way back, yeah?'

Asta was looking forward to squiring the newlyweds around London. 'As long as you don't mind the sofa bed.'

'Of course I mind the sofa bed. If you weren't so bloody-minded you'd have moved out of that stupid flat by now.'

'I like that stupid flat. I brought up Kitty there.'

'If you'd only spend your husband's loot, there'd be a guest suite waiting for me, with a gold-plated bidet and a butler called Jenkinson. But no, you have to make your silly point.'

The point that Asta made didn't seem silly to her.

'If I had a squillionaire in my grasp,' said Oona, 'I'd wear crystal knickers and wee champagne.'

'Thank God,' said Asta, 'for Peg. At least *somebody's* flying the flag for Girl Power in this family.'

'Peg?' snorted Oona, eyeing their mature relative, who was leaking puritanical disapproval on the edge of the dance floor in a new, horrible dress. 'She thinks *feminist* is code for *raving lezzer*.'

'She's financially independent. She answers to no man. She lives the life she wants to live.' Peg was a real person to Asta now; the portrait Asta had carried around during her years of exile had been a crude daub. Peg Looney had depth. She spoke out. Even when Asta didn't agree with her – which was ninety-nine per cent of the time – she respected her. Having Peg on your side meant never having to be afraid. (Although she was, sometimes, still afraid of Peg.)

'Look at her,' laughed Oona, fondly. 'She's bullying the new Father. Straightening his jacket. Like he's a five-year-old.'

'He's letting her do it,' said Asta, touched that Father Babashola, a confident, vigorous Nigerian man with a gap in his front teeth, understood his housekeeper and gave in to her fussing. She spoke loudly and clearly to her new charge, using simple words and phrases. Father Babashola, who had graduated with a first from Oxford, nodded patiently. 'He knows how much she misses Father Dominic.'

'Kitty cried all day, you know,' said Oona, half respectful, half disbelieving. 'Even I was shocked. I thought he'd live forever. Just to spite us all!' She lowered her voice. 'That boss of yours is a one. If I wasn't an old married lady . . .'

'Easy, tiger. He brought a plus-one.' Titled, thin and languid, Conan's date looked like all his other girlfriends, but Asta nursed high hopes. The woman's IQ was well into double figures and she took no nonsense; perhaps she'd tame Conan, help him be happy at last.

'Do you ever regret turning him down?'

'He's family. It'd be incest,' said Asta. The thought that she could regret plumping for Jake amused her. Conan had taken her pregnancy as a personal affront, but was already showering the unborn dot with unsuitable gifts.

Jake and Angie tangoed over. His tie was around his head: Phase Four of wedding drunkenness had been achieved. 'Look at Gerry!' he said, delighted; watching his bird's family was one of his chief pleasures in life.

They looked. All in taupe – dress, bag and silly hat – Gerry had rugby-tackled Father Babashola and was introducing him to the man she'd chosen from her many, many beaux on www.catholiccanoodling.com. No doubt she was reciting Olaf's online profile, of which she was inordinately proud. Olaf's long and varied list of interests included not only the clichéd long walks and open fires, but also Pekinese breeding, speed-walking and taxidermy. Despite all this, Olaf was dull; so dull he was almost interesting. 'My sister's in love, ladies. Can you feel the glow from here?' Asta winced as

Gerry bent double at Olaf's side, honking like a goose having a heart attack at some insipid joke.

Martin was never mentioned. He'd been eradicated from history. Gerry had a whole new life; she'd bought a cat, holidayed in Majorca and had her moustache lasered. Olaf was an important girder in this decadent new structure.

Occasionally Olaf stayed overnight at the Big House, where Gerry now lived along with her mother and her niece. Jake referred to this living arrangement as 'a sitcom waiting to happen', but Asta loved the stories that emerged as three generations of Looney gals rubbed along together. Kitty punched the air when Olaf slept over; Ma pretended not to notice, and said a fervent *Hail Mary*.

'Laters, bitches.' Oona had spotted Declan talking to a woman under sixty: this was against the rules, and he knew it.

Asta stood, and a scuffle broke out between Jake and Angie to help her up; they almost knocked her over in the process. This pregnancy had brought out a competitive streak in her family and friends, all of them keen to check her hydration levels and check she'd taken her vitamins. Angie sent her emails with headings like 'SORE NIPPLES?' and even Oona repeated 'Are you tired? You look tired. Sure you're not tired?' on an endless loop.

As ever, Gerry went further: during the wedding ceremony she'd swivelled around in her pew to mouth the immortal question, *Are you constipated*?

When Asta had ignored her, Gerry leaned over to hiss, 'Come on, level with me, when was the last time you had an honest-to-goodness poo?' Asta took it all patiently; she'd seen how Gerry had swallowed hard at the announcement of her little sister's second baby.

This pregnancy was different to her last. Gratitude bloomed in Asta's chest. She put out an arm to Angie, a constant in both her babies' lives, and Angie grinned. With the telepathy of great friends, she knew what Asta was trying to say.

This time around there was no fog of guilt, just a straight path ahead. This time last year Asta had left behind a befuddled, hurt Jake at the airport. 'But why?' he'd said, refusing to let go of her, unwilling to relinquish her to Duty Free.

'Because I have a life,' she'd said. That had been clumsy; Jake had snapped, 'Yeah, and I'm part of it, I hope!' She'd carried on, muddling through, wishing she had a speech-writer for times like this, to iron out the creases and make it all clear. She loved him, but she was leaving him; how to convince him that those two things could be true at the same time?

'I built my life on my own. I placed every brick with my bare hands. I can't just pretend it's not there, close the door on my little flat where all the milestones of my life with Kitty took place.'

She'd asked Jake what she'd do if she stayed. 'Would I be on your payroll?' Asta, after so long as a soloist, wanted a strong partner. 'Don't you want the same, Jake?'

He'd visited. She'd flown to him. After he'd finally stopped carping about her 'defection' they'd blossomed, like the geraniums that rioted in Ma's window boxes at the first hint of sunshine.

And then you happened, said Asta silently to her bump.

Unplanned, but more welcome even than Christmas, the baby made perfect, wonderful sense. And forced its parents to make some decisions.

'It's time for me to come home,' Jake had said. There was more opportunity for the fledgling company in London, and Steve was missing the ale, the litter and the less sarcastic women.

The Regency house Jake bought – three floors of creamy stucco – had taken Asta's breath away. The plans drawn up by Jake and Steve (now one of the family, and prey to Asta's consistently poor matchmaking skills) would rescue the Grade II gem from dereliction, and deliver a home full of light and space and folksy elegance for the blended Jones-Looneys.

Showing her around, hard hats on, Jake had said, 'While we're refurbishing we can rent somewhere near your flat, but, you know, *nicer*.'

'Excuuuse me?' Asta's expression had been colder than the snow that brought them together.

Jake soon learned just how stubborn a Looney could be; they stayed put. Asta refused to let him help with the rent. Every now and then, she reminded him that he was a kept man.

'Our girls, together again.' Angie brought her friend back to the present, pointing at Kitty and Maisie flirting with the local boys. 'D'you think Kitty will ever come back?'

That 'ever' was casual, and not designed to hurt, but it did. 'Hope so,' smiled Asta, watching Kitty nudge Maisie, blushing and happy. She'd changed her hair: Asta didn't approve, but hadn't said so. The truth was that Kitty had found her calling. The Mill Hotel ran like clockwork, thanks to the fusion of Kitty's energy and Ma's experience. Jake said Kitty was 'an old soul'; Asta liked that.

'She'll come back when she's ready,' said Jake, who was paternal (as Kitty wanted) but hands-off (as Kitty also wanted). 'Come on, Angie. Dance with me! You know you want to.'

They strutted off. Angie was pro-Jake, always siding with him in any spats. She did her own thing to the music, while Jake . . . Asta couldn't really describe what Jake was doing.

'Greetings, Fatso!' Conan rocked up, keeping that force-field between them he'd activated on her first day back at work.

His plus-one clobbered him with her dainty evening bag. 'Hey! Apologize, you swine. She looks scrumptious.' She winked at Asta.

Do you know more than you're letting on? thought Asta, liking her even more.

'You look pale,' said Conan. 'Do you need to sit down?'

Asta would have liked to shout, exasperated, for every-body to stop asking if she needed to sit down, and that it was a myth that pregnant women need to sit down a lot. Except she did want to sit down. 'I'm fine,' she said. 'But thanks for asking.'

Later, alone on the terrace, she pulled the concertina door across and muted the party. Finding a chair, she sank into it without any help.

The baby was lively. Possibly it was a dancer like its dad – last seen either doing the twist or having a fit, it was hard to be sure. Asta sighed, partly with fatigue, partly with con-tentment. She was overwhelmed by both.

Sometimes, to pleasantly scare herself, Asta imagined how her life would be if she hadn't taken the dare held out by Conan. It would be a fine life, admittedly, one to be proud of. But it wouldn't have the lengthy cast list of the current one. It wouldn't boast a boisterous, loving Ma or an infuri-ating, unique sister or a formidable, awe-inspiring aunt.

Kitty would be mummified in cotton wool. *And my heart would be alone.*

This new life, her rebirth, stretched Asta. She worried about Ma's health; she fretted about Kitty having so much responsibility; she yearned for Gerry to meet a baby who needed a mother as much as Gerry needed a child.

Jake slipped out to join her, and the party roared for a moment before he closed the door he'd designed.

'I'd forgotten how exhausting this little village can be.' Jake flopped beside his other half, throwing a drunken arm that landed a little too heavily around her shoulders. He could never keep his hands off Asta; if she was within touching distance, she got touched.

Resting her head on his shoulder, she murmured, 'Me too.' They looked out at the chilly darkness, framed by the soft glow of the fairy lights Ma had strung everywhere, cutting-edge design or no cutting-edge design. 'Do you ever miss it?' Along with her other worries, Asta somehow found time to wonder if she'd forced Jake's hand, if he might be happier in Ireland.

'Um . . . not really.' Jake sounded as if he was in two minds, both of them a bit pissed. 'I'm glad to get here, but I'm even gladder to get home.'

Never smug about the micro-world she and Jake had built – she'd been through too much to take happiness for granted – Asta nonetheless had confidence in it. 'And to think I had you down as a heartbreaker.'

'Strictly a pipe and slippers man, me.'

'Never!' Asta loved his rakish looks, his naughtily premature white hair, his repertoire of winks and his long, languid limbs. Jake made domesticity sexy, and he made a woman of Asta.

'Your ma's been dropping hints again.' Jake pronounced it *hintsh*.

'I know.' *Wouldn't it be grand to have another wedding here?* or *I see all them fillum stars are getting married!*

'Would you like me to make an honest woman of you?'

'Ask me again when you're sober.'

'I *am* shober!'

Asta was already married in her heart, where all the important stuff happened. Maybe, after the baby arrived – this pretty, football-playing, poetry-writing baby – she'd have the energy to pull on a white dress and invite three hundred of her closest friends to the Mill, but she'd never been a greedy girl. She had everything she wanted, and that was surely enough for anybody. 'Let's talk about it when we're in the new house.'

Jake was sombre. 'This time next year we'll have an actual staircase and a kitchen you can swing a cat in, and we won't have to smile at your weird neighbour when we meet him on the landing.'

'Here you are!' Kitty joined them, pink of cheek and trendy of dress. 'Do you need a cushion, Mum?'

'Not you as well,' smiled Asta. 'Just be my little girl for tonight, sweetie. Let me look after *you*.'

'If you like.' Kitty had expressed no envy of the latecomer who would end her reign as only child. 'Just think, next Christmas'll be the baby's first! We'll have to come to you, won't we?'

'Jesus, KitKat, let me get labour out of the way before we plan next Christmas.'

'But it's the best time of the year,' insisted Kitty. 'It's magic.'

Jake took Asta's hand and squeezed it.

'Christmas is when we all get together.' Kitty took Asta's other hand.

We're always together, thought Asta. Her heart was full; this time it wasn't heartburn. She carried them all inside her, felt them nourish her, keep her going. It was so ordinary, her life. And so special.

'It's snowing!' squealed Kitty, leaping up. Merrymakers flooded onto the terrace, exclaiming at the white floss raining down. The darkness transformed – miraculously, some might say – into a translucent dreamscape.

'If it's heavy,' said Ma, ever hopeful, 'youse can't go home!'

'That's fine by me,' said Asta, who knew that home wasn't a mark on a map. Home was wherever she lay down alongside Jake, their baby safe inside her, her other baby not too far away, and Setanta snuffling at the foot of the bed. Last night, the dream had returned.

Asta sits on a branch of the highest tree on the highest hill. It's snowing, yet she's as warm as toast. A bird sings. Drums sound, in rhythm with her blood.

She is happy.

EXCLUSIVE Q&A
WITH CLAIRE SANDY

1. Why did you decide to write a book set at Christmas time?
Well, that's easy! Christmas is so magical it *begs* to be written about. Unlike other big occasions, such as birthdays or weddings, which focus on individuals, *everybody* looks forward to Christmas. It belongs to each of us and we all invest so much in it; can there be any worse recrimination than 'You ruined my Christmas'?

2. What does Christmas mean to you?
The word conjures up so much. When I was a child it meant: presents! Now that I'm older, I don't even think about what I might receive; it's all about the ever-growing list of presents to buy/meals to plan/strange dietary needs to accommodate. The real meaning of the season – and look away now if you're allergic to sentiment because there's a lorry-full of the stuff headed right for you – is being with the people who are special to me. Some of those people have gone now, so Christmas is bittersweet these days, but no less meaningful.

Oh, and Christmas means Quality Street. Obviously.

3. Do you have any family traditions you look forward to at Christmas?

Apart from the Boxing-Day row, you mean? Like any family, we have little rituals and touches that personalize Christmas. The starter at lunch *has* to be smoked salmon, just as my mother-in-law *has* to wrap a Terry's Chocolate Orange for everybody. After the meal, my dad always used to say 'That was the best turkey I ever ate in my life'; now that he's gone, I find myself saying it for him.

4. What is your favourite Christmas memory?

They jostle for position. My whole body can remember how it felt to be muffled up in coat and hat and scarf, standing between my parents at Midnight Mass, thrilled to be up so late and entirely confident that Santa was on his way. There's also the year we stayed at my uncle's farm and I looked out of the window on Christmas morning to see a cow with tinsel on its horns. My very favourite memory, though, is of being a tiny thing, just sitting and gawping at the Christmas tree. I was gormlessly happy, not a thought in my head, transfixed by the bright ethereal points of light. Nowadays, I need to be drunk to replicate this feeling.

5. Did you *write* Snowed in for Christmas *at Christmas time?*

I wish I could say I wrote this book wrapped in fairy lights, mince pie crumbs down my front and glitter in my hair, but the truth is more mundane. I wrote it just *after* Christmas, which made all the descriptions feel poignant, as if I was writing about a land I'd been banished from. Maybe you can feel the yearning in the pages!

6. Are you a last-minute Christmas shopper or are all your presents wrapped six months in advance?

I've always been highly organized (and highly smug) about Christmas presents. I plan, I plot, I save. I put aside an evening to wrap. Until last year, when even I got sick of my goody-two-shoes ways. *Wing it!* I told myself. I left everything until the last minute, anticipating a glorious adrenalin buzz, thinking *God, I feel so ALIVE!* as I dashed through John Lewis on the twenty-third of December.

Never. Again. I could feel Christmas falling apart as I spent twice as much on half as many gifts as I usually buy. They were wrapped as if I'd done it in the dark with a gun to my head. And adrenalin tastes much the same as cold, naked fear . . .

7. Do you have a favourite Christmas book?

Perversely, my favourite Christmas book isn't about Christmas. When I was twelve years old, my mum gave me a copy of *Gone with the Wind*. *Yuk,* I thought. Expecting it to be soppy and dull – and looooong – I only picked it up late on Christmas night when I'd exhausted the novelty factor of my other toys. I was transfixed, hanging upside down on the sofa (why do kids do that?) and had to be prised off the cushions to go to bed.

8. Do you prefer writing novels with Christmas or summer settings?

That question is so unfair! There are pros and cons to both. The truth is, once an author finishes a book they long to work on something different, so if you ask me while I'm writing a Christmas story my answer would be a loud and clear 'summer'. And vice versa.

TOP FIVE CHRISTMASSY DRINKS

1. My very first taste of alcohol was a glass of **Advocaat** at Christmas. Suspiciously yellow and ever so eggy, I'm surprised it didn't put me booze off for life. I recall my mum ceremoniously placing a scarlet maraschino cherry on a cocktail stick in the glass. Technicolour nostalgia!

2. These days, Christmas kicks off mid December when I offer round the **Aperol Spritz**. Well, I don't *offer*: I foist. A measure of festively orange Aperol plus a blast of prosecco, topped off with soda water and garnished with a slice of orange spells Christmas to me.

3. For the non-drinkers, a **Virgin Sea Breeze** looks and tastes sophisticated. Pour half and half grapefruit juice and cranberry juice over some boulders of ice, and knock it back happily, knowing there's no hangover in the offing.

4. My parents always started Christmas day with a **Bucks Fizz**. I remember gagging at the thought of champers in the morning and I only overcame my aversion when I tinkered with my mum's recipe. Back then, people used too much orange juice. I pour out a small measure, then fill the glass with prosecco and consider myself ever so Jackie Collins-ish.

5. When I was small, people had drinks cabinets. These were ornate beasts, only opened on high days and holidays. Every single cabinet in the land had a bottle of **creme de menthe** lurking in its mirrored innards. This alarmingly green liquid was always brandished at Christmas but never actually found its way into a glass. Perhaps now is the time to bring it back into vogue. Let's all demand creme de menthe this Christmas!

SURVIVAL TACTICS IF YOU EVER GET SNOWED IN FOR CHRISTMAS

This is one of my most cherished fantasies. A log cabin in the wilderness, smoke curling out of the chimney as the snow banks up against the door. But what would the reality be like?

1. Food
Let's hope you've already done the yuletide shopping. If you've been diligent and traditional, you'll be up to your hips in poultry and carbs and sweet delights. Graze. This is no time to diet, people! No rules apply. If you want After Eights and stuffing on the same plate, go for it.

2. Games
No, not mind games – this is no time to undermine your sister's confidence in her potato-roasting methods (although that *is* very popular at my house). Crack out the board games. Nothing says Christmas quite like a sore loser turning over the Monopoly board and storming off to bed.

3. Knitting
As a seasoned knitter I can verify that it's the answer to world peace; nobody who's made a Fair Isle coat for their dog could countenance genocide. Likewise, when tempers

are frayed in your cabin, when you're having a sugar come-down, or you just lost at Hungry Hippos for the third time in a row, sit down with your needles and run up a scarf. (If it's nice, keep it; if it's revolting, wrap it up and give it away.)

4. Talk
Like, *really* talk. Tackle the big questions. Life. Love. The universe. Why men have nipples and why only offensive people say 'no offence'.

5. Sleep
Because we're all sleep deprived these days. My friends and I compete over who's done the most on the least sleep. I used to go on holiday to dance and flirt and get tiddly on cheap and peculiar foreign booze; now I go on holiday to sleep. Let's hope that cabin contains a big comfy bed.

TOP FIVE CHRISTMASSY DISHES

I'm no Nigella, but I take the art of feeding guests very seriously. Especially at Christmas time, when too much is not enough and nobody can quibble that there was no need to go to all that fuss.

1. My favourite Christmas nibble

Gotta be a fondue. If you can get your mitts on a small fondue set, and you can cope with the idea of lava-temperature cheese so close to your guests, then a fondue is an excellent way to get everybody mingling. There will be scoffing, but soon even the scoffers will be elbowing children out of the way to dunk their bread cubes in the delicious cheesy gunk. You show me a person who can't be won over by melted cheese and I'll show you a liar.

2. My favourite Christmas starter

Smoked salmon is king here. Buy the best you can afford and pile the slices on a dish. Scatter chopped spring onion and some vinegary capers all around. These days I make like a Swedish person and boil two eggs before separating the whites from the yolks and crumbling them up. The little piles of white and yellow rubble look otherworldly against the vivid orange of the salmon. Elegant *and* moreish.

3. My favourite Christmas main

This is one area where nobody can dictate. Whether it's turkey, ham, a nut roast or a re-heated Chinese takeaway, this bit truly is up to the individual. As long as it's cooked and served with love, there is no way to cock up Christmas lunch; just volunteering to do it means you deserve a medal!

4. My favourite Christmas dessert

Not Christmas pudding. Not ever. That dark, menacing mound with a sprig of anaemic holly doing its best to render it 'fun'? Nope. My preferred Christmas dessert is pear trifle: poached or tinned pears face down in a bowl along with slices of madeira cake that have taken a long bath in some elderflower cordial, all topped with a layer of custard and a layer of cream. As I crumble a Cadbury's Flake over the whole concoction I reflect on how much fun it is to be both tasteless and greedy.

5. My favourite Christmas titbit

I'm already looking forward to standing by the open fridge late on Christmas night, possibly in my pyjamas, tearing at cold roasties and slapping bread sauce into a baguette. Why is there no epic poetry written about leftovers?

What Would Mary Berry Do?

By Claire Sandy

The perfect bake is no piece of cake

Marie Dunwoody doesn't want for much in life. She has a lovely husband, three wonderful children, and a business of her own. But her cupcakes are crap. Her meringues are runny and her biscuits rock-hard. She cannot bake for toffee. Or, for that matter, make toffee.

Marie can't ignore the disappointed looks any more, or continue to be shamed by neighbour and nemesis Lucy Gray. Lucy whips up perfect profiteroles with one hand, while ironing her bed sheets with the other. Marie's had enough: this is the year it all changes. She vows to follow – to the letter – recipes from the Queen of Baking, and at all times ask, 'What would Mary Berry do?'

Husband Robert has noticed that his boss takes crumb structure as seriously as budget cuts and with redundancies on the horizon, he too puts on a pinny. Twins Rose and Iris are happy to eat all the half-baked mistakes that come their way, but big brother Angus is more distant than usual, as if something is troubling him. And there is no one as nosey as a matching pair of nine-year-old girls . . .

Marie starts to realize that the wise words of Mary Berry can help her with more than just a Victoria sponge. But can Robert save the wobbling soufflé that is his career? And is Lucy's sweet demeanour hiding something secretly sour?

A Very Big House in the Country

By Claire Sandy

One house. Three families.
What could possibly go wrong?

For one long, hot summer in Devon, three families share one very big house in the country. The Herreras are two tired parents, three grumbling children and one promiscuous dog. The Littles: she's gorgeous, he's loaded – but maybe the equation for a truly happy marriage is a bit more complicated than that? As for the Browns, they seem oddly jumpy – especially around each other.

By the pool, new friendships blossom, but at the kitchen door, resentments simmer. Summer-crushes form, secrets are swapped and when the adults loosen their inhibitions with litres of white wine, they start to get a little too honest . . .

Mother hen to all, Evie Herrera has a life-changing announcement to make; one that could shatter the summer holiday and rock the foundations of her family. But will someone else beat her to it?

extracts reading groups
competitions books new
discounts extracts
competitions
books
new
reading groups events
events books
extracts new
new titles reading groups
interviews
events extracts
discounts
new books events
events new
discounts extracts discounts
www.panmacmillan.com
extracts events reading groups
competitions books extracts new